JACK GLASS

·JACK GLASS·

A GOLDEN AGE STORY

•

ADAM ROBERTS

GOLLANCZ

LONDON

The right of Adam Roberts to be identified as the author
of this work has been asserted by him in accordance with
the Copyright, Designs and Patents Act 1988.

First published in Great Britain in 2012 by Gollancz
An imprint of the Orion Publishing Group
Orion House, 5 Upper St Martin's Lane,
London WC2H 9EA
An Hachette UK Company

A CIP catalogue record for this book
is available from the British Library

ISBN 978 0 575 12762 3 (Cased)
ISBN 978 0 575 12763 0 (Export Trade Paperback)

3 5 7 9 10 8 6 4

Typeset at The Spartan Press Ltd,
Lymington, Hants

Printed and bound by CPI Group (UK) Ltd,
Croydon, CRO 4YY

The Orion Publishing Group's policy is to use papers that are
natural, renewable and recyclable products and made from wood
grown in sustainable forests. The logging and manufacturing
processes are expected to conform to the environmental
regulations of the country of origin.

www.adamroberts.com
www.orionbooks.co.uk

To Merryl Wynne Roberts

This narrative, which I hereby doctorwatson for your benefit, o reader, concerns the greatest mystery of our time. Of course I'm talking about McAuley's alleged 'discovery' of a method of travelling faster than light, and about the murders and betrayals and violence this discovery has occasioned. Because, after all – FTL! We all know it is impossible, we know every one of us that the laws of physics disallow it. But still! And again, this narrative has to do with the greatest mind I have known – the celebrated, or infamous, Jack Glass. The one, the only Jack Glass: detective, teacher, protector and murderer, an individual gifted with extra-ordinary interpretive powers when it comes to murder *because* he was so well acquainted with murder. A quantity of blood is spilled in this story, I'm sorry to say; and a good many people die; and there is some politics too. There is danger and fear. Accordingly I have told his tale in the form of a murder mystery; or to be more precise (and at all costs we must be *precise*) three, connected murder mysteries.

But I intend to play fair with you, reader, right from the start, or I'm no true Watson. So let me tell everything now, at the beginning, before the story gets going.

One of these mysteries is a prison story. One is a regular whodunit. One is a locked-room mystery. I can't promise that they're necessarily presented to you in that order; but it should be easy for you work out which is which, and to sort them out accordingly. Unless you find that each of them is *all three at once*, in which case I'm not sure I can help you.

In each case the murderer is the same individual – of course,

Jack Glass himself. How could it be otherwise? Has there ever been a more celebrated murderer?

That's fair, I hope?

Your task is to read these accounts, and solve the mysteries and identify the murderer. Even though I have already told you the solution, the solution will surprise you. If the revelation in each case is anything *less* than a surprise, then I will have failed.

I do not like to fail.

part I

•

IN THE BOX

'Hey Liz! What's in the box?'
'It's my little voice of self-doubt.'

Liz Phair, 'Smoke'

The prison ship was called *Marooner*. The name had nothing to do with its colour.

This was its sixth run, and, as it had done five times before, it began by unloading its kit. The remaining seven prisoners waited in the hold. There were echoes as they coughed, or kicked their heels against the plasmetal wall. Still, it was hard to believe that when they left 8Flora the space had been crammed with more than forty human beings. It was surely not big enough for so many bodies.

There it was – the growl. The shudder.

'That bump,' said Gordius, 'is them unloading the fusion cell. I heard it's possible to short it – to explode the whole asteroid, which is a way of saying, by way of saying, transforming it into a shell of rapidly expanding dust and—'

Lwon said: 'Stop talking.'

But Gordius couldn't stop talking. He had watched all the other prisoners being unceremoniously unloaded; each batch to their own prison. Now, finally, he knew his own time had come and his nerves had got the better of him. 'You know what space is? It is a moat. It is an uncrossable million-mile moat. *We'll* never see home again. Eleven years? There's no way we'll last it out. And if by some impossible fluke we do, then we *will* have gone insane and won't want to go back.'

Lwon repeated his instruction, with a more ferocious emphasis.

'There!' said Gordius. The ship was jettisoning its cargo packages into the hollow: a cylindrical scrubber, for the air; a lightpole; a small pack of spores. Finally, and – most important of all – three excavators, cabled together. The momentum of the package, and its Newtonian equal-and-opposition, made the plasmetal structure of *Marooner* as a whole wobble and chime. Boom, boom, thrum. Outside, as each package flew into the cleft, and collided with the wall, or wedged in at the narrowest point, of course there was no noise at all. But the seven prisoners were inside the ship, listening to the activity. It was the sixth time they had heard it: they all knew what was going to happen next and could not help but be apprehensive. The voices of stevedores could be heard, the content of their shouts muffled by the intervening structure of the ship, leaving only a rhythmic groaning musicality. 'It'll be hard enough work,' said Gordius, 'digging out, and not *only* the digging, but the *architectural* business of designing the – of making the most of – making the most of – but even *harder* work will be finding a way to live together without killing one another.'

'I'll kill you right now,' said Davide, 'if you don't shut up.' And the wall, to which they were all of them strapped, said: grrrmmm, and there were intimations of certain other, unfathomable noises.

The terms of the sentence were that these seven be deposited in the hollow of the asteroid known as Lamy306 – 200m across, this worldlet, this little-princedom. The hollow was a crescent-shaped valley in the surface of the rock, the residue of some long ago impact (of course), one which had deformed the material of Lamy, twisted it, broken and folded it over, leaving a long, thin, pocket-shaped cave: it stretched some fifteen metres along the surface of Lamy, extended, at its deepest, ten metres into the worldlet. It was no more than a metre wide at any point. Into this irregular-shaped cavity *Marooner* had deposited all the relevant gear, and there were only two further tasks for it to perform. It deployed its foam hose, and applied a skin of gluey sealant to seal over the long slit-mouth of the declivity. The ship worked from one side to the other. The seal set almost instantly upon being exposed to the vacuum outside.

The seven all knew what was imminent. Lwon spoke up:

'Listen everybody,' he barked. 'We'll more likely survive this if we work *together*. No fighting, no panic – we'll need to get the light on first, and then the scrubber—'

Ejection cut him off. Then the cargo hold shuddered and shook and the seven humans inside it felt the startlement of anticipation. All seven hearts pumped suddenly harder. Some of the seven readied themselves, some were too flustered to do so, but it came, irrespective of whether they were ready or not.

A hatch opened in the hold, and the rail to which all seven were attached came free from the wall. They went in this order: Gordius, three times the weight of any of the others, a near-spherical man; Mo, his mouth set in a line and his eyes tightly closed; Davide, roaring; Lwon, calm, or seemingly so; Marit looking startled; E-de-C waving his heavy fists as if he would fight the very air; and at the end of the line, the feeblest of them all, Jac, with no legs, looking idiotically placid. As if he didn't quite grasp what had happened to him!

Then they were sucked out and down, smacked on the front and back by the cold, flexible material of the discharge schute and into the swirling microgravity darkness.

It was perfectly dark and very, very cold. Jac, sensibly enough, clutched his head with his arms as he shot down the schute, but as soon as he was aware that he had emerged into the cavern itself he put his arms forward. A painful, jarring collision. He caromed from a rocky surface, and was able to quench his speed. Naked skin touched naked asteroid, that mystic Sistine-chapel-ceiling moment of contact: the first person to lay hand upon it since the unpolished globe had formed out of its dust and ice. There was no handhold, of course, and although Jac's fingers scrabbled at the rock he could not anchor himself. Lacking legs, it was harder for him than it was for the others. The air inside the pocket was gusting and burlying, yanking him one direction and then an-other. It was disorienting, monstrously disorienting; the black density of that lightless place, his ears filled with white noise and pain. He flew backwards, collided a glancing blow against some unyielding plane of hardness, smacked frontways and bounced back.

This is what was happening: the *Marooner*, having pumped the cavity full of air to a higher-than-sea-level pressure, was now sealing the last gap in the seal. Jac had been inside the cargo hold during the six previous iterations of this procedure, and so he knew what the ship was experiencing right now – linked to the sticky matter of the seal by the tether of the very hose that was laying it down, and buffeted by the venting gases from the (shrinking) hole into the aerated cavity. The seven of them had sat tethered in the same hold, crammed with prisoners, as the *Marooner* leapt and shook until the conniption motion subsided and the vessel detached and angled itself about and accelerated away. They had sat there with thirty-five others whilst that happened; and then with twenty-eight people, and with twenty-one, and with fourteen, and now it was only them. Now the *Marooner*'s cargo hold was empty, and when the shimmies and shakes diminished, and the seal was completed, the sloop would turn about and navigate back to 8Flora.

No spacecraft would come this way again for eleven years.

When a ship finally did return it would find one of two things. They would be alive and the work done; or they would be dead and the work not done. Perhaps the seven prisoners (or whatever proportion of them survived) would have excavated the interior spaces of the asteroid into a series of habitable chambers – or perhaps they would have hollowed one great chamber and adapted the fusion engine to shine in the midst like a sun; or else they might have carved a beehive of cells and zones; or a thread tangle of tunnels.

If they – or some of them – were still alive, then the Gongsi would recover them. Mostly, when this happened, the survivors were pathetically grateful, eager to climb back on the prison ship. Very occasionally the survivors would resist; would have gone rock-native, would scatter from the retrieval officers and try to hide – or fight. But in that unlikely eventuality they would not be permitted to stay; for the rocks were most valuable to the Gongsi as vacant possession. Land a touch-up team, put in some windows, tow it into a more advantageous orbit, and sell it. Real estate. And the prisoners? Released, sent back onto the cavernous freedom of the Ulanov System.

Free.

But first you had to survive the sentence. And that meant you had to turn a tiny pocket of air filling a declivity no larger than a room, near the surface of a frozen asteroid, into an environment that could support seven human beings for a decade and more. You had to do this *yourselves*, without external help or guidance, and using as few items of equipment to help you as the Gongsi could, always mindful of its profits, get away with supplying. It was a simple and indeed (that overused corporate term) *elegant* business model. The Gongsi was one of four working in this field; their name – it happened to be *Diyīrén* – was hardly important. It had won the contract for handling convicted criminals by agreeing the lowest per capita fee per delinquent. From this baseline they worked to extract the maximum profit from the situation.

This is the way the worlds work. It's always been like this.

Of course, none of this was in the minds of the seven prisoners. The entire, pitiless horizon of their existence was as close to them as the jugular veins in their necks. Everything was swallowed up by the pressing need for immediate survival. There was a mighty rushing sound, and an acrid gunpowder stench, a tingle of sand blown upon the face. Jac coughed, and coughed again. Everything was black. But in the commotion he was thinking: *how large is this space*? Not large. *With seven men breathing it, how long will the breathable air last*? Not long.

Somebody's voice, muffled by the rushing, in the dark: 'the *light* – quickly – light, or we're *dead*!'

Jac bounced again off the wall, cracked the side of his head painfully, and lurched forward. Putting out his arms he scraped rock on both sides, and pushed with all the strength in his shoulders. He wedged himself still, and for a moment all he could do was blink and blink and cough. The darkness was complete; the rock felt killingly cold against his flesh.

'Find the *light!*' somebody bellowed, again, his voice distorted. 'Or else—'

There was light. A strip of yellow-white, and the whole narrow chamber was illuminated with a gritty, cloudy radiance. It stung Jac's eyes; or else, the still-swirling dust did that.

Jac blinked, and blinked. He was able to make out the shapes of his fellow prisoners, some stationary, some still hurtling. It was Davide who had grasped hold of the light pole and turned it on – indeed, Jac could see the ingenious way he had used it as a brace to hold himself steady in the swirling air, wedging it between the angle of two walls. The space they were in was really not very large. A wedge of pitted black-grey rock above and below tapering to a stocky dead-end. And at the formerly open end of the declivity, a new ceiling of red-brown of permaseal, the fabric of which was wobbling slightly in the gusts. Jac thought exactly what everybody else was thinking: *we must survive here for eleven years. We must take a pole of light, and a bundle of equipment you could pick up for a couple of thousand credits in any Mart, and with that we must somehow keep seven people alive for four thousand days.* It seemed flatly impossible. Of course Jac knew, as they all did, that many prisoners did manage to do it – the Gongsi's business model depended upon this, in fact. But the Gongsi's business model also accommodated the death of a proportion of prisoners; for in almost all cases they could retrieve the kit they had supplied, and even in death the fees they took from Ulanov police authority administrations per prisoner more than covered the costs of portage and sundries. If they survived and turned the asteroid into saleable real estate the Gongsi made a lot *more* money, of course. But there was no incentive for them to offer a helping hand. The question for Jac was: if they did survive, then in what mental state? On the other hand, such questions were a less pressing concern than imminent death.

Alienated from his bId for the first time in his life, Jac was unable to call up the numbers – how many prisoners, as a whole, died during their sentence? And of that number, how many were instances where the whole group of seven died? And of that number, how many such deaths occurred within the first few hours of being deposited?

They were all thinking it. Eleven years in the most hostile environment imaginable, entirely dependent on their own resources, with no hope of assistance. A prison made of rock insulated from the rest of humanity by millions of miles of vacuum in every direction. Eleven years! Their only hope was to endure the full eleven-year term and pray that the Gongsi hadn't forgotten them by the end of it, and was still trading, and had the incentive to come collect the hollowed-out globe.

Jac had more to fear from the end of that eleven-year period than from the sentence itself. Of course, he didn't tell the others that.

'Now! Quick!' Davide was shouting, indistinctly, his mouth caked with dust. 'Locate the scrubber!'

Now that the lightstick was on, those who were still being burlied about by the breeze were able to orient themselves a little better, and brake their velocity against the walls or in at the thin end of the wedge. In moments, the only things still moving were the items of kit the *Marooner* had unloaded into the cavity. Even in tumbling motion, bashing dust from the walls as they bounced, it was easy to see which was which: the largest was the fusion cell, knocking ponderously between wall and wall; only slightly smaller, on account of it being three machines strapped together, was the bundle of excavators – the irregular shape of this package together with its size meant that it had become stuck in the wedge. But the rest of the kit, the tree-trunk-shaped scrubber, the spore pack, a sealed box of biscuits (Lembas brand) so small a child could hide it under her tunic – these things continued to bash and rattle about the claustric space.

Jac wiped his face with a dusty hand, leaving it no cleaner than before. To his left, the great globe-shape of Gordius was squashed between the walls, his arms waving, and the fat of his flesh rippling. It was hellishly cold.

To his right, Jac could see the other five. Marit made a swipe at the scrubber as it flew past him, caught it with one hand and tipped it about in mid-air. But before he could make a second swipe and actually grasp the device, Lwon kicked off with both feet, shot across the space from the far side and scooped the scrubber into his open arms.

'Hey!' cried a hoarse-voiced Marit. 'I had it!'

Indeed, Lwon had put himself at some disadvantage by leaping the way he did. He collided almost at once with the other wall and had to yank his head round to an alarming angle to avoid smashing his skull. He sprawled on the rebound. The scrubber spun about, and he thrashed to steady himself. Finally Lwon managed to get his heel into a kink in the rock and settle himself. But he had achieved his aim: he had the scrubber.

'Listen to me!' he cried. 'Heed me! The next few hours are the *most* dangerous. One false step and we *all die*. We can't afford to fight amongst ourselves.'

'Turn the damn scrubber on,' said Marit, aggrieved. 'No sermons!'

'That's no sermon,' boomed E-d-C. 'He's running for office!'

Somebody else booed, or groaned, or perhaps coughed. Through the dusty air, Lwon called: 'I'm not saying I should be leader,' though that was obviously exactly what he was saying. 'I'm not telling anyone what to do. But if we start fighting amongst ourselves, we might just as well wreck this scrubber here and now – choke to death in hours, instead of dragging out the agony for years.'

'I'll tear your head off,' growled Davide, although without particular belligerence. After all, he had the light pole.

'Turn the scrubber on!' said Mo. 'Turn it – *on*.'

'Wait,' said Lwon, putting his hand up. 'We don't even know what model it is.'

'What's to know?' said Marit, slapping his legs to warm them. 'A scrubber's a scrubber—'

'We can't afford any mistakes,' said Lwon, turning the bulky device over and over. 'A single mistake could kill us all.' But there were no instructions printed on the machine; and he couldn't draw out the theatre of his moment for much longer.

So he turned the scrubber on. It made no sound, but the dust near one of its circular apertures stirred and started drawing slowly in.

'Why don't we all take charge of a different thing each?' said Gordius. 'Then we all got a stake – yeah?'

All faces turned to the far end of the cleft. The light was strong, the shadows it threw black and stark, stretching oddly over the slant surfaces of the walls. 'What's you say there, fat-boy?' demanded Marit.

'I'm only saying,' said Gordius, his voice audibly quivering with retreat, 'is that – look, there's seven of us. The fusion cell, the scrubber, the light, the, uh, the spore pack, the, uh, uh, the biscuits – that's five items. Divided equally between . . .'

'Oh, you want the *biscuits*, do you?' bellowed E-d-C. The effort of shouting caused him to cough violently. 'Those biscuits got to last us until we get the spores growing their *slop*. You eat them all up, what *we* going to eat?'

'We could eat *him*,' said Mo, showing thirty-two teeth. 'He'd last us a while. And as for half-man there,' Mo gestured towards Jac, 'I guess you don't eat as much as a regular guy?'

'Hey, don't misunderstand. *I* don't want the biscuits,' insisted Gordius. Even in the bitter cold of that space, he was perspiring. 'I wasn't saying that! I mean – sure, I'd like a biscuit, but, sure. The food should be equally divided, until. Sure. But, look, I *don't* mind, and I guess Mr No-legs here doesn't mind either. Why don't you five divide the five items between you? And then you could – you could—'

Lwon interrupted him: in a loud, stern-to-be-kind voice. 'Your best bet, Softbody, is keep your opinions to *yourself*. We got a lot to do just to stop ourselves dying right here and now.' He looked in turn at the other four: Davide, Mo, Marit and E-d-C. 'I know you, Ennemi-du-Concorde, and you know me. I know you are strong, and that you got the willpower. You know the same of me, I think. I'm not setting to boss you – I'm not setting to boss *any* of you.' The scrubber in his arms was carving a spectral Doric column out of the floating dust near his shoulder. 'I tell you what,' he said.

'What?' boomed Marit, with sarcastic emphasis.

'I say *when* we get ourselves sorted, and the air and water and food supply is settled, when that's done I say we excavate seven completely separate chambers, and have one each. Then we don't need to be in each other's hair. Then we can just wait out our time best as we can. But until then . . .'

Davide, evidently, had a practical mind. 'Break that lightpole into seven,' he said, 'and I don't reckon you'd have enough light to even *grow* the spores.'

'They'd grow,' said Marit. 'But slow – slow – and small. But you're right, the better bet is keep the pole in one piece. Or maybe break it in two.'

'And there will be time to discuss all these things,' said Lwon. 'But not right now! Now, we have more immediate concerns!'

Jac examined the whole space. It didn't take him long. 'We could make a window,' he said.

This was the first time any of the others had heard him speak, for he had kept his peace on the outbound flight. The sound of his voice made all eyes turn towards him. 'You say – *what* was that, Leggy?'

'We could make a window,' Jac repeated. 'Let sunlight in. I know we're a long way from the sun, but we'd still ensure a degree of . . .'

Mo started laughing: a curt, barking, aggressive noise that transformed almost at once into coughs. Lwon said, dismissively: 'sure, half-man. You *do* that. You conjure your magic window and set it in the side of the rock.'

For some reason, Jac persevered: 'there must be silicates in this rock. It wouldn't be hard to run a line from the fusion cell, melt the—'

'Talking of which!' boomed E-d-C. 'I'm cold as the grave.' He started an ungainly, ill-coordinated crawl over the surface of one wall towards where the fusion cell was lodged. Lwon followed him with his gaze, but did nothing to stop him. He still had the scrubber, after all.

E-d-C's large hands grabbed the cell, turned the massy object easily in the microgravity, and dialled up some heat. As soon as he did so, the others began to shuffle, or scramble, over towards him. The air was horribly, horribly cold; and although the fusion cell put out only faint warmth it was better than nothing.

All except Lwon. 'Don't get too cosy,' he yelled. 'We need to find *water* before we can get ourselves all warm like a cat on an exhaust plate. We need to find some ice or we'll all be dead in days.'

The other four alpha-males ignored him. Gordius was whimpering a little as he tried to extricate his bulk from where he had wedged himself. Jac made his way hand-on-hand over to the big fellow. 'You're stuck in there pretty good,' he observed, bracing his thigh-stumps against the rock and pulling at an arm.

'I bounced in the dark,' said Gordius, struggling, 'and then – wham. It shot me in here, like a . . . like a . . . *ouf.*' He came loose and floated out.

They gathered their various bits and pieces and tucked them all into the cleft to keep them from moving about. Davide propped the light pole at an angle, wall to wall, somewhere near the middle. Then they all set about unpacking the three excavators with which they had been supplied. The scrubber would keep the air fresh, but without water they would not last long. That meant digging through until they found ice. 'What if we don't find any?' asked Gordius. He knew the answer to this question as well as any of them; but that didn't stop him asking it aloud. 'We die,'

Jac told him. 'What if we find *some*, but not enough to last us eleven years?' Gordius pressed. 'What if there isn't enough ice in this rock to last seven men eleven years? What then?'

There was no point in answering him.

E-d-C had brought out the first of the excavators, and was examining the device. 'Anybody here ever worked as a miner?' he asked.

The scrubber had cleared some of the dust out of the air; and the breeze had settled, running toward the scrubber along one wall and away from it along the other. Jac found that he was able to cough up and moisten his mouth sufficiently to get most of the grit out of it. 'I dated a Moon Miner once,' Mo said. 'She was tough as a battlebot.'

'She ever impart the wisdom of her profession *to* you?' E-d-C enquired.

'No.'

'Then press your lips *tight*, idiot,' E-d-C snapped.

Mo glared at him. Lwon spoke up, to defuse the hostility. 'By the time we've finished our term here,' he declared, 'we'll all be *expert* miners.' He had the second excavator and was examining at it. 'It is a series of problems to be solved,' he announced. Even with the heat from the fusion cell, their environment was extraordinarily cold. Breath spumed from his lips with every word Lwon spoke. 'That's all it is. If we take each problem in turn and solve it, working together, then we'll get through it. It's a series of problems to solve – all that's left, after that, is the will to endure our time here.'

All that's left after that, Jac thinks, is the will.

'So I'm no expert,' E-d-C, 'but these look like utility models. Decades old. Second-hand. I can tell.'

'You amaze me,' said Davide, in a perfectly unamazed voice.

'Eleven years,' said Gordius, apropos of nothing.

'There must be a schute,' said Marit. 'An schute. Ein schute. I,' he said, rummaging. 'This?' It was a coil of black cable, about as thick as a man's wrist. There were three schutes, rolled to-gether: one for each digger.

They unspooled one of them, and found its business end: a pen-nib-shaped bit. 'All three together,' said Lwon. 'E-d-C – and Davide take first shift. We dig until we find some ice.'

Davide, holding the third excavator, removed his attention from the controls to angle his face in Lwon's direction. 'That sounded very much,' he said, 'as if you were giving me an order.'

The tone in which he said this, as much as the words them-selves, brought a frozen quiet to the space. Everybody looked at Lwon.

'If you'd prefer not to, Davide,' Lwon said, in a low, measured voice. 'That's fine. But if we don't find water, we will die.'

'*I'll* have a go!' said Gordius, brightly, holding his arm out for Davide to pass him the excavator.

Saying nothing, Davide uncoiled his own waste schute, and fitted the open end into the port at the back of the excavator.

E-d-C had already fitted his schute to his digger. 'So, the exhaust,' he said. 'Through the rock? Or through the stuff they sprayed to seal this cave?'

Marit, near the ceiling, reached out and thumped the artificial substance with his fist. Then he wrapped his arm back around his knees and hugged himself. Jac, from the other side of the cleft, saw how vigorously he was shivering. In the microgravity the little muscular tremors made him jiggle in position slightly, as if he were being agitated from without, like a particle in Brownian motion.

'The thing about the seal,' said E-d-C, 'is that at least we know it's not too thick.' He pushed off with his feet, dragging his excavator with him. On reaching the ceiling he pressed the sharp end of his schute against the material of the ceiling, and turned the device on. Jac expected – he didn't know what: whirring, lasers, something. But the point simply sank into the material. It pulled a metre or so of hose after it. Then it stopped.

'I'm going to try this one on rock,' said Lwon, scrabble-pushing himself to the other side of the cavity and pressing his waste schute against the wall. This time there was more noise: a coffee-grinder whirring sound. The schute-point burrowed more slowly into the rock, and tugged one, then two, then three metres of hose after it. Then it stopped.

Davide had picked a third place on the rock, and his schute dragged less than two metres of hose. The three men took their respective machines to different parts of the cavewall, and set the drillmouth against the rock.

'Is there no way we can – what's the word—' Marit said, evidently unhappy that he didn't have one of the drills. 'Dowse?'

'Dowse?' Lwon repeated.

'You're just going to dig? That's blind luck. What if there's no ice in the direction you choose to excavate?'

'Then,' said Lwon, 'we try another way. We keep digging until we find it.' And he started his machine.

It wasn't an excessively loud sound, but it wasn't restful on the ear either, and there was no escaping it. Lwon, E-d-C and Davide ground at the rock in sweeping or circling motions. The first two were able to provide traction by setting their feet against the other wall, and Davide dug his heels into the edge of the ceiling. But it did not go quickly, and there was nothing at all for the other four prisoners to do but watch. The fusion cell was giving out a modicum of heat, and although it did little to warm the air more generally, Mo, Marit and Jac clustered around it, and Gordius got as close as his great bulk would allow. 'Why isn't the fusion cell hotter?' Mo wanted to know. 'It's got enough energetic potential to blow the whole asteroid to dust. I mean, if all released at once. So why did they set the heating element to max-out at such a *low* threshold?'

'Why do you think?' growled Marit. 'They're sadists. Low-level bureaucratic sadists.'

'I think,' Jac put in, emphasising the first word, and continuing in a singsong voice, 'there's a more practical reason. It's cold now, and will be for a while. But there *will* come a time when our main problem will be finding ways to radiate excess heat.'

'Shut your head-hole, Leggy,' said Marit. Jac looked away, smiling.

Grrn, grrn, grrn, went the drills.

'I'm thirsty,' said Gordius, eventually. 'Would it have killed the Gongsi to maroon us with a couple hundred litres of fresh water? Would it? How much would that add to their precious expense sheet?' He kept chattering on. His was the type of personality, Jac noted, that was unable to leave well alone.

The dark grey walls made a Λ. The air was filled with scraps and orts of dust, crumbs of rock. The smell of cordite was in Jac's nostrils. Stenchy, stenchy.

'It would only be postponing the inevitable,' said Jac. 'They could hardly supply us with eleven years' worth. We *will* have to shift for ourselves. Might as well start as we mean to go on.'

'But,' said Gordius, pressing his fists into his ample stomach. He didn't say anything else.

'You sound like you're on *their* side,' observed Mo. 'That's a provoking attitude to take.'

'I will say it one more time, Leggy,' said Marit. 'And no further warnings. Keep your head-hole shut.'

Jac regarded him with a sly eye. But he didn't say anything else.

'Eleven years,' said Gordius. 'We won't last *one*. We'll die of thirst in a week. There's no ice in this rock. There ought to be a law. The Gongsi ought to be compelled by the Lex Ulanova to survey their prison stroids, to ensure—' He petered out.

They fell into an unhappy silence. Jac watched the three diggers. Davide was the most aggressive, straining his muscles to try and force the drillmouth hard against the rock. Jac wondered if that would make a difference; presumably the machine processed as much matter as it did, regardless of whether it was pressed or merely set against the rock. But Davide was an impatient man. Everything about him made that fact plain. He would have to learn to shed his impatience, Jac thought, or he would not last very long. Lwon was more methodical, moving the drill in a tight circle and slowly carving out a metre-diameter circular space. E-d-C was making more dramatic, sweeping left-to-right gestures with his machine, scraping out a shelf. It required considerable muscular effort to move the excavators – weightless but nonetheless massy – through this shuttling series of motions. Jac wondered how long it would be before he exhausted himself. From time to time E-d-C and Lwon would stop, examine the area they had carved out, and check their machine. Davide did not stop.

Time passed. Nobody had any way of measuring the time: none of them had any bId connection any more. Jac cast his mind idly back to his schooldays. How had ancestral humans done it – measured the passing of time? (He was going to think: how did *cavemen* manage? But that seemed, in his present situation, too much like irony.) Water clocks. Pendula. Both things that depended on gravity. What sort of clock could they build in this gravityless environment? Sundials. There was no sunlight, here.

It didn't matter. Time didn't matter. Only the will mattered.

Davide was sweating, despite the ferocious cold.

Jac watched the particles of dust sliding slowly-slowly in beautifully coordinated trajectories, slowly, in towards the intake end of the scrubber. Gordius saw that he was looking. 'I know what you're thinking,' he said.

'You do?'

'You're thinking: what if the power chip in the scrubber malfunctions?' Jac hadn't been thinking that, actually, but he didn't say so. 'Well,' Gordius went on. 'I was thinking that too. Without the scrubber, we'd all asphyxiate in a very short time. But, see, *if* that happens, we can hook it up to the fusion cell.' He said this as if he had spotted something terribly clever and useful. Jac went back to watching the dust patterns.

Time passed. The next thing that happened was that Davide

broke off from his digging. 'Somebody else have a go,' he gasped. 'I need a rest.'

'You're straining at the machine,' observed Lwon, over the noise of his own digger. 'You need to take it easier.'

'Two-and-a-half-hours a day,' Davide snapped back. 'Minimum – *minimum*. Any less than that, and your muscles will waste. You'll end up looking like Leggy, there.' He nodded in Jac's direction. Then he pushed off and flew slowly over towards where the biscuits had been stowed. Lwon saw what he was up to, quickly enough. 'Wait!' He shut off his digger.

'I'm either having some biscuit,' Davide announced, 'or I'm eating your flesh, raw, Lwon.'

'We *all* eat *at the same time*, and we all take the same amount,' announced Lwon, forcefully. 'That way we avoid falling out. If we start fighting amongst ourselves, then we might as well cut our own throats. And the biscuits won't last us long, anyway. We should keep them till we're really hungry.'

'I *am* really hungry,' Davide barked. 'Did you just see the job of work I did?'

Jac watched Lwon's face, as he sized-up the situation – whether this big man was going to back down, or not. Lwon evidently decided the latter was the truth of it. 'In that case, we all get one Lembas. All of us – one each.'

Davide growled, but made no objection. So E-d-C shut off his digger too, and the seven of them gathered around the food. Davide took it on himself to hand out the supplies: one biscuit per person. 'Leggy here don't need a whole one,' he said. Marit laughed. 'I'd be happy with half,' Jac said, mildly. But Lwon spoke up: 'give him the same as everyone else, Davide.'

Nobody got very far with their biscuits. Without water, it was too parching a meal, not calculated to please dusty mouths. Jac ate some few nibbles, and put the remainder back. Davide went to the far side of the cavern, turned to face the rock, wedged himself in, and went to sleep. Or perhaps he didn't: he was shivering pretty violently, and it was hard to imagine he got much rest. But he made a performance of sleeping, and of do-not-disturb, and everybody else let him be.

'Come on,' said Lwon. 'We need *water*.' Gordius again offered to take his turn, but Marit overruled him and took the spare machine. Drrn, drrn, drrn.

They laboured for a long time. The relatively high pressure in their pocket meant that the air was dry, and that fact combined with the dust meant that everybody felt terribly thirsty. 'Could they not leave us a single keg of *water*?' groaned Davide.

'The scrubber will produce a little water, I think,' said Jac. 'The reaction takes the carbon from the see-oh-too and—'

'You'll be quieter,' snarled Marit, 'when I rip out your tongue.'

Jac, smiled, but said nothing more.

It was colder than could easily be expressed, colder than any of them had known before. As Davide said, repeatedly, in tones of gruff incredulity, it was amazing that human beings could exist for any length of time in such cold without simply expiring. They were wearing whatever they had been wearing when they were arrested – tunics, trows, dish-shoes. None of them were in cold-weather gear. Their breath burst from them in great cloudy bursts like ectoplasm; their eyelids kept sticking together as the moisture froze. Working helped a little; and a couple of them imitated Davide's exercises: furious running up one wall and down the other. At other times they clumped together, scowling, for shared warmth.

The cold was very hard to bear, but the thirst was worse. The dry air and the effortful labour of drilling parched their mouths; their tongues felt like dry horns, the roofs of their mouths were swollen and hard and caked in dust. Their muscles ached from operating the machine, or else from the constant shivering. The seven of them bickered amongst themselves constantly, and there were occasional flare-ups; but nobody had the energy to pursue it. Rock crumbled laboriously from the biting parts of the drills.

They stopped continually, examined the face of excavation and checked for ice. It was only rock, nothing but rock.

'Days,' said Lwon. 'Without water, we won't last more than that. We may not even last that, given that it is so *cold*.'

But Jac was right; one of the side-effects of the scrubber clearing CO_2 from the air was a thin trickle of water from a spigot on the cylinder's side. It was barely enough to wet a single tongue, let alone supply seven labouring men with sufficient fluid. And given that fact, it possessed the potential to focus strife amongst the seven of them to dangerous levels.

Lwon announced that they would take turns at this trickle, and although Marit loudly challenged his right to make this announcement, everybody agreed. There was no other way. Davide went first, and then Lwon. But it took many hours for the spigot to refill, and with each person to wet his whistle the mood of the group as a whole became more sour.

Matters came to a head quicker than Jac expected. Ennemi-du-Concorde broke off digging and floated towards the spigot. As he approached the scrubber, Marit said: 'I am next. You take your turn – after me.'

Without so much as looking at him, E-d-C growled: 'try to stop me and I'll tear your jaw off.'

E-d-C lifted the massy, weightless scrubber in both hands to bring the spigot to his mouth. At once Marit struck. He launched himself from the wall with both legs and collided hard with E-d-C. The two men spun about in an arc, pivoting over the sliding scrubber. But the space was so confined there was hardly any room for them to scrap. E-d-C's spine smacked audibly against the wall. Marit started landing blows, like a boxer at close quarters, in at E-d-C's ribs and stomach. Jac could see that he was holding a piece of rock in his right hand.

But Lwon acted with impressive speed. He was on Marit's back almost at once, calling to Davide to help, and in moments the two of them had disengaged the struggling Marit. In the course of this, Davide received a stone-holding fist blow on the side of his head, and this did not improve his mood. But then E-d-C swam over to join in, and the three men began pounding Marit.

This punitive battery didn't last long. The next thing was that Marit, solus, was rotating slowly in the middle of the space, curled into a ball, coughing and shivering. He was a human spindle, and he was drawing a thread of tiny red beads about himself. The thread was coming from his mouth. E-d-C took what little water was in the spigot into his mouth, and, watching him, Jac felt the dryness in his own mouth that much more intensely.

They dug on. Marit sulked in the corner for a bit, but when Lwon kicked him gently and told him to take a turn at the digger, he did as he was instructed.

They dug, thirsting and frozen, for hours. 'I've never felt so physically miserable,' Mo announced to the group, finishing a shift with the digger, hugging himself and pressing himself close to the fusion cell. 'It is literally impossible that I could sleep. Sleep is simply an impossibility.' But he fell instantly into unconsciousness anyway, and Lwon moved his body away from the vent.

Gordius said: 'we are going to die.'

'This headache is enough to make me want to excavate my own skull with the digger,' growled E-d-C.

There was nothing to do but go on. Their environment acquired a hallucinatory aspect. The dark grey walls. The way the continuous brightness of the lightstick laid a straight set of bars and shafts and lines through the cluttered, dusty air of their space. At one point Jac thought the walls were sweating, and pressed his face against it to discover only icy dryness and bitter-tasting dust. There were ashes lining the inside his throat. There was a throb to the fabric of spacetime. The box was not shut sufficiently tightly. The voice was leaking out. Jac listened to the voice, or ignored it, indifferently. It hardly mattered. He was hours from death. They all were.

24

The drill ground on. Jac felt it inside his own teeth. There were microscopic people trapped in his teeth, clearing the space with minuscule diggers. His nerves sang.

His turn on the machine. He pressed it against the rock, and it moved through the material with a painful slowness.

Everybody's lips were the colour of the walls.

'Wait,' cried Lwon. 'Wait.' He was poking his hand at the front of his digger, the skin on his neck twitching with micro-shivers. Jac had this thought: if I lean over and turn the switch on his machine, the digger will devour his hand and arm, and he will die. He restrained the impulse, of course. He felt giddy, nauseous, freaky. Punchy, skittish. Ill, dry, dry, dry.

Lwon was holding something in front of him. It looked like a piece of coal. 'Ice,' he said.

Lwon had hit a seam: some cometary body folded into the making of this rock billions of years ago, either dragged in by gravity, or arriving via random collision. Ancient water, older than the oceans of Earth over which the Ancient of Days had brooded in the Book of Genesis. The frozen apotheosis of the origin of things.

They scrabbled enough ice for everyone from the wall. It was painful to suck on it, and it tasted foully of the gunpowdery dust with which it was mixed, but – enduring the cold of it and ignoring the shivers – it was water, and water settled into their stomachs. With water came an awareness of profound hunger, and the seven of them raided the biscuits. Jac decided the best bet was to crunch crumbs together with ground-up ice and take it into the mouth all in one go.

They ate and drank. They shivered and shivered. Nobody drilled for several hours. Instead they clustered together about the fusion cell and dozed, or simply hung there. They were too tired even to celebrate.

Lwon soon roused them. 'The biscuits will soon be gone,' he said, forcing his shivering lips around the words. 'Now we have the ice, we need to grow the spores, and that won't happen overnight.' Sluggishly, they gathered ice and tried to arrange it near the lightstick. Microgravity made this hard, until Davide suggested gouging a trench in the rock and packing it with ice.

This took several hours, and when finished there wasn't enough ice to fill it, so Lwon took the digger back into the seam to extend it. Finally they were able to pack chunks of ice into the trench. Everyone's fingers were purple with cold. E-d-C broke open the first of the spore envelopes – they had only been supplied with three of them – and pressed the glucky contents onto the ice.

'Now, we wait,' he said, trying to warm his hands again by hiding them in his armpits.

'No,' said Lwon. 'Now, we *dig*.'

There was no day and no night. The light pole shone all the time. E-d-C started scratching a tally on the ceiling – no point in scoring it onto the rock, he observed, since over the years ahead of them they were going to dig all of that away. He marked it by his own sleeps, figuring that from waking to waking was roughly one mondial day. Jac suspected that E-d-C was a napper; that he might sleep ten times in two days, only ever brief periods, easily woken by the slightest jolt. But he didn't say anything. It hardly mattered. And prolonged sleep was hard for all of them, because it was so cold. Exhaustion would overtake them and they would slumber, but then after a short time their own shivers would wake them.

Soon enough E-d-C gave up bothering with his tally.

The biscuits were all gone, but the ghunk had not yet bloomed from black to green. Davide tried eating the black paste, but ended up throwing it up. 'So it doesn't taste like caviar?' Lwon asked, sarcastically. 'Be patient, boys! It's the *green* stuff we want, *green* is the ghunk with all the necessary nutrients. It won't be long now!'

They went hungry. There was at least water, now; ice from the vein they had discovered, to augment the dribbles from the spigot of the scrubber.

Davide gave up his exercise regimen. He simply didn't have the energy.

It was still shiveringly cold, all the time. They kept the fusion cell continually on, heating at the top of its range; but its range had been deliberately limited by the Gongsi, and although it put out some small warmth the rock around was so very cold that it chilled the air. 'We're not going to warm our air pocket until we've raised the temperature of this whole blocking *rock*,' growled Mo. Gordius started to say that, since rock was a poor conductor, they wouldn't need to heat the whole thing; just enough of the rock immediately around them to insulate them from the larger cold. But the others yelled at him, and Marit threw a shard of stone with a baseball pitcher's force and accuracy straight at his head. It cut a ◇-shaped gouge in Gordius's forehead. Blood beaded out. This made Jac angry. 'What are you doing?' he yelled. 'Hey!' The others had never seen the legless man angry before, and decided to find it richly amusing. Gordius had gone silent and pale. Jac tended the big-fellow's wound, pressing the corner of his tunic until the bleeding stopped.

'I think that upset *you* more than it did him, Leggy,' taunted Marit. 'You in love with the fat boy, or something?'

'He was explaining the problem of heating this space,' Jac replied. 'It's no reason to cut his skin.'

The others laughed some more, and gave up.

They didn't understand the situation, anyway, Jac thought. The slow action of the fusion cell *was* heating such of the icy rock as was exposed to the air. But every day they cut away precisely that rock, and ejected the gravel to space. They were, he reflected, inadvertently working to keep their own environment chilly. Still: there was nothing they could do about that, except endure it.

They went hungry for days. This did nothing to improve their tempers. But finally, one day, one batch of ghunk went green.

The first meal was special. As they ate it, the group almost approached a kind of camaraderie. The first crop of ghunk was plentiful enough for everybody to have as much as they liked, and it tasted – well, it tasted like the starvation had been pushed away to arms'-length again. Stomachs shrunken by hunger were soon filled; and afterwards everybody hung in space or lay against the wall, hugging themselves to try and stay warm. From time to time, somebody would go to the scrubber's spigot and gather a bundle of glass beads of water. 'Can we modify the spores?' Davide asked, after a while. 'Tweak them? Encourage them to make alcohol?'

Nobody answered, so Gordius, looking timidly from face to face as if expecting immediate rebuke, said: 'theoretically it ought to be possible. But I'd bet you a credit to a crater the strain they've given us has been gene-tagged to block developments like that.'

'That *would* be just like them,' E-d-C agreed, placidly. 'Not that it would cost them anything. What do *they* care how we wait out our time here? Drunk for eleven years straight – or enforced sobriety – it'd be the same to them. They choose the latter because it is more cruel. That's all.'

'Cruel isn't right, I think,' suggested Jac. 'It's business, not sadism.'

Marit laughed at this, as if to say; *you see a difference?* And E-d-C growled: 'there you go again, defending them.' But Jac went on: 'none of this is random, none of it is careless. They've done this with thousands of prisoners. Tens of thousands, probably. They've been doing it for decades and decades. They've got it down to a fine art. This is *how* they extract the maximum productivity out of – us. This is how they ensure the asteroid has been most thoroughly mined and worked through.'

'We put all the labour in. Then at the end they take it away, sell it and pocket our money. It makes a man want to mess the whole rock *up*,' said Mo. 'Just to spite them.'

'Jac's right,' said Gordius, emboldened by the success of his previous contribution to the exchange (success being measured, of course, in the absence of physical assault). 'If we mess up their rock, we're only messing up our own environment, only hurting ourselves. There's nothing we can do. They've got us very neatly stuck.'

'Still,' said Mo, stretching, and talking in an expansive tone. 'There ought to be a way we could . . . let's say, near the end of our sentence, drill new tunnels that compromise the rock's integrity in some way. Not to actually cause us danger, just to make it impossible for the Gongsi to sell it on.' When nobody replied, he added. 'Like, lots of shafts *near* the surface – or.' But then he laughed, and added: 'It's never going to work! There *is* nothing we can do. They've set us on the cable and we got to ride it all the way along! Though they're bastards, you got to admire their cleverness!'

'I don't like to think there's nothing we can do,' said Davide, darkly.

'Come—' said Mo. He was near enough to Davide to be able to reach out and slap his flank. 'Don't fight it! You'll only fret yourself to pieces. Eleven years isn't *so* long. We have food now, we can keep busy, with the drills. Before you know it we'll be free.'

But Davide shook his head. 'You want to make yourself into a drone, you go ahead. I refuse to accept that they got me beat. There has to be a way out of this cell.'

'For instance?' asked Lwon.

Everybody looked at Davide. He blushed, his dark skin going a red-granite colour. 'Agents of folly,' he said, turning his eyes to the wall. 'All of you.'

'Drill through to the outside,' said E-d-C, grinning, 'take a deep breath, and jump through? Is *that* it?' It wasn't so very funny, but it made Marit and Mo laugh, and Gordius followed a few beats later. 'A *real* deep breath?' E-d-C pressed. 'Jump all the way back to Earth?'

'Bit of re-entry heat,' Marit put in. 'Warm us nicely.' They *were* all shivering.

Davide, finally, was goaded into replying. 'There's no way off without a ship, sure' he said. 'But who says the first ship that comes by has to belong to the Gongsi?'

'So you're going to signal a ship?' asked Lwon, his voice level and serious. 'You have a transmitter somewhere secreted about you, do you?'

Davide stared furiously at him. 'Or even if the first ship that comes along *is* the Gongsi retrieval vessel,' he said, shortly. 'Even if we *do* have to wait eleven years – why should we just troop aboard meekly and go back to 8Flora? Eh? Why not *take* the ship?'

'Take it . . . how?' Lwon gave the impression of somebody who genuinely wanted to know.

'There's metal in this rock,' said Davide, turning his eyes to the wall again. 'There must be. Why not extract it, and make weapons from it? Then when the Gongsi team land to collect us – bam! We take them *and* their ship.'

Nobody spoke for a while, until Lwon did. 'A plan,' he conceded. 'But there are at least three-bit problems with it. How do we turn this ore into metal? Smelt it?'

'Smelt it,' repeated Davide, perhaps agreeing with Lwon, or maybe blankly questioning his words by repeating them.

'We were wondering why the fusion cell has its threshold set so low – yeah? Wouldn't it be *nice* to warm this place up more than we're managing – yeah? Well maybe this is why the Gongsi has set it up the way they have. If they gave us unlimited heat that's precisely the sort of thing we'd be doing: smelting, forging big-old swords, making ourselves troublesome for the retrieval crew.' He shook his head. Dust came off his beard and swirled slowly through the air both sides of his face. 'They're ahead of us there.'

'There has to be *something* we can do,' insisted Davide.

Jac spoke up. 'Metal may be beyond us. But what about glass?'

'Hah!' said E-d-C. 'This again? You still want *windows*, Leggy?'

'It's just that I've noticed, during my shifts on the digger,' Jac

30

said, 'when I'm digging through silicates – I've noticed that I get beads of glass. They're thrown off by the friction, I guess. Well, mightn't there be a way of . . .'

'You know the difference between *ingenious* and *clever*, Leggy?' Davide broke in. 'Maybe you're the first but you surely aren't the second. Think it *through*. What good are glass beads? If we can't generate the heat to smelt metal, how can we generate the heat to work glass? And if we made a window – how could we fit it into the side of the stroid? How, exactly, would we cut out a window frame without losing all our air? And even if we could? Say we're talking about a piece a metre wide – sand-glass would be so full of impurities it'd crack at the slightest knock or deformation. It would be a suicide portal.'

Jac said nothing. Everybody was silent.

'You know what?' Mo said, suddenly. His own beard was growing out in straggling curly sideburns, and not – it seemed – on his chin at all. He twined dusty fingers into his face hair and tugged. 'We've never had the conversation about why we're here.'

'You mean, in an existential sense?' asked E-d-C.

'No,' said Mo. 'I mean – what did each of us *do*, to get an eleven year sentence. I'm thinking: not murder, or we wouldn't have got off so . . .' He rolled his eyes around their coldroom confinement space: 'lightly. So what?'

'I bet I can guess,' said Davide.

Everybody looked at him. 'Go on, then,' prompted Lwon. 'Guess.'

'Well, well,' said Davide, stretching. 'So: you and E-d-C know one another. You said that, during our first day here. I reckon you're part of the same criminal milieu. Which suggests organisations, which in turns suggests illicit portage about the System. Or maybe trespass. Contraband, smuggling, hocked-ships, taking-and-flying-away. Which?'

E-d-C nodded. 'Something like that,' he said, with some peculiar, unreadable tone to his voice. 'It's true I *do* know Mr Lwon, a little,' he added. 'Though only in a business capacity.'

'And then there's Leggy here,' said Davide, turning to look at Jac. 'You can tell a lot about a person from observing the things their mind gets hooked up on. For you, it's making a *window* for this place. Eh? Yeah. You want to have a view *out*. It's like an obsession. What does that tell me? Well, combined with the fact that you're not built for violence,' – Davide gestured at the place below Jac's pelvis where his legs ought to have been '—makes me believe that you're a *political* prisoner. A dreamer, an idealist, somebody who hasn't come to terms with the fact that the Ulanovs run things now. Am I right?'

'Not built for violence,' repeated Jac, meditatively. 'Doesn't that depend upon what you mean by violence?'

'Sure, sure,' said Davide, dismissively. 'The oppressive state is inherently violent, we can all agree. Property is violence, trade is violence, I'm sure you're capable of all *sorts* of revolutionary action – planting dangerous software that does horribly violent things to accountancy programmes and bId access, for instance. Sure. But, for all that, I look at Marit and I know he's capable of tearing a man's throat out with knives, and I look at you and I see you're *not*.' He favoured Jac with a lowering wolfish grin, just to show that *he* was capable of the more physical forms of aggressions. 'Nothing to be ashamed of, being a political prisoner. Just so long as you don't forget your place in the pecking order.' Then he turned his attention to Marit and Mo. 'You two,' he said. 'Forgive me, but you don't strike me as management-level criminals. Hired muscle, enforcers, something along those lines.'

'Go take a swim in space,' snarled Mo.

'Which only leaves our fat friend, here. You're the odd one out, aren't you, Gordius? *Odd* odd-one-out. What did *you* do to get yourself mixed up with such noxious company, my pally?'

A tomato-red flush was spreading over Gordius's ample neck and chins. The diamond-shaped scar on his forehead had healed to a pinker colour than the surrounding flesh, and it went livid as he blushed. 'You don't want to know,' he muttered.

'Sure we do,' grinned Davide. 'Don't we?'

'I've been unjustly imprisoned,' he said. 'I was only doing what my religion required.'

'Hoho!' boomed Mo. 'You a *religious* maniac? What did you do, big boy?'

But an impermeable membrane had snapped into place around Gordius's mind. Though the four alphas (Lwon only excepted) teased and provoked him for a long time, he would not listen, and nothing could entice him to speak. He folded his limbs around his large frame and put his face to the wall. Jac watched him. He knew this for what it was: a retreat into a profound misery, the prison of melancholy that had memory written on its door. Soon enough the others grew tired of taunting him, and with food in their bellies they disposed their bodies as best they could, floating in proximity to make the most of mutual body heat, and fell asleep.

Jac remained awake for a long time. He was thinking of glass.

It took them a great many more days – or what passed for days in that clockless place – to get a proper rhythm of ghunk growing right. First of all, individual crops grew out of sync. They had groups of days when there was too much of the slop to eat, and groups of days when none of it was green at all and they had to go hungry. But trial and error meant that they eventually arrived at a situation where there was food every day, even if not necessarily enough to completely satisfy everyone's hunger. Familiarity did nothing to endear them to the stuff. It was the texture of it, as much as the taste. Glop.

They decided to expand their growing space. It took Jac and Gordius a couple of hours to dig out a trench, and adjust the position of the lightpole a little so as to shine into it. A soaked rag was pinned to the bottom of this with stone-chips, a smear of spores scratched up by fingernails from underneath the edible green bloom, and the marginally more sheltered growing environment meant that the ghunk grew not only quicker but seemed – everybody agreed – even to taste a little less noisome.

But it was hardly food. It never *fully* satisfied hunger. It lay slimily in the stomach; it emerged unsatisfactorily from the other end of the digestive tract. This was also a problem, of course, in that enclosed space. They debated what to do with their bodily waste. Urine, soaked into rags, helped the ghunk grow even better; but they could find no useful function for faeces. Although everybody assumed that it would be somehow useful when it came to growing the food, in fact the ghunk was perfectly indifferent to it: as happy to grow on bare rock as on a frozen turd. So over two days E-d-C and Jac between them dug a cul-de-sac shaft, into which such waste could be disposed.

Otherwise the main activity of any given day was digging. As the cavity space expanded, they used the fusion cell to break oxygen out of the ice – indeed this, rather than heating, was the reason the Gongsi had gone to the expense of providing it. The scrubber was fine at refreshing air; but new space needed new atmosphere to fill it. The cell worked efficiently enough, and the seam of ice seemed big enough to supply both drinking water and new air. Their voices slipped up the register, a semitone higher, a tone. Some of them spoke more squeakily hilariously than others – the hydrogen, of course. Lwon grew worried about fire: should any of the diggers strike a spark from some nugget of meteorite iron, or something. His worry was contagious, but day followed day and the level of hydrogen in the air stabilised. It seemed that the scrubber, for all that it was an antique model, was as well suited to the task of processing the hydrogen out of the air and into carbon. From time to time they discussed, more or less idly, how it was doing this. Methane was one possibility – just as flammable, of course. Nobody could tell if the air smelt any worse than it had before. 'It smells absolutely bad already,' was Davide's opinion. 'It could hardly smell any worse.' Maybe the gas was being processed into some more complex hydrocarbon chain. The scrubber's filters did need scraping out from time to time. They took it turns to clear its tube of blackened powdery residue, making sure to do so near the digger so that the clogging stuff could be passed through the exhaust hoses. 'All our lives depend on this machine,' said Gordius, uncharacteristically minatory.

The scar over the cut on his forehead looked like an unpolished ruby set into his flesh.

Life inside Lamy306 had settled into a routine. It was dull: physically uncomfortable (especially the cold) and monotonous. But it was bearable. There was food and water, and there was work to occupy at least some of the time. They were still alive. A stratification in their respective relations had very quickly established itself. At the top were the alphas: Lwon, Davide and E-d-C, the latter not conceding Lwon anything so dignifying as 'leader' status, but neither challenging it outright. Then came Mo and Marit. Finally, at the bottom, were Gordius and Legless Jac. The hierarchy was made most manifest in the group's sexual arrangements. Gordius got the worst of this, unluckily for him, with everyone but Jac taking humiliating advantage of his body in various ways. To begin with he wept openly at his cruel usage, complained, begged them to leave him be. But after a while he seemed to become habituated to it, in a glum sort of way. The other men would often discuss him as a sexual object, combining many taunts at his obesity with more admiring observations that his extra weight at least gave him a feminine quality, at least from certain angles. With respect to Jac their comments were more dismissive: his deformity was, all agreed, a repulsive thing. It meant that they left his rear-end alone, although all five of them did insist upon other ways in which he could gratify them. Jac seemed to take these indignities with a quiet stoicism; but then it was hard to tell what he was really thinking. He kept his thoughts to himself.

In a way, Mo and Marit had a more troublesome time. Sometimes they were treated as *de facto* alphas, and the five men would laugh and joke together. But sometimes, without warning, the top three would treat Marit and Mo as betas, almost on a par with Gordius and Jac. This was mostly a question of penetrative sex, which quite apart from causing them physical discomfort provoked a more grievous psychological hurt. Mo suffered from this latter to a greater degree than did Marit. When it became apparent that Mo found his treatment peculiarly oppressive, Davide took a particular delight in singling him out for his sexual attentions. In the aftermath of such encounters, Mo would become surly, and would strike out at Jac, but more often at Gordius, in unpredictable ways.

That said, the group's sexual interactions were neither frequent nor prolonged. The environment was too public, too draining, above all too *cold* for any of them to maintain prolonged erotic appetite. Sex, when it happened, tended to be a rapid and more-or-less brutal process of masculine discharge.

For Jac it was one more discomfort to put on the same level as the constant cold, the unsatisfactory food and the general monotony. He did not dwell on it. But he could certainly see it was gnawing away at Gordius's peace of mind. 'You need to think about something else,' he advised the big fellow. 'Don't let it fester in your thoughts.' Gordius glowered at him, and Jac thought he was going to turn away and sulk. But instead he burst into tears. 'I can't bear it! What else is there to think of? I'm always cold, and always hungry! The others show me no mercy! What else is there to think of?'

Marit, Mo and Davide were on the drills; the noise of their action against the rock, now as absolutely familiar to all seven of them as the sound of their own blood pulsing in their ears, droned in the background.

Jac wasn't sure what to suggest. 'Put your mind outside the rock,' he suggested.

'How? If I look to the future, it just seems an impossible long period of time! And if I look to the past – oh! The past!'

'Do you know where the past and the present intersect?' Jac asked him.

'Where?'

'In your mind, only. It's the only point. Otherwise, the past is further away than the furthest galaxy. We know it, intuitively, because we understand the irrevocability of past action, and sometimes that makes us sad.' He looked into Gordius's face, trying to read his expression, but the fellow wouldn't make eye-contact with him. 'But it ought not to make us sad. Another name for that irrevocable gap between past and present is – freedom. Only our minds hold us back.'

'Freedom,' said Gordius. 'Oh, you're speaking ironically! Look where we are! There's no freedom here.'

'Oh there's always a way out,' said Jac. As he said it, abruptly, his heart started thrashing in his chest. It felt as if it wanted to kick its way out. Fibrillations, and the sweat rising shudderingly upon his skin. Had he said too much? But Gordius, of course, was too caught up in his own misery to take the words further. He said: 'I killed my father.'

Jac took a moment to calm his own thrum-thrumming core. Then he said: 'is that why you are here?'

Gordius seemed cast into the most profound glumness. He nodded, and his chins took up the motion.

'Eleven years for murder?' said Jac. 'That seems rather . . . lenient?'

'There was mitigation,' mumbled Gordius.

'For *murder*?'

Gordius seemed to hiccough, or cough, and a shudder passed through his frame. Then it all came out: 'I come from a sunward settlement,' he said. 'A thousand people in a near Venus bubble, all of whom share a religious faith. And believe it or not, and of course you wouldn't believe it, seeing the degradation to which I am presently reduced – I am a, am a – a very important man in my community. I was a god-child, a globe-being.' He started sobbing, and the little muscular spasms that crying entailed caused his body to shudder and begin to rotate in space. 'I am the sun!' he said, bitterly, or else he said 'I am the son', Jac couldn't tell. And then it occurred to him, perhaps that was precisely the point. 'I have been fed and oiled since before I can remember. All through the cosmos God-the-All-Around has shaped His Will into globes: suns and planets and even little planetesimals, such as this, even this benighted worldlet where we are incarcerated. And we worship Him by . . .' But tears overtook him: slow, regular, low-volume sobs.

After a little while, Jac said: 'killing your father was by way of . . . a religious rite?'

'A sacrifice,' gasped Gordius, his face in his hands.

'Your father a willing victim?'

'Of course! It is the *greatest* honour . . . no greater honour is imaginable. When *my* time comes I will accept the destiny with . . .' But the sobbing got the better of the words once again. 'Oh but my time will never come, now!'

'The Ulanov enforcers didn't see it that way, I suppose,' said Jac. 'You poor man. No! You poor – god, I suppose. How are your people managing, whilst their god is in jail?'

'The congregation has my sister,' said Gordius. 'She is much less perfectly globular than I, but at least she *is* of the divine cell-line.'

'There's no chance,' said Jac, a tone of calculation entering his voice, 'that your people would seek you out? Perhaps bribe the Gongsi to find out where they have stuck us? Send a ship to rescue you?' He was thinking: what *wouldn't* a people do to save their god? He was thinking: perhaps befriending this man would be the *politic* as well as the humane thing to do – for a friend might permit him to come along when his people rescued him. But Gordius answered: 'I'm not a god any more. I *was* a god, but I'm not one any more. I'm nothing to the Faithful of the Spheres any more. It is exactly as if I am already dead. They could never locate me, anyway; and they never would try. What – vex the Ulanovs? They would risk the destruction of their whole settlement. One Forward Cruiser could punch holes in the fabric of their bubble from a hundred thousand clicks away.' He shook his large head. 'So you see what my problem is? You talk about my past – what have I got to remember except exile? And what have I got to look forward to? – even assuming I survive eleven years in

38

this hellish place. I could never go home. I have no home. I was a god once, and deapotheosis leaves not a man but a . . . nothing.' He started crying again.

Jac was surprised how disappointed he was to discover the unlikelihood of rescue from this quarter. Perhaps his willpower was not the tightly focused thing it had once been. He scratched an itch in his stump. But then something occurred to him and he smiled broadly.

'You're smiling,' Gordius noted, in a flat, disappointed voice. But at least he had stopped crying.

'I'm sorry. I can't help it. Those others are here for their various crimes, and they all think you're as mild as a kitten. But you're the murderer! You're the one with the actual violence in your past! They don't know the half of it.'

'Don't tell them,' Gordius begged, in a panicked voice.

'Of course I won't,' said Jac. 'You and I – we're in this together, aren't we? I just think it's funny. What people don't know generally makes me laugh; especially if they're simply too dense to see it when it's right in front of their eyes.'

It was pitiful to see how much emotional sustenance Gordius took, immediately, from that mere statement of mutual misery: *we're in this together, aren't we?* He pushed his wrists into his eyes, and grinned, and nodded. 'And what did *you* do?' he asked, in a thick-as-thieves voice. 'To end up here, I mean?'

'What I did,' said Jac, smiling again. 'You mean – what was I sentenced for? Well, I I I was not sentenced for the right thing.'

'I knew it,' gasped Gordius. 'Like me – you're an innocent, unjustly convicted!'

'No,' said Jac, in a neutral voice. 'That's not what I mean. I deserve to be here. There's no question. It's just that I was not guilty of the specific thing for which I was sentenced. And,' he added, deciding that it was only fair, all things considered, to take the big fellow into his confidence: 'and that's my dilemma. Eleven years. Long before the sentence comes to an end the Ulanovs will discover what I *really* did. And the punishment for that is . . . well, rather more severe than eleven years inside an asteroid.' Gordius was making round eyes at him now. 'So, I am in a particularly difficult situation,' Jac said. 'I cannot say that I am enjoying my present lodgings. But however horrible they are, they are better than what will happen to me when the Gongsi ship finally docks to retrieve us. I cannot look forward to *that*.'

'What will you do?' whispered Gordius.

'I,' said Jac, looking around him, gauging whether he had told Gordius too much, or just enough to bind them together in the friendship of victimhood, 'I shall make glass.'

Gordius blinked, blinked, and then grinned. Suddenly he clasped Jac to his bosom in a wobbly embrace. 'You and your window!' he cried, joyfully. 'Don't ever stop dreaming of your window, Jac! Keep your dream alive!'

Disengaging himself, Jac said: 'well, yes. A window would be a useful thing. Even a small one. With a window you can . . . see the outside world.'

The group discussed their situation, talking round and round the topic, but really there was nothing to discuss. The one thing they all wanted was privacy. So the only conceivable course of action was to excavate a series of separate chambers, and link them together with tunnels. That was the most pressing goal. 'Seven chambers first off,' Lwon said. 'One each. And then we can warm the air in each, and it will in turn warm the rock, and instead of stripping that warm rock away it will act as insulation and we might start feeling something like comfortable.'

'Music to my ears,' said Davide.

Jac figured that the top three would dig themselves chambers, and possibly that they would let Mo and Marit dig themselves rooms as well; but that some other plan would come to play before he and Gordius got a room of their own. But eleven years is a long time. He figured he'd be able to make himself a cubby hole at some point.

In the meantime he gathered glass. When he was digging

through silicate-rich areas, little beads and minuscule lumps of the stuff would be shed from the drilling point. He turned off the waste schute, and spent time picking these out from the general chaff. They were never very big – ten could fit in the space of a fingernail – but they were the real thing, actual glass.

So he tried an experiment: he carved out a shallow depression, gathered as many of the tiny marbles as could be persuaded to float inside it, and then covered them with the drill. It took a number of attempts, but he ended up with a larger lump of irregularly shaped glass, fused by the excavator from the smaller pieces. When he held this, it sat neatly in the middle of his hand.

Davide mocked him for it. 'Some window! That's barely enough for a monocle!'

'A glazier has to start somewhere,' said Jac, mildly.

'Never mind glassmaking,' Davide snarled, displeased by this reply. 'You keep digging. I want a room of my own. You hear?'

'Dig your own room,' Jac said, slipping the lump of glass inside his tunic.

'What?' roared Davide.

'I'm *digging* your own room,' Jac clarified. 'Is what I said. I'm doing it *now*.' He turned on the waste hose again and began once more grinding away at the rock.

After his shift was over, and after he had eaten a little ghunk and drunk from the scrubber's spigot, Jac took out his lump of glass and examined it. It was opaque on the outside, and shaped with as many bulges and prongs as an amoeba. Taking a piece of abrasive rock he began to rub away at the outside. He fell into an easy-enough rhythm, and the action helped keep him a little warmer. But the others only mocked him.

'Hey – what you doing?'

'What you rubbing there, Leggy?'

Jac smiled, and shook his head. 'What is it?' E-d-C demanded.

'It's his chunk of glass,' said Gordius, eagerly. 'Hey, are you *grinding* the glass?'

'Is that your window, cripple boy?' said Marit, with an unfriendly laugh. 'Window big enough for a cockroach, maybe?'

'I think he's going to make a microscope,' said Mo. 'And then what? With your microscope you'll – what? Look for your legs?' Everybody laughed at that.

Jac kept grinding. After a while, Davide said: 'how did you *lose* your legs, anyway, Jac-my-lad?'

'It's a long story,' said Jac.

'Oh,' said Marit. 'You think maybe we won't have enough *time* to hear it?' He laughed, without warmth. 'Tell the story, cripple boy.'

Jac stopped rubbing. All eyes were on him. 'Well, Marit,' he said. 'What happened was: I was pleasuring your mother and she got so excited she snapped them both off with her muscular thighs.'

There was the briefest pause when it looked as though Marit might launch straight for him, strangling-hands first; but then everybody laughed, and the fury receded back deeper into Marit's eyes.

Later, with Mo, Marit and Lwon on the drills, Gordius came over and asked: 'how *did* you lose your legs, friend?'

'It's neither a long nor a boring story,' said Jac. 'But I'd rather not go into it here.'

'Oh,' said Gordius, disappointed. 'I thought you were brave, talking back to Marit. He's a violent soul. My father used to say: one thing about being a god is that you can see into the souls of men and women. You can see the gravity that keeps their spirit together, and perceive whether it be evil or good. He has a violent soul, I think, does Marit.'

'You think?' Jac asked, drily.

'Oh! Yes!' said Gordius, ingenuously. 'Davide is,' he looked around, lowered his voice, 'Davide is angry too, but it's a *regular* sort of anger. Marit is different. He is cruel. He likes to pass the time by flicking chips of rock as hard as possible at me. He likes to aim for my face when I'm not expecting it. I think he wants to

42

get one of my eyes out. I think, if he managed to knock one of my eyes out, he'd laugh!' Gordius shuddered. He had not maintained his original bulk, what with the limited diet of ghunk and the hard work of drilling; he had shrunk, and his skin lay in folds about his frame, like drapery.

'We'd best keep our eye on him,' Jac said.

You and me together, friend!' said Gordius, with a catch in his voice.

Day followed day. Jac kept his eye on them all. Marit had a cruel streak, no question; but Jac figured Davide was more immediately dangerous, for his frustration was working alchemically upon his rage. Although for the time being the laboriousness of the work and the exhaustion of rest soaked up his rage, there was no knowing how long that would last. Lwon and E-d-C were too focused on manoeuvring for position in the group as a whole to divert energy towards persecuting Gordius or Jac. No: Mo and Marit were the most immediate threat. Already Jac could see that even the incessancy of the tasks needful for immediate survival was not enough completely to distract them from their own dissatisfaction. They were bored, resentful, and although their surly gazes mostly followed the three alphas, Jac knew that it was only a matter of time before they kicked downward. Sooner or later they were going to take out their bitterness on either Gordius or him. That would be at the least painful, and at the most fatal.

Eleven years: he would never last that long. Neither would Gordius. They had to get out. Or at any rate: he had to.

For the time being, though, the three alphas and two alpha-betas spent a good deal of their energy upon dominance games. 'I was the number one thorn in the Ulanovs' side,' claimed Davide. 'You know who arrested me? Bar-le-duc himself! In person!' Jac's attention was snagged by that. 'You *that* important, are you?' asked Marit, sourly, 'that the Ulanovs' top arrest agent came personally for you?'

'Bar-le-duc!' repeated Davide.

'I don't believe a word of it,' said E-d-C. 'I reckon a low-ranking policeman snagged you up, same as the rest of us.'

'Well that shows what *you* know!' said Davide. 'Bar-le-duc, the famous Bar-le-duc, took me *personally* in hand. I had cost the Ulanovs billions of credits. I was Solar System enemy number one.'

'In the old days,' said Marit, 'they used to put delusional lunatics in hospital, not in a prison like this! I'll tell you what, though; true fact, not fantasy like Davide's boasting. They made a *movie* about me! *I'm* the metrical Jesse James. I'm famous in a hundred communities.'

'Shanty bubbles, maybe' said Davide.

Lwon refrained from boasting, but the others indulged themselves freely. And Jac watched as Gordius, childlike, strained to join in. One day, unable to keep his secret to himself, and hoping to ingratiate himself with Lwon, Gordius indulged in a bit of boasting of his own: he revealed that he had been a god to his own people. This was a mistake. Lwon relayed the information directly to everyone, and Gordius held his knees to his chest and rotated slowly in the air, his skin flushing with embarrassment, as E-d-C, Marit and Mo brayingly mocked him. 'So you're the *God* my preacher told me about!' 'Hey, God, why don't you perform a miracle and get us out of here! Go on – jaunt us clear and free, take me to . . . someplace warm.' 'His magic only works,' said Mo, sarcastically, as if explaining an important theological crux to everyone, 'after we crucify him. Once we've tortured him to death, *then* he comes back, and *then* he can do the magic.'

'You don't understand the revealed truth of cosmic religion,' blurted Gordius, goaded beyond caution. 'I'm not the *spiritual* god. *She* is Omni – I'm but the material god, englobed in flesh. Or,' he faltered. 'I was. I was, but. Now I'm nothing.' He started crying, tears coining from the corners of his eyes as little silver globes and floating way. 'Now I'm nothing at all, less than nothing!' he wailed. 'I have lost everything! You might as well kill me now and get it out of the way!'

'Stop your noise,' snapped E-d-C, crossly. He was close enough to be able to kick out, and he caught Gordius in the middle of his loose-skinned stomach. The big man mooed like a heifer in pain, and bent double as he slid backwards through space and pranged against the far wall. Jac watched carefully. Everybody was laughing. E-d-C had a severe grin on his face as he slid back away from his blow; Lwon and Mo were laughing, but it was Marit who was laughing the hardest. Jac thought to himself: maybe he *is* the one nearest to cracking, after all.

It would either be him, or Davide, he was sure of that.

'Bar-le-duc, bar-le-duc,' sang E-d-C, tunelessly. 'Nabbed us all, nabbed us all – except for god-boy who was betrayed by Ju-u-das.'

There was no escaping their labour, though. When the others took their turn on the diggers, Jac worked at polishing his lump of glass. It was slow work, and after several days it all came to nothing: a carelessly too-forceful thrust to try and erase a small protuberance caused the whole piece to crack into three pieces. Jac breathed deeply, and breathed out. Then he bundled the pieces together, gathered some more miniature marbles, and spent a portion of his next session at the digger pressing them into a new lump. Davide saw what he was doing, and for a while the whole group – Gordius amongst them – gathered around Jac to mock him for his self-appointed Sisyphean task. But Jac was placid, and non-confrontational, and eventually they grew bored and left him to it. After a good deal of careful effort, he managed to produce a slightly larger, flatter lump.

Then, after his stint on the diggers: back to scraping and abrading.

'You're just doing that to pass the time,' said Davide, dismissively.

'Just to pass the time,' agreed Jac . 'Though I suppose time will pass, in any case, regardless of what I do.'

Work continued. The three diggers were diversely employed, each excavating a chamber. Lwon himself struck lucky one day, discovering a second vein of ice, bigger than the first. He turned the extractor off, and used the drill to whack chunks of it out. The others stopped whatever they were doing, or not doing, to grab these and pass them back. 'We can grow a lot more of that delicious ghunk now,' cried Davide. 'Can any man boast a greater joy in his heart than I?'

'I'm so sick of your voice,' said Marit. Then, looking around, and to make clear that he wasn't picking a fight with Davide, he added, 'I'm so sick of *all* your voices.'

'Well,' said Lwon. 'We've got eleven years. You'd better get used to them.'

'How can it still be *eleven* years?' Marit growled. 'Surely we've been here a year already!'

This, of course, was a real issue. How were they going to keep track of time, in the longer term? Should they even bother trying? Lwon finished pulling the ice from its seam, or all the ice he could reach. This left an overhang of rock that was easily broken and chipped away by the digger. It felt like a day on which something had been achieved, actual structure added to the interior space; so everybody stopped work and ate some ghunk and drank a little, and lay about the walls or the ceiling. 'Ice is easier to mine than rock,' said Davide, as if uttering a profound and original truth. 'A few more veins like that, and we'll very soon have a room each.'

E-d-C broke wind, and everybody yelled in mock-protest and spoke disrespectfully of his fundament.

'You know what?' said Mo. 'I think it *is* a little warmer.'

'Barely,' said Marit, shivering. But it was true: the worst of the arctic chill had gone out of the air. 'We should hold on to the memory of this cold,' said Lwon. 'Soon enough, it'll get *hot* in here, and then our problem will be finding a way of disposing of the heat. Then we'll look back on these days with fondness.'

'Better be too hot than too cold,' said Mo, earnestly.

The thought that they would one day look back on these times – that there might actually be a future for them – mellowed the group as a whole. It made them meditative. 'There must be ways to dump the excess heat,' said E-d-C. 'Thousands of prisoners survive their term. The majority, I reckon. They find a way, and so will we. There's no problem this rock can throw at us that we won't be able to solve.'

Jac held his peace.

Mo started speaking about his time on Earth, working hauling luggage for a wealthy fretman. 'That full gravity,' he said, 'it's tiring, sure, like they say. It tires you because it's there even when you're sleeping, so you never sleep quite right. But my god and lord how it tones your musculature! It was just hauling bags, not even specially big ones, but my arm muscles got big as boulders.' He displayed his arms. 'Not so bulky now,' he conceded, sadly.

Gordius farted. 'Hey!' Davide objected, loudly; and then, as the stench penetrated even over and above the foul smells in which they habitually lived, everybody groaned and spoke threatening words. Gordius started giggling. 'Sorry, guys,' he said, but he didn't stop giggling. The giggles made the folds and curtain-drapes of his flesh wriggle and flap like a flag in a strong wind. His laughter acquired that hysterical edge, that grating edge. 'Sorry! Sorry!'

Marit roused himself, and floated over to Gordius. He reached out and slapped him in the face. The sound of a wet cloth on a riverside stone. Gordius's head turned quickly to the right, but the laughter didn't stop. Marit drew back his arm again, folded his open hand into a fist. Then he thrust it hard against Gordius's cheek. The giggling stopped. The sound of a bat hitting a ball. The sound of butcher's cosh hitting flesh. Marit's arm was back out, and down again: punch, punch, again in the face. Gordius was making a high-pitched warbling noise, and wriggling to get free; his own arms stretching and trying to push Marit off. Another wet thwacking sound, this one right in the eye. Marit had hold of Gordius's long hair with his left hand, and was holding it tight. Again, another blow, on the nose, and an adder-shaped strand of dark fluid leapt out into the air. Gordius's struggles meant that the two of them were rotating, their feet coming up to where their heads had been a moment before, but all of Marit's attention was on where his blows handed: his fist sank into cheek, his fist hammered into the eye socket a second time, Gordius's cries increased in volume. Finally Marit's fist made a booming noise as it cracked against forehead bone, and Marit released his grip. He floated back, nursing his right hand. 'You hurt my fist!' he snarled. 'You've done something to my knuckles – you bag of blubber.'

Gordius was foetally clutching himself, sobbing, his great bulk rotating slowly. Trails of sticky-looking bloody mucus extended and curled oddly in the zerogravity.

Lwon said, 'are you OK, god-boy?' But got no reply.

Marit came back over to the new bundle of ice, where it floated, and tried to apply some to his reddened knuckles. 'You *smelt* what he did?' he demanded, of nobody in particular. 'We got to breathe all that? No way. Not me.'

Jac went over to the big fellow and tried to soothe him. It took a long time before he could coax him to take his hands from his face, and when he did he saw what a mess it was. Seaweedy extrusions of blackened blood hung from his nose and his left eye was swollen and sealed shut. There were many contusions, and the bruises were already showing, knuckle-shaped fairy stepping stones across the expanse of white cheek. Jac fetched some of the new ice, made Gordius suck on a piece to try and reduce swelling inside the mouth, and scraped the worst of the blood away. 'It's not so bad,' he said. 'Though your eye is going to be swelled shut for a few days.'

'Why didn't Lwon stop it?' Gordius sobbed, indistinctly, his mouth full of ice. 'Marit just went on and on. Why didn't Lwon intervene, and stop it?'

'Why would he risk antagonising Marit? For you? Not worth it. On the contrary,' said Jac. 'He'd rather Marit blew off steam thwacking you than – you know. Attacking him.'

Gordius's battered face acquired a sulky look. 'Isn't he supposed to be in charge? He ought to act like he is.'

'I'm not sure you grasp what being in charge in this place, with these people, means,' said Jac. 'Anyway, I don't think your nose is broken.'

For some reason, this news made Gordius start to weep. 'Here,' said Jac, uncertainly. 'Have some more ice.'

'We're never going to survive here, you and I!' Gord said, through his sobs. 'They're picking on me now, but it'll be you tomorrow. Every time they get a little annoyed, they'll take it out on us two. We'll be beaten to death. Literally to death. And the worst thing is – there's nothing we can *do*!'

'We need to get off the rock,' said Jac, looking over his shoulder.

Behind him the sound of the drills had started up, in their respective chambers. Davide, E-d-C and Mo had resumed digging; Lwon was watching them, Marit was nursing his hand.

'There's no way off this rock,' moaned Gordius. But he peered at Jac with his one good eye. 'Is there?'

'You tell me, god-boy,' returned Jac.

'You're planning something. What? What will you do?'

'To begin with,' said Jac, wiping his bloodied hands on Gordius's tunic. 'I'm going to finish making my piece of glass.'

'Is that the key to it?' He explored his own bashed face, gingerly, with his fingers-ends, wincing. '*Is* that it? But your window would only be the size of a hand – maybe smaller – what good is that?'

'Nothing,' agreed Jac. 'No good at all.'

He was about to push off, when Gordius grabbed his elbow. 'Take me with you.'

Jac looked over at Marit again. Then he looked back at the big fellow.

'I'll keep it to myself!' Gordius said. 'I promise! I won't tell them. And anyway, I can't give away what you're planning, because I don't *know* what you're planning. I just know you're planning *something*. And when you do it, whatever it is. And when you,' He coughed on the blood coming down his throat from the inside of his nose. He gulped. 'And when you do – take me with you. If you don't, I'll die here. The others, they can simply serve their time. They won't miss us.'

'They'll tear themselves apart,' said Jac.

Gordius chuckled, but it turned into another cough. 'Look,' he said, when he regained his breath. 'It's true I'm no longer a god, but my people are rich – they pay tax at 22%! The Ulanovs classify them as a special contributory community! It would be to your profit, helping me. And – and – and anyway, to leave me behind would be murder.' Gordius turned his now-misshapen, bruised head from side to side. 'What *are* you going to do, though? What are you planning? Why do you need a window?'

Jac looked at him. 'I would like,' he said, enunciating clearly in a low voice, 'to be able to see outside.'

'You're going to summon a ship,' said Gordius, in an excited-little-boy voice. He put up his hand. 'It's OK! I won't tell them! Globe, *I* don't even *know* how you're going to do it! There *are* no ships out here, and a window the size of a button isn't going to enable you to – no, never mind. I don't need to know how. I just need to know that you'll take me with you.'

Jac directed a steady gaze at him.

'Jac,' Gordius pleaded, whisperingly. 'Look what Marit did to me! For no reason! These are violent men. These are murderous men. We're not – I'm here on account of my piety, and you're a political. *We're* different. But these men are like – tigers. We can't stay here for very much longer. Not if we want to stay alive.'

'Tigers,' said Jac, meditatively. It was as if the word reminded him of something. Then, returning from some distant realm of thought, he said: 'you should have some more ice.'

'This ice is all dusty,' said Gordius, sulkily. Then he hissed: '*say* you'll take me with you. Please! Please! My people will make you rich. Just say you'll take me with you! Promise it!'

Jac held his thumb up, and pressed it lightly against Gordius's bruised lips. 'I promise,' he said. 'I will take you with me.' There was something in his voice that sounded like tenderness. And maybe it was.

Jac did his best to work on the lump of glass when nobody was paying him any attention, but in such close quarters it wasn't easy. He was grinding with a more careful, laborious motion, taking pains not to crack the piece. It took a long time.

The first chamber having been completed, there was a general agreement that the digger in question would best be used in carving out a corridor into the heart of the stroid. New chambers could be budded off this central line. And so the interminable labour continued.

Jac finished his turn with the digger, excavating this new tunnel. He was sweating, and floated to the spigot. 'Yours,' he gasped to Marit.

'My hand is still sore where Buddha-boy there hurt it,' said Marit. 'You take another turn.'

Jac was far too tired to do anything but sleep. He made his way over to the scrubber. He didn't say anything; all he did was shake his head, wearily. But then as he bent to put his lips to the spigot he felt a sharp pressure on the back of his head. His mouth slammed against the tap, and his front tooth clicked back like a switch. The circulation inside his head made a sudden loud noise and he pulled his head back in. His vision had become ruddy with pure fury. He looked around. Pain sang its terrible song inside his mouth and at the back of his head simultaneously. Everybody was laughing at him, although the cacophony of his own pulse sprinting round his veins and arteries dampened all other sound. Marit had thrown a large chunk of stone at the back of Jac's head: the impact had smashed his mouth onto the unyielding substance of the spigot. He put a hand to the place where the skull overhangs the back of the neck. His hair was stickily wet. He looked from face to face. The lightpole was gleaming Hadean rouge; the faces looked demonic and red as sunset. He took a deep breath. Now?

He released the breath. No, no, no.

The colour drained from his vision, and the sound returned to normal. He breathed in. Breathed out.

'Your *expression*!' laughed Marit, seemingly well-pleased by what he had done. 'You should have seen it.'

Looking left. Jac felt his front tooth; it had been knocked more than forty-five degrees from true; and the gum raged with a resentful pain. Looking right – there was the missile, still rotating and moving slowly away from its own recoil; a chunk almost as big as Jac's own skull.

'It's OK, little legless man,' said Marit. 'You know what? I'm feeling the chill. I'll work after all, to spare you the labour. No, to warm *myself*.' He went through to the barely-started new tunnel and, still chuckling to himself, started up the drill.

Jac looked from face to face. Lwon, E-d-C and Mo were bored now; their attention had moved on to other things. Davide was laughing, though, and – away to the right – so was Gordius, his bruised face twisted into as much of a smile as the swelling and soreness allowed: a freaky-looking half-smile. He caught Jac's eye, and the half-smile wilted.

But Jac needed a drink now, more than ever. He needed to wash the blood from his mouth. Leaving the spigot alone he took a piece of ice and fitted it between his lips, past the raw, bent tooth. The back of his head stung fiercely. He felt the cut in his scalp with his fingers. It did not seem too deep. But the tiny space had an aura of unreality to it now; as if he had been jolted out of a particularly cheap virtuality. He went to the wall and tucked his heel into an anchoring declivity. Then he surprised himself again: he fell fast and instantly asleep.

With every waking Jac made a careful examination of his environment, as if looking for something about it that had changed. Of course nothing had: the same rock, black as squid ink; the same ashen taste in the mouth; the same weary shine of the lightpole, the same unappetising strips of ghunk.

Two more chambers were finished, and the other two diggers

were moved to join the first excavating the central tunnel. The aim was to make this as wide as possible, and to run it ten or twenty metres straight in before adding any more rooms to it. Lwon, Davide and E-d-C took up residence in the three chambers that had been made, of course; and whilst Jac was glad of the extra elbow-room in the original cavity – miraculously, their absence made the tiny space seem cavernous – the others were less content. 'Twenty metres of tunnel?' roared Mo. 'I want a room now! Concentrate all three diggers, and you can scoop me out a room quick as mustard.'

'I'm in front of you in the queue,' said Marit, knocking his two fists against one another.

'You ladies can fight for it later,' said Davide. 'We need to dig some tunnel before we can make your chambers.'

'Not *twenty metres* of tunnel, though!'

'No,' said Lwon. 'Just enough as we need.'

So the new task was tunnelling. The bruises on Gordius's face thinned and went brown and yellow, and his swollen eye slowly returned to normal. But Marit continued his idle persecution of him, with an irregular regimen of random slaps, pinches and punches. One day he announced that he'd decided they needed to increase their growth of ghunk, and that Gordius's tunic was the ideal growing medium. At first the fat man took this for a jest, but it quickly became apparent that Marit was in earnest.

'Sure,' agreed Davide. 'Why not?'

'I'll freeze!' complained Gordius.

'Oh, it's much warmer than it was when we arrived,' said Marit. This was true, although the slight increase in warmth did not change the fact that the main cavity was still refrigerator-cold. The individual rooms were more comfortable: each of the three alphas had taken turns with the fusion cell in each chamber, leaving it there whilst they slept: the smaller space had warmed nicely, with some of the chill taken out of the walls. The fusion cell was back in the main cavity now, but only because Mo and Marit had complained so loudly. 'Come on,' Marit pressed, with sadistic glee. 'Take your tunic off! I'm doing you a favour – you've lost weight, my boy. I'll grow more ghunk, you can eat a little more heartily and you can put a bit more fat on your bones.'

The others were smiling, and Gordius looked with mounting panic from face to face. Then he made a mistake. 'Lwon,' he said, appealing directly to him. 'Don't let them do this . . .'

'What are you begging *him* for?' roared Marit. 'You should be begging *me*, you slug!' In a moment he was on him, slapping him – open-handedly this time – on his face and about his ample torso, tugging at his tunic and screaming 'off with it! Get it off!' directly into Gordius's face. Whimperingly the victim complied, and soon enough he was clutching his naked chest and shivering visibly. 'I'll freeze to death!' he wailed. 'I mean it – I'll die of the cold!'

'All that seal fat?' said Marit, pinning the tunic to the wall near the lightpole with stone chips. 'You'd be warmer naked than any of us fully clothed.'

'You're god, ain't you?' said Mo. 'Miracle up some heat for yourself.'

Mo and Davide helped Marit rub beads and pearls of water over the fabric, and then they applied some of the black spores. When they were finished, Marit looked well satisfied with what he had done.

More digging. E-d-C found a prize, buried in the core of the rock: a piece of metal. It was black as space, and palpably denser than the rock around it. 'Meteorite iron,' said E-d-C proudly. 'Actual metal! All that anxious talk about how we were going to smelt metal – there's no need! Here's an actual piece of the early solar system, embedded in this stroid!'

'We still need to think of a way of working it,' said Lwon. 'It's harder than the rock.'

So they all gave up tunnel-digging for a while, and instead clustered around, proposing various strategies for working the iron. Davide tried grinding it with the business end of a drill, in the hope that friction might heat it and make it malleable; but it only shattered the lump into two. Everybody screeched, as if the chunk were a complex machine that had been broken irreparably. Then, at Mo's suggestion, they tied it to the fusion cell's heated plate. It warmed, a little, but become no more workable. Then they started a lengthy debate about whether it could be beaten into malleability. Davide's idea was: put it to the wall, and use the scrubber as a blacksmith's hammer; but everybody else thought this a terrible idea. 'If we damage the scrubber we will all die in hours,' Lwon said. There were similar objections to using the fusion cell. They took turns with the densest chunk of rock they could find, smashing first one then the other piece against the wall; but it made no difference whatsoever to the material.

Still, the iron was a prize. E-d-C took the larger of the two pieces, and Lwon took the other.

Another day, when Mo, Marit and Lwon were on the diggers, and E-d-C and Davide sleeping, Gordius shuffled over to Jac. 'I was thinking about what your plan might be,' he whispered, excitedly. As Jac started to say something he added, 'I know! I know! But I won't tell *them*. I know it has something to do with the window you're making.' He pointed at the spot under Jac's own tunic where he had the piece of glass tucked. 'I think I have it figured. You make your glass *transparent*, and fit it in the side of the stroid. I thought: it can't be that; it won't be big enough to look out of. But then I thought: ok, logically then, you're not *doing* it in order to see outside. So I thought about it, and I figured it out.' Gordius chafed his own arms, and rubbed his palms over his ample, loose-skinned front, to warm himself a little. 'See, I thought: if it's not for you to see out, it must be for others to see *in*. Am I right? I don't mean, putting their eyes to the keyhole, of course. But I mean . . . I mean, if I were piloting a spaceship, checking stroids for my compadre Jac the Legless. I know he's inside one of them, but there are tens of millions of steroids! How can I know which one Jac is *in*? Well – maybe the one with a little light shining out of it?'

The grin on his face made Jac's heart wince with pity.

'Doesn't sound entirely plausible to me, Gordius,' he replied, as gently as he could. 'You'd have to be pretty close to exactly the right stroid even to *see* a light so feeble as our lightpole shining through a piece of glass no bigger than a hand. And there are plenty of random lights on inhabited stroids, some of them no bigger than this one. Also – how am I supposed to fit a window to this place without decompressing all our air into space?'

'Oh I haven't got all the details worked out yet,' Gordius agreed eagerly. 'But I'm on the right lines – aren't I?'

'Did you consider,' suggested Jac, gently, 'that I'm making the glass just to keep myself busy, to use up some of the four thousand days we're stuck here?'

'Oh it's *more* than a pastime,' said Gordius, with a certainty born, Jac knew, of desperation. 'It's part of your plan. Are you a pirate? Do you have a crew?'

'No,' said Jac, a little sadly. 'And no. I'm alone.'

This took a little of the wind from Gordius's metaphorical sails. But he still said: 'remember your promise. You're going to take me with you.'

'Rest assured, Gordius,' said Jac. 'I won't be leaving *you* behind.'

He was inside a box: the box was made of stone, and it was passing around the sun at a distance of many hundreds of millions of miles. Its path was a perverted circle. He was inside the box, with no possibility of help, with men who would kill him soon enough – out of sheer boredom if nothing else.

And as the digging part of their waking hours became more habitual, boredom became an increasing problem. 'Almost,' E-d-C said, one day, 'I preferred the first few days of our time here. Almost.'

'Are you crazy?' said Davide, working his way through his beard, pulling each strand of hair straight, one by one. After he had finished this he would go back through, braiding strands together, and then platting the braids. 'Don't you remember how cold it was? I hope I never experience that level of cold again, long as I live.'

'That's true, Mr Arrested-by-the-famous-Bar-le-duc. But we were at least *busy*,' said E-d-C. 'We were occupied. It was cold, sure. But I hardly noticed it – because I was so busy just keeping alive.'

'I'd rather be warm and bored,' said Davide, 'than busy and . . . and so *cold*.'

It had grown noticeably warmer inside Lamy306. Not yet body temperature, of course; and the main space was notable chillier than the three new rooms occupied by the alphas. But even the main chamber was much less severely frozen than before. Of course Gordius, naked from the waist up, complained continually that he was cold. And, truly, he shivered like a man with Parkinson's disease. From time to time, Marit would bellow 'you're *cold*? I'll soon warm you up, god-boy!' and he'd launch himself at Gordius, slapping and hitting. When this occurred, as it did frequently, the victim would shriek and curl himself, as best he could, into a ball. Usually Marit quickly grew bored, and floated away.

Boredom was not a problem for Jac. He watched, and watched. He was inside the box. He *was* the box. What was inside *him*? He knew, of course, and you know too. But even the little voice of self-doubt has its moment of catastrophic certainty.

He couldn't get out of the box, that was a certainty. How could he get out of the box? Putting it like that constituted a practical reframing of the situation, but that only snapped open all the possible trajectories of the future. *If* he got out of the box – the conditional mode. But the idiom of the conditional is possibility and possibility is just another name for uncertainty, and there it was: doubt. His one point of certainty, his dubiety. The material out of which his personal box was built.

'You really think they are coming back?' asked Mo, one day. It happened to be a time when all three alphas were digging. The other four were floating idly in the main space together.

'Sure,' said Jac. 'Eleven years? It's not so long. In the larger scheme of things.'

'Why should they bother, though?'

'Because,' said Marit, evidently irritated by this question, 'they need to recover their investment. That's *all* this is, you understand? It's not punishment. They're certainly not interested in rehabilitating us. Everything in space is expensive. Everyone's margins are filament-thin. They spent money porting us here, and money on the devil-scum equipment with which they supplied us – those diggers, that scrubber, even the tiny handbag of gutrot spores. Cost credits, all of it. It's credits, credits, cre*ditto*. They get that money back with profit. We *make* their profit, by turning this rock into a saleable real estate. That's all. That's all it is.' He was making himself angrier with each sentence he spoke.

'Sure,' said Mo. 'They'll swing by and collect Lamy306 at some point, and fix a buttonthruster, and push it into a saleable orbit. Sure. But why should they do so in the eleventh year?'

'That's our sentence,' stammered Gordius. His shivering had affected his ability to speak; his words stuttered and blurred. 'They *have* to come back – once our sentence is served, and we've paid our debt to solar society.'

'God has *spo*ken,' spat Marit, and threw a stone at him.

'The Gongsi aren't primarily in real estate, though,' said Jac. 'Their primary profit comes from taking prisoners from law enforcement and processing them, for a fee, in accordance with the sentences handed down by law.'

'Sure. But no company lasts long with only one profit stream. The Gongsi diversifies. And profit means cutting all overheads as far as possible. Our *sentence*? If they come when our sentence is finished, they got to come with a large ship, put us in a pressurised hold, feed and water us, take us back to 8Flora, process us – that all costs,' Mo said. 'Let's say they come back in *fifteen* years. Or a hundred.'

'That *would* be a long-term investment,' said Jac.

'These Gongsi think long term!' said Mo. 'That's my whole point. If they come back in a quarter century, we're all dead. They don't have to do anything other than chuck us spaceside. That would be cheaper for them. And cheaper means more profit.'

'Think of the smell!' said Gordius, wide-eyed. 'It would be horrible!'

'The savings would be tiny,' said Jac. 'Hardly worth factoring in. And there would be associated costs. Indeed, I reckon it would cost more.'

'How you reckon that, half-man?' Mo wanted to know.

'Mainly,' said Jac, 'the cost of delay. Every year that they *don't* put this box on the real estate market is a year of lost revenues. I'd bet the Accountancy AIs would rather not wait the full eleven years – I mean, that'll be the term of the contract they signed with the Ulanovs, but I'm sure they'd rather come collect us as soon as we hollowed the rock out. They can't, of course. But I'm saying they'd prefer sooner to later. And if they left us to die, there would be ancillary costs. If we were all dead and decayed they'd have to clean the whole interior. I'm guessing that would be more costly than simply flying us back to 8Flora.'

'Yes,' said Gordius, with a big smile on his trembling face. 'See? They'll definitely come for us.'

'You think bodies would decay in this chill?' said Mo, disinclined to concede the argument. 'I'd say we'd keep pretty fresh. It's cold as any freezer.'

'Two more years,' said Jac, 'with the fusion cell pumping out heat, plus our body warmth, and bearing in mind how good an insulator space vacuum is – two more years, and this place will be hot as a sauna. Our main problem will then become how to lose heat. We'll be digging just to find colder rock to bring the temperature down. And when we've hollowed the whole place out we'll have to start thinking about how to radiate away waste heat.'

'Ah,' said Mo. He was near enough to the fusion cell to give it a slap. 'That's assuming this junk is still heating in a year's time.'

'Fusion cells last decades,' said Marit, sulkily. It was as if he resented the endurance of the technology. 'That light pole will still be shining for *decades*. The heater will work *just* as long.'

'Fusion cells generally speaking – sure. They'll keep generating power for decades. But we don't know what's inside the box we got, do we? Its top temperature is capped, isn't it? Sure.'

'Your point,' said Marit, gruffly. Gordius was whimpering in time to his shivers. Conceivably he was unaware that he was making any noise.

'You know what I'd do?' said Mo. 'If I were in charge, in the Gongsi? For the first few months, sure: without heat we would simply have died – sure. But what if the box has an internal timer? A thermostat? It waits until the temperature reaches a preset level – zero, say – and then it cuts out.'

Everybody pondered this possibility. 'That would be sadistic,' said Gordius, shaking slurs into the 's's.

'You think sadism is beyond them? Look at it this way: it's not quite cold enough to kill us, but not warm enough to keep us comfortable. And though vacuum insulates, we'll still lose heat to radiation. And anyway, the bulk of this rock is colder than ice, and we're chopping into it every day. That'll more than counter-act our collective body heat. What if we *never* get warm? What if, on the contrary, we get colder and colder? So we carry on work-ing, because it's the only way to keep warm. But it gets colder, and colder, and soon enough we freeze to death. *Then* the Gongsi sends a ship along; it's all been calculated by the AIs, down to the hour. They open up this box, and inside all they have to deal with are our freeze-preserved corpses. Maybe they don't even chuck up spaceside! Maybe they grind them up and grow tomatoes in the mulch! I don't know. My point is – wouldn't that be more *economic*?'

'Eleven years,' said Gordius. He wasn't smiling any more.

'That was our *sentence*. It was judicially determined. It would be against the law to . . .'

'If we die in service of our sentence,' said Marit, in a growly voice, 'then the Gongsi is not liable. Legally speaking. That's *our* look-out. Staying alive.'

'They wouldn't do that,' said Gordius, not meeting anybody's eyes. 'What Mo said. They *wouldn't* do that.'

'I still say it would cost more,' said Jac. 'If nothing else, there would always be the risk that they would be found out, and fined. And Gongsi hate risk. Risk is expensive.'

'You know what I studied at Gobi?' said Mo, bringing both his arms out in an expansive gesture. 'Economics. You know what I learned? There are only three things in the universe. *Only* three things. There's raw materials, there's energy, and there's labour. Now energy's expensive. Yes, it's cheaper than it used to be in the chemical age for sure, but it still costs. And raw materials are more expensive than they've ever been. They're abundant, but only in space, and space is a horribly expensive environment in which to harvest them. Energy is scarce, and raw materials are scare, and scarcity means more cost. The only thing that isn't scarce? Labour. People keep spawning *people*. The poorer they are, the more kids they have. It's one of those crazy counter-intuitive laws of the natural world. Because, really, it ought to be the other way about; it ought to be the richer you are the more kids you have. But that's not how it is. Earth is exhausted, in terms of raw materials, and is very poorly positioned in terms of energy, because it's got this blocking veil between it and the sun called "atmosphere" and because its gravity degrades the efficiency of fusion cells to the point they're ludicrous. But it is super-abundant in people. It's a crazy – breeding – manu*factory*. And that's the physics of economics: scarce means expensive; abundant means cheap. Supply and demand. That's the system we live in, gentlemen – and god-boys. It's a system where raw materials are costly, and energy is costly, and the only thing that isn't costly is human life. This box made of rock is worth more to our Gongsi than any number of human lives.'

This was a long speech, and it left Mo hoarse. He floated to the scrubber and took a sip from the spigot.

'That's a rather . . . ,' said Jac, treading cautiously, unsure of the volatility of Mo's mood. 'A rather *nihilistic* view of the state of things, maybe?'

'You think?' said Mo, darkly. 'I was raised a Trickledowner. I was raised on Earth, too, not in some shanty bubble made of plastic that you can watch degrading around you in real-time. No, I was raised in a gated city in West Africa. God-boy here had it easy, compared to me. The *functioning of economics* was the Newtonian mechanics of our world. My fathers studied and *worshipped* economics. You know why?'

'Because they believed economics explained the whole cosmos,' said Marit, with the tone of somebody who knew whereof he spoke.

'That of course,' agreed Mo. 'Sure. But you know what, friend? Something more, too. Because they believed that economics *preserved the special place for humankind* at the universe's heart. We used to think the Earth was the centre of the cosmos, and *that* meant we were special, until science told us we're marginal creatures. Then we thought the sun was centre, until science told us not even that was true. We used to think God made us in His image, and that meant we were special, until science told us we just evolved that way because it suited a landscape of trees and savannas. That's what science does: it says, look again and you'll see *you're not special.* But economics? Economics is also a science. And what does it say? Ask my fathers, and they'd tell you. It says: there is energy, and there are raw materials, and that's the cosmos. But without *us* the energy is random and the raw material is inert. It's only labour that makes the cosmos come alive. It's only us that make economics happen at all. And *that* makes us special.'

'It's a good point,' said Lwon, diplomatically.

'I thought so too. You tend to believe what you're taught, growing up, I guess. But then I went to Gobi, to study. Economics, of course; I was hardly going to study anything *else* at university. I majored in Chaos Exchange, and the philosophy of money. But I also took a course in historical economics. The point of *that* course was to show how inefficient antique human economic systems were, because they didn't understand the physics of the systems they were trying to operate. But it didn't have that effect on me. On the contrary. It opened my eyes. It made me lose my faith – not my faith in economics, which is as immutable as entropy. But my faith in the idea that economics preserves a special place for humanity. Suddenly I saw. Economics preserves a special place for *value*, and value is not the same thing as people. For a while, in Earth's earlier development, the two things happened to coincide. But not anymore. Not since we used up the mundane raw materials. Not since we stepped into space. Listen: economists on Earth used to say that sending human beings into space could never be cost-effective. Imagine! For half a century, Earthen governments spent billions of credits shooting *robots* into space on chemical explosions. Oho, *that* was cost-effective, was it? Robots are expensive now; but they were *vastly* more so then. People, though, are cheap, and getting cheaper. They keep breeding, and that means they're always becoming relatively *less* valuable. We're always the cheapest option. We're *always* the cheapest option. We're losing absolute value with every generation. So I quit school, and I went into crime. My fathers disowned me. You know what? I don't think that was really fair. I was only following their precepts, after all. I started leveraging profit from the only superfluous resource available. I joined a gang of people smugglers. I did that for pleasure and profit for ten years – until the Ulanovs caught up with me.'

Mo had worn himself out speaking; and he turned to the wall and went to sleep. 'He makes it sound like he's a grand philosopher,' grumbled Davide. 'But I'm the one here arrested in

63

person by the great Bar-le-duc.' Nobody even had the energy to mock him for this ridiculous affectation of his. Silence fell.

Marit passed the time chucking stone the length of the main space at a protrusion on the ash-coloured walls. He hit it dead-on nineteen times out of twenty, but still he continued practising. Tock, tock, tock. It was a maddening sound. It had the relentlessness of water-torture. But there wasn't a way Jac could tell Marit to stop without redirecting the fellow's anger onto himself. He tried to ignore it. Tock, tock, tock.

Gordius floated over to Jac. 'I'm cold,' he said. 'Give us your tunic.'

'It won't fit you,' said Jac. This was a simple statement of fact.

'I'm *cold*. It's better than nothing. I could die of this cold! It's more than a human body can bear. You're my friend. Come *on*, Jac! Let's *share* your tunic – that's what I'm saying. I wear it until I get a little warmer, then you can have it back.'

'No,' said Jac.

Gordius's big face shuddered, and then crumpled, like a toddler about to burst into tears. But it wasn't tears that came. Instead he scrunched up his brows, and glared demon-eyes, and unleashed the tanked-up anger of the downtrodden. 'Yes!' he squealed. 'Yes! Yes! Yes!' And his hands were on Jac's neck, and the loose skin of his arms flapped and slapped against Jac's shoulders.

The suddenness as well as the ferocity took Jac by surprise. Gordius's much greater mass carried the two of them hard against the wall. Jac felt the crash painfully. The skin at his neck was being wrenched most uncomfortably.

He withdrew deeper inside himself, put himself away from his own pain. Where did he go? Hard to say. Perhaps he went into the box. But if he did, the box remained intact, unopened. There – on a completely different orbit, much further out in the darkness beyond Jupiter – was his own heart, though it was thrumming too rapidly. That wasn't good. The skin of his neck was rasping. It might tear, and blood would come out. That wasn't good either.

He calmed his thoughts. Here was his brain. This was what was inside the box of bone that was his head. Under his right hand was a rock. He felt it: loose, sharp-edged. He grasped it. His fingers ends just missed it, and it span in mid-air. He reached again, tickled it closer, and grasped it.

This was a delicate situation. He wanted of course to minimize physical damage, and most especially to avoid serious cuts, wounds or even major abrasions to the skin. But he had to act.

It was not going to be easy.

He calmed his heart.

Here were his eyes, and they transmitted the action of photons striking the retina along the optical nerve to his brain. There were two holes in the box of bone. He put himself back into his eyes, and saw Gordius's face leering and fury-gurning close up against his own. The diamond-shaped scar in the middle of his forehead glowed red, like an angry eye. The third eye is the one linked to the soul. But Jac's own vision was oddly distorted, distilled into a central oval with darkness all around. He realised that his eyes were bulging, and that he had not taken a breath. There was no point in trying to take a breath, so he didn't bother with that. He had to think what to do with the rock in his hand.

The options slotted into place beside him. To strike repeatedly at the body, or the neck, or perhaps at the face. That would surely encourage Gordius to cease his attack, but it would surely open wounds in the skin. To knock him on the back of his head, where the long and matted hair would soften the blow; such that the skin would probably not be broken, but where there was no guarantee the knock would be enough to make Gordius desist. The third option was the only one that remained.

His vision shrank further. There was a gargling, choking somewhere in the vicinity. It belonged to him. Jac considered the trajectory, felt for the sharpest edge of the rock he was holding, lifted it.

He jammed it as hard as he could into Gordius's eye.

It was a sideways trajectory, coming in at an angle, and their two faces were so close together than Jac couldn't quite avoid hitting his own head too. But the sharp point of the rock went into the eyeball.

Gordius howled, and released his grip on Jac's neck. In a way that was the hardest moment; Jac's diaphragm sucked down instinctively, air flowed down the rasped-raw windpipe, the heart burst into a drumroll of rapid beats, and the physicality of it all almost drew Jac back from his calm-place in the box. But he couldn't afford to lose control. Not if he wanted to minimise physical damage.

Barely, he clung on to his internal composure. He flipped his left hand round and got it to the back of Gordius's head; with his right hand he ground the sharp point of the rock hard as he could into the eyeball. Gordius's scream rose exactly a tone and a half in pitch. His own hands were at his face, trying to pull the rock away.

It was enough. Jac let go, slid himself along the wall, and fully re-entered his body. This was not pleasant: his throat burned with a horrible pain, a blend of crushed and abraded sensations. A different, distinct pain was banging rhythmically inside his head. His eyes were watering, his lungs retching with some acidic, uncontrollable coughing. He doubled up and rode out the initial hump of hurt. As the worst of the physical distress began to recede he became aware that the drills had stopped. Marit's toc-toc-toc was absent too. The only sound was Gordius's screeching. No – there was another sound. It was a rainfall sound.

He opened his eyes. The other five were floating, applauding him. That's what the noise was. 'Bravo, leggy,' said Marit, his face one big beaming smile. 'I thought you were a casualty there, but you showed . . .' he flourished his right hand, rolling it over and over like an antique courtier underlining a point, 'commendable resourcefulness.'

66

'That *was* entertaining,' agreed Davide. 'Maybe we should get you guys to fight on a regular basis. Break up the tedium.'

E-d-C chuckled. 'Like Ancient Greek Gladiators!' he said.

'Roman,' said Lwon.

'Whatever! It passed the time.'

Jac took three deep breaths to try and settle his scorched lungs, and pulled himself over the wall towards Gordius. The big fellow's screeches had shrunk a little, and he had hidden his face entirely in his hands. When Jac touched his shoulder he flinched. 'Let me see your eye.'

'I'm sorry, I'm sorry,' he squealed.

'Come along, Gord,' Jac said, taking his large hands and moving them gently aside. 'Let me see the damage.'

'I don't know what came over me! I'm so sorry – you're my only friend! I'm sorry!'

'There there,' said Jac. Gordius had scrunched his good eye closed; but his left eye was a mess. 'Come over to the scrubber,' he said. 'I need to wash this at the spigot.'

'It's just I've been so cold – so long, so cold—' Gordius let Jac bring him over to the scrubber, and only flinched a little as he rubbed myriad little ball-bearings of water over the wound. The others were still watching. 'Give him a kiss,' called Marit. 'Kiss it better.' He laughed harshly. Jac glanced up and then back. His worry was that he might have done more than crush the eyeball; he might have cut open the skin around it, gashed the cheek or the brow. It wasn't the cut as such that worried him – a simple cut would scar over quickly enough. But the environment was not healthy; hygiene was very difficult to maintain in such a place, there was so much crap and crud, so many bits and pieces floating through the air, that a cut might very easily become infected. And once infection took hold, who knows where it might go – it could suppurate, whole patches of skin could become open sores. Gordius might die in agony. Jac didn't want that. The cut to the forehead had been bad enough, but luckily it seemed to have healed cleanly. He might not be lucky again.

Prising the eyelids apart made Gordius whimper, but nothing more: the pupil had been pushed into the body of the ball, and a rip opened that had let out the scrambled pale jelly inside. But Jac assumed that was a sterile matter and would – he didn't know; set, or scar, or something. He closed the eyelid and washed it some more. 'Don't touch it,' he instructed Gordius. 'Leave it alone to heal. In a day or two it will stop hurting.'

Gordius's emotions had now cycled from rage to remorse to indignation again. 'My *eye*!' he cried. 'You've blinded my eye!'

'You've still got another one,' called E-d-C. 'Count your blessings, you sack of ghee.' This made the five of them laugh heartily, and Mo started doing an impression, pitching his voice high and effeminate: 'my eye! Oo my eye!'

'You didn't have to *blind* me,' Gordius wailed. 'What have you done? I'll never get an artificial eye in *here*!'

That made the other five laugh even louder.

'I thought you were my *friend*!' Gordius wailed. 'Why did you *blind* me?'

'You *were* trying to throttle me,' Jac pointed out, mildly.

This was too much for Gordius. He started crying. 'You'd think with only one eye you'd cry half as much,' said Marit. 'But *listen* to him!' This was pitched to the others as a comic ob-servation, but nevertheless the general laughter grew less. E-d-C, Lwon and Davide floated back into the central tunnel and started up the diggers again. Gordius curled into a ball and sobbed to himself. Mo went back to sleep, and Marit went back to toc-toc-tocking shards at the far wall.

Jac took himself into the corner, and got out his piece of glass. Smoothing it, working it, grinding over its surface in a circular motion; it was calming. He contemplated his own body as he worked: his throat was very sore, and his bronchial tubes rasped and wheezed as he drew breath. That wasn't pleasant, but it would improve. There were specks in his vision. That, in a way, was more worrying. If the violence of assault had detached a portion of Jac's retina it would be very bad. Probably it was only a matter of some broken blood vessels. Hopefully it would improve.

He put his mind from his own pain, and concentrated on working the glass.

Later, the three alphas came out of the tunnel, dusty and panting. It was Gordius's shift now, but although Jac felt weak, still in pain and little inclined to the work, he took the god-boy's place. He was worried that working at the digger might send bits of grit into Gordius's still raw eye socket. An infection could be fatal. It was not as if they had medical facilities, where they were.

So Jac worked his shift. The tunnel was now fifteen metres long, stretching deep into the heart of the stroid. Marit had decided, unilaterally, that it was long enough; he had turned his digger and was starting to excavate a room of his own. Mo followed suit, and Jac didn't see any reason to do differently. The way things were in the group at the moment, they really needed at least the semblance of some time apart from one another, or they were going to detonate. So the diggers were working their way, slowly, into three separate chambers. If there were six rooms then Gordius would be the one left in the main space.

Not that it mattered. Each room was a box within the box. What's in the box?

The voice was in the box. Still inside.

Much later, after Jac had finished his shift, and as he settled himself in the corner to sleep, Gordius came over to him. He was due to work on the drills. Though he complained, and whinged, there was no shirking his turn now; but before he slipped into the tunnel he put his wounded head close to Jac's. 'I'm sorry, I'm sorry,' he said, in a pitiable voice. 'It was a crazy madness. I should never have done it. You were right to take my eye.'

'That's alright,' Jac told him, embarrassed by his fawning. 'But I am very weary, now, after everything. I must sleep now.'

'I just wanted to say I'm sorry! You were *right* to take my eye! I acted abominably! Will you forgive me for attacking you? You're my only friend in this hellish place! Will you—'

'Come on, god-boy,' yelled Lwon, from the tunnel. 'Time to work. Come along *now*.'

'Will you,' he dropped his voice, and spoke with a pitiful urgency, 'will you still take me with you? When you go?'

'I promised, didn't I?' replied Jac.

'It's just that – I should never have grabbed your neck. I'm so sorry I did. You haven't . . . changed your mind?'

'When I go,' said Jac, closing his eyes, 'I shan't leave you behind, Gord.'

The big man was weeping again, but tears of joy, and from one eye only. 'Thank you, my friend. I won't forget it. We're in this together, you and I. It's crazy for us to fight.'

'Come on, god-boy,' bawled E-d-C, 'or I'll have your other eye.'

Gordius went into the tunnel. Jac felt sleep flood up around his consciousness, like the warm water in a station bath. He was gone, or almost, when he felt a hand on his arm.

His eyes opened with an almost audible snap. There, right in front of him, was Marit's grinning face.

'What do you want, Marit? Sex, is it? I'm pretty tired. Let me sleep first, and I'll be able to do more for you.'

'I heard what you told god-boy,' said Marit.

Jac processed this. He ran through the various possibilities, selected a reply. 'So much hair growing in your earholes, it's a wonder you can hear anything at all. Really it's like toothbrush bristles in there.' But he said this with a half-musical lilt, as if feeling his way.

'Hah,' said Marit, mirthlessly. 'I heard you plain enough. He thinks you got a way out of this rock?'

'That's what he thinks,' said Jac, carefully.

'He's weak in the head. His will is weak, and he's none too bright. How can any of us get away from here?'

'There's no way,' agreed Jac.

70

'Unless that somebody come get us. And only the Gongsi know we're here.'

'Only them,' Jac said, nodding. For this was true enough.

'And they won't be back for a decade or more. Right?'

'Right.'

Marit leant in closer. His breath was a thing of sulphur and decay. 'So why does god-boy think different, eh? What have you been telling him?'

'I haven't been telling him anything,' said Jac, choosing his words with care. 'But he's clinging on to his sanity by a fingernail's width. Let's say this: if he has gotten it into his head that I have a magic road out of this box – well, I certainly haven't directly contradicted him. Let him hope.'

'Hope grows,' noted Marit. 'Kill it young and it'll hurt him. Kill it old and it'll end him.' He floated away.

Jac shut his eyes again. Nothing could keep him from sleep. But as his consciousness did the slow dissolve of the cheaper bitFlicks, he heard Marit's harsh little voice coming, as if from a long way away: 'I'm watching you, Leggy. Always watching.'

Time passed. They dug and dug, and soon enough three new rooms were ready. Then the alphas discussed amongst themselves and decided that the tunnel should be extended five metres, and then a second large chamber cut out. 'We can break the lightpole in two, and have two separate lit spaces. Grow twice as much ghunk!' said Lwon. Jac didn't want to contradict him with the obvious – that with half as much light, the spores would grow half as quickly. Making a second chamber seemed as good a use of their time as anything else.

Gordius's eye healed, more or less. There wasn't any infection, although the top and bottom eyelids on that side were, he reported, 'glued shut'. Jac wanted to test to see whether they were actually sealed together, or whether Gord only didn't open them because it was uncomfortable for them to move over the deformed, whited-out surface of the dead eyeball. But he couldn't think of a way of doing it.

So instead he worked at his glass. The piece was nearly complete. The thing to do after that would be: to make a second piece. Every now and again, his time at the drill threw up little pieces of new glass. It was never anything substantial, and he didn't bother trying to build a larger lump. But he took a few likely looking shards: two handsome sicklemoons in brown-green (once the crap was scraped and polished off them). A straight piece like a miniature sword, or a cocktail stick. A few tiny little D-shaped chips, such as would have delighted the heart of Neanderthal men.

He was nearly ready.

Then two fairly serious problems presented themselves to the whole group in quick succession. The first was something of which they all became only gradually aware, but which shook them into desperate action. It became incrementally clear that the air pressure was lessening, very slowly. That was worrying enough, but even more alarming was the fact that the air was growing less wholesome. Everybody grew breathless with the slightest exertion. They checked the scrubber, and it was working fine; but of course it could only recycle what was there, and the excavation was continually making the interior space larger. More ice was needful, to generate more oxygen. There wasn't enough in their drinking supply. 'Feed in what we've got,' said Davide, with an anger that did little to disguise his anxiety. The thought of slowly suffocating, Jac thought, was a larger terror to his mind than the thought of dying of thirst. 'And drink what?' countered Lwon. 'Our own piss? No, we need to *excavate* a *whole lot* more ice.'

The practical upshot was that they started the second chamber sooner than they anticipated, as they swept the diggers round in a wider arc looking for another seam of ice.

This precipitated the second problem. The waste schutes, attached to the rear of the diggers, had been near full extension for a while. This new direction pulled them taut. That was alright; when E-d-C pulled his schute from the socket it had burrowed through the rock wall, the hole sealed itself. Looking at the tapering point, it seemed that it was designed to fill its own tapering hole with rubble. At any rate, it proved easy enough to reposition the schute. E-d-C set the mouth of it against the rock, inside the tunnel itself; and over the course of about an hour and a half it dug through to the outside again. The same thing was true of the second drill's waste schute. The problem came with the third digger, the one whose schute had been pushed through the artificial barrier of the seal laid down by *Marooner* at the very beginning of their stay. Putting the waste schute through *this* material proved, in retrospect, to have been a bad idea. When the schute was extracted it did not seal the hole, and with a horrifying rushing sound the air in the cavity began to gush into space.

Lwon, Davide and Marit gawped in horror. Mo began shouting incoherently. Everything in the main space was being drawn towards the leak point.

Even Jac found it harder than usual to remove himself from his own somatic responses (pounding heart, adrenalised bloodstream) and find his calm place. He managed it, though. He selected a likely looking rock and placed it over the hole. This slowed the leak but did not stop it, for air was still seeping round the edge. So he retrieved some of the abject matter from the hole in which they stored toilet waste, and worked it with some water from the spigot to make a clay, and with this he made a seal around the rock and the stuff of the ceiling.

The leak was stemmed. 'Nobody,' Jac gasped, 'nobody knock this stone.'

This eventuality had not improved matters, though. The air pressure had been lowered even further, which made everybody yet more breathless. Even the simplest action had become massively laborious and exhausting. For Gordius and Jac there was a single, wan upside, insofar as none of the alpha or beta males had the energy for sex. But the situation was desperate. If they failed to find ice, they would all die soon. It was as simple as that.

So they dug, wearily and inefficiently. They fell into narco-leptic sleeps whilst still operating the machinery.

Day followed day.

Davide, fretfully, blamed E-d-C for this infelicitous turn of events. 'Why did you think the *seal* would be a good material to put the schute through, man?' he said. 'You can see the schute's designed for rock.'

'Shut up,' gasped E-d-C.

'*You* shut up! Your stupidity is choking us all!'

E-d-C growled, plucked a rock from the air, drew his arm back. Davide flinched, visibly, but didn't back down. 'Go on then,' he snarled.

E-d-C's eyebrows went up. You could see the muscles in his neck tense as he readied himself.

'Hey!' yelled Lwon.

Both men snapped their gazes round.

'Let it go, Ennemi,' said Lwon, speaking clearly.

Everybody looked from Lwon to E-d-C. 'I *asked*,' he said. 'I asked everybody. I said, shall I try it? Everybody said, yes. You all said so.'

'None of us said *not* to,' said Davide. 'That's not the same thing.'

E-d-C's eyes widened; he glared at Davide, as at a betrayer. 'This *little* man doesn't get to rebuke *me*.' He held the rock up, and drew his arm back.

'Let it go,' said Lwon, enunciating each word with precision.

E-d-C turned his eyes on Lwon. His face had fallen. Nobody in the space could mistake the look of hurt in his eyes.

Lwon returned his gaze, levelly.

Jac watched with interest.

'Let it go,' Lwon said again.

E-d-C unwrapped his fingers from around the rock, and left it hanging in mid-air. 'The celebrated arresting officer Bar-le-duc never came within one AU of *you*,' he said. Then he pushed himself, wearily, away and went back into the tunnel. Shortly the sound of a digger started up.

Jac went back to polishing his glass. The piece was pretty much there. Rough at the rim, but that didn't matter. He looked up. Marit was having an animated conversation with Davide. Jac was struck by the scene: Davide happened to be floating in the same orientation as Jac. Marit's body, however, was one-hundred-and-eighty-degrees turned about, his mouth near Davide's ear. The oddity of the orientation, and the almost but not quite audible murmuring, gave the scene a diabolic quality. Perhaps the paucity of oxygen in the air that added the shimmery, hellfreeze atmosphere to it.

Time moved on. The black walls darkened in hue. They became essence of black, a perfectly scorched black. They burned, they gleamed, they shined with black. The colour was the truth about the universe. This cosmos that had gleamed for some hundreds of thousands of years with Big Bang light, and now existed in the scorched carbon of the afterburn.

The lid on his box rattled and bulged.

There was nothing to do but hope for water, or they would all die there. Jac considered: there were worse things that could happen than him dying. Of course, there were much better things too.

He tucked the piece of glass away under his tunic. If they didn't find ice soon, it wouldn't matter, and none of it would matter, and nothing would matter ever again. That thought was almost restful. The thought hardly disaffected him at all; although it did disaffect him a tiny bit, in the Will at the heart of his being. And he wanted at least to have finished his window. His miniature window. Tiny little window.

Any of them could rip the temporary seal away from the hole in the wall, the rock with its faecal cement, and kill everybody. It would be a simple matter.

*

He dozed. He dreamed an incoherent dream. Some of the Ulanov deputies dream lucid dreams in which they solve problems, deduce mysteries, uncover conspiracies, get to the bottom of crimes. Such clarity of dreaming was beyond Jac.

Mo shook him awake: it was his time on the drill. His head felt too small for the high-pressure lava his brain-matter had become. Headache, headache. It was very unpleasant, and in a grimly fascinating way; for he could not remove himself from the discomfort, the way he could with conventional pain. He withdrew his mind from the carapace of his nerves and muscles, but the exhaustion and ache was still with him. Its misery had stained his soul grey.

Nothing but dry stone. Slow process. Jac turned his schute off, churned the rock with the digger's business end, and then sifted through the floating rubble. Black crumbly carbon, or cold igneous chunks hard as sin, or silicates – but no ice. Then Jac turned the schute on and worked the same area, drawing the debris away and clearing away at least some of the rubble.

He fell into an uneasy, unrestful sleep; but he was still at the digger, and he woke to the punches and slaps of a wearily furious Lwon. 'Leggy! Leggy – wake!'

He had chanced upon ice, but the schute was drawing it away and depositing it into space.

The next hour passed in a delirious, agonised fog. They brought all three diggers to bear on the seam – a deep reach of blue-black ice – and carved out big pieces; and they carried it through and fed it into the scrubber. Ice! At last! The device's onboard fusion cell worked, and the water was processed and, slowly, the oxygen levels began to rise. It took a long time for the worst of Jac's physical misery to recede.

Replenishment.

Nobody did anything for a long while, except suck some of the renewed supply of ice and munch some ghunk. Everybody was intensely relieved at the find.

The alphas lurked in their chambers, the rest floated in the main space. They had their own rooms now, all save Gordius; but the rooms were cold and lonely, and they preferred to float together. Gordius, who had acquired permanently blue lips and a thousand-metre stare, and whose shivers appeared to have fallen into odd regularised patterns and echoes, was muttering something to himself under his breath, over and over.

Marit had put his head in at Davide's room and was whispering something – fomenting rebellion presumably. Jac was too drained and worn-through to care.

Dust and debris in the air, everywhere, slowly and inevitably drawn into helices and whorls by the stately rotation of Lamy306. Their world, and prison, turning over on itself in space, like a restless sleeper.

Jac dozed, woke, dozed, woke.

The box was sealed. It felt as if it had been locked beyond the ability of mortals to undo. Only the very faintest noises from inside to indicate that there had ever *been* anything there at all.

Buzz, buzz.

He took out his piece of glass and began working over it, polishing and smoothing. Nearly there. But he worked slowly, and without panache. Nearly was the asymptote of eternal existential disappointment. This was the geometry of the cosmos. Black and lady grey and blue and purple and –

'Leggy!' said Marit. He had floated across to him, and his reeking mouth was close by Jac's face. Only exhaustion prevented Jac from starting in surprise, or shrieking. 'Marit,' he croaked.

'You finished that window, then?'

He looked at the other man. He almost said: *you're* a window, so transparent is your scheming. But there was nothing to be gained in Marit knowing how much Jac knew. 'What?'

'I've been meaning to ask you, for a long time,' said Marit, keeping his head where it was but pulling his body closer to Jac's. 'How *did* you lose your legs? Or were you born that way?'

Jac put his thumb to the middle of his chin, and pressed hard.

He drew himself, inwardly, and readied his spirit. 'One of the two, certainly' he replied.

Marit wasn't really interested in that, of course. 'E-d-C's been *watching* you work on your glass, you know. Watching you! He told me he's going to take it, when you finish it. What for, I said? But that doesn't matter. He doesn't want it *for* anything. He just wants it. He's a bully.'

Jac cocked his head. 'You planning something?'

Marit's eyes shimmered, left-right, left-right. 'Look,' he said. 'Things can't go on the way they have. We almost choked to death! E-d-C is a *liability*, man. Surely you see it? It's a matter of self-preservation. Davide understands that. And I'll tell you what I think. I think you're canny enough to see it too.'

'So, my support and loyalty to – you, Marit? And in return?'

Marit stretched a ghastly smile out of his blue lips. 'You get straight to the point, don't you Leggy? That's good. I like that. OK, straight to the point. Davide and Mo are with me. You saw how Lwon feels about his so-called *deputy*. E-d-C is isolated, out on a limb. What do you get in *return* for your support? You get a better situation inside our little prison. You move *up* in the world.' His eyes shimmered, left-right, left-right. Jac almost chuckled: he could do the maths, as well as anybody. Not that it mattered.

'How?' Jac asked. 'E-d-C is a big man, a strong man. Hit him with a rock, you might not kill him.'

'I've something denser than rock,' said Marit, with another disagreeable smile. 'Don't you worry about *that*. I'm not asking you to – get your hands dirty. All I'm asking for is: your support. And . . . talk to him. Davide won't, and he doesn't trust Mo or myself. Talk to him, distract him.'

Jac almost laughed. 'And?'

'You'll see.'

'What about Gordius?'

This, clearly, had not factored into Marit's calculations at all. He glanced at the fat man, and back again. 'What about him?'

'You don't think . . .' Jac began, but Marit spoke over him.

'He's neither here nor there. Him?'

'He's losing it,' said Jac. 'His mind – you see the way he's muttering to himself, over and over?'

Marit curled has lip, scornfully. 'So?'

'You don't know which way he might jump. He was sentenced for killing a man, after all. He's killed before. What if he does it again? What if the violence freaks him out?'

Marit nodded, slowly. 'You think he might freak-freak out? You know him better than me. OK, OK. I'll have Davide watch him. Good! You see! – when we work together, things get sorted. Don't they? Don't they, though?'

'Sure,' said Jac. Maybe there *was* more oxygen in the air. He was starting to feel the tightness and misery go out of his soul a little.

Jac observed. He marvelled that E-d-C couldn't tell that Marit and Davide were plotting something, so theatrically obvious did their behaviour seem. But maybe it was the still-too-thin air, or maybe the tipping point had been reached and E-d-C was giving up, on a subconscious level. Giving up was a worry for all of them. Jac couldn't stay in this stone box for eleven years. He couldn't stay in it for much longer. It didn't matter, except that it mattered. It was important, it was unimportant.

In the end, he didn't need to engage E-d-C in conversation. E-d-C engaged *him*. Presumably he could sense that something was up, without necessarily being able to put his finger on what it was.

'I was talking to Lwon,' he said, out of the blue one day. 'And we had a disagreement. He said, because you've less blood in your body – because you don't have the legs – you feel the cold *more*, since it's our warm blood keeps us warm. But *I* said, less; since you don't lose heat through the extremities, the legs I mean, the way the rest of us do. Which is it?'

'Having no-one else's experience to compare mine to,' Jac replied, 'I couldn't say.'

79

E-d-C nodded at this, as if it were wise. But his attention was not on this. Then he said: 'the new seam of ice looks like it'll give us both water and air for years. Really years! I was chatting with Mo. I said to him: you really think the Gongsi would maroon us on a rock without *surveying* it first? Of course they checked to make sure it had the necessaries to support life. He said he wouldn't put it past them. But they're not psychopaths! Maybe they are cruel, yes. Inhumane, all that. But not *insane*. Now that we've unlocked this seam, we are guaranteed water, air and food for years. We can concentrate on making this place a nicer environment to live in. Am I right? A room for everybody! Warmed throughout!'

'Sure,' said Jac, distractedly.

'I'm not trying to gloss over the hardships we've suffered. I've suffered them too! It *has* been hard, hasn't it?'

'On balance I'd have to agree,' said Jac.

E-d-C sucked his teeth for a while. 'We've only one chance, you know.'

Behind him, Jac could see Marit putting his hand inside his tunic. 'Only one chance?' he repeated.

'Good order. It's our only chance. If we keep a lid on our tempers, and keep good order, then we can last the time – last all eleven years, and come out of the other end free men, with our dignity intact. But if we give way to anarchy we'll all be dead in a week. Die like beasts, or survive as men? Is that really even a *choice*?'

'Die like beasts,' repeated Jac. 'Or?' He kept flicking his glance over to where Marit floated, on the other side of the main space. He had removed his hand from his tunic, empty. As if he had been scratching an itch. But he hadn't. Jac knew he had the meteorite-iron cosh in there. He was readying himself, psychologically, to use it. He was checking where everybody else was. Davide was in the tunnel, digging, and so were Lwon and Mo. Should he go fetch his ally? Should he wait until the shift ended?

It was as if his inward thoughts were projected across the screen of his face for all to read.

- Do it now?

Jac forced his eyes back to E-d-C's face, met his gaze. He was listening to what the man was saying, but all the time he kept thinking: eyeballs are very fragile, the skull can be so easily cracked open. Blood yearns to free itself from the body. 'Sure,' he said.

'Shall I tell you how I ended up here?'

'Alright.'

'I killed a man.'

'Really?' said Jac.

'Oh I know what you're thinking: there must have been mitigation, or they would have done worse than just lock me in a box for eleven years. And, yes, there was. There was mitigation. But – do you know what I used to do?'

'What?' He glanced over E-d-C's shoulder again. Marit had his hand inside his tunic again; and his eyes had narrowed. Jac could see that his breathing had become more shallow. From the other end of the tunnel, the sound of the diggers, working the seam of ice, buzzing and purring.

Cold, cold, cold.

'You know how Lwon said he knew me from before – you know *how* he knew me?'

'No,' said Jac.

'I used to be in the Civvies. I wasn't some low-grade grunt, either. I was a *marshal* in the civilian-military force. When the Ulanovs took over, all those years ago, they kept the structure of the Civvies pretty much as it had been. New top brass, or course; and some new rules. But basically the same. And I was a marshal! I say that, so that you can understand. You can understand that I *know* small-group dynamics. I have a lot of experience in running them, keeping them going, keeping order. I know that without good order we have nothing.'

Jac nodded. Behind E-d-C, Marit had half-brought-out the

black phallus of the iron club from his tunic. But then he stopped, spooked by some real or imaginary danger, and tucked it hurriedly away again.

They were all losing their minds. Jac realised it, then. Paranoia and anger and self-pity and suffering and the toxic proximity of other human beings.

'One of my duties,' said E-d-C, 'was to carry out executions. I didn't like doing it; but it had to be done. Follow orders, that was my world. There was this one cadet, and he assaulted a senior officer. The officer had had sex with his girl, or something – or made a pass at her, it didn't matter what. The cadet had no business attacking him. No matter what the provocation, a junior officer cannot just punch a senior officer! They went drinking together. Cadet got the lieutenant drunk, and then broke his legs with a tungsten spar. Afterwards the officer was full of remorse – believe that? Said he'd been wrong to go after the other boy's girl. But it didn't matter. The cadet had to be punished. He took it well, too; he knew the rules. And that's what I mean! We don't have to *like* one another, or to like the situation here. But we do have to endure it, and that means we got to have a code. Lwon understands that. Davide too, though his temper *is* awkward. But he understands it at least. Marit – is a more difficult problem.'

'So,' said Jac. 'You didn't say how you ended up here.'

E-d-C smiled thinly. 'I executed the cadet,' he said. 'He struck a superior officer. Broke his legs! The rules were clear, so I OK'd the order, and he was executed. Only afterwards did it turn out he'd *previously* applied for discharge from the Civvies. His discharge had been granted, too, although the notification had got delayed in a spamstorm. I didn't know! How could I know? That didn't save me. I'd been the one who killed him, thinking him subject to civilian-military discipline. But it turned out that at the time I performed the execution he wasn't civilian-military, he was an ordinary civilian. I pled ignorance. The court said it took my plea under advisement, but the fact remained. I killed a citizen. So here I am.'

The drills stopped their noise, one after the other. In a moment, Davide, Mo and Lwon would come through. Then, Jac thought, it would happen.

'Jac,' E-d-C was saying. 'I think you're hearing what I'm saying. Am I right? I was talking with Gordius a while back, and he told me you were sentenced for political crimes. That's what we all thought, of course. Yes? So – I just want to say: I understand the urge to oppose the Ulanovs. Of course I do! I respect the desire to oppose authority. All I'm saying is, not here. Yeah? Not now. I know Marit's been stirring things up, but you need to listen to me. Survive this, get back out into the wider System, then you can carry on with your political, er, agitation to your heart's content – yeah?'

'Get back out into the wider System,' echoed Jac. 'I hope to.'

E-d-C was about to say something encouraging, when he finally saw that Jac's eyeline was not on him, but over his shoulder. He turned. Lwon was emerging from the entrance to the tunnel. Davide was just behind him. E-d-C looked straight at Marit, with his hand down inside his tunic. The latter froze.

Jac read the situation. He reached out with both hands, touched the two walls, and drew himself closer into the corner of the space.

There was a hitch in the passage of time. Time held the second for a moment. Then it let it go.

It was Davide who acted. He saw at once that Marit had frozen, and that there was panic evident on his face. Davide's own face distorted with anger and frustration. He roared. It was a shattering sound in the enclosed space, a great bellowing bull-like noise. Because he was still half in the tunnel, Jac didn't see Davide bring out the second chunk of iron. But it was in his hand, and it struck Lwon audibly across the back of his skull.

E-d-C called 'no!' and launched himself through the intervening space. Lwon's head had gone floppy, and his body was moving towards the far wall. As E-d-C hurtled towards him, Davide just had time to bring the black cosh up and sweep it down a second time. A baseball professional could not have timed the blow better. It caught E-d-C in the centre of his forehead, whipped his head back and to the side, and sent a spur of blood out into the air, a tumble of beads and slugs of red. E-d-C's momentum carried his body forward, colliding with Davide, and the two men tumbled against the wall together.

With an eerie chimpanzee screech, Marit leapt at Lwon's unconscious body. He brought his own metal club down twice in quick succession, on the side and the back of his head. Then, clumsily, but with increasing regularity, he began pounding Lwon's responseless form. Some of the blows missed, or glanced away, but others dinted the skullbone or pulled divots of flesh from the scalp. Very quickly a debris cloud of red dabs and dots and droplets filled the air around his head.

'Marit!' Davide cried. 'Enough!'

And, as abruptly as he had begun it, Marit broke off his assault. Jac caught a glimpse of his face as he pulled away. It was acned and spattered with myriad red dots. The features were drawn up in an expression of pure ecstasy.

The coup was effected as simply as that. For a while nobody said anything. Gordius was no longer muttering to himself and was instead staring open-mouthed at the mess: two corpses floating, trailing blood from their wounds in myriad beads and lumps and dots. Indeed, as their prison itself slowly rotated the blood-field was slowly folded over on itself, wrapping into incrementally appearing patterns of twist and helix.

In the immediate aftermath, Davide and Marit brandished their iron clubs, and Mo whooped and cheered and applauded them. Gordius and Jac were silent.

Eventually Davide made a speech: 're-birth,' he said. Then, more loudly: 'renaissance! Things are going to be *better* from now on. Nobody elected Lwon boss! Nobody voted for him! He was a tyrant and a bully. We're all in this together.'

They weren't, though. As the adrenaline from the attack faded from their bloodstreams, the two assassins became grumpy and peevish. 'You two!' Marit ordered Gordius and Jac. 'Clear this mess up!' Gordius didn't respond at first, but when Marit rushed at him brandishing his club the fat man squealed and scrambled to the side.

'I said clear up the *mess*,' bellowed Marit. And Mo, eager not to find himself falling on the wrong side of the divide in this new dispensation, added his support to Marit's new authority: 'you two do as you're told, or I'll break your bones!'

'How do you suggest we clean it?' asked Jac, mildly enough. Mo snatched a smallish rock from the air and threw it at his head. It was slowed by passing through the sticky matter in the way and Jac was able to duck out of the way.

'Strip the bodies,' said Davide, in a deep voice. 'Use the clothing to net some of this stuff out of the air – and wipe the walls down with some crushed ice.'

Jac and Gordius did as they were told. 'O brave new world,' whispered Gordius as they worked, the first thing Jac had heard him say in a long while. 'We'll be next, you know,' he told Jac. 'It won't be long now.'

Jac thought: it won't be long now.

Gordius got E-d-C's tunic off first; it had less blood on it than the other, and he wrapped it around his own torso like a cape – it had been a long time since he had had his own upper body clothing. Then he and Jac got E-d-C's trousers off, and then Lwon's tunic and trows. Then Gordius took Lwon's corpse, and Jac took E-d-C's; they crammed them into one of the rooms off the corridor. It was a waste of one of the rooms, but better that than have to live in the open space with two dead bodies.

When they came back through they were covered in blood; but then so were the other three – there was no way to avoid it in that confined space.

It was a tricky business sweeping the blood out of the air, and wiping the walls just tended to smear the stuff about. After a great deal of labour they had cleared some of the air, and they went back into the corridor, and stuffed the bloodied clothes in at the mouth of the chamber, packing the bodies in.

Back in the main chamber, Davide and Marit still looked a little stunned by their victory. 'This rock will support five more easily than it could ever have supported seven,' said Mo. 'I'm not sure seven could have lived here the full eleven years anyway.' This wasn't true, of course, but nobody challenged him. 'It was, it was a *long*-term solution to the, to the, the *problem*,' he said.

'It'll certainly be less crowded around here now,' said Marit.

That wasn't right, though. Though there were fewer people now, the space felt paradoxically more crowded. It was impossible to put out of one's mind the fact that two human corpses were stuffed into the chamber on the left as you passed down the tunnel. They loomed larger in death than they had done in life. But there was nothing anybody could do about that. Worse, the spectre of murderous violence had been summoned from its interstitial reality; and that's a ghost that makes very uncomfortable cohabitation.

Over the next few days, Davide instructed Gordius and Jac that they, now, would do all the digging – that, indeed, he and his two friends were *sick* of digging. But it didn't take long for that to change. The truth was, digging, though tiresome, was at least a distraction. Within two days, everyone was taking turns at the diggers again, as before.

Davide took Jac's piece of glass too. 'I deserve some kind of medal,' he said. 'And this will have to do.' Jac surrendered it without protest. It hardly mattered. 'You were never going to fit it as a window, were you,' sneered Marit. 'You won't miss it. You can make yourself another one!'

Jac didn't reply. He had no new lump of unworked glass; all he had were the various chips and shards he had picked up along the way, and which he kept about his body tangled in with his body hair. When he had an unobserved moment, he might bring one of these out and polish it. But he was content not to work any more on the larger lump.

The shift in the power seemed to bring little satisfaction to the top three. Conversation was sparse. The seam of ice was excavated, ghunk grown, and work begun making the three alpha chambers bigger. The truth of their circumstance was: *waiting*. There was, in essence, nothing else for them to do. Davide in particular sank into what looked very like depression.

'What will you tell the rescue crew when they come in a decade?' Jac asked Davide one day. 'We'll tell them *you* killed them!' crowed Marit, overhearing. 'You and fat-boy! Or – we'll say, they killed one another! Who'll contradict us?'

'Nobody,' conceded Jac.

The one positive result, if it could be phrased that way, was that events had shaken Gordius out of his fugue. He no longer muttered to himself, and as the ambient temperature crept marginally up, he was shivering less. From his newly acquired tunic he ripped a strip of cloth and tied it around his dead eye like a pirate. Otherwise he began to revert, although intermittently, to his earlier garrulousness.

'They're quiet now,' he told Jac, in a low voice. 'You know why? They've vented their frustration. But it'll build up again, and next time the victims will be – you and me.'

'Very likely,' Jac agreed.

'So your escape plan?' Gordius hissed. 'Can you bring it forward?'

'If you like,' said Jac, in a tired voice.

Gordius peered at him, to try and see if he was joking or not. 'Seriously? Because, I tell you: we've *got* to get out of here. The others have gone over the edge! We'll be next! Don't you need your window, though? Your piece of glass?'

Jac shook his head. 'It doesn't matter,' he said. All he felt, now, was sadness. And sadness, like the horrible physical discomfort he had experienced when the oxygen levels had dropped to dangerously low levels, was not something from which his soul could withdraw itself.

'It was a *red* herring, all that glass polishing?' Gordius pressed.

'Distraction? Clever! Throw them off the scent. So what is your plan? If ever there was a time to tell me, it's now, surely!'

'It's all distraction, Gord,' Jac told him. 'There is no escape plan. There never was one. How could anybody possibly escape from this prison? It was all about filling the time until the Gongsi send a ship along, in ten years, or whenever they decide to swing by.'

Gordius stared at him, and then decided not to believe him. 'Sure!' he said. 'Sure!'

'I'm not here for political crimes,' Jac told him. 'I know you think I am; you jumped to that conclusion. I never said I was. And it's not the case. I'm here because the authorities mis-identified me. They will have realised their mistake by now; and if they haven't they soon will. They want me for something much worse than regular political crimes. Much worse. When they come back for the rest of you, it will be mindwipe for me.'

'Are you innocent?' breathed Gordius, wide-eyed.

'By no means,' said Jac. 'In fact, I'm guilty of things far worse than even the authorities know. They'll work out who I am. And when that happens, I believe they'll send a ship over here im-mediately to retrieve me – this is no bravura on my part; this is a simple statement of fact. I've no idea what that would mean for you – maybe they'd reseal you back in, and leave you all to complete your sentences. Maybe they'd bring you back with them, bail you, who knows. I'm afraid I can't bring myself to care; because as soon as they come back for me, whether it's in the near future or at the end of the sentence, things are going to be much worse for me even than now. And even more than that – well, there are *other reasons* why the authorities must never apprehend me. When they put me here, they didn't realise what they had. So – here I am. But I won't be so lucky again. I can't permit it to happen.'

Gordius looked very serious now. 'I've been a fool,' he said, in a low, thrumming voice. 'All this time, you *said* you had to get away. But you didn't mean *literally* get away, did you! You meant – escape. You mean . . . suicide. Self-murder, and you the murderer!'

Jac looked into his big, baggy face. 'According to you,' he said, 'neither of us will have to bother with suicide. You say those three will kill us anyway.'

Gordius started to laugh at this, stopped, and then looked terribly sad. 'I feel a double-fool for not seeing what you meant,' he said, in a doleful voice. 'I guess I was so hopeful about getting out of this box, I was prepared to believe anything at all.'

Jac smiled. 'Endure the sentence,' he said, 'and the Gongsi will ship you away from here forever. At least *you* have that prospect to hope for!'

Mostly Lamy306 was cold enough to keep the spilled blood from rotting; but near the Fusion Cell and around the light the stuff curdled. It went bad and began to reek. Marit ordered Gordius and Jac to clean the foul material away, but they couldn't get rid of the smell.

It was almost time, and it was almost time, and Jac got used to living in that on-the-cusp state of mind. Almost. Funny, that the word should include the totalising *all* and the majoritarian *most* and yet signify the state of neither.

But then, with a natural rightness, it *was* time. It came, unforced, unhurried, like a machine's component slotting into place. Like a puzzle coming together and revealing its solution in one glorious moment of coherence.

To everything, its time.

Davide and Marit were drilling, at the far end of the corridor. Mo was in his room; Jac and Gordius in the main space. When Mo emerged, Jac could tell from his expression that he wanted sex. 'Come'n, Leggy,' he ordered. 'In my chamber. I don't want god-boy watching.'

Something inside Jac's spirit snagged, or snapped; some final-straw-like sensation. But it wasn't a breakage. It was only the component slotting into place. He had waited a long time, after all. Not eleven years, true, but a goodly time. As he floated through after Mo, into his rock-hewn cell, he fiddled one of his glass shards free from his hair. His own hair, under his fingers, was clogged and matted, as oily and repellent as tentacles.

What's inside the box?

Doubt is there.

What's another name for doubt?

Death is another name for doubt. Death is what inflects the immortal certainty of the universe's process with uncertainty.

When they were both inside the smaller space, Mo said: 'I'm going to shut my eyes and pretend you're my wife. Don't *say* anything to spoil the mood, and keep your snaggle *teeth* out of the way, OK?'

'OK,' said Jac.

The box-lid swung wide. There was no longer a box. It was all gone, and dissolved in a heat and a light. Everything clarified for Jac. Light is a form of heat. Everything in motion is a form of heat. Even the massless drive of protons.

Jac's blood flowed swift and smooth, after many months of moving more sluggishly.

He took Mo's member in his left hand. Then he rose up along the other man's body, and brought his face close to the other's face. 'My love,' he whispered, and kissed him.

Mo reacted badly. He said, angrily, 'what are you *doing*?' But Jac was a good kisser, a strong kisser, and he forced his mouth upon the other man's, and muffled the words.

Jac had the shard of glass in his right hand. With one gesture he passed it through Mo's member. He felt the hot pulse and the gush of blood. Mo screamed, but Jac pressed his mouth harder down upon his bristly lips. Jac brought his two hands up, one holding the amputated flesh, the other the glass shard, and waited until the stifled scream came to an end. Mo, writhing and bucking, sucked in a breath to scream again. Then, finally disengaging from the kiss, Jac stuffed the severed item into Mo's open mouth, crammed it hard in. The second scream never emerged, although

Mo bucked and struggled and thrashed about. But there was hardly any space inside the chamber, so there was no way of throwing his assailant off.

Jac held him until he had bled out. Felt his whole body weaken under his grasp and eventually stop moving. The whole chamber was filled with blood, Jac himself completely covered in it. He cut himself a stretch of cloth from Mo's tunic, and tied it around his own mouth to filter out the blood, to stop himself choking on it. He was warm, now, and inside his skull he felt brightness. He attended to his own heart. It was still stepping through the moves of its four-part pavane, no quicker than before. He centred himself. He could keep it that way. Neither panic nor elation. Calm. Calm.

Jac slipped into the tunnel, and slid along the wall towards the far end, where the two men were digging. Marit was further along, at the extreme limit of the tunnel, excavating its end. Davide was widening the passage closer to, and had his back to Jac. The noise of two drills; the double vibration. Jac's hands felt the thrum in the body of the stone. The shine from the main chamber was a long way behind them, and only the headlights on the individual diggers gave out any illumination. It was a confusion of dust and small debris, and black shadows in jiggling motion cast back from the excavation. Jac slid through the murk easily enough, as if it was his natural medium. He appeared, as if from nowhere, all his skin bright red and slick, and forced two shards into Davide's neck from behind, one at four o'clock, one at eight. They went in easily enough, although the pressure required to ram them home cut Jac's own palms. His hands were wet as he pulled Davide's bucking body out of the way, and grasped the controls of the digger. Marit only realised something was happening right at the end, when the endlessly hungry mouth of the excavating machine reared up at him.

Placuit.

Afterwards, Jac floated in the tunnel, reassuring himself of his calmness. He looked inside himself. There was his heart, still moving regularly on. It was alright. He had to wipe his mouth-guard, his strip of cloth, free of blood from in front of his mouth. But it was still possible to breathe. And then, from the light at the end, where the main chamber was, he heard Gordius's voice, wheedling and anxious. 'Guys? Guys! What's going on? I heard screaming.'

'It's alright, Gordius,' he called back, his voice strong and clear and audible. 'I'm ready for you now.'

He started back towards the brightness.

Afterwards, he brought the drills out of the tunnel and back into the main cavity. He laid out the necessaries.

The hardest part was holding the shards of glass in his bloodied hands. Without a handle the blades were too slippy, and of course they tended to cut his own palms. But everything was nothing except a problem to be solved, so he applied his practical reason-ing and solved it. Bone made a good handle, and his victims had plenty of that.

There was no hurry.

He worked carefully, methodically, cutting open Gordius's corpse with as few and as small incisions as he could manage. He removed a great quantity of the innards. The skull came out once he had severed the spine and optical nerves, and felt his way in around the cavity with his slippery fingers and long nails. 'What can I tell you?' he told him, as he worked. 'This is the truth on which space settlement is founded. Energy is valuable, and raw materials are precious, but human beings are mere resources to be exploited.' He had learned the lessons of his time in prison.

He kept the ribs, embedded in their leathery tough membranes and the medium of their subcutaneous fat. But the spine came out, the arm bones and muscles, the tibia and fibula, yellow and red in the incessant brightness of the light pole. The pelvis was harder to extricate, but he got it out eventually.

He slept when he was tired, ate as much ghunk as he could,

and then he turned his attention to the legs. The glass went blunt, of course, and he kept having to sharpen it. But he was patient, and careful, and he was used to working with the material.

Soon enough he had finished.

He contemplated his next move. He knew, of course, that the excessive cold would be a problem for a while, and that after that excessive *heat* would become the problem. He didn't have the resources to manufacture a heat-transfer or radiative solution to this latter; the best he could hope for was to endure it, and to get where he was going before it became fatal. Ice would help.

So he focused on solving the practical problems. He made a chunky sewing needle from bone, and fitted the large gash at the base of Gordius's back with laces made from tendons. Mostly deboned, Gordius's large frame was now as floppy and foldy in the zero-g as an un-put-up tent.

Next Jac packed ice into one of Gordius's hollowed-out arms. Then he did the same with one of the legs – forcing it in until it looked from the outside as if it suffered from elephantiasis. Into the other leg he packed the foot and lower section with ice, and then carefully manoeuvred the scrubber in, entire. The skin of the leg stretched to receive it, like a boa constrictor swallowing its lunch.

Almost time to go.

He sewed the fusion cell to the shoulder blades, like a back-pack. The heat vent was on the lower side, within easy reach of Gordius's boneless hand, had that hand been capable of reacting any more to the volition of reaching.

Three more things.

He took the clothes from the various bodies, and tied them together into a carryall. Into this he placed all the remaining free ice. There was no need to excavate more ice from the seam. The sack, when finished, was full. Jac sewed two edges of it crudely to the skin of Gordius's belly.

He went to Davide's body and retrieved his piece of glass. Davide, dead, surrendered it without objection. Now Jac began the fiddliest and most crucial part of the whole undertaking. The eyelid over Gordius's damaged eye was sealed pretty effectively shut, it seemed to Jac; but he took the eyeball out and filled the cavity with a putty made of fat, water and waste. The other eyeball came out too, of course. Jac trusted himself (working by touch, with very limited tools) to be able to fit the glass circle inside in such a way as to guarantee a seal against the outside. Fiddly, fiddly. Finally it was done, and he cleaned it as well as he could.

Almost finished. He positioned a digger, mouth-first, against the stretch of artificial membrane, the stuff that had originally sealed them in. It seemed like a long time ago.

Finally, he pulled the corpses of Lwon and E-d-C out of their temporary mausoleum, and left them in the main chamber. When he broke through the membrane and vented this space, they would join their former cellmates in deep space. The authorities, returning, would find the prison empty. He couldn't rid the place of all traces, of course; there was a lot of blood, on the walls and in the tunnel, and it would be a simple matter for the Police to DNA it and determine from whom it had come. But it was as much misdirection as Jac could manage.

Jac was smeared and covered in blood; his hair was solidified with the gel of human offal. He thought to cut it off, but his glass scalpels – all save one – were all now irretrievably blunted and broken, and he had no time to dig out more. He kept his one, unblunted glass scalpel; and one of the iron clubs, and stowed them inside his new suit. Then he readied himself. Even in microgravity it was a tricky business pulling himself inside the new suit; and the last bit of sewing, using a sheet of pleural membrane to ensure the seal, took him a long time. More sealing work with his makeshift putty.

It was cold inside; the ambient temperature plus all the ice in the leg and the arm, of course, but nothing he couldn't endure.

At least he was ready. He slid his right arm inside its new sleeve, and turned the digger on. A moment of nothing – external

94

sound was completely muffled – and the view through his one glass porthole took some getting used to. Then he felt a lurch and a pull, and the chamber filled with glittery rubbish. The digger plunged through the opening it had itself made, and Jac was pulled through as well.

He was outside.

The first thing that happened was that Jac's new suit swelled prodigiously, like a balloon pumped hard past its capacity. He had expected this, although there was always the chance that his seams would burst, and everything would end before it had even begun. But this didn't happen. The suit became perhaps twice as spacious inside, which was a good thing. The bad thing was that, fitting his arm inside the right sleeve, he could no longer manoeuvre fingers or even bring the arm down to the side. This was a real, and pressing problem; for if he couldn't move the arm at all he would be condemned to simply drifting through space until he died. But Jac discovered that by swivelling himself about and putting both his arms into the right sleeve he just about had enough muscular strength to overcome the high-pressure stiffness, to move the arm and clench the puffed-fingers.

He was spinning round and round. Beyond even the chill of this ice-packed suit, Jac could feel the outside cold: an intense, primal, terrifying thing – an absolute chill. Its name was Death. Death had many names. It was an environment to which no human was suited. It was implacably, monstrously opposed to every spark that animated the living body. But there was the sun, a bright coin of light that moved smoothly from top right to bottom left of his little eyeglass window. With some effort, and some misfires, Jac fed ice in at the warm vent of the fusion cell, and used the resulting thrust to take the more ragged edges off his tumble.

There was a hissing sound, which meant air escaping. But Jac located the leak and sealed it with his putty, working the stuff first with his fingers to loosen it up.

There was Lamy306 swinging down through his line of sight

and disappearing. It looked bizarrely tiny, as if a fairy had shrunk it away. So, so. It came back in at the top of his line of sight, and moved down again and vanished out the bottom. With some more angling of the fusion cell, and more application of ice to the heated vent, he settled into a less hectic axial rotation. Then, with a final struggle against the stiffness of his suit, he put out enough blasts of gas to still even this.

He was hanging in deep space. He got his bearings: sun, stars. Then he waited. He was shivering, but happy. He waited, and watched, and he was good at both things. The scrubber thrummed in the leg, so he had air. He breathed in and breathed out.

It took several hours, but his patience was rewarded. He saw a blinking light; one of the other asteroids, at who-knew-how-many million miles distance. That would do. He fed his fusion cell vent with ice, and slowly began to accelerate himself through space. It was slow, but the nature of acceleration is that it becomes steadily less slow. Keeping the blinking light in his eyepiece, and working as a stoker to generate gas, he accelerated slowly at first. But there was nothing to stop him, and he kept applying small amounts of thrust. It would take a while, but he had plenty of time. Not all the time in the world, it was true; but enough. Enough. Or too much!

part II

•

THE FTL MURDERS

DRAMATIS PERSONAE

Diana Argent
Eva Argent
Our heroines

Iago
Their Tutor

Berthezene
Dominico Deño
Jong-il
Their bodyguards

Carna
D'Arch
Faber
Leron
Mantolini
Oldorando
Poon-si
Sapho
Sun-kil
Tapanat
Tigris *and nine others*
Personal handservants to Miss Diana and Miss Eva

Police Inspector Halkiopoulou
Police Subinspector Zarian
Local police, investigating the murder

Miss Joad
Personal agent of the Ulanovs

Jack Glass
The notorious criminal

1

The Mystery of the
Hammered Handservant

A month before she turned sixteen Diana got involved in a real-life murder mystery. It was was was *too* exciting.

So, she and Eva came down to Korkura for a spell of gravity – which is to say, so as to spend a month before the birthday party getting used to Earth again. And whenever she thought about this trip afterwards she associated her legal majority with mystery and the death of a servant. A problem to be solved! And who was better at solving problems than her? (Nobody! *Her* problem-solving is second-to-none: intuitive, human, chaologic – it's what she was bred and raised to). Eva told her to be careful; said it might be dangerous, was best left to the authorities, all that manner of chaff. But Eva was a fuss; and Dia had her bodyguards to look after everything, and had Iago to help her too, and anyway. It *was* her birthday. It was *almost* her birthday.

The trip down was yet another springy plasmaser descent, yet another sicky feeling in the gut, and the added horror of increasing *density* for lord's sake. When she was older, she decided, she was going to travel up and down *in a sloop*, and watch the reëntry burn colours of lit stained-glass glow outside her porthole. Sloops rocket up, and when they want to come in again they just fall straight down; and something about the thought of *freefalling* through the hot, vacant ocean of air excited her. But for now it was the plasmaser capsule again, and the slow elevator descent, and not even the satisfaction of seeing the counterthrust capsule going *up*, for at the relevant moment of crossover the window was blanked with hazy cloud.

Anyway: they came down somewhere in Turque, and then there was a tedious shuffling short-hop flight to the island. The MOHmies had more-or-less owned Korkura since before the sisters had been born; and Diana and Eva often spent time there. As ever, this was holiday and relaxation time, of course, and the build-up to Dia's sixteenth birthday, but *at* the same time MOHmie put a rather tiresome emphasis upon the benefits of a spell of gravity, don't you know. In fact, both MOHmies were cross, for neither of the girls had been doing their exercises. 'Three hours of centrifuge a day is a minimum,' they said, several trillion times every *hour*. '*Five* hours a day would be better. But it doesn't seem to matter how we scold, you won't even do *three*. Your bones will wither! You'll become permanent uplanders! Cripples!' Such *nagging*. You wouldn't believe it. And anyway, they had a whole month of actual Earth gravity now – down they went: riding the plasmaser. In their car: Diana and Sisterissima Evissima, and the twelve people whose business it was to look after them.

The ones whom Dia actually knew were the bodyguards, of course. Necessarily they had the closest relationship with their personal guardians: Dominico Deño and Jong-il (of course), and the new one, Berthezene. *He* seemed alright, actually. She also knew Iago, of course – Iago with his old-world manner and his immaculate clothes. Iago, though, wasn't a bodyguard. He was something else; halfway between a servant and an actual person. Dia pronounced his name *eye-ah-go*, and Eva *ee-goo* and he smiled and declined to say which pronunciation was correct. Perhaps neither. Then there were the others, whose names had to be prompted to Dia's mind by her bId: Faber, Mantolini, Oldorando and Poon-si, Sapho, Sun-kil, Tapanat and Tigris. Eight handservants, all of them dosed with so much CRF they could not help themselves loving Dia and Eva more than anything else in the whole solar-windy, asteroid-rainy System.

The remaining servants came in a second car, the to-be-murder-victim amongst them. That meant (afterwards, Dia shivered with grisly delight to think of it) that Leron – the victim's name – had *sat* there, in the company of the eleven other house-servants, waiting patiently all the way down to the ground. How strange a thought that was! He'd sat there strapped in his seat whilst the car fell down and his stomach registered the plummet-ous motion, but actually he was hurrying towards his own death. Down to his last few breaths of air. His last hours alive. But he didn't know!

None of us *will* know, of course. The weird grammar of death. You die, he or she dies, they die but there is no genuine form for 'I'. Not really. All know *that*, none know *when*.

Anyway, the car came to a halt on the ground, and the full weight of gravity chomped on Diana's limbs and stomach and chest, and made her head loll and strained her neck. She regretted not putting in her three-hours-a-day *now*, of course; and she had to be physically carried (hu-mi-li-*ating*!) to the short-hop runner and fitted into the seat with the high back cradling her head. Eva, on the other hand, was unrepentant. 'We could have spent five hours,' she gasped, and drew a breath. 'Centrifuge's isn't the same as,' gasp, gasp, breathe, 'actual gravity.' Gasp. Pause.

The short-hop flier buzzed and did its salmon leap into the air, and caught itself up there and flew on.

There is nothing to *do* with the misery of gravity but endure it and get used to it, and *gradually* overcome it. But Eva felt a momentary fury as the flier ascended and gravity got *even worse than one g* for a few seconds. Lady, that was hard! But then the craft settled into flight, and she turned her head a little, and watched the landscape slide past her porthole. It was a stupend-ous sight, really it was, stupendouser even than orbital vistas, because it was so *much* more varied and brightly lit. The sky down here was not one colour, as space is: it was rather a smooth gradation from smoke blue and pale in the dome to flowerpetal purple nearer the deckle-edged horizon. Mustard-coloured hills and peaks, green-yellow scrub and grass, polygon shapes of human habitation. The flier passed west over the coastline, and land drew back as though on a rail, and there was nothing but sea, which possessed the hard-faceted look of a solid, though she knew it was trillions of tonnes of *water*, get that, just sloshing and lying in a huge geographical basin, against all the promptings of common sense.

Soon enough they passed another coastline, and almost immediately landed at the house. The girls were deplaned and carried inside, and they both fell asleep straight away, because the gravity was so exhausting. But sleep was an uneasy business, and Diana kept waking herself up with the pain of lifting her own ribcage to draw breath, or with the strenuous effort of turning herself from her left side to her right. Come evening, they had a long bath. The handservants laid actual candles all around the pool as they wallowed and swam – candles! Like they'd descended not just down the gravity well but down the time well too, to *ancient* Greece or something like that.

There was other stuff too, of course; but Dia could remember none of it afterwards. It was retrospectively overshadowed by the events of the following day. Murder, the immense fact of it, blotting out all earlier memories – that's not a surprise, surely. *Presumably* the two girls spoke to their MOHmies, and I guess they slept. The sun must have come up, because it always does. They probably didn't have the energy for much by way of games or fun. The solar flare of memory illuminates only that afternoon. Murder – and, maybe *revolution*! *Faster* than light.

This is how it happened:

Diana and Eva were in the main house, of course, and doing nothing more than lying about, exhausted. Most of the servants were in the servant house, similarly worn-out. Eva was asleep, although Diana couldn't get to sleep, or couldn't stay asleep, because of the goddessdamn asthmatic sense of *constriction* in her lungs that came from just *breathing*, for out-loud-crying. She'd unblanked the walls, and was staring listlessly out across the estate. A hot, bright Mediterranean day. She was pondering things. For instance: she wondered at the merit in bringing servants down with them, rather than just hiring Earthly servants who were already used to the gravity. Of course there *were* many native servants here; they maintained the estate when nobody was in residence and so on and so *forth*. But to come down was to bring your own people with you from zero-g, and that seemed egregious to Dia.

The lawn was olive-green, sun-heated. The grass was bristly as a man's beard hair. Plane trees nodded indulgently in her direction. The sky was the colour and thickness of a bluebird's eggshell. Away to her right was an orchard of olive trees, its foliage a mass of hyacinth blue against the white air. Dia sighed. The sun was very bright and white and throwing dark purple shadows from anything vertical. It seemed off that the sun could be brighter at the bottom of the Earth's gravity well than it was in space, when they were actually closer *to* it for lord's sake. The servant house was a single-storey structure away to the left with black solar convertor peat on the roof in which red and yellow flowers bloomed. But the best part of the view was the way the garden ended, and the prospect dropped away down to the sea. Such colour! You look down upon the Med from orbit and it looks blue like any ordinary blue; but then you lie on a couch on the actual shore and it looks *completely* different. One thing invisible from the uplands is the way the *shuffling* of its surface shakes two dozen different shades of marine from the sheet of colour. Gorgeous.

Across the bay was the town – Kouloura, 55% owned by Dia's MOHmies, and, like, *totally* dedicated to her. All the people there; they revered the MOHmies, they really did. Hundreds of white-painted houses, like teeth, filling the jaw-shaped cove. Dia shifted her position and took a gasping breath. Deño coughed, quietly. He was on duty in the corner, sitting in a chair with his weapon in his lap. Dia's bId told her he had another hour, and then Jong-il would take over.

She watched, and before the moment everything changed it was as banal and ordinary as ever it had been. She watched. Everything changed, as she watched. Her life would never be the same again.

She saw a strange thing. Servants came running out of the servant house. They were just as afflicted by the gravity as she was, of course; more so, if anything, since their duties meant they generally didn't get the time or facilities to do their exercises. But something had *really* spooked them, because they all came out through the main entrance, limbs ropey, lurching and staggering and tumbling like newly-born calves, the lot of them. Arms akimbo, legs refusing to bear their weight, falling over and picking themselves up. It was a little comical, until she understood the reason for it. Dia even started laughing, although that only reinforced the sense of constriction in her chest, so she stopped.

But she saw soon enough that something was amiss. Reedy, plaintive cries became audible, across the lawn. Some of the servants were pulling at their hair, faces like tragic masks (her bId pulled up a dozen examples, so she could see the appropriateness of the comparison). Their howls were *clearly* audible through the wall. 'What's going on?' Dia asked. She checked her bId, but all it could report was that the house systems were reporting everything AOK. So it wasn't the house. If not the house itself, then – something in the house?

She made the couch sit her up. 'Dominico,' she said. 'What's going on?'

But Deño had already risen, slightly unsteadily, to his feet. 'Berthezene is checking,' he said. And it was true: for there, through the wallglass, Berthezene could be seen, stalking awkwardly over the dry grass towards the servant house. He and Jong-il and Deño, who had a professional reason to keep up their upland exercises, did five or six hours every day. Still, even they found the first couple of days back under the haul of gravity a strain (of all her personal staff, only Iago seemed to shrug it off); but this was a serious matter.

Dia hopped into the security channel via her bId, which meant that she heard the news as soon as anybody – as soon as either of her MOHmies, back up in space. The news was that one of the servants was dead. And then, almost at once, the news updated: name Leron, murdered, actually murdered.

'This,' she gasped, 'I have *got* to see!'

It took Dia moments to fit her crawlipers, and then she was away, plocking out through the door and across the grass. The fragrance of lavender and brine. Sunlight striking down like the wand of Apollo, bright and hot. The low, flowery roof of the servant house lurched closer with each step, rocking a seesaw boat-like motion as her braces moved her towards it, and then she was at the entrance. A servant (Dia's bId pulled up his name: Tigris) was lying on his back gasping; another (Sapho, the name) was crouched on the stoop, weeping. Dia didn't have time for *them*! She had to get inside! She wanted to see the body.

Deño was at her side. 'Miss,' he said, laying a hand on her shoulder. 'Are you quite sure you want to go inside? Are you sure you want to see—?' 'Are you *joking*, Dominico?' she replied. Murder mysteries were her *passion*! And here was a *real-life* one! Miss out on this?

No. Wavey. *Way.*

She stalked inside: a moment for her eyes to adjust, with the bId display gleaming distractedly bright. Then she got her bearings. The hall, the central corridor, individual rooms coming off left and right. The ceiling was tuned to a low light. She could smell that food had been cooked: cheap and spicy. There was some other odour, too: metal, or fear, or excitement, or – Deño touched her shoulder again. 'Permit me to go first, Miss,' he said. She thought about brushing him aside, and dashing down the corridor herself. But that *would* have been reckless. She was excited, but not stupid. Deño's brow had that /—\ shaped crease running over his eyebrows and down the sides of his face. He only got that when he was really concentrating. It probably meant something was really amiss.

He held his weapon out in front of him, walking slowly down the corridor, and she crept after him. He looked in each of the open doors, one after the other, and all the cubicles inside were empty. Dia kept checking her bId, but it was reporting the whole building Normal. They reached the far end; and there was only the storeroom left, and Diana was pretty worn-out, let me tell you, with all the excitement and the walking and this was *despite* the crawlipers. But Deño ordered the door open, and it melted away to reveal – the murder scene.

Leron was the victim's name. A mature male originally from (her bId told her) a large shanty bubble called Smirr. Recruited as a houseservant along with seven others not one month before. And now he was dead!

He was flat on the ground, pressed against the stuff of the floor by the remorseless Earth gravity. His chest was not moving up or down. The flesh of his head had been pulled aside and the serrated join of his skull plates unzipped, and a copious amount of blood had come out – a beachball's worth of blood. The weirdest thing about the scene was the way the blood was pressed flat and spread wide, adhering close to the concrete floor. The fatal wound was near the top of his crown, and it had yanked the expression on the face into a bizarre mask. Both eyes were open, although the left one had been inked black.

Eew.

Diana turned to see Jong-il and Berthezene lumbering up the corridor towards her. 'Miss! Be careful!' And behind them came Iago; walking smoothly and without apparent effort, as he always did. The suavest of the suave. 'Miss! Miss!'

'I'm fine,' she called back, annoyed at the interruption. They loved her, she knew; but it could be a drag-drag-drag sometimes.

'Come out, back to the house, Miss,' said Jong-il. Berthezene was pointing his gun into each room in turn, standing beside each opening with his weapon vertical near his chest, and leaping out to level it at possible assailants, over and again. The gun's barrel: vertical – horizontal. Vertical – horizontal. 'The servants are all outside,' Dia called, peering at the corpse. 'There's nobody *in* here! You worry-warts!'

'Death is never a safe environment, Miss,' said Iago.

'*Please* be careful, Miss!' cried Jong-il. 'The police have been notified!'

She ignored all this nanny-nonsense, and turned back to the victim. If she had to describe her immediate reaction to seeing this dead human body – the first she had ever seen – she would say: disappointment. It was not just that it looked disconcertingly like a live body in repose (although it did, the dent in its head notwithstanding). It was that it lacked any other qualities at all. She supposed she had been expecting something profound and existentially jarring; some objective correlative to death itself. Personal extinction, the unthinkable asymptote of life. Perhaps she had even been *craving* such a conceptual shock. Not that she wanted to die, of course; but that she expected there to be more of a buzz, more startlement, more *thrill*. But whatever this was, it wasn't that. She adjusted her crawlipers to crouch beside the body, and then reached out with her right hand to touch the inertness of the corpse's right hand, like God on the Sistine Ceiling. Nothing.

And here was Iago, lifting her up again. 'Better leave well alone, Miss Diana,' he said. Of all the servants, only he used her first name.

'I was just,' Dia began to say, but she didn't know what she was going to *just*. With an enhanced iQ, and some of the best data access algorithms in the whole Ulanov protectorate, she *ought* to be able to work it out. Presumably the 'just' had to do with the imminence of . . . something. All of us are only a moment away from death. There will come a moment which will be the last one we experience, the last moment before we lose everything. It ought to be something to cast the delicious, ghastly shiver through the soul. But Dia didn't feel anything like that.

So she stood there, next to her Tutor, and looked at the corpse on the floor, whilst her three bodyguards arranged themselves about her and aimed their weapons at imaginary foes. Until she decided to leave that place there was nothing else for them to do.

'His skin-tone is surprisingly light,' Iago noted, shortly.

It was true: dead Leron's colour, under the ceiling lights, was somewhere between mud-brown and amber. His spilt blood was much darker than he was. She posed the question to her bId, but it had very little to say on the topic, the sparseness of the data presumably reflecting the fact that the life he had lived had *been* sparse. Name, Leron: one of the Greenbelt poor, born in a certain shanty bubble, unofficial name Smirr, with such-and-such official designation – like trillions of System poor, raised on unrefined ghunk and 80%-recycled water. There was a data-trail as to how the Argent family had hired him, but it was absolutely and depressingly and boringly unexceptional. He had been put forward from his home globe to a broker, on account of his better-than-average looks, and better-than-average iQ, and better-than-average reflexes; and passed from that broker to an-other, and then through the long trail of good service to a variety of positions until he came to the attention of one of the Argent factotums. An important family like theirs was always on the lookout for good servants. From his point of view, Dia reflected, it must have been winning the golden ticket. The bId noted that Iago himself was involved in the vetting process, this being one of his duties for the family. What then for Leron? Initiation in the family Lagrange, and beefing up the bones ready for 1G service, and dosing with CRF and all that. But he had barely started his service He hadn't *even* started! This was the first time Dia had ever laid eyes upon him, and he was a corpse! To go through all that, and finally get the big break, and to come down to Earth . . . only to be killed straight away! There might be something poignant about it, if it weren't so absolutely ordinary and boring and regular. At least, Dia thought, at least he got to put foot on Earth before he died – how many of the trillions of shanty-bubble-poor could claim such a thing? At least he had stood on the homeworld. But then she thought to herself: he's only been down a day. There's a good chance he hadn't yet acclimatised to enough to place the soles of his feet against the ground. And that thought made her a little sad.

//Why is his skin colour the shade it is?// she asked.

//Human beings born to live in upland environments must deal with much higher than Earth-standard ambient radiation. Dark skin pigmentation is both a common augmentation and is strongly selected for in brevet-evolutionary terms.// quoth the bId.

Tch! Tch and *tuch* you ask a *specific* question and the Biolink iData gives you a *general* answer. Useless, useless.

'That there's the weapon, I'd guess,' said Iago, nodding. And there it was, the modern Club of Herakles, a great plasmetal hammer; plasmetal, or conceivably solid metal. It was lying on the ground beside the victim. 'It would require somebody of great strength to lift such a thing,' was Deño's opinion. 'Even assuming they were acclimatized to the gravity.'

This was self-evidently true. So do you know what Diana thought? She thought: since that suggests the murderer is a person of great physical strength, the murderer will *actually* be a very weak individual. A fellow with a small physique! That was her *first* thought. Diana knew murder mysteries, you see. She had played a thousand Ideal Palace whodunits. A thousand, at least! Oh, she wasn't a fool. She knew this was different – that this was life, not a story. But she had spent as much time solving real-life historical crimes as she had solving made-up puzzle stories. And the unexpected was as much key to real crime as to made-up!

She looked about, to get a sense of the immediate environment of the crime. The room was full of *stuff*. The hammer on the floor, with the blood on its metal snout, was only one of a whole series of implements for bashing and digging and all the other incomprehensible business required for tending gardens. In the corner of the room a robot sat motionless. On the far wall a chainweave sheet hung; and in front of it a stack of plastic barrels and boxes. There were odd-looking fins sticking out from the wall, like the heat-radiator panels of an upland house although for some reason here fitted to the *inside* of the building. What was the point in that? To her left were myriad pots of paint and plasmetal lacquer, and long tubes of some description, and who knows what else.

'Lots of possible weapons here,' she observed.

'Yet the murderer chose a heavy hammer' said Iago.

'Or made it *look* as though he did,' Diana said.

'Miss Argent,' urged Deño, at her side. 'Please! Let us leave this place. I am not happy here. This space does not permit me to maximise the security coverage.'

'Sure,' she said, absently, running her eye round the variety of stores. There was nothing else to see here. And she *was* feeling tired again. This gravity is a crushing thing; an unrelenting thing. And so they went out.

It was slow work coming back across the dry lawn.

Back in the house, and Eva hadn't moved so much as a centimetre. Diana stripped off her crawlipers, and made it back to her couch, supported part of the way by Iago's gentlemanly arm. She saw that her sister was plugged into Ideal Palace.

'Eva!' she hooted. 'Evissima!' But she didn't have the energy even to wave her arm, and certainly didn't have the oomph to get up and go over to her. So she left Eva idling in her worldtual, and slipped into an uneasy doze.

2

The Police

She was woken by Iago. 'The police want to have a word, Miss Diana.'

She stared at his old face, as creased as any druid's His short hair; his muscular torso, his long legs. He was leaning over her, but he made even this look as though he was bowing. She said: 'You love me, don't you, Eye-ah-go?'

'Of course I do, Miss Diana.'

'What I mean is: it's not just that you're dosed up with CRF?'

'All the family servants are so dosed, Miss.'

'But it's not *just* that?'

'It's not just that.'

'Would you love me even if you had no CRF in your system at all?'

'Of course I would, Miss.'

She smiled. '*You* want to have penetrative sexual intercourse with me,' she said.

His reaction was priceless! 'No!' he replied. 'Certainly not, Miss Diana!' His eyes were round as coins, startlement and wounded pride. 'The very idea! My love for you is pure as Plato.'

And she laughed out loud. 'I'm only teasing you,' she said, making the couch sit her up a little. As if that needed saying! Iago was old enough to be her *mother*. He was old as a druid. He was ancient as chaos and old night. 'Come on then, let's have these police in. I shall answer their questions.'

'Do you want me to stay?' Iago asked.

But his question only annoyed her. 'You think I can't answer some police questions without your chaperoning me? Go away, you hideous, lined, wrinkled, mottled *old* fellow.'

'You MOHparents asked me to stay whilst the police speak to you, Miss,' he murmured — although he did back towards the door.

'I'm sixteen,' she said. 'I can look *after* myself.'

'*Will be* sixteen,' Iago said. 'In three weeks.'

'Close enough for government work. And anyway, Deño is here if I need looking after from these gargoyle *policepersons*, so you can – shoo – shoo – shoo.' Her Tutor bowed, and walked out of the door. Here's the thing about Iago: he made it look *easy*. Her three bodyguards made it their business to train all the time so as to keep their muscle tone. She couldn't believe Iago followed that kind of regimen, being a Tutor rather than a bodyguard. Indeed, you could see, from the condensation of sweat on his upper lip, that moving around in this gravity was a terrible, painful strain for him. But he never complained; he never so much as *alluded* to his discomfort. Iago walked as soon as they landed, *sans* crawlipers, moving his long legs, spine straight, arms at his side. He bowed. He insisted on standing whilst they sat. It was, in its way, heroic. She knew *what* he was doing, of course. He was trying to impress her. Never mind the CRF, he loved her true as any knight in romance loved fair maiden. To admit that his legs ached, or his lungs burned, would be to let her down.

So Dia readied herself, and two police officers came through: one female and one male. Both had the same stocky, troll-like solidity of people raised in this horrible gravity. Both bowed their heads when they came to stand beside her.

'Good afternoon, Miss Argent,' said the female. Dia's bId supplied the necessaries: she was Police Inspector Halkiopoulou, in company of Police Subinspector Zarian, and both were retained by a Ulanov-accredited legal enforcement agency. She waved all that away.

'My sister is lost in the Ideal Palace at the momento-tomento,' she told them. The slightest delay in the arrival of their smiles suggested either that they were dense, or else that they were both using translation bugs. *That* was poor form, really. It was English Dia was speaking, after all: not Potpourri or Tidharian or Pidgin-Martian. And this island was *majority owned* by the Argents, after all!

'Woh, though, isn't this a terrible thing?' she said. 'A dead body! A dead servant!'

'It is clear the individual *has* been murdered, and it seems death has occurred following a mighty blow to the cranium,' said the man-police in accented tones, presumably reading the phonetic transcription from across his lenses. She hated that. That was excessivo cheap.

'I saw,' she said. 'It was *super*-woh.'

'It is unclear who has committed the crime,' the female one was saying. 'Certainly it was another of the servants present in the building. We have checked the House AI, and nobody else entered the servant house, or left it, during the period prior to the murder. When the body was discovered the nineteen servants housed there all exited the place in distress, but they are all counted, and nobody else was inside. So the murderer must be one of the nineteen—'

'That's exactly, boringly, exactly what you'd expect!' Dia broke in. 'I have solved literally *hundreds* of whodunits in the Ideal Palace, and I know how important it is to keep an open mind. It might not be any of those nineteen at all!'

The two policepeople looked at one another, and then at the floor. Their evident embarrassment infuriated Diana. 'The House AI,' said the female, 'tracked the victim, alive, entering the house. Since then nobody else either entered or left, until after he was dead. Accordingly . . .'

'Oh I know,' she snapped, 'of course I know that real life is different to IP-stories. Of course I know that! But I also specialise in *real-life* whodunits. Really, I've cracked hundreds and *hundreds*.' She paused to get her breathing back to normal. How could she convince these professional policemen of the genuineness of her passion? 'I'll send my scores to your bIds if you like – there's a girl in Mars orbit who has slightly better metrics, in terms not just of picking the right murderer, but in the identification of the right clues, and in time markers. But the thing the thing is is *is* she's better on made-up murder mysteries, and those are *easier*. I mean, they're usually more *complicated* than real-life, historical murders—' Dia gasped, and snatched a breath, and went on '—but the thing is, they're complicated in a kind-of *predictable* way. You know what I mean? An invented whodunit has the same relation to real life as a chess puzzle has to an actual game of chess. You look at the classics: Poe! That woman from the Christ family, whatever, and Dickson-Carr, and Queen Ellery, and Jay Creek, and Rajah Nimmi. To solve those sorts of stories your starting point needs to be, like, *what would be the most ingenious solution*? Throw likelihood away, and look for impossible ingenuity, and you're halfway there. Of course real life isn't like that!' She was wearing herself out, what with the gravity and everything, but the thrust of her enthusiasm carried her through. 'I've played hundreds of real-life murders, from history. I've solved murders and kidnappings. I solved *four different* Rippers. Tonks – that's the girl in Mars, Anna Tonks Yu, *can* you imagine a stupider name? – she does histories too, but she's only better than me on the *made-up* whodunits. Do you understand?'

'She is a member,' said the female policeperson, tentatively, 'of the *famous* Family Yu?'

'Yes, big-big family, but don't get distracted,' said Diana, crossly. 'You're not dealing with her, but me. This has happened right on *my* doorstep! You need *my* help to solve it! She'd be no use to you anyway. I can help you!'

These long speeches had worn her out, so she sank back into her chair. She was expecting the policepersons to make polite noises of discouragement, perhaps vague promises and dismissals. But instead they seemed genuinely pleased. 'We would very much welcome your assistance, young Mistress,' said the man – Zarian, her bId reminded her – 'your help would be an *invaluable* addition to our investigation.'

Diana was sufficiently taken aback, and tired enough, to say nothing at all to this. She widened her eyes.

As the silence started to become awkward, the female policeperson, Inspector Halkiopoulou, spoke up: 'I'm sure you understand, Miss Argent, that we are very aware of the *sensitivities* of . . . conducting police investigation into the internal matters of a family with such a . . . great eminence in the affairs of the whole System.'

The male one added: 'we are perfectly well aware that your two MOH parents have – personal connections with the Ulanovs.'

'The Argents are much . . . loved, on this island,' the female policeperson said, with a smidgen too much tentativeness about the main verb. 'Quite apart from the fact that you *do* own more than 50% of the town.'

'My MOHmies do,' said Diana. 'Which amounts to the same thing.' She was feeling a little miffed, if you must know; although maybe it was just the tiredness and the general discombobulation. But she wanted the police to want her because of her Ideal Palace expertise! – not just because she was a scion of a highfalutin friends-of-Ulanov *family*. What she *really* wanted was for them to take one look at her stats, and see that if you broke them down properly – broke them down in the way that was most relevant to the sort of crime we're talking about here – then there was *literally nobody in the Solar System* to touch her for solving who-dunits! Or, nobody in her age group. Which is to say, of the three dozen or so teenagers who hung-out on the (alright, she admitted it) most expensive IP realms, only Anna Tonky-wonks Yu even came *close* to her.

It was absolutely a lie to say she had a crush on Anna. That was as absurd as absurd could *be*. She would fight anyone who said so.

But instead of that these policepeople were giving her the usual sycophantic stuff, on account of how her MOHmies were *players*. Of course, it was true. And besides, the victim *was* an Argent servant; and the murderer was probably an Argent servant too. These people were *hers* – not the policepeople's.

'Of course, Your MOH parents have spoken to us,' said the man. The woman glanced at him, and then turned her eyes back on the floor.

'Of course they have,' said Diana, sourly.

'You'll understand we have certain legal processes we must pursue, to remain within the terms of our commercial contract as Ulanov sanctioned police,' the woman purred. 'But we would be pleased to . . . defer to yourself in the business of determining who – has committed this crime.'

'I'm very tired,' Diana told them, with imperious suddenness. 'I *will* help you solve this murder mystery. Tomorrow I shall interview all the servants, with help from my bodyguards and my Tutor. We will let you know what we come up with.'

The police bowed, and went out. Diana lowered her couch and turned cumbrously onto her side, to give her squashed spine a rest. And as she moved she caught Deño's eye. There was a sparkle in it. It made her smile. He felt it too. Her own murder mystery! Too, too, *too* exciting.

3

The Utility of Dreaming

The girls spoke to their MOHmies later that same day. The link was relayed a hundred times or so, just in case somebody chanced upon it and tried piggybacking through the source (and nobody must know where the girls were – danger! danger!), so the quality wasn't good. But their parents were perfectly recognisable: arm in arm, floating in one of their great green globes up in space. 'You'll never guess, oh-my-MOHmies!' blurted Dia, as soon as the connection was secured.

Both MOHmies smiled their identical smiles, but only MOHmie Yin spoke: 'we have *some* idea, my dear – Iago informed us; and the police have communicated through official channels.'

'An actual murder mystery! A dead servant – murdered, and nobody knows by whom!'

'So we hear. We instructed the policepersons that you should help them.' Those smiles, in separate faces, so perfectly identical they looked like one of the dimensional superposition problems you get in kindergarten.

'I'll work it out,' said Dia proudly. 'I'll have the mystery cracked in – oh, a day, I should imaginate. A day and a half, I should imagi*nation*ate.'

'We don't doubt *that*,' said MOHmie Yin. 'Will you help her, Eva?'

Eva looked sulky. 'Now you *know* I have my PhD to finish. I'm closing in on a solution to the supernova problem. An actual solution! And, MOHmies-dearests, if I *might* say — there are problems that are trivial, and problems that are profound. When you bred us to solve problems, surely you had the *latter* sort in mind?'

'Ah, but,' said MOHmie Yin, turning to look into the face of MOHmie Yang, 'which is which? Are exploding stars profound because they are very big and very far away? Or is it precisely that that makes them *trivial*?'

Dia wasn't slow to pick up the hint. 'A human being is dead,' she said. 'Importance and triviality are value judgments that apply only to the human world. And in the human world death is precisely the profound thing.'

'You do talk nonsense, sister,' said Eva, annoyed that her MOHmies seemed to be siding with Diana. 'You couldn't care less about this human being, dead or not! You feel nothing for him one way or the other. How could you? You never met him. He's just another servant. To you this is simply a problem to be solved, just like the Champagne Supernova problem is to me.'

'Life is more important than data,' Dia retorted, piously.

'When you saw the body — did you weep?'

Diana glowered at her. 'Don't be obtuse,' she retorted. The blithe smiles of their parents, rendered in scratchy-scratchy dynamic 3D right in front of the girls.

'There's one thing, MOHmies,' said Eva. 'One thing that does puzzle me. When I think of the trouble you take to keep us both *safe* . . .'

'Of course,' said MOHmie Yang. 'Nothing is more precious than you two girls. The future of the Clan *depends* upon you.'

The expression on Eva's face tightened a little, but she pressed on: 'surely, surely, but . . . *given* that such is the case, aren't you a little alarmed that somebody has been violently murdered within

– within metres of us, literally? Shouldn't you . . . I don't know – shouldn't you pull us out?'

For the first time MOHmie Yang spoke up: 'pull you out? No, no. You need your *gravity*, dear girls.'

'There's no threat to *you*, my darlings,' agreed MOHmie Yin. 'The servants are all dosed with CRF. All thoroughly dosed *and* conditioned to the *nines*.'

'To the ninety-nines,' agreed MOHmie Yang.

'They could no more harm *you* than cut off their own legs! Don't worry about *that*. And as far as this murder is concerned – well, it's a problem to be solved. And who is better at solving problems than you two, my darlings?'

'There's always Anna Tonks Yu,' said Eva, under her breath, as the call ended. Diana heard this, but chose to ignore it. Chose to ignore and snore. The Yu Clan would chop their heads off (literally, no doubt) given half a chance. It was actually quite insulting – *actually*, in fact – for her sister to mention *that* little flatface idiot. Close to Clan treason, actually; and, at the very least, *hurtful* to say that Anna Tonks Yu could outperform Diana in problem solving. On the other hand, if Dia challenged her, or bridled, or reacted in any way, Eva would only ramp up the taunting; and it wouldn't be long before it got to 'you *love* her' and 'you want to *marry* her' and so on. Marry her! She'd never even *met* her in the flesh. As if Eva had any conception of love what! so! ever! She was cold as a comet, all rational thought and data crunching. She might as well have been an AI.

Their quarrel didn't last long, of course. The two girls said their prayers together, and afterwards kissed and went to their respective beds.

Eva fell asleep easily. Both girls slept a lot: and *falling* asleep was never a problem. (The problem, in this gravity, was *staying* asleep.) If Diana lay awake for a while, reflecting upon the day that had been, it was not because she was too excited to sleep. It was more pragmatic than that. She wanted to process the day's input a little before the dreams came.

Dreams! Any old AI can crunch data, draw hypotheses and spot patterns. But there are no AIs, and precious few *human* minds, that can intuit solutions from interacting chaotic systems. This is what made Eva and Diana special, and that specialness – exhibited in their MOHmies too, of course; and in various other siblings and buddings, to much lesser degrees – was the foundation of the Clan's success. They served the Ulanovs directly, and how wealthy it had made them! As far as dreams were concerned – well dreams are generated by the random processes of neural oscillation during the brain's rest phases. What dreams do is cycle and recycle images and feelings, rationalisations and fears. There's nothing special about that. It's not the *dreams* that matter (chaff, mental turbulence, the rotating metal bars moving endlessly through the transparent tub of metaphorical slushy). It is what the problem-solving circuits in the mind *make* of the dreams. Dreams iterate and test mental schemas, discarding the maladaptive to return the adaptive to the slush to be reworked. Dreams are emotional preparations for solving problems – that is why we have evolved them, because problem-solving abilities are *highly* adaptive and thus strongly evolutionarily selected. Dreams intoxicate the individual out of reliance on common sense and preconception, and tempt her into the orbit of private logic. Dreams have utility.

Dreaming was central to what the girls did, not because of what the dreams contained, but because of what the urge to interpret sparked inside them.

Diana liked to prepare her thoughts before descending to her personal dream-avernus. She sorted the events of the day, mentally. She rehearsed all she had seen and heard, and thought for a while about her emotional reaction to what she had seen. It was odd how much of her feelings were ones of unsatisfactoriness. The corpse itself. She had expected to encounter death as a kind of existential depth and had been disappointed. But maybe there *was* a deeper truth there. Maybe profundity actually *is* a mode of disappointment. The rhythm of the climax – joy and despair, sex and pain – is of course the currency of *life*. Death can only ever be a sort of anticlimactic belatedness.

It hardly mattered: because tomorrow she would begin investigating her very own murder mystery! There was no question that she could solve it. Too too *too* exciting.

She composed herself, and went straight into sleep. Of course she dreamt. She always dreamt.

She saw the whole Solar system: the incomprehensible sprawl of it. Planets blotted with people; and the billion or so globes and houses orbiting in free space – a foam of bubbles, tinting the sunlight green and ochre where they clustered together. So much plastic, extruded from rocksilicate and algae oils in the endless manufactories. Some of these zero-g houses were mansions, sparsely populated and expansive; many more were rock homes, hollowed-out asteroids and brick-moons. By far the greatest number were shanty bubbles: cheap balloons of inch-thick transparent plastic, crammed with the poorest of the poor, subsisting on a diet of ghunk augmented by whatever plants they could coax into growth. Pass through the shoals of these crowded homes: the ghunk soaking in sunlight within, and hundreds of faces pressing up against the walls to watch you pass. Many of them were dirty, greying or black or blue-black, blistered and scabbed by long years of exposure to pitiless sun-radiation. Or –

Stop. Something odd here.

It occurred to Dia, inside the dream, that she rarely dreamed such bigness. That was more Eva's kind of thing: the vastness of space, orbital mechanics and faraway stars. Diana usually dreamed on a more intimate and human scale. Yet here she was, taking in the entire System. She looked down at herself, wondering how it was she could hang in space and see these sights without dying. But she saw that she had been gifted the body of a spaceship; a sloop hull, painted white (why *white*?), and inscribed upon her flank the legend: FTL. But the odd thing was that her fuselage was positively bristling with wings, fins, vanes and struts. Wings – in space? Fins are perfectly purposeless in zero-gravity. Yet there they were: all manner of them, bristling all over her spaceship body. Why?

'Where am I going?' she asked herself; and the answer came back to her like an echo: 'into the sun'. Past the foam of houses and bubbles and the population of human beings in their trillions she saw the sun. It had a human face; and although it didn't look like Leron, the murdered handservant, Dia somehow knew that it *was* him, nonetheless. 'My spaceship body is hard. If I fly into the sun,' she thought, 'I shall smash his skull and kill him. Does that matter?'

Does it matter? The voice said: 'the shrapnel will scatter and kill all of humanity. Does *that* matter?'

Does that matter? She woke up, suddenly, breathing hard. But her heart was not hurrying; and the room was calm. It was the gravity that made her haul her own ribcage in gasping breaths. *Bristling*, she thought, *with wings, fins, vanes and struts*. Odd. She thought about the dream for a while, and then she sent herself back to sleep.

4

The Mystery of the
Champagne Supernovae

Eva Argent, five years older than her MOHsister, had been shaped in slightly different ways. Not *too* different, obviously, or the whole point of the Argent family would be obviated. The *physical* differences between the girls were minor; but mentally they were star and black-hole. Both, of course, lived for information – they were *moved* by it, they delighted in it, they immersed themselves in it. It was what they were *for*. The Argent family had made its fortune, and had risen to its Systemic eminence, on the back of suchlike information skills, and accordingly the new generation – both Eva and Diana – had been made with the same passion for problem-solving. But Diana's mind worked best when she could *personalise* the information. Hers was a creative sort of problem solving, freewheeling and intuitive. Eva was different. People-problems did not interest her. Data seemed to her a larger, purer, more transcendent quantity than *Homo sapiens*ness. Human-to-human interactions were, effectively, all just politics, and politics bored her. It wasn't that she actively *disliked* people. For example; ironically enough, her dispassion meant that she had already engaged in a good deal more sexual experimentation than her virgin sister; both with her peers, and with some of the more physically attractive servants. But she was able to do this precisely *because* she ran no risk of emotional entanglement. No; what set her mind alight were the problems far removed, in a literal sense, from the worlds of humankind.

Right now she was working on her seventh PhD. That was why she was spending so much time in her Worldtuality rather than engaging with reality (not that there was much point in even *trying* to engage with the real world until her body had adjusted a little to the horrible pressures of gravity). This would be her third thesis on Supernovae, her fifth on astrophysics more generally, and she was close to completion. And it *was* interesting! The development of specialised AIs had made available a quantity of raw data on supernovae unimaginable even a few decades before. It gave data artists a wealth of new ways of addressing the several dozen as-yet-unsolved astrophysical mysteries.

Eva's current work was on a particular kind of Type II Super-nova. Normally, such events only occurred to stars that had at least nine times the mass of the Sun; for a certain minimum threshold of mass was absolutely necessary for the supernova reaction to take place. Which is to say: it was (of course) possible for less massive stars to go supernova, but they generated a different data-profile, in terms of the balance of hydrogen and helium, than was the case with Type II. In an earlier PhD Eva had addressed the problem of stars that generated a Type II supernova despite lacking sufficient mass. Now she was looking at a different variety of stars; ones that achieved Type II supernova luminosity without generating a debris shell and despite being *much* too small; far smaller than any other examples observed. Only four such cases had been identified – the first, observed in the early twenty-first century had been given the name 'Champagne Supernova'. After a song, apparently (that was the great era of the *song*, of course; that was when everybody had been crazy for the *song*). Since then, only three more of the champagne type had been located amongst the trillions of observed stars. Extrapolating proportionately from the parameters of observational capacity (a simple algorithm) suggested that this was a phenomenon that had happened maybe two dozen times *in the entire history of the universe* – which made this 'anomalous superluminosity' problem vanishingly rare and extraordinarily interesting. *Something* made these tiny stars *mimic* supernovae explosions! And Eva was determined to find out what. The data was rich, although not rich enough to propose 90th-percentile explanations. Nevertheless she had three working hypotheses, and two of them 50th-percentile likelihoods, which was enough for a PhD.

She had not been made as any kind of child prodigy, but nevertheless Eva was awarded her first PhD long before she was sixteen. Diana, on the other hand, was different: her sixteenth birthday was only weeks away, and she had nothing more to show for herself than a regular Tertiary School degree. The truth, Eva knew, was that Dia had a *distractible* mind. She lacked the staying power required for higher-level information work. And since the family's eminence, its usefulness to the Ulanovs, *depended* upon information work of the very highest calibre, that might prove a problem in the long run.

In the long run the Clan needed a clearer vision in charge.

For Eva, all these Whodunits her sister loved were nothing more than symptoms of an unshed immaturity. 'Who is the killer?' was never a serious problem – not in the cosmic sense. Take the recent unpleasantness: one servant amongst a group of nineteen had killed another servant with a hammer. There was no question that it *was* one of the servants – nobody else had gone into the building, and nobody else but billeted servants had come out. So the only questions that remained were: which one of the nineteen was guilty? Why did they do it? And did the act constitute any sort of threat to either Eva or Diana? Had Dia canvassed her opinion, Eva would have answered those questions in a moment, to within data-tolerances with which any reputable information explorer would have been more than satisfied. But Dia would never ask – because she was hooked on precisely the romance of the crime mystery. Romance!

Put silly romance to one side, and take those three questions in order. First: who committed the crime? Narrowing the group of suspects down to only nineteen people already placed the solution in the 99.9+++th-increment. Even if you limited yourself to the population of the island (though, since the whole Argent group had only just landed, and had not yet interacted with any island natives, the murderer was massively unlikely to be found outside the group – but for the sake of argument) we were talking about 19 out of 102,530, which was the 99.998+th percentile. Eva had never reached such levels of near-certainty in any of her PhDs! It was ridiculous to ask for more. Trillions of people in the solar system, and Diana wanted to waste her time sifting through a group of nineteen? Let her. If Eva had been in charge, she would have treated all nineteen as guilty – and then either execute them all, or perhaps treat the group conviction as a technical mitigation and sentence them all to long prison terms.

Second: *why* did the one-in-nineteen do what he or she did? Here the increments weren't so good; but even idling in the relevant section of the Imaginary Palace for ten minutes gave Eva enough data to arrive at an 85th-percentile or higher probability. The motives that explained human murder bunched, historically, into three groups: material gain; personal grudge and sociopathy.

Since these were close family servants, all carefully vetted by the Argent's systems (they would hardly have been assigned to attend directly on the girls, otherwise), Eva could rule out the last of these. The first also seemed unlikely. They were servants, not citizens. They had grown up in solar orbit shanty bubbles, on the edge of the Sump, subsisting on ghunk and living by cheap scrubbers and fusion cells. We're not talking about the more durable rock houses, excavated out of old asteroids and the like – only the relatively wealthy could afford those sorts of homes (and only the superwealthy, like Eva's family, could afford the massive multi-part plasmetal structures *they* inhabited). No: shanty bubbles were designedly temporary structures, alright for a few years, until solar radiation began to degrade the structural integrity of their plastic. When you bought them, you agreed to a warranty that specified no longer than three years' use. Then, on pain of prosecution under the Lex Ulanova, you were supposed to buy a new one. But the Sumpolloi, the very poorest – of course they couldn't afford that. So they lived on and on in those deathtraps, patching leaks and fractures, overstraining the fabric with a much higher population than they were designed to hold. Or, worse, jerry-rigging them – all warranty immediately voided by such action, two-year maximum prison sentence possible (though who could be bothered to police it?) – drilling windows and linking the holes by crawlskins, tying Globes together in clusters. Horrible, vulgar, teeming humanity. Bodies in constant proximity. The smell, the threat, the waste. Usually even the data access was held in common, so there wasn't even the possibility of privacy *there*. Often the Bubbles would break wide open and everybody inside would be killed; or only a few desperate survivors would be able to suit themselves up, or scrabble, ratlike, along the crawlskins to a neighbouring shanty. It didn't stop them. 'They' kept on breeding. And there were *billions* of these bubbles in solar orbit, staining the sunlight dark green! The limitless poor.

These servants, the Argent daughters' personal handservants, had been uplifted out of that morass. By virtue of taking on

Argent livery they were automatically wealthier than anybody else they had hitherto known. It was actually low-level stuff, of course; a pittance. But it was a lot *to them*. Why would they want more? Indeed, since their contracts were all-time, it wasn't as if they would ever have the leisure to spend extra credits. So, although Eva couldn't rule out the possibility that the crime had been committed for reasons of material gain, it seemed unlikely. By far the most probable explanation was personal grudge. You might delve deeper into circumstances and uncover exactly what the grudge was, but why would you bother? Here was an explanation any professional information artist would be happy with. At least: anyone who worked in the sciences.

And that only left the third question: did the crime constitute a present threat to the sisters? Cursory thought might imagine it did. Somebody capable of murderous violence was in physical proximity to the girls. But the girls were surrounded by expert bodyguards; the nineteen suspects had been confined pending investigation, and – above all – the girls themselves could never have been the target. All the Argent servants were dosed with high levels of CRF, geared to generate not just feelings of loyalty but, actively, of self-sacrificing love, the real thing, towards the core members of the MOHfamily. Quite literally, they would sooner chop off their own limbs than hurt either Eva or Diana.

The clincher, as far as Eva was concerned, was the way her MOHmies had reacted. If they had the slightest fear their daughters were in actual danger, they would have pulled them straight back up into orbit. But not only had they not done so, they were actively encouraging Diana to indulge her hobby and investigate the crime – on site. Evidently the crime posed *no* direct threat to the girls.

Not that the two girls were ever *safe*, of course. On the contrary, danger was a constant part of Eva and Diana's lives. They were the chosen key daughters of the Argent Clan. Their family was one of five MOHfamilies that were, collectively, second only to the Ulanovs in the Solar System's hierarchies of power. Below them, thousands of Gongsi corporations, of varying size and aggressiveness, jockeyed for position. Any one of them, or (of course) any of the other four MOHfamilies, might have good reason to want to hurt the Argents. But none of that had anything to do with one servant bashing another servant on the head with a hammer! Most servants had only the vaguest sense of the structured hierarchy of power's upper echelons – beyond the sense that the Ulanovs had won the war all those years ago and gifted order and law to the System. The MOHfamilies, and below them the Gongsi, and below them the myriad bands, police, civvies, conventional genetic families, cults and mafias, and below *them* the Polloi, the hundreds of billions of ordinary citizens – all arranged in concentric circles around the Ulanovs, like medieval species of angels around the throne of God. And below the Polloi, only the sub people, the *Sump*, the dregs – the trillions. One less, whether dispatched by natural causes or by a hammer to the skull, hardly mattered.

Insofar as she dipped into political data – and she could hardly avoid doing so, however much she preferred the chillier perfection of physics – things seemed, presently, stable in the System. It had been three decades since the last attempted coup, when the Palmer MOHfamily had tried to eliminate the Ulanovs with one strike and usurp their place. Of course, it was safe to assume the other families, and Gongsi and lower-ranking organisations too, were *plotting*. Eva assumed her own MOHmies were plotting too. It would be longer-term suicide not to lay-in plans, possible strategies and the like. The Ulanovs would expect as much, however much the Lex Ulanova forbade it. But Eva couldn't see anything that was likely to lead to upheaval or bloodshed in the immediate future.

Still, it was only sensible to take precautions. The Palmer Clan had been annihilated; and neither MOHfamily nor Gongsi would be so foolish as to attempt a direct assault again. But it was certainly possible than either might attack either; and a strike against the Argents – the information guild, particularly vital to the Ulanovs – could achieve a great deal for an ambitious lower organisation. Indeed, the chances of such an attack increasingly edged from possible into probable as time went on. Dia and Eva were not yet ready to assume the mantle of command. To strike now made more sense than waiting until they consolidated their inheritance.

The iRumours, of course, were all about faster-than-light travel. If you believed the gossipoppers, the Ulanovs were on the verge of discovering, or rediscovering, of uncovering (or something) *a technology that permitted FTL*. Idiocy. It was impossible, of course. The laws of physics forbade it. But the mere rumour was enough to throw the Data Markets into array. It was as if somebody on the Dutch stock market in the seventeenth-century had announced: 'tomorrow I shall have an actual, working technology for turning lead into gold!' The markets tended to go borderline chaotic at the mere *idea*; and data markets were more volatile than other kinds of markets. But that didn't mean it was actually going to happen.

As for Eva, well: she had six PhDs in physical sciences, and was about to submit a seventh. She knew perfectly well not only that FTL was impossible, but that its impossibility was of a particularly glaring kind. This Mc-whatever he was called, this fellow who was supposed to have stumbled on the means of breaking the light barrier – he had disappeared, of course. Eva doubted he had ever existed. And if he had, he was only a crank. His 'discovery' amounted to somebody saying: *I have created a perpetual motion machine*, or *I have invented a square circle*. But she didn't have to believe the technology existed. She only had to believe that *people believed* the technology existed. People, being stupid, believed all sorts of things.

If this impossible device were to tumble into the hands of the Ulanovs, it would represent – of course – unimaginable power and wealth. It would consolidate their power in an absolute sense. They would control humanity's migration to the stars. Of course, people would be prepared to kill for such a thing. To kill on a vast scale. And of course, the Argents, as the Ulanovs' information clan, would be assumed to be hand-in-hand with any such discovery. All of this, just the idea of it, put them at terrible risk.

But Eva and Diana were well protected; their location a secret close-guarded, their every hour guarded by the best bodyguards money could buy. The island was ringed and littered with defence systems. A landing and assault would have a low probability of success. Of course, a rival MOHfamily or Gongsi – assuming they knew where the girls were staying – could just bomb the entire island from orbit. But that would be an act of war; not a step lightly taken. An assassination attempt would be safer, and whilst that could come at any time it wasn't terribly likely.

And all of this was a *parsec* away from one servant clocking another on the head with a hammer. Only an idiot would think that this sordid crime constituted the first of what a crime narr-ator might call 'The FTL Murders'.

Eva put the whole thing out of her head. She worked on her anomalous supernova problem, and refined her possible solution from 52% to 55% probability. Then she washed, and ate, and played chess for a half-hour. Then she played with her sister in the IP, and they both chatted remotely to their MOHmies – Dia, of course, excitedly gabbling about this *real-life murder mystery*, and how she was going to find out which of the nineteen servants was responsible, and their parents smiling indulgently. Eva found herself obscurely angry. But then she slept in a gel tank, and woke the next morning feeling a little better about the gravity. She got on with her research.

The murder was a trivial matter. She carried on thinking so, right up to the moment when Ms Joad arrived.

5

Ms Joad

Ms Joad worked directly for the Ulanovs. It didn't *get* more (*up!* *up!*) elevated than that! The fact that she had come down to the island to speak to the girls face-to-face threw everything Eva had assumed about this mystery *in the incinerator*. Pff! Gone. As Diana put it: there was no wavy *way* the Ulanovs would be interested in this crime if it were truly just one servant killing another.

Ms Joad had the physique of someone for whom the uplands were a habitus: long and loose-limbed, skinny wrists, big hands. Her eyes were large, but not in an animé little-girl way. On the contrary, they were a Shiva-coloured dark purple-black, and capable of an intenser gaze than is usual for the human eye. Her features were never anything other than serene and controlled, and the elements of her face were regular and balanced in a way that ought to have been handsome. But there was some quality about her, some indefinable edge, that parsed her beauty through *terror*. Whenever Ms Joad turned her bland gaze upon her, Eva could almost see through those eyes into the sandstorm of her mind. She was violent not in a crude, bashing-people-about way. She was violent, as it were, ontologically. She was dangerous as a scorpion. But that was clearly stupid, because she was much much more dangerous than any scorpion!

Because she travelled up and down all the time on Ulanov business she was used to gravity, and took only a couple of hours to acclimatise – enough time for Eva and Dian and all three of their bodyguards to assemble in the mansion's main hall to meet her. Iago brought Ms Joad through. He came into the room first and she followed him; but the door squealed and shook when *she* passed through it, as if possessed by the spirits of several devils.

'My oversight! I forgot,' she said, in her inky voice. The expression on her face made it clear that she never forgot anything about anything, and that oversight was alien to her nature. Without ostentation, but in a way that made it clear she was performing the action for the benefit of her audience, she pulled a metal firearm from inside her jacket. This she handed to Berthezene, who slipped it in a smartcloth pouch. Then, smiling slightly, she stepped outside and came back in through the door.

It had no complaint to make about her second entry.

She was walking with crawlipers, but she moved easily to her chair and settled herself unfussily. 'My dear girls,' she said. 'My employers have sent me to make sure you are *well*.'

The girls, seated, didn't get up (in this g? Are you crazy?). 'We are both *very* well,' said Diana. She looked over at Iago – characteristically, he was very deliberately *not* sitting in the available chair, but was instead standing with his back to the wall a little way to the left of Jong-il. He did not return her look.

'Both very well,' echoed Eva.

Joad looked from one girl to the other. 'There has been a murder, I hear. On your property. Metres from this house. Isn't that extraordinary?'

'Is this what has brought you down here, Ms Joad?' asked Eva. 'I can assure you that the Ulanovs need not be concerned with something so trivial.'

'*I* am investigating the crime,' said Diana. 'Although, of course, Ulanov law is being observed scrupulously; two accredited policepeople,' – the flicker of her eyelids as she drew their names from her bId – 'Inspector Halkiopoulou, and Subinspector Zarian, visited yesterday. It's all in order.'

Joad blinked, forcefully, once. Thus she took on board the necessary information. 'Very good. Of course my employers are anxious to ensure that you are both perfectly safe.'

'We had all the servants' CRF levels checked straight away,' said Diana, rather superfluously. 'There's nothing amiss.'

Joad looked at Diana, and then at Eva, and then she smiled.

'So you are to try your hand at investigating crime, are you, my dear?' she said. Although she was speaking to Diana she was looking straight through the main window at the garden outside.

'Yes,' said Diana. 'I have a great deal of experience in World-tuality at . . .'

'Believe me it's different in real life,' Ms Joad interrupted her. 'I know what it means really to investigate a crime.'

'The murder *is* a simple matter,' said Eva, a little too urgently. 'One servant killed another, probably for reasons of sexual jealousy, or personal grudge. The killer must be one of a group of nineteen servants. It's an unfortunate but eminently containable and, eh, indeed, *contained* event. My sister is looking into which particular servant is responsible. I myself spent some time yesterday ascertaining whether there was any chance the crime was symptomatic of a larger threat to our family – it isn't.'

'And you,' said Ms Joad, smiling amiably but speaking with a voice that could freeze starfire, 'have six PhDs already!'

'I,' said Eva, wrong-footed, 'I do.'

'My *dear* girls. I'm sorry to be the one to tell you that the matter is more dangerous than you realise.'

Dia's heart lolloped in her chest. Was Joad was going to *stay*? Had the Ulanovs sent her down to *monitor* the sisters, to spy on them, browbeat them? The thought of this individual contaminating her personal space, her own house, *was* intolerable.

'Really?' she said, in as ingenuous a voice as she could manage.

'You have played a great many of your whodunit games, in Worldtuality and so on,' said Joad to Dia, again without looking at her. 'So tell me. *Have* you ever heard of Jack Glass?'

Glass! 'Of course,' said Diana.

Ms Joad curled her mouth into a smile. 'I've been on his trail, you know,' she said. Nothing Ms Joad said could be described as offhand, exactly; but the way she imparted this piece of information came close.

And poor foolish Diana was enough of a fangirl in her chosen hobby to squee at this news . 'No! Really? Seriously and really?'

'Oh my *dear* girl,' said Joad, deadpan, looking through the window again. 'You have no idea. He's more dangerous even than his reputation suggests. Do you know what? We had him!'

'Had him?' repeated Eva.

'What – arrested?' asked Dia.

'Arrested *and* imprisoned.'

'I had no idea!' gasped Diana. 'That's not data available in any of the usual locations.'

'And I'll thank you to keep it that way. Leak it, and I'll trace it back.'

'Ms Joad!' said Diana, genuinely affronted.

'Of course,' Joad continued, without pause and without altering her murmurous monotone. 'You are your MOHmies' daughter. You understand the importance of informational hygiene and secrecy and,' she lifted her right hand, as if testing the gravity, flipped the hand over, and concluded, 'all that bag and baggage.' The hand came down again. 'I feel confident that I can tell you this, in confidence. We *caught* him. He was working under an alias of course, and was tried and sentenced for a minor crime – sent out to an asteroid called Lamy306, a long long way away, in a distant orbit. He was supposed to serve eleven years. It took us six months to realise our mistake – a lamentable lag, really. But then we realised what we had – *whom* we had, I mean – *him*, in other words, *Jack Glass* himself. So we hurried on out to Lamy306 in four ships to pick him up. Do you know what we found?'

'He was dead?' asked Eva. 'Suicide?'

Joad moved her head smoothly about on its frictionless neck and directed her gaze upon the sister. 'Certainly not. He wasn't. All his *fellow prisoners* were. Or – traces of them. Mutilated. Carved into,' and she gave this next word a peculiarly lubricious intonation, as if it chimed with some part of her inner being: '*chunks*.' She all but licked her lips. 'Their bodies were gone, but their blood was all over the walls.'

There was a silence. Cicadas tut-tutted distantly in the fields.

'Bad luck for them,' said Eva, eventually, trying not to flinch as Joad looked hard at her.

'Indeed.'

'At least you recaptured *him*,' asked Diana.

Joad swivelled her head back. 'We did not. He wasn't there. Somehow he escaped. Alas.'

Both daughters took this in, and a beat later both spoke at the same time, 'how is that possible?'/'How could he?' They stopped. Diana said: 'He wasn't there in the first place. Is that it?'

'It's a proper locked-room mystery,' said Joad. 'How did he escape from one of the best-locked rooms in the entire solar system!'

'He must have had help,' said Eva. 'A friend must have cracked the encryption, worked out where he was serving his sentence, and sent a ship out to pick him up.'

Joad shook her head, a series of short tight shimmers from left to right. 'The Gongsi in question has AIs surveilling all its many prison asteroids. Naturally, it saves money by surveilling them from a distance, and by AI. That means that, *had* a ship come to rescue him, they wouldn't necessarily have been able to do anything to stop it. *But* they would at least have recorded footage of the rescue, and could have used that as the starting place for investigation and recapture. The footage of Lamy306 is uninterrupted, complete, and a perfect blank. Grainy, and low-res, but complete. The quality is enough to have picked up anything so prominent as a sloop energy drive or any other kind of propulsion exhaust. No ship visited.' She looked slowly from sister to sister. 'Quite apart from anything else – how would Glass's contacts have known which asteroid to visit? Your family's expertise in data protection ought to tell you that encrypted data is not so easily cracked. And there are hundreds of thousands of possible locations. No. Nobody rescued him.'

'He never went,' said Diana. 'That's the solution – which is to say, that's the trick. The trick with *locked-room mysteries*, at any rate. You – we – are supposed to believe that the murderer either broke into or escaped from an impossible-to-enter-or-exit space. But that's never what happens.' She blushed. 'What I mean is: if it's impossible for Jack Glass to have escaped from this asteroid, then . . . well, he didn't escape. That's what impossible means, after all. And *that* means, he never went in the first place; somehow the authorities were fooled into thinking that he *had* gone. He was never there. The other prisoners all murdered one another.'

Joad nodded. 'But, my dear, his DNA was found in the innards of this asteroid, along with everybody else's. Oh, he was there. He was inside the impossible-to-escape room for a while and then – suddenly – mysteriously – one might almost say *magically*, he vanished. Pff! Teleported right out of there.' Abruptly, Joad laughed, a crow-like sound.

'He *must* have had a ship.'

'There was no ship.'

'Nobody can just – teleport,' said Diana. 'There's no such thing. That's magic, not science. There is a rational explanation. Even if we haven't deduced it, right now, it will be there.'

'He has no legs,' said Eva, suddenly.

'Quite right!' barked Joad, delighted. 'Did you pull that out of your bId, my dear?'

Eva shook her head. 'I don't want to look into his bId entry. It surely contains horrors and I'm a . . . touch squeamish about such things. I just remembered. That's one of the things that everybody knows about him,' She looked at her sister. 'I prefer the inanimate to the animate. It's more . . . manageable. Physics, chemistry, iDynamics.'

'Where *you*, my dear,' said Joad, angling her head a little to the side and regarding Diana like a velociraptor. 'You prefer the human stuff – hmmm? What we hear, up amongst the Ulanovs, is that your MOHmies have high hopes for you when it comes to *personnel management*. Problem-solving and investigation with a skill-spin in *people*, yes?'

'I suppose I prefer the animate to the in,' said Diana, warily. 'For Eva it's the other way about.'

'So *that's* your fascination with whodunits, is it?'

'I suppose so.'

'Don't be alarmed, my tender morsel,' said Ms Joad. 'The Ulanovs, whom I represent here, have no problem with the Argents training up a next generation of information experts. But you can't blame us for being curious as to how that training is *going*. The divide is as neat as MOH sculpting would lead us to expect. A hard-body problem girl in you, Eva, and a soft-body problem girl in you.'

'How did he *lose* his legs?' asked Eva, unable to leave the gruesome image alone.

'Nobody seems to know for sure. Oh, there are various theories,' said Joad, airily. 'Get the better of your squeamishness and pull his details from your bId and you'll see.'

'It's common enough, in the uplands,' Diana pointed out.

'Indeed it is, soft-body girl!' said Joad. 'And why not? If you never plan on coming down the well, then you won't miss them. Legs are of little use in zero gravity, after all. Some people go so far as to have them deliberately amputated – or to sell them. People will sell anything if they're poor enough.'

'The fact that he *has* no legs,' said Eva, 'rather suggests he's an uplander-only kind of fellow.'

'That's a reasonable assumption to make, I suppose,' said Joad, indulgently. 'Though some of his victims have been murdered at the bottom of gravity wells. Glass isn't his real name you know. People call him Jack because, well, it's a serial killer-y name. As for his surname, well. We're not entirely sure what his real surname *is*. It may be Prytherch. I don't know what sort of a name that's supposed to be. Do you know how he acquired the name *Glass*?'

'How?'

'He acquired that surname for reasons to do with his – *work*. It's how he kills, our Jack-the-Ripper of the spaceways. It was the same with the victims in Lamy306; he killed them all and cut their bodies up with sharpened *slivers of glass*.' Ms Joad was looking directly at her.

Her black eyes. Oh! Totally shiversome, Dia thought. Then she thought: maybe Eva *is* more squeamish than I, but – oh!

'They say he has hey-ho murdered more than a *thousand* people,' said Diana, with a touch of awe in her voice.

'Or a million,' said Joad. 'Depending upon which story you believe. What is certain is that his murder rate has reduced recently. Until his spree on Lamy306, in fact, he hadn't killed in quite a long time! Of course, it is getting harder for him. We are *making it* harder for him. After Lamy306 we disseminated his DNA details to every policeperson, civvie and personnel checker in the System. With that, no legs and a bad reputation, he's starting to sore-thumb *stick out*. Each new murder is a risk for him. He can no longer be, eh, *gratuitous*. My belief is that when he murders, now, it is only for a *very* good reason.'

'And *has* he?' Diana asked. She could not keep the eagerness from her voice. '*Has* he murdered again?'

'My love, why else do you think I am here?'

The two girls looked at her. 'You don't mean to suggest—?' began Eva.

'It's *not* possible,' Diana said, loudly, at the same time.

There was a moment's pause.

'And *one* of the remarkable things about Mr Glass,' said Joad, with a serious face, 'is the knack he has for *making the impossible happen*. Indeed, indeed, indeed. Escaping Lamy306! Well, I am still chasing him, and I have reason to believe that he has his sights set upon your precious selves, my dears.'

'No,' said Dia.

This was the wrong thing to say – not just the word but the tone. Joad turned her eyes upon Diana. They were black in the way that tsunami water is black as it washes through the ruined town, black because it has churned up the living and the dead.

They were the colour of hope liquidised into despair. 'I beg your pardon?' she said, with a formal chill.

'Please, eh, forgive me for *contradicting* you,' said Diana, sweat tickling her upper lip. 'But, if we all remain cool and chilly for a moment, you're saying our servant was murdered *by Jack Glass*. You're saying that *the famous Jack Glass* came here and murdered our servant?'

'That's exactly what I'm saying,' said Ms Joad, sombrely.

'And then – what? Then he left?'

'Since he's no longer here,' said Joad, 'Yes. Your security people have searched the whole estate of course. The police have searched the surrounding territory.'

'But – *why*?' asked Diana. 'Why would he come here, go to the bother of breaching our security only to kill a *servant*? Why not us?'

'I'm not saying,' noted Joad, her smile returning, 'that he has finished.'

There was a moment of silence.

'But why *us*?'

'Oh, my dear thing! Your sister, with her attention wholly focused on those anomalous supernovae, I might expect her not to know! But you? Surely you've deciphered what the hidden thing is – the thing that *nobody* is talking about, and that the Polloi don't even know exists, but the thing everybody who *knows* is *secretly* talking about?'

'What?' asked Diana, flushing with embarrassment. 'What is it?'

Joad looked at the guards, and replied. 'FTL of course! A thing worth killing for. Something the possession of which will give the owner unprecedented power and wealth. A *functioning* faster-than-light technology.'

'But,' said Diana, again. 'What's that got to do with *us*?' Even as she asked this, she knew the answer. Because the Argents' reputation was based on their knowledge-wealth, their skill at finding things out. If anybody knew about a mysterious new technology it would be them.

'Never mind *why*,' said Eva, with a single horizontal fold in her clear, beautiful brow. 'I want to know *how* he is supposed to have done this.'

'Of course my wonder child,' said Joad. 'You *would* be more interested in practical hows than fiddly human whys.'

'I'm serious,' said Eva. 'There is unbroken surveillance of the servants' house – of the whole estate. For the entirety of the relevant period nobody entered or exited the house. *How* did your infamous Jack Glass get inside the storeroom to bash the servant's head with that big hammer?'

'The how *is* an interesting question, isn't it?' said Joad. 'The who has been answered, so the how remains.'

'How did he get on the island, never mind anything else. How did he get down to Earth, through all the security checks? How did he even know we are here?'

'All good questions,' said Joad.

'And *how* did he get inside a locked house without being noticed by any of the surveillance systems?'

'You might ask: how did he get out of Lamy306?' Joad replied. 'I don't know. But he did.'

'What *evidence* do you have that he killed our servant?'

'You'll have to believe me. I can't tell you exactly how I know. You'll understand that there are levels of secrecy within secrecy. I shouldn't even, strictly speaking, have dropped those three little letters into the conversation.'

'FTL?' said Diana, again. 'Why? Why come down here, sneak inside the servants' house, bash out his brains – for FTL? I don't, I *don't* understand, I don't *understand*.'

Ms Joad rose, smoothly enough, but with a slight wibble of her leg muscles inside their crawlipers. 'It is a puzzle, I agree. I'll admit the how baffles me as much as it does anybody else. But you can surely work that out! After all, your MOHmies have the highest regard for your problem-solving abilities, my dears. The highest regard.'

'Are you saying,' Eva pressed, 'that Jack Glass *teleported* into our servants' house?'

'There's no such thing as teleportation, my dear,' said Joad. 'Might I have my weapon back please?'

Berthezene brought out the smartcloth pouch.

'I'll have the handservants get a house ready for you, Ms Joad,' said Eva, remembering her hospitable instincts rather belatedly. 'Do you have a preference – inland, or by the coast?'

'Oh I'm not staying, my darlings,' said Ms Joad, looking at neither of them.

'Oh!' said Eva, as if slapped. 'You're going straight back up?'

'The Ulanovs are not people to keep waiting,' she said. Then, she turned her black gaze upon each of the MOHsisters, one after the other. 'You have bright futures, as information artistes, my dears, I have *no doubt* of that. And so you will learn: there are things you can learn by being in the same physical space as somebody that you cannot learn from an ideality, no matter how fine-grained it may be.'

'And what have you learned from us, Ms Joad?' Dia asked, emboldened.

'I have learned,' she said, her glance settling momentarily upon Dia. 'Which of the two celebrated MOHsisters is the one *to watch*.'

Diana felt giddy, as if removed from the usual rubrics of caution. 'But at any rate, Ms Joad, we must *thank* you for letting us know that our servant was actually killed by Jack Glass, no less. Though I do still wonder how he magically got inside the servants' house.'

'I've no idea!' said Ms Joad. 'Goodbye my loves.'

As soon as she had gone, and whilst Deño supervised a new search of the area (there was nothing to find; his people were nothing if not *thorough*), Eva and Dia called up their MOHmies again – an awkward, blurry, nauseous image, since the security routers sent it through nearly a thousand-or-so random pathways before making the connection. But there they were: both parents, arms linked, floating in space, and the space all around them coloured bright with the force that through the green fuse drives the flower. Diana told them that Ms Joad had visited, although (of course) they already knew that. Nor did they seem particularly worried by this. 'You two can solve this horrid mystery,' they said, in one voice. 'Work together, daughters!' 'Ms Joad said the murderer was Jack Glass,' said Diana. 'A lot of *nonsense* is spoken about that fellow,' said MOHmie Yin. 'If you listen to the rumours he's ninety-percent Grendel and only ten percent man! But I refuse to believe he's a superman. He's only a man. He's not even the shadow of his own reputation.' 'I don't see *how* he can have done it,' said Eva. 'I don't understand, practically speaking, how it can have been done.' 'You're a smart girl,' said MOHmie Yang. 'You will figure it out.'

Just before the conversation ended, Diana said: 'Ms Joad said it had to do with FTL.' Hard to gauge it on so shimmery a skyline, but at those three letters it was almost as if both MOHmies shuddered. Did they? Or was it a flaw in the image rendering?

'Hard to see what a *servant* could know about such a thing,' said MOHmie Yang. 'Or what it might have to do with murder.' But there was a strange tone to her voice. Was she angry? Diana got that seventh-sense intimation that she had touched on an unmentionable matter; although a strangely involuted one whereby the fact that it was unmentionable was itself unmentionable. 'FTL is a hippogriff,' said MOHmie Yin, grinning unconvincingly. MOHmie Yin added: 'it's a nonsense, it's a no-thing. It's impossible, you know. The laws of physics forbid it.'

'And talking of laws,' said MOHmie Yang. 'We have accredited you both as crime investigators under Ulanov law. The local policepersons must defer to you, now.'

'Oh they're already doing *that*,' said Diana, dismissively.

'Sort this mystery out!' the MOHmies sang, in unison. 'Make us proud, daughters!' And that was the end of the conversation.

The sisters sat together for a while. Diana worked more-or-less idly through what her bId had on the legendary Jack Glass. Three quarters myth and improbable fantasy; the rest the usual life of a political dissident with murderous and terroristical-violence proclivities. There was nothing in any of the easily accessible datafields about him being captured, locked away in an asteroid, and then – impossibly, magically – escaping his prison. The Ulanovs were keeping that fact tightly controlled, it seemed, for whatever reason. Assuming Ms Joad hadn't simply made it up, for her own reasons. She stared at the image of his face. It looked as bland as any other face. Murderers often did.

'I still don't see why,' said Eva, unable to get Ms Joad's black gaze out of her mind, 'she had to come in person. All the way from the Ulanovs! To *us*?'

'Something *is* wrong,' said Diana. 'She didn't come down here just to meet *us* in person. We're hardly important enough. And there's literally no reason why she should be interested in the death of a servant.'

'So she came just to intimidate us, then. A personal visit *is* more intimidating than an appearance in the IP, after all.' And then: 'which is to say, she came to intimidate *our MOHmies*. Not us: *we* hardly matter, in the larger scheme of things, after all. This was her way of saying to our MOHmies – we're watching your daughters, we can get to them, we can reach them.'

And it was at that moment that Diana had one of her intuitive leaps of comprehension, the sort of instinctive human-nature-based insight of which Eva was not capable (for all her five years of extra life and her six PhDs). 'They're scared.'

'What?'

It was almost a criminal act to say this; and Dia could not help glancing nervously around. Almost certainly this space was shielded and protected against direct Ulanov surveillance. But *almost certainly* was not as reassuring a form of words as you might want, where the ultimate powers in the system were concerned. 'The Ulanovs are scared – of us, of the Argents, of our MOHclan.'

'Why?'

'Do I have to spell it out for you, Eva? Those three little words, I suppose. Do you think I even *know*? I'm fifteen years old, and politics and conspiracy and power-jockeying and all that are beyond *me*. But they won't be forever. And you can bet your bippy the Ulanovs have an enhanced sensitivity to the pre-tremors of rebellion. They're scared that the Argents are about to – I don't know what. But *something*.'

Eva was wide-eyed. 'Do you think we are? Our MOHmies, I mean?'

'*I* don't know, do I? But that would explain her strange insistence that it was Jack Glass who killed our poor little handservant Leron. Why him?'

'Explain it how?'

Diana pushed some tagged data into one of her sister's IP atria. 'See for yourself. There's nothing in this data to upset a squeamish MOHsister, I should add – though he *has* done some horrible things to his fellow human beings. But I've tagged up a dozen or so key semes, and the main one is: his close association with the Revolutionary movements.'

'The Terrorists,' Eva said, automatically, a more-or-less superstitious reflex.

'Sure. Terrorists. Antinomians. Followers of Mithras. All that. Glass is a kind of figurehead, or inspiration, for these groups. He has devoted his life, apparently, to overthrowing the Ulanovs.'

Eva whistled a C# through perfectly pursed lips. 'Is that what Joad was saying? Was that her coded way of warning us that the Ulanovs suspect us of having *Antinomian* sympathies? "Jack Glass is your murderer" . . . means *that*?'

'Or if not us, then maybe amongst our servants?'

'Oh how could that even *be*? These are carefully selected handservants! They go through – goddess, I don't even know *how many* layers of preselection and vetting. How could they slip through that degree of checking?'

'It doesn't make sense,' Diana agreed. 'There are too many levels on which it doesn't make sense. Unless.'

'Unless?'

'Unless our MOHmies have some new leverage. Some new means of applying pressure. Those three letters Joad made such a fuss about accidentally-on-purpose letting slip.'

'Don't be ridiculous,' said Eva.

That evening the girls ate together in the snug. Deño and Iago ate at a separate table. An open window let in odours of salt-water and lavender. The seesaw of the cicadas swelled and shrank, as if the air itself were pulsing. Or yawning. The view was of the stalagmite silhouettes of the cypresses, and above them was the black-blue nightsky, speckled all over with lights. More of these were in motion than were stationary.

'When I mentioned FTL to our MOHmies,' Diana said, because she had been ruminating on this for a while, 'it was as if I had uttered a profanity.'

Eva looked at her. 'You think?'

'Why should it be a secret?' Diana asked. 'If somebody has developed the technologies of faster-than-light travel – well, then, that's a cause of collective human celebration! It would mean the freedom of the stars! Why would it need to be kept secret, why would people kill for it, why would MOHmie Yang flinch when I said it?'

'Maybe it was only a wobble in the image,' said Eva.

'It would be like the Wright brothers discovering heavier-than-air flight, then sealing the data in a chip and *telling nobody*. Surely it would make sense just to . . . disseminate the knowledge? To lodge a copy in a public IP, something?'

'There's no FTL technology,' said Eva. 'It doesn't exist. Any such thing would violate the laws of physics. It's a nonsense.'

'Wouldn't that make it more ironic, though? People killing one another over what they *think* is a new FTL technology, when such technology doesn't even exist! Killing people just over a rumour.'

'Anyone with a kindergarten education knows that faster-than-light travel is a nonsense,' said Eva again. 'Anybody not actually a member of the Sumpolloi knows it.'

'It's exactly the Sumpolloi who are likely to believe it, though,' said Diana, thoughtfully. 'Perhaps that's the point. If there really were an FTL technology then people could use it to flee the System . . . couldn't they? They could use it to escape the Lex Ulanova altogether.'

'And if there were a technology to make us all-powerful and immortal then we'd all be gods,' said Eva. 'But there isn't.'

'You're missing my point. The point is that the *idea* of it could become a symbol, a flag. A banner. A rallying point for revolution.'

Eva shuddered. 'I do wish you'd stop using that word.'

After supper they prayed together, and kissed, and then they went to their separate bedrooms.

6

The Gate of Horn
and the Gate of Ivory

Diana's head was filled with motion and electricity. All our heads are, of course. But hers was of a degree of sophistication unusual amongst human beings. She was thinking: and if there were a technology that violated the laws of physics and permitted FTL travel. Would it, having violated one law of physics, allow the user to violate other ones? Teleportation, for instance? As Deño made a final check of her room, she asked him: 'Dominico, am I safe here?'

'Yes, Miss,' he replied. 'As safe as we can make you.'

'What if a murderer could teleport directly *into* my room?'

Deño's face registered puzzlement. 'But Miss,' he said. 'There's no way anybody could do that.'

'You're right,' she said, settling inside her gel-bed. It was a delicious sensation: for the gel took the edge off her gravity-fatigue. 'Is Iago outside?'

'Of course, Miss.'

'Send him in. I want to say goodnight to him.'

Deño left, and Iago came in. He stood, as if to attention, beside the bed. 'Oh sit down, Iago,' Dia chided him. 'You only stand up to try and impress me – and I'm not impressed.'

'I prefer to stand, Miss,' he replied. But little dots of sweat were evident on his forehead, and the muscles in his thighs were visibly trembling under the effort of keeping him upright. Pride, Dia decided. That's all it was. Well: she wasn't going to insist.

'Eye-*arrr*-go,' she drawled. 'Do you think the solar system's most infamous murderer is going to materialise in my bedroom out of thin air and kill me?'

'No,' he said, levelly.

'Oh, come, come, Iago. You *heard* what Ms Joad said. You were right there.'

'Nevertheless, I'm still not sure I understand who this gentleman is supposed to be. A myth, is my guess.'

She smiled. 'You're right, of course. It's all politics, isn't it? It's all jockeying for position amongst the MOHfamilies and the Gongsi, isn't it? We are *intimidatable*, I suppose. Killing Eva and killing me would harm the Argent family, and would benefit our rivals, I suppose. And by the same logic, even just *scaring* us has some small benefit. But, goddess! – if they wanted us dead, wouldn't they just blast the whole island from orbit?'

'That,' said Iago, shifting his weight slightly from his left to his right leg, 'would be an act of war.'

'But maybe war is where this is going?' She said this languorously, sliding deeper into her gel-bed. It was a real enough worry, she supposed; but a point is reached, as sleep comes over a body, when even the most acute worries lose their sting.

'The Clan's power and influence is based on *influence*,' said Iago. 'Any of your rivals, any organisation who wants to supplant you in the hierarchy below the Ulanovs – well, they need to do more than just wipe you out. They need to *take your place*, and that means they need your *information*. Without it they wouldn't be able to consolidate their power.'

'Indeed,' said Diana. Sleep was coming. Hello sleep!

'My understanding, Miss,' he went on, in a pleasant-enough lullaby-y drone, 'and of course I don't know the specifics – but my understanding is that there are caches of extremely valuable information encoded into the fabric of this house. To destroy it would be to destroy that information.'

'So,' said Diana, not really paying attention, and drifting away. '*Would* it make sense to send a ninja assassin inside the house to put a sword through my heart and cut Eva's head off?' But she was mumbling now. Bowing awkwardly on his trembling legs, Iago left the room and sealed the door.

Diana slept.

She dreamt about trees. A baobab tree filled the entire solar system, which, according to the logic of dreams, had become a human-scale space, like a medieval cathedral vault or a sport's venue from the Martian Olympics. The tree was as tall as Saturn's orbit, and the detail of its trillion leaves would baffle any engraver who wished to illustrate it via ink on paper. In this tree lived all of humanity who mattered; the great folk, the MOHfamilies, the Gongsi and their executives, police, army, engineers. You could see them easily enough, in amongst the branches, perched like birds. But then, in her dream, Dia looked again and saw that every single leaf was a woman or a man dressed in a curious green costume; a dark green tubular outfit around their torso and legs, and a paler green cape that wrapped all about. There were trillions of such individuals, clinging desperately to their stems and twigs. And at that point Dia noticed that there was a great breeze blowing through the branches, and that they were rocking and shaking, and that the myriad greenclad members of the System Sumpolloi were all of them in danger of being blown off. That was why they clung so desperately. Of course Diana knew that there is only one wind in the System, and that it is the solar wind. So she looked down the main trunk of the tree towards its base. The great tree had its roots planted in the sun, coiling about and interpenetrating the material of the burning star. Of course, Diana thought to herself: how could it be otherwise? The sun was still shining as fiercely as ever it did, though clogged and tangled with roots that were as fat as a hundred Jupiters. The solar wind still came blasting up at her. But as she watched a change came over the substance of the sun. Its luminescence began to fade, and it turned the colour of blood, the colour of a dark red-chilli pepper, and molten and roiling. Somebody was there. She looked again, narrowing her eyes against the blast of the solar wind, and looked, and looked. It was a man, a giant, an impossibly huge man. She knew who it was. None other than Jack Glass himself; and he was holding an antique book, clasping it to his chest. He stopped and looked up at her, as she hid amongst the high branches, and spoke directly to her. He didn't shout, or bellow, and pure vacuum intervened – yet she heard him very well. 'The sun is become a sea of blood mixed with glass,' he said. 'The roots of this tree are sucking the life out of the sun.' 'What is the tree?' she called back. But he did not reply, and the dark red colour darkened further to black-brown. It solidified and cooled to the colour lava assumes when it is chilled by the ocean into new and ruffled granite. 'When it has sucked the life out of the sun,' Jack Glass boomed, suddenly loud, 'the sun will die, and so the sun will die. It's happening right now!' 'The tree can't die,' she said. 'Vital information is encoded in its branches. Secret information is hidden in its matter.' 'Too late,' said Jack Glass. The black roots of the tree were now indistinguishable from the black matter of the sun; and Diana knew that death was passing up the tubercles and passages of the tree, and that soon the entire arboreal growth would wither and turn to flakes of iron and clumps of soot. Jack Glass was still visible, in amongst the tangle of the tree's roots; but visible from the back, like God in the Garden of Eden. She wanted to cry down to him: who are you? And: why do you want to kill me? And she wanted above all to ask him: what is in your book? But she knew that the book contained, written on pages of treated and bleached animal skin, the entire and copious secret of *faster-than-light travel*. And that the book contained the answer to the other two questions as well. So instead, as the leaves began decaying in great scatters from the branches all around her, she yelled: 'what *is* the tree?'

Then she woke up. As she opened her eyes, somebody inside the room with her – invisible, just to the left of her field of vision, or maybe just to the right of it, whispered: '*you* are the tree.'

She squealed, and struggled to sit up and look about; but the gel made it harder than it might otherwise be. She called the lights, and looked left and looked right.

There was nobody in the room.

And now the doorpanel brightened, and a representation of Deño (hooded, to signify his modest respectfulness) asked her if she was alright, and did she need any assistance?

Her heart was trembling like a leaf in a breeze. 'It's alright,' she replied. 'I'm alright. But I see now how Jack Glass can creep into my room, despite all the security in the world, and without need of teleportation.'

'Shall I stay in, Miss?'

'No,' said Diana, speaking the lights down again and slinking back into her bed. 'It's a dream, only a dream.'

Eva also dreamed.

She didn't go to sleep straight away. After the meal, and the prayers, and after Jong-il had checked her room, she found she wasn't particularly sleepy. The day had been an eventful one; and perhaps the visit of Ms Joad had unsettled her. Or the mere fact of an unsolved problem, and the lack of sufficient data to address it, bothered her. That a human being had died did not distress her. Had it been somebody she *knew* it would have upset her; she wasn't a monster. Had it been somebody she cared about. But it was nobody she knew, and it would have been disingenuous to pretend that the death of somebody she didn't know affected her on an emotional level. What bothered her was the problematic; the lack of resolution to the dilemma. This in turn fed into the incompleteness of her current research.

So she went into her worldtual for an hour or so, and did some more work on anomalous supernovae. Her main supposition had to do with the Pauli principle, and the hypothesis that, under very unlikely and therefore very rare – but possible – physical circumstances, the degeneracy pressure of certain states of relatively low-gravity matter could undergo catastrophic shear. She played with some creative equations for a while, and borrowed a good proportion of the house computionality (it was night; it was being underused anyway) to crunch some millions of regular equations. The heart of the neutron-dedensification would – assuming it happened this way – be an inequivalence governed by a particular set of criteria; but she was starting to think that standard inequivalence theory did not provide the sort of range of solutions her problems required. She trawled through some of the indexically recognised Speculative notions, but none looked useful. And by this stage she discovered – with that strange belatedness that often characterises the experience of those absorbed in research – that she *was* tired, actually. She came out of her IP, and got into bed. For a while she did nothing but concentrate on settling her breathing in this choking gravity. She was missing something. What was she missing?

Something was niggling her about this stupid murder. She didn't need to go back into the Worldtuality; it was enough to call the data up on her bId. She checked quickly through the relative locations of people. After the servants were all billeted, on arrival, nobody had gone into or come out of the servants' house all day. All the bodyguards, and Iago, were tagged to one another, so that they could call on one another's assistance in an emergency, and the datahistory of the tags showed that they had been in the main house the whole time. Nobody had crossed the perimeters of the estate. The murderer had to be (a trivial logical deduction) one of the servants inside the servants' house. There was no other explanation. No Jack Glass had levitated down and slipped through the interstices of matter so as to penetrate the roof.

Joad had been messing with their heads. Nothing more. Even if she meant 'Jack Glass' not in the specific sense of the actual human being who bore that name, and was using it instead in a sort of generic sense to mean 'any dangerous murderer', it was not possible for this individual to have done what he did.

She put it all from her mind, and readied herself for sleep. At first sleep was shy and teased her; but it didn't stay away for long.

She dreamed.

The neurones inside her head made patterns of electrochemical discharge curl and fold across the material of her brain, as a breeze rummages through the leaves on an ash tree.

She was in her MOHmies house, in space. But she was not alone, and neither was she with her MOHsister. She was with a male stranger. She didn't know his name. 'I have invented a new way of transporting people from a planet's surface into space! Surely you can see that plasmaser descent-ascent is cumbrous and infrastructure heavy; and free ballistic flight is wasteful and expensive and dangerous.' 'What is your new way?' Eva wanted to know. 'What's it to you?' the stranger said. Eva was trying to work out if his skin was as dark as it looked, or whether this was simply a function of the darkgreen light in that place. *Did* she know him? She thought she knew him. 'What's it to me? Astrophysics is my special expertise, I have six PhDs,' she told the stranger. He chuckled. 'Of course you do: but that's all to do with distant stars. Stars that explode even though they shouldn't! *I'm* talking about a technology that is much more down to earth!'

'Tell me,' she pressed.

'Oh, it is a question of spacetime origami, that's all. If this place is tucked *into* that place, then that place is also tucked into *this* place. It's because the universe is infinite. Regular geometry no longer applies in such a manifold.'

'That doesn't make any sense,' said Eva.

The stranger gestured. She saw then that his hands were red. She looked again, and saw that the skin had been peeled away, as a glove is drawn off, and that the workings of muscle and sinew beneath were visible, slick with blood. 'Step through that door, and see what I mean.'

It was a door made out of light. With no sense of apprehension, Eva pulled herself along a guy-rope and passed effortlessly through the door. On the far side was darkness, and gravity, and she stepped down onto a flat floor. Where am I? she wondered, but she knew where she was: the darkness around her was crowded with lumber, tools and machines. It was the storeroom in which the handservant had been killed. Somebody was here.

'Who is it?' she said aloud.

'Leron,' said the voice. Eva went, instinctively, to her bId to locate the name, but in her dream she had no bId – indeed she had, weirdly, never even been fitted with one. Not that it mattered: she could remember the name. Leron was the servant who had been killed.

'I can't see you,' she said.

'Nobody can see the dead,' he replied. But, despite this, a foggy kind of illumination was starting up about his head. She could see his features. His face was shining, like an angel's.

'How are you *doing* that?' she asked him.

'You are the expert on stars,' he replied. 'Not I.'

The glow was beginning to bring into vision the indistinct shapes of all the objects in the space around her: two garden robots, silent and static, loomed to her right. All about her were stacks and containers and globes; strange shapes and geometries.

Mysterious fins and vanes on the wall. Prongs and poles from the ceiling.

'I must warn you,' she said. She was conscious then of a tremendous sense of urgency, a need to communicate to Leron the danger he was in. 'Somebody is coming here to kill you! You must vacate this place. We don't know why, or who, although it may be the infamous murderer Jack Glass.'

Leron shook his shining head. He gleamed brighter and brighter. Shadows shrank and spooled-in amongst all the objects about him. It was so bright as to hurt her eyes.

'Go!' Eva called.

'There is no *go*,' he said.

The hammerhead appeared in space beside him. It was in ballistic flight, guided by no-one, and moving towards him; sweeping up over and down in a parabolic arc. What she saw then was the collision between a lozenge-shaped chunk of iron (the matter out of which black dwarf stars might be constituted) and Leron's shining head. The skull collapsed under the impact, pieces of shell breaking in; she caught a momentary glimpse of the magma-red innards, the grotesque distortions of face. But the pressure down – she knew how this worked as well as any person alive – generated its subatomic counterforce. In flawless silence, the head bloomed outward and every direction spilled with searing white brightness. Eva could see nothing now. She was standing in a tempest of light, blowing back her hair and rushing whisperingly past her. Everything was white.

She woke.

Somehow she sensed that her sister was awake, in her room. She ticticked Diana's bId and received an immediate answer. 'I have just had a dream,' she said.

'So have I,' said Diana. 'I dreamed that I met Jack Glass. What about you?'

'I was talking to the murdered servant. His head went super-nova. It happened right in front of me! I almost *never* have dreams like this,' said Eva. 'But it has left me with a sure conviction.'

'A conviction of what?'

'This murder,' said Eva, speaking slowly, amazed at her own words, '*is* connected to my research. The two *go together*.'

Dia waited before she replied. Then she said: 'my lovely sister, it's a little *hard* to see what the two have in common. A servant gets his skull bashed in on Korkura. A star millions of light years away explodes. How could they possibly be connected?'

'It's an intuition I have,' said Eva. 'Intuition makes me uncomfortable, of course it does. This is not how I *work*. Nonetheless. There it is. I feel sure of it.'

'Good night, lovely sister,' said Diana, through the bId.

'Good night, lovely sister,' Eva replied,

But Diana didn't go straight back to sleep. The glow of light inside her solar plexus; the excitement. She had one last tour of her personal worldtual before sleep. It was constructed to grant her access to data fields, but it lacked the capacity to send or receive messages. This was a matter of protection, of course. In theory, nobody at all was supposed to know where she and Eva were right now. In fact, as the appearance of Ms Joad made plain, the Ulanovs knew – but it was a fair assumption that the Ulanovs knew everything. The more pressing question concerned the other MOHfamilies, the lesser organisations (the Gongsi, the militias and cults) and everybody else. *They* could never be allowed to know. The temptation to strike the mighty Argents in a tender spot would be too great.

Her bId was a complex, secure system. But Diana was more than clever: she was *made* to feel her way around complex systems. She could do what no AI could, and intuit pathways through the chaos algorithms. The hard part wasn't cracking the communications blackout; it was cracking it in such a way that nobody knew it had even been cracked.

It took her twenty minutes; that was all. Then she set up a

bumper-bumper set of message relays to protect her location and directed her message.

Anna Tonks Yu was asleep, in a Mansion orbiting Mars. But she woke up as the message alert hummed. Anna Tonks Yu: Diana's rival, her enemy. The great love of her life.

'Diana!' Anna cried. 'Is that you? You foolish and ugly girl, you woke me up!'

'What did you do to your *hair*?' returned Diana. 'It looks terrible. You might as well cut it all off.'

She filled in the delay-time in the conversation by playing a game of Go against the House AI. But the delay did not annoy her; on the contrary, she found it added spice to the conversation. What is love without anticipation?

'So you called me just to abuse me!' cried Anna, throwing her arms wide. 'It is emotional harm – I shall sue you through every court under Ulanov jurisdiction.'

'When we are married I shall beat you,' Diana said. 'Like an old-fashioned spouse. I shall beat you with a stick.'

The game clogged in the bottom left quarter. Dia cleared it and rebooted it as a three-dimensional game on a toroidal grid.

'If you beat me, I shall kill you,' returned Anna. 'It will be justifiable femicide.'

'And the last thing I see will be your stupid flat face!' cried Diana, in an ecstasy, adding, 'oh I love you, I love you!'

The flare of emotional intensity fizzled and died as she waited for the reply; but it sparked up again as the countdown approached zero.

'I love you too, Drop-dead-Di. Is that why you called, just to say that? What a risk! You're not supposed to call. I might work out where you are, and betray you to your enemies. Only I would never do that, because if I did they would kill you, and only *I* am allowed to kill you.'

They were never going to get married, of course. Their respective MOHfamilies would never allow it. But even if *they* could be persuaded the Ulanovs would regard an alliance between the

Information and the Transit branches of their own structures of power as too great a threat. Anna and Diana both knew that; and Diana knew more – though she wasn't sure if Anna had as much insight into human nature – that the intensity of their affection for one another was a *function* of its impossibility. Were all the obstacles between them removed, the love would surely wither. Not that any of *that* mattered.

Diana gave her the news. 'I have a *real-life* murder mystery to solve,' she boasted.

She finished the game, and dismissed the board. As the countdown slid away she prepared herself for Anna's reaction. It did not disappoint.

Anna made her mouth a perfect O. 'No wavey *way!*' she yelled. 'A real-life one – where? You're trying to de-arrange my *sanity!*'

'Right on our doorstep! One of our own handservants, his cranial bones all bashed and dinted and cracked, dead as an iron star.'

The interlude flew past.

'That's the most amazing. That's most amazing. That's *the* most. Have you solved it?' asked Anna. 'Do you need my help to solve it? I'm the best brain at solving whodunits in the So-so Solar System, you know.'

'Such delusions!' said Diana. 'I have to go now, my love, my life. When I've got to the bottom of things here I'll parcel up the data – the solution in a different package, of course – and see how *you* do with it.' The walls of her IP were throbbing, which meant that her network of buffers was about to tumble in on itself. She disconnected.

7

The Investigation Begins

The next morning Diana began her very own murder investigation: she was Holmes, and she appointed Iago her Dr Watson. 'It's quite alright and spot-on,' she told him; 'check your bId and you'll see Watson was *quite* a bit older than Holmes.' Iago wrinkled the skin next to his eyes with < and > as he smiled. They were in the bright morning sunlight, and by *golly* he looked old. 'And Eva can be Mycroft, since she's so very clever,' Dia added.

'How do we begin?'

'With the autopsy; but that's done, and the results are on the bId. Have you checked them?'

'I assume,' he said, saluting the scene so as to shade his eyes. There was a gauzy haze over the sea, but the dun-green trees and sand-coloured fields all stood out with hyperreal vividness; as did the white houses of the distant down. 'I assume the autopsy confirms that death occurred as a result of cranial damage.'

'He was bashed. He was dented and dinted and dashed to death. No surprises there.'

They set off towards the scene of the murder, and it ought to have been more exciting. But something was corroding her enjoyment. In fact, several things were. One was Eva. They were hardly the first sisters in the world whose love for one another waxed and waned; but Diana couldn't help thinking it was *her* birthday in three weeks – and *she* was the one with the passion for murder mysteries – and now a real-life murder mystery had happened right on her doorstep and you might think Eva would be more pleased. Especially since last night she had almost opened up to her; a little intimacy, her strange dream.

But this morning, she had been all stand-offish, had breakfasted alone in her room and then vanished inside the IP for more stroopid-stroopid work on her stroopid-stroopid PhD. She tried not to care; but her stand-offishness was more than a touch *piss-offish*.

The best analgesic for mental discomfort is work, of course. Dia ran through the surveillance footage of the servants' house one more time, making sure that nobody *had* gone in or come out for seven hours prior to the murder. Immediately after the murder, of course, people spilled and staggered from the main entrance, doing their weird contorted grief-dance. This was all negative data; just like the House AI surveillance record that told her Deño, Jong-il, Berthezene and Iago had all been inside the main building for the whole of the relevant time. Not that she suspected any of *them*, of course; but it was good officially to (as the phrase so splendidly put it) *eliminate them from the enquiry*. There was no House AI data on Eva, of course; any more than on Diana herself – they were the daughters of Argent, and beyond surveillance. That was the least they could expect, in their eminence; although there were also practical advantages in minimising their data profiles. After all protection was the name of the jeu; the name of the jeu was *protection*.

But Diana knew she wasn't the murderer, and it made no sense to think Eva was.

There was the question, of course, of who was to *serve* them, now that all nineteen of their remaining handservants had been locked up. But they still had Deño, Berthezene and Jong-il – not to mention solid old Iago – to give them their food, and sort out their needs. And they could dress themselves, if they had to. Other stuff would have to be postponed, or else go hang. Besides, as soon as Dia worked out who the *real* murderer was, the servants could all be released and things could return to normal. So! So –

The *next* thing to do was to examine the crime scene itself, and then (she slid the palms of her hands across one another, trying to work up a little excitement) interview the suspects. Interview the suspects! She would Poirot them good and proper. They would be *properly* Poirot'd.

So Dia had put together a message to her sister and sent it into the Worldtuality: saying, only, 'please be my Mycroft! I'm setting out to solve these FTL-murders (thank you, Ms Joad) and all help is good help if it's *your* help. I know you're working and working and working, and trying for the good of all humanity to explain why that minimum-fraction-tiny-number of stars blew up, so I won't ask you to do the crime scene investigation. But shall I come to you with my theories, and shall you help me put all the pieces together?'

Nothing came back from Eva for a long time, and when something finally did trickle out of the IP it wasn't even delivered by an Eva-avatar. It was a plain statement of three things:

One. Ms Joad was trying to unnerve us, either for the hell of it, because the Ulanovs benefit by sowing confusion and dissension amongst the MOHclans, or possibly as some small play in part of a larger specific strategy. It doesn't matter. Ignore her. The fabled Jack Glass has probably never been to Earth, and is certainly not involved in all this. She mentioned him as a nurse talks about Boojie-monsters to little children, and for no other reason.

Two. Talk of 'the FTL murders' is folly, folly and nothing else. Nobody can go faster than c. Saying 'FTL murders' is just another way of saying 'the impossible fairy-story murders'.

Three. One of the other servants murdered Leron, probably for reasons of some personal grudge. That's all there is to this regrettable business.

That put a crimp in Dia's good spirits, right there. So formal! And although it was rather grimmish to talk about the death of another human being – and so on, and so forth – there was no reason why it couldn't be *fun*. Still, hey-ho and hoopsa-girlagirl-hoopsa. Diana tried to keep her spirits up. She finished her breakfast and as she was spending ten minutes flexing her limbs and getting used to the crawlipers (the gravity was a *little* less oppressive today) another message pinged out of the IP. This one was at least delivered by an avatar:

Sis: I'm sorry I woke you last night. My dream was mental rubble from the day, randomly arranged. You were right. How could there be *any* actual connection between unexplained supernovae millions of light years distant and the sordid murder of one servant by another here on Earth? Ignore me, and enjoy yourself. Love, Eva.

But, oddly, that only made Diana more despondent. Eva probably *was* right. It almost certainly *was* nothing. Iago, who was present when the avatar delivered this message (so was Jong-il), seemed quite struck by it, pushing his wrinkly brow deeper into wrinkles and quite lost in thought. 'What ho, Tutor,' she asked him, with a forced jollity. 'You think there might be a connection between this murder and the explosion of distant supernovae after all?'

He rearranged his face into a proper servantly blandness. 'It would be hard to see,' he deadpanned, 'what the connection between those events could *be*, Miss.'

She wouldn't let it go. 'You had a look on your face, just then—'

'What sort of look?'

'As if you had suddenly realised something.'

'Realised?'

'Exactly,' said Dia. 'You had the look of somebody who had just realised something deep and important.'

'Very shrewd, Miss,' he said. 'I had indeed suddenly understood the secret of life, the meaning of the universe and the key that would unlock this particular mystery.'

So she slappit his arm, and told Iago that he could stop being Jeeves for the day and ordered him instead to have a go at being Doctor Watson. But Diana's spirits refused to buoy- themselves up, however much she primped them.

They went out into the sunshine and walked awkwardly down to the servants' house. It was already very hot, the air blue as cigarette smoke, the heavens taut above them. A scramjet, very high overhead, cut a white slit in the sky. You could hear its faraway rumble. Otherwise it was perfectly still.

They crossed the crinkly grass: Diana going first, Iago and Jong-il, scanning the scene for possible assailants.

The inside of the servant house was empty (all the servants had been detained in a secure building a kilometre or so away, on the far side of the olivetree forest). Stepping into the gloom from the brightness of the day, Diana felt a tingle of anticipation in her stomach; but it soon dissipated. There was nothing here. She started going through each of the rooms, one after the other, but they were all the same: a bed – regular mattress, no gel-beds for the servants of course – and a sphere, unlocked, that contained a few trivial personal possessions. A few datachips easily scanned by the House AI, and usually containing only religious texts. Odd toys and mascots and trinkets. But she didn't go into all twenty rooms; she got bored after five. So they went back into the store-room.

It seemed both larger and less cluttered than it had done when Diana had visited before. That was one of the things about gravity, of course: when you first got back under the strain of it, things appeared to constrict about you. No, it was something more; a sense that the excitement of the moment had drawn the space around her, like a shawl. Now it was receding. She knew why. The truth would be banal, obvious – like Eva said, another servant smacked his head with a hammer, over some petty jealousy or grudge. The day before she had believed that it might be a really crunchy, chewy mystery; a whodunit as gnarly as any she had ever played in IP. But reality wasn't like that. This was what they called 'the cold light of day'. Except that the light was not cold. It was hot and sunny.

She took an inventory: storage boxes and spheres; bags, implements for tilling and turning, trimming and toiling. Her bId tagged each of these items with their name and the chance to find out more if she happened to be interested. But she wasn't interested. The hammer was gone. //Where's the weapon?//

//?? – A weapon is a device for causing harm, or defending one's . . .//

She had meant to ask that out loud. She turned to Iago. He was wrinkling his nose up; his face like an ancient turtle's. 'Where is the weapon?'

'The police removed it, Miss. It is evidence, and there are legal requirements.'

'I wanted to see how heavy it was.'

'It was a hammer, for banging in pegs and posts and the like. There's another over there just like it.' He pointed.

Without the bId tagging everything, the storage room had reacquired a little of its former, estranging tang. Incomprehensible grids stacked six-deep leant against the wall; weird wide horizontal fins embedded into the wall itself; a pendule with curious attachments hanging from the ceiling. She located the hammer and grasped the handle. The shaft moved towards her, like a lever being pulled, but there was no way she could move the dense metal head up from the floor. It was simply too heavy.

'This is too heavy for me to lift.'

'It is solid metal,' Iago agreed.

'I don't believe any of the servants, decanted from a zero-g environment directly into one full g, could lift such a hammer.'

'Somebody did,' Iago noted.

'Ah, but I have a *theory*.'

'Miss?'

She gestured towards the garden robot in the corner. 'I was thinking: of course, normally a servant wouldn't have clearance to operate something as expensive as a robot. But that one is specifically for garden work, isn't it? And many of these servants must have been here *pour cultiver le jardin*! Maybe one of them took advantage of the fact that they could manipulate this heavy-duty ordnance to kill the victim.'

Iago made a moue with his wrinkly old mouth.

'Oh don't be like *that* ee-arrr-*gow*,' she said. 'It's a neat theory, no?'

'I was only thinking, Miss,' he said, not meeting her eye. 'Why get the robot to *pick up a hammer* and hit the victim? Why not just use the robot to strike the victim directly?'

'You're just hole-picking. You hole-picker. These robots are – there was something about them that caught my eye. When we were here before, I mean. Something.'

They went over to the hulking great machines. 'This,' said Diana, excitedly, drawing an open-brackets in the floor with her toe. 'Do you know what this is?'

'The floor, Miss?'

'Dust! I read about it – tiny particles of matter. Usually it just floats in a suspension of air; but under gravity, like here, it *settles* . . . accumulates. Look.' She was proud of herself for knowing about the action of dust in gravity. Details like that could be important. 'The dust is on the floor, and the implements. But look *here*.' She gestured to a patch on the robot's inert arm, and another on its shoulder and head. 'The dust has been disturbed! It snagged my attention without my even *realising* it. I'll tell you, Iago: I dreamt that night of the whole solar system seen from a long way out, with all the billions of home globes in orbit. At the time I thought it looked like foam; but now I know what my dream-mind was trying to tell me. Dust!'

'It *has* been disturbed,' admitted Iago, examining the robot. 'But I'm not sure I see what that means. Or whether it necessarily means anything.'

'It means the *robot* is the one who lifted the hammer and brained poor Leron. Which means the murderer is the person who *controlled the robot*.'

'Miss, we can easily check the machine's record of work.'

Of course they could. 'I expect it to confirm my theory,' said Dia. They had to call up the House AI in order to access the robot's CV: it hadn't been so much as switched-on in over six months.

'Six months?' cried Diana. 'I don't believe it!'

'I'm afraid it's undeniable. And look, the dust forms an unbroken skin over the device's feet and the floor. This robot hasn't moved in a long time.'

'This stupid great machine, just *standing* here in the corner of this storeroom?' Dia snapped, angry that her theory had so summarily been disproved. 'What's the point in that?'

'Robots are expensive, Miss,' Iago pointed out. 'People are cheaper. Apart from very specific jobs – large-scale construction, or the use of RACdroids in contract work – it's almost never cost-effective to use a robot.'

'Then why have the brute at all?'

'It's anomalous, I suppose. A piece of old junk. It was probably bought for some specific, larger job, and then mothballed afterwards.'

Diana took a deep breath. Ghastly gravity, making *breathing* so hard. 'So that's not it. Never mind,' she said. 'But *somebody* lifted that hammer and smashed it down on Leron's head.'

'That's the position we started from.'

'Never mind that, Wats-loon,' she said, angrily. 'I want to ask the suspects some questions now!'

Iago said: 'I'll order a car.'

They came back outside, and waited a minute or so in the hot sun until the car buzzed over. 'Roof down, I think,' Dia announced, settling into the seat. Jong-il sat close beside her, his weapon out, and Iago opposite her. Then the platform buzzed away – a little shakily over the grass until it found a road, where it could pick up speed.

They soon left the main compound far behind. To Diana's

164

right the Mediterranean buzzed blue and white with light; the morning sun still fairly low in the sky. There was a breeze too: clean and salt-cool. Then they turned inland, and passed at speed alongside a straight row of cypresses. Sunlight epilected between trees. Dust blowzed over the road in spectral tan-coloured folds. Diana watched the landscape in motion. Her mind wandered.

'Here, Miss,' Iago announced.

They were at a squat white-flanked building without windows. Jong-il went first; then Diana climbed awkwardly out and stood for a moment. The grassy odour of olive oil. The sound of the cypresses hushing her. Beside the building was a swimming pool, ten metres across, filled, it appeared, with green tea. The shadow from the building printed a trapezoid over the dry grass, and dipped its apex into the water.

Subinspector Zarian was waiting for them in the block's main doorway, out of the sun. 'Good morning Miss Argent,' he said. 'With regard to these nineteen suspects – do you wish me to be present when you question them?'

'No,' said Diana, irritably.

Diana's legs were aching, but it was nice to get out of the heat into the cool entrance hall. Two black-uniformed functionaries – policepersons too, according to her bId – stood to attention. 'Is this, then, a police facility?' she asked Zarian. Her bId knew the answer, of course. But she wanted to remind the officer who was really in charge.

'No, Miss,' Zarian replied. 'This facility belongs to the Argent family – to yourself.'

'Do you have a chief suspect?'

'Initial enquiries suggest that a twenty-year-old female called Sapho may have been responsible.'

'Has she confessed?'

'She has not. But she had a grudge against the deceased.'

That unlovely clenching sensation inside Diana's chest was incipient disappointment. The danger here was that the mystery might be so cut-and-dried – so banal – that it was already solved.

165

'Don't tell me any more,' she said. 'I want to speak to Sapho myself.'

They all went through to a well-furnished room, with one small window in the wall. There was no other light. Dia wondered if murk were better for interrogation than brightness; but decided that the plain light of day would be her ally in illuminating the truth. So she talked to the wall and widened the window until a great fall of light shone into every corner.

With a sigh, Diana settled onto a soft gel-filled couch. Jong-il took up a position next to her, and Iago leaned, standing against the wall. Zarian set a chair in the middle of the room and one of the other functionaries (Officer first-class Avraam Kawa, said the bId) brought Sapho through.

She was a typical shanty-globe girl: long trembling limbs, some difficulty holding her head upright, sweat on her face from the effort of everything. She had to be helped to the chair by the Officer, and she didn't so much sit as coil loosely onto the seat. Her hair was close-trimmed, and her skin a patchy brown-black all over. She looked ancient, but was probably not much older than Diana herself, the gravity tugging her face into all the shapes of old age. 'Hello Sapho,' said Diana. 'Do you know who I am?'

Sapho, oh she looked *corpse*-tired, she really did: sagging particoloured skin and deep bags below her bovril-coloured eyes. Yet, it occurred to Dia, there was something pretty about the girl too, despite her gravity exhaustion. A directness in her gaze, a good line along her long nose, a strong chevron-shaped chin with a neat point at the end. An attractive girl. She blinked. Panic, or exhaustion, possessed her.

She repeated her question. 'Know who I am, Sapho?'

Sapho nodded, fractionally, and then began to cry. 'Oh Miss,' she said. 'Oh Miss.'

This, Dia knew, was the CRF acting on heightened emotions. It was one of the awkwardnesses of dosing one's servants with the treatment. It did make them loyal, of course; and it didn't interfere with most of their functions – but it made them much more emotionally volatile, and oh my *lord* it robbed them of initiative and agency.

'You knew Leron, Sapho?'

'Yes, Miss.'

'Somebody killed him. Somebody cracked his head open like a revolutionary shanty globe!'

Sob, sob, sob.

'Who killed him, Sapho?'

More staccato sobbing. 'No, Miss. Don't know, Miss. I'm scared, I'm only young, I'm scared, and I don't want – I cannot – oh Miss, oh Miss!'

'A little difficult to see,' Iago murmured, his arms folded, 'how she could lift that heavy hammer, in this gravity. She can barely keep her own head up on her neck.'

'Sapho,' said Diana. 'They are saying that you killed him. Why would they say that?'

'They are saying hateful things about me, Miss, because I love the Argents, and I love the Ulanovs.'

'They tell me you hated him. Leron. Did you?'

'Leron was from my globe, Miss. He was a bad man. And when we were being made ready to come down here and serve you, he would put his – I cannot say the word to you Miss, it is too vile, into my – I cannot say the word to you Miss, it is too vile. Oh Miss!' She started sobbing again. 'I love you so heartily, Miss! Please do not be disappointed!'

This was surprising news, and it took Diana a moment to digest it. 'Which globe do you come from, Sapho?'

She reined in her weeping. 'It is called Smirr, Miss.'

'And you're accusing the murdered man of being a rapist?'

'He was a bad man, a bad man.'

'Do you know who killed him?'

But Sapho only wept and shook her head. 'He was a bad man, Miss! I love you – and I love the Ulanovs! But *he* – didn't have the same love in his heart.'

'Didn't love us?' Diana was startled to hear this. From her

reaction, so was Sapho. 'No Miss! Of course he loved *you*. He had as much CRF inside him as any of us! But CRF of course,' she made a mucus-thrummy noise behind her nose, coughed, and resumed, 'but CRF means you are loyal to one group, not two. And he hated the Ulanovs! He was a terrible man, a bad man, a terrorist and an anarchist and an antinomian – he used to say he wanted to break the Lex Ulanova into pieces.'

'Was that was why he was killed?'

Sapho blinked, and blinked. 'He was a terrible human being, Miss,' she said again, in a low voice. Then she resumed sobbing.

Diana was interrupted by a message alert through her bId. But when she checked, there was no message. Wait up. What? She brought her attention out into the world, and heard the drone of the alert again. It only took her a moment to locate the source of this buzzing. A *wasp*! A real live creature, butting its head against the plain section of wall, as if it could break through and escape. Dia watched, fascinated. Nothing discouraged the beast: it went back and back at the window. Dia leaned over and used her bId to zoom the creature in. It was striped like a cartoon tiger; an anvil-shaped head and those little tight half-globes of black-bubblewrap for eyes. Its wings were smoky blurs. Even setting the bId to its maximum slow-down setting didn't resolve them into discernible organs in motion. She moved the bId focus to its wasp head: curled antenna like ram's horns. Anvil-shaped cranium. A monster.

'They sting, Miss,' said Iago, from the other side of the room. 'You don't want to get too close.'

Diana glowered at him. 'Sapho – Sapho – tell me: who murdered Leron?'

'I think it was justice, not murder, Miss. I think he was a bad man. I say he deserved it.'

'The policepersons – they are saying you killed him. *Did* you kill him Sapho?'

But her only reply to this was disbelieving, self-pitying tears, and a series of gaspy incomprehensible words. Diana was bored with this display. She sent Sapho away: Officer first-class Avraam Kawa led her out.

'*She* seemed pretty happy to see him dead and gone,' Diana observed. 'What do you think, Iago?'

'I think, Miss,' said the Tutor-who-was-no-tutor, 'that I personally vetted all twenty of these servants. I did so in direct, personal consultations with Ms and Ms Argent. These were to be personal handservants to yourself, Miss, and to Eva as well. We took no chances, in terms of their moral character.'

'You don't think a revolutionary and a murderer could slip past such a vetting process?'

Iago made his right eyebrow go from — to ^. Just his right one! His left stayed where it was. Such a clever trick. He did it from time to time, but no matter how much Diana practised in front of the mirror she had never been able to emulate it.

'Alright,' she conceded. 'But if he's not a revolutionary, why does Sapho call him one? Why baa-baa *blacken* his name? No, don't bother answering the . . . don't bother answering. Bring me another servant to question, and I shall proceed with the questioning.'

'Shall I kill the wasp, first?' asked Jong-il.

But the truth was, questioning servants was a *bore*. It was a well-bore; a gravity-bore; a boffo bore. Many tears were shed, by men and women both, boys and girls, all weeping as if weeping had just come into *fashion*, goddess-love-it. And there were lots of tediously repeated assurances of their undying loyalty to and love for the Argent family, prompted by the heightened mood and the fear and above all by the CRF. There was very little actual informational content.

What Dia gleaned, by this increasingly frustrating and tedious sifting of emotional blurting, fell into one of two categories. On the one hand, some servants – the bId gave her names, and personal details, the skill quotients and coordinations, the birthmarks and disease actuarial of all them – thought that Leron was a bad man. When pressed for specifics they all said the same thing: he was a terrorist and an anarchist and an antinomian, and he hated the Ulanovs and all that was legal and right and ordered in the System. Some (Mantolini, Tapanat and Faber) also alleged that he was a sexual bully, and forced both females and males into unwanted sexual congress.

But on the other hand, other servants – Poon-si, Tigris and Oldorando most forcefully – put forward a completely different version of events. According to them Leron was a thoroughly good man, almost a space-saint. So far from being a terrorist, or plotting from his lowly position to bring down the Ulanovs, he was dedicated to the System-wide rule of law, and moreover he worked to expose disloyalty in others. According to these people, this fact explained his demise. 'He was killed before he could reveal that *she* is a traitor and a revolutionary,' said a servant called D'Arch.

'She?'

'Sapho! You have spoken to her? She is a traitor to the very bone! Look in her eyes and you can see it!'

'A traitor to the Argents?'

Again, at the merest suggestion of such a thing, the servant looked genuinely shocked. 'No, no, no,' she said. 'Who could be disloyal to *you*, Miss?' And then the gusty tears came. 'Never that, Miss! The thought hurts my heart, just the *thought* of it!'

'Then you mean – a traitor to the Ulanovs themselves?'

But it took a long time for the weeping to settle to the level where meaningful communication could continue. 'Yes! Yes! She is the serpent in the globe of Eden, she is the spider. She hates law and good and right and order and everything that has made the Solar System habitable and free of war. She is a killer!'

'And – Leron was about to report her, was he?'

'Yes! Yes! So she killed him. She tried to do it before, but now she was able.'

'But,' she had to check the bId again to remember this one's name; the servants were all more or less indistinguishable from one another, 'but D'Arch, why hadn't he *already* reported her? He had many weeks when he could have done so, before you all came down here.'

The confusion in D'Arch's eyes was unmistakeable. 'But he was a good man,' she said. 'The killer is Sapho. I told the police already!'

From his position near the door, Iago interpolated a question: 'have you heard of Jack Glass?'

This had an immediate effect. D'Arch's eyes went wide, and colour dimmed in her dark face. She stared at Iago as if he were the devil made flesh. 'Jack Glass?' she repeated. 'He is – the father of lawlessness.'

'Did he ever visit your globe, D'Arch?'

'No, never! Yes, he is everywhere! But *I* never met him – not I. They say he can kill anybody in the entire System, and that he is dedicated to bringing down the lawful, harmonious rule of the Ulanovs!'

'If he can kill anybody in the system,' said Diana, reasonably enough, 'then why doesn't he just kill the Ulanovs and be done with it?'

This was, she realised as soon as she had said it, a shocking thing to voice aloud. If D'Arch had looked shocked at the name of Jack Glass, she looked flabbergasted that anybody could say such a thing aloud. *Kill the Ulanovs* – just putting the words together like that was probably a legally actionable thing.

'Never that!' gasped D'Arch. 'Nobody could do that!'

Officer first-class Avraam Kawa took her away and brought in another handservant: this one called Carna. Diana's bId sketched her in terms of basic data, but didn't explain how her gristly hair had turned such an antique shade of grey at the age of only twenty-one; or what had caused the old, chevron-shaped scar over her right eye, like a corporal's stripe. As to this latter, Diana got the sense quickly enough of a combative personality only imperfectly controlled beneath the more appropriate veneer of handservant deference. She met Diana's eye without flinching, and unlike most of the other interrogates she did not cry. But she also had definite ideas about who had killed Leron.

'*She* did it.'

'Who? Sapho?'

'That's right. She tried it once before, in the dizzy dummies you know.'

'The what?' Dia asked.

'The,' said the woman, enunciating more clearly, '*dizzy* dummies, Miss.' Dia's bId popped up with: //*large scale centrifugal devices in which simulated gravity is used to bulk up bone and muscle prior to transferring a servant from zero to fractional g*//. Intrigued she scratched up a little more data. These were not like any machines with which Dia was familiar, except in underlying principle. They were, for instance, much larger and without any of the more civilised trimmings. It seemed that servants would spend *whole days* inside fast-spun cages. The system had a grille and sluice, since the speed was rapid and continuous, not like the machines Dia was used to. Accordingly vomiting was common, as likely (statistically) at the end of the procedure as the beginning. Fatalities in the .07 to .15 range, depending on the make of the device. Stress fractures in subjects' bones occurring in the .35 to .45 range, but most of these being relatively easily fixed.

Dia asked: '*how* did she try to kill him?'

'Miss, have you ever seen the dizzies?'

Dia laughed. 'I'd never even heard of them until now!'

'Oh, Miss, there are lots of ways to harm someone in there. It was in there that Petero was killed.' Her complexion was an even dun-colour, but the skin on the inside of her eyelids – the little ledge of flesh visible between the eyeball itself and the outer skin of the face – was black, like natural mascara. It made her look almost soulful.

'Who?'

'Petero was Leron's *best* buddy. They were oh-ho *friends* from years back. But Petero broke his neck in the dizzy dummies, learning this gravity. It's a hard lesson.'

'So – Leron's best friend was killed before he even came down here?'

'He died, yes.'

Diana looked over at Iago. 'Is that true?'

Iago checked his own bId, or he didn't and just pulled the fact from his memory, it was impossible to tell with his impassive face. 'Broke his neck, yes.'

'Was it an accident?'

'Accidents do occur in these gravitational acclimatization devices, Miss,' Iago said. 'And sometimes such accidents are fatal.'

'But did somebody *kill* – eh, him?'

'Petero Grenadine, of the shanty globe Smirr?'

'Him, yes.'

Iago pursed his lips, noncommittally. 'It was investigated, of course. There was nothing to suggest it was murder. The worst you could say is that it wasn't reported very promptly. If they – the other servants in the device, I mean – if they had raised the alarm straight away, he might have been saved. But by the time he was noticed, he had expired. Brain dead.'

'Why *didn't* they immediately sound the alert?' Diana wanted to know. 'Good goddess, a man's life could be saved!'

'Perhaps he wasn't popular,' Iago suggested, vaguely.

'He was plenty pop-u-lar!' snorted Carna, scowling at Iago. But then she looked back towards Diana, and winced, and her eyes went moist. 'I mean, Miss,' she said. 'Not to be contradictory – but he was a fine man. And Leron was too. They neither of them deserved to die.'

'Did you,' asked Diana, feeling the transgressive nature of the question as a warm gleam in her chest and the buzz of adrenaline – she was the investigator! She could ask anything no matter how outrageous! – 'did you have sexual relations with Petero?'

Carna looked horrified, and then immediately abashed, and finally she looked at the floor. 'Oh, Miss,' she said, in a shamed voice. 'Such a question from a young Miss!'

'Did you?'

'Miss, you must understand how the world works, when you grow up in a shanty globe – the high morals and purity and the goodness and the order of *your* life, of the blessed Argents, is hard to maintain in *such* a place. The Argents shine silver with the light of Ra'allah Himself! But in the globes . . .' She trailed off.

'I'll take that as a yes,' Diana stated, elated at having (as she thought) touched on an important point. Not only important but properly grown-up! But then, she *was* going to be sixteen in a fortnight. 'And Leron too?'

Carna didn't say anything.

'I see,' Dia said, sternly; although her external performance of disapproval didn't reflect her inner glee. This was something key – wasn't it? She tried another stab in the dark. 'Now, he was also having sexual relations with Sapho, wasn't he? Leron?'

Carna's looked back at her, open-eyed. The expression was either one of astonishment at such a wrongheaded assertion, or else astonishment at Diana's perspicacity. Dia wasn't sure which was more likely. She pressed on:

'Was that *it*? Was it sexual jealousy – did *you* kill Leron because he was having sexual relations with another person?'

'No,' gasped Carna, her brow creasing. She looked baffled. Or furious. Was it fury? And if so was she furious at being found out? Or furious at being unjustly accused?

'Leron and . . .' But the name had gone out of her memory; Dia cycled quickly through the day's order on the bId, 'Leron and *Sapho* went into the storeroom to have sexual relations. You followed and killed him.'

'No!' snapped Carna. 'I am no killer. And besides you are suggesting I – did – did – the physical activity I am too embarrassed to name – *that*? In *this gravity*?' And Diana finally recognised the expression on her face for what it was: incredulousness.

All the servants were questioned eventually, although Dia rattled through the last five in short order. There was a huge amount of redundancy and noise in the data; and taking it all in, after the manner of the great mystery detectives, did not leave Dia much wiser. About half the servants thought Leron had been a minor devil, a traitor, bully, rapist, revolutionary and thoroughly bad man, and that his death had been well-deserved. About half talked of him as a force for good in the cosmos, a kind-hearted, loyal supporter of both the Argent family (of course) and the Ulanovs, the principle of good justice in human form. The latter tended to believe that the handservant called Sapho had killed him. As to how she had been able to lift a heavy hammer and thwack it down on his head – and as to why Leron hadn't simply dodged the blow – nobody could say.

'You've questioned everybody,' Iago noted. 'Now?'

The two of them were alone in the interrogation room. The policepersons had discreetly withdrawn. Diana lolled in a gel-chair, breathing shallowly.

'Not everybody,' she said. 'I haven't questioned *you*.'

'Me, Miss?' the Tutor replied, retreating into the evasive formality of his old-world butler manner. 'I remind you that my whereabouts during the murder have been determined with a certainty that puts me beyond suspicion of the crime.'

'Not as a *suspect*, ye-are-goh,' she drawled. 'You *are* silly.'

'I am happy to answer any questions, Miss, of course,' he said, frostily.

'Oh don't get all crusty-crusty on me, you old satyr. I only want to ask you about politics.'

'Politics,' Iago repeated. 'How do you mean?'

'I know you like to *veil* your true importance to this family under a cloud of unknowing,' she said. 'But though I'm young and *sometimes* giddy I'm no fool. What shall we call you – consigliere?'

Iago couldn't stop a smile! He even snorted a brief puff of air out of his nostrils, which was the closest he came to laughing. 'I wouldn't use that particular vocabulary in the hearing of your MOHparents, Miss Diana,' he advised.

'Oh?'

'It's a mafia term, you know.'

'So? Mafias are perfectly respectable organisations. They have their place within the structures and hierarchies of power, all beneath the umbrella of the Lex Ulanova.'

'Quite right,' said Iago. 'Trillions of human beings, most of them living in the Sump with nothing to lose – it's a vast potential for chaos, anarchy and destruction. Order can only be maintained with a large and various body of well-motivated enforcers. Mafiosi have their place in that larger framework of power, as you say. But it is a place *several ranks below* the Clan Argent. You might just get away with calling me a non-executive director; if only because the language of the Gongsi is less *infra dig*. But one thing Mrs and Mrs Argent are very particular about . . .'

'—is our pre-eminence. I know. We're second only to the Ulanovs themselves. I know. You think I don't? It will be my family, one day; my *Clan*. Mine and Eva's.'

Iago didn't say anything to this; but he didn't say anything in a way that somehow implied that this eventuality was far more conditional than Diana's confidence suggested. She looked at him, through the clear air and the fog of gravity.

'What?'

But he shook his head, still smiling.

'It's a test, I know,' she said, feeling suddenly tired. She even closed her eyes. But this wasn't a time to go to sleep. 'Everything's a test. I don't doubt our MOHmies love us both, but everything *has* to be a test, doesn't it? To discover whether we're yet worthy, or if we'll ever be, or goddess-help-me which *one* of us will be worthy. It's such,' she gulped air, opened her eyes wide and sighed out the contents of her lungs. 'Bore!' she concluded. 'Bore, bore, bore.'

'You ask me about politics, Miss Diana,' said Iago. 'I can tell you this: for somebody like you, an important member of one of the most powerful families in this System of trillions – everything *is* politics. It's true as well for Miss Eva, however much she tries to flee into the furthest reaches of deep space with her abstruse astronomical research. Your presence on this *island* is politics.'

'You're expecting an attack on the family?'

'Yes.'

'From which direction?'

'From one of the other MOHfamilies,' he said.

For a moment Dia felt a pang at her illicit communication with Anna Tonks Yu. But Anna would never betray their love. And anyway, nobody knew about it – not her family, not Anna's. Not even Iago knew that she had sent the message; so it was unlikely any enemy had been able to break it.

'Which one?' she asked.

'We're not sure. Maybe the Clan Aparaceido. Maybe the Clan Yu.'

Diana's heart gave a little shudder at that; like the epileptic shiver that a fly does in between passing from perfect stillness to perfect stillness. The shudder passed, as they always do. Foolish as it was (and she *knew* it was foolish) the love she and Anna shared was not for here-and-now, but for the ages. It was a love that only came into human affairs once in a hundred years. And they had never even met!

'I can see why the military might – ,' she said, looking at the floor to cover the momentary wetness in her eyeballs. 'I mean: I can see why the Clan Aparaceido might think they could land a blow on us. They have their own information-gathering systems – not as effective as ours, of course, or as deeply integrated into the System population. But at least they have them. But the Yu family?' (just saying the name made her heart hurry!) 'How would it benefit the *transport* clan, savaging our information capacities? They have nothing comparable. Would the Ulanovs even permit it? It's an inevitably losing play, surely?'

'A fair analysis, Miss,' Iago said, tartly. 'But an analysis deficient in certain respects. For one thing, it is old-fashioned to regard the MOHfamilies as single-skill entities. We are no more limited to information and problem solving than the Clan Aparaceido is to military operations, or the Clan Kwong to taxation.'

'Do you say *we?*' she asked, a little stung by the severity of his response.

In turn she saw something she had literally never seen before. She saw Iago blushing. Or, at least, she saw two Jupiter-spots of red fade into view in each of his cheeks, stay there for several seconds, and then dissolve away again. He looked straight at her, and when he spoke his voice was level, but she could see that she had rattled him.

'You're quite right, Miss,' he said, stiffly. 'I ought not to talk as if I am part of your MOHfamily. I am not; I am only a servant – a Tutor. Nonetheless, I trust you'll permit me to add nuance to your analysis. The Ulanovs preside over a hard-fought peace, one they have maintained by the strictest application of the Lex Ulanova. Simply enforcing that law absorbs the lion's share of their energies. They have no personal attachment to any of the five MOHfamilies, any more than they do to any individual Gongsi lower down, or to any particular militia, police force, mafia, cult, band or religion. Whether these entities preserve good relations amongst themselves or whether they destroy one another is ultimately a matter of indifference to the Ulanovs, I believe, unless such conflict threatens the Lex, and therefore their position. Squabbling, provided it falls short of all-out war, is unlikely to do this. Should it turn into a war, then they have the means to intervene and stamp it out. Indeed, historically, the Ulanovs have feared only one thing.'

'Popular uprising,' said Diana, placatingly. She was feeling sheepish at having goaded him; for though he was cranky and awkward and unbelievably old and wrinkled, she did have a soft spot for the old fellow. And you couldn't fault his loyalty.

'That's it. It is the numbers involved that make it potentially an unmanageable eventuality,' said Iago. 'But until recently they – the Ulanovs themselves, the MOHfamilies below them, the

Gongsi below *them*, and all the other enforcement organisations – *have* kept the peace. The Sump is crowded with human life, it is true, but it is an intrinsically disorganised swarm, massively internally variegated. And life in the Sump is precarious; if any region of shanty bubbles shows any overt signs of popular unrest, it is a simple matter to break a representative sample of globes, kill an example-making number of malcontents.'

'You make it sound so clinical!'

'What it *is*,' Iago replied, blankly, 'is an actuarial matter: the loss of present life balanced against the much larger loss of life a full-scale revolution would entail. But things have changed.'

'How have they changed?'

'Ms Joad herself brought the three letters concerned to your attention yesterday.'

'FTL?' said Diana. 'The impossible FTL?' And then she laughed out loud. 'I suppose that explains why the Yu family might be interested. Transport *with added FTL* would open up a whole new avenue of wealth-creation for them! And the Aparaceido: the military are *obviously* going to have an interest in making their craft faster. Faster than possible.' She slapped her own leg. 'They think we have the secret! They think we have it! We're information, after all. Is that why they want to destroy us, all-of-a-sudden? Oh, I know they've wanted to destroy us for a long while, but this would explain why it is so *suddenly* a threat.'

'There are various imponderables, should the technology become reality. Although of course you're correct that it would potentially generate enormous wealth.'

'Enough wealth to enable a MOHfamily to challenge the supremacy of the Ulanovs, perhaps?'

'Miss!' Iago snapped. 'To speak those words is to commit a crime of lesser treason under the terms of the Lex Ulanova.'

'Alright, alright. *I'm* not advocating revolution. But that would be another of the worries, wouldn't it? If there were such a technology, and let's for-the-sake-of-argument say it's reasonably cheap . . . then the whole game would change. The Polloi would all buzz off to distant star systems, out of the reach of the long arm of the Ulanovs. Far from the remit of the Clan Kwong taxation and revenue capacities.'

Iago gazed steadily at her for several long seconds. Then he said: 'indeed.'

'Iago – *do* we have this FTL technology?'

'By "we", Miss, you mean the Clan Argent?'

She clucked at him: 'alright, touchy-touchy Tutor type. I didn't mean to make you feel *excluded*, you know. *You're* a vital part of the Clan, too, for all your genetic difference. But you haven't answered my question: do we have it?'

'No, Miss.'

'The actual technology? Or the information leading to the technology?'

'Neither, Miss.'

'Of course we don't!' she said, triumphantly. 'Because it is an impossibility according to the laws of Physics. But do people *believe* we have it?'

'There are,' said Iago judiciously, '*suggestions* that the data concerning the building of such a drive might exist somewhere.'

'In the Sump, of course. It starts to make sense. This was presumably what old Joady was on about – if Jack Glass (we read: revolutionary agitators) got hold of the plans for an FTL engine, it would make red rebellion much more likely, and more likely to succeed. When these twenty handservants landed on the island, did you deal with them?'

'Deal with them, Miss?'

'Yes: debrief them, check on them, anything like that?'

'They fall within my purview, yes. Myself and various other people. I had prior dealing with them, and – yes I did visit the servants' quarters on the night before the crime.'

'And?'

Iago looked at her. 'And what, Miss?'

'Is there anything you can tell me that will help me solve this ma-ma-*mystery*, my dear Tutor? Were there tensions? Did you walk in on an argument and somebody threatening to kill some-body, anything like that?' When Iago shook his head she added: 'but were they discussing FTL in hushed tones?' She was watching his reactions, but – after the startling faux-pas of the blush – he was too controlled to give anything away. 'What about Jack Glass, did they mention him? Was he lurking in the shadows?'

'This fishing is rather a clumsy strategy, isn't it, Miss? For someone of your – talents?'

She glowered at him. 'Oh I think I've done enough of questioning people for today, thank you *very* much.'

8

The Deep Blue Sea of Why

Diana stumped right out of the building under crawliper power, straight past the waiting policepersons. She didn't reply to their plaintive 'farewell Ms Argent' and 'let us know if I can be of any other assistance.'

The heat and glare of the unremitting sun. A choir of cicadas making the sound of friction.

She got to the car a little ahead of Iago. 'I want to go for a swim,' she told him. 'You know the place.'

It was a short drive to the coast, and then only a few bumps and shakes as the car's gelwheels deformed to lumpy legs and walked them down the rocky headland. The beach itself was smooth and broad and white; perfectly deserted, of course. When Diana opened the car door boiling air flowed inside. 'Gracious,' she said, struggling out. The afternoon was extraordinarily, vastly hot. As Berthezene and Jong-il climbed back up to find the best places on the rocky headland to keep guard, and with Iago waiting on the lunula-shaped arc of white sand with her clothes, she stripped off and lumbered into the little waves. The water was so fresh with cold that it made her scream with laughter.

She lolled, and basked, enjoying the support of the water against the unrelenting gravity. It occurred to Diana (she wasn't certain of this, rationally; but it felt intuitively correct) that she had all the pieces of data she needed to solve this mystery. But there were a number of different ways she could piece them together, and her brain refused to bring the conceptual mosaic into proper coordination. Vetting the servants. Bashing in somebody's head. FTL. Revolution. Fins on a spaceship. Fins? What has *fins*? Fish do.

Why did *fins* keep reoccurring to her?

She breaststroked further from the shore. The sunlight fell in curling folds and shafts through the water. Such clear water! Ice and blue and Perspex-coloured down to the sandy bottom except where the sunlight struck it, and made something yellower and smoky out of the medium.

But she was easily tired, and soon made her way back to the beach to sprawl on the smartowel Iago had laid out for her. He sat facing away, and for a while she just lay there letting the sun press down upon her flesh. She was very soon dry.

Birdsong was audible, a constant dribble of flute-like noise, rather lovely-on-the-ear, actually. The breeze smelt of sea salt and olive trees and resin and *heat*. So hot! It was tantalising that she could hear the birdsong so clearly and yet not see the birds. Craning her neck a little, she had a view of the knot of trees at the top of the rocky slope, with their sugary load of blossom. Maybe the birds were in there.

After a while she asked: 'how old are you, Iago? *Very* old, aren't you?'

'Older than you, certainly Miss,' he said, without turning around.

'But how *much* older?' She sat up and pulled the towel around her. 'Turn around for she-heaven's sake, won't you? Golly I can't talk to your *back*.'

Iago got to his feet – actually stood straight up, as if to attention, and turned to face his charge. 'It is in your bId, of course.'

'I'm asking you.'

'I'm 45 years old, Miss Diana.'

'Oh that *is* old! But you look even older, you know.'

'I've spent a good amount of my life upland, and time goes – differently there.'

'I've spent almost *all my life* upland!' said Diana, with a little shriek. 'Oh don't I know how time drags!'

'Well, when I say upland,' Iago replied, with a queer, unreadable little look in his eye. 'I suppose I mean further up than that.'

But Dia wasn't particularly interested in that. 'So you are forty-five, regular, and I'm sixteen. That's a gap. We could never get married, with an age chasm like that, could we?'

'The difference in our ages is certainly a barrier,' agreed Iago, coolly. 'In addition, in terms of status, wealth, political influence and every other consideration, we are spectacularly ill-matched. You are beautiful and I am ugly. Your mothers would have me killed if I took any sort of advantage of my position. And quite apart from anything else, you are female and I am male. I believe your mothers have higher hopes for you than that you marry a – man.'

Dia shrugged; for on this matter she had no strong views one way or another. It was as distant from her current life as the universal background radiation. 'You know I'm only teasing you, Ee, ar, goy? I'm not in the least *atom* interested in sex or marriage or boys or even girls at the moment, and certainly not in an old relic like you.'

He smiled a chilly smile. 'Precisely, Miss Diana.'

'Maybe I shouldn't tease you. I am a shocking tease, I know,' she said. 'But you don't mind?'

'I don't mind.'

'You love it, actually.'

'Well—' he started to say.

But before he could contradict her she added: 'you love *me*, at any rate?'

'Naturally I do, Miss,' he said, in a formal voice.

'Oh that's the CRF speaking! If you were a free agent, you'd hate me. And anyway I've *much* more pressing things to worry about than that. I have to solve this murder! A real-life murder!'

Iago didn't say anything; he didn't so much as raise an eyebrow. But Diana knew him well enough. 'Don't take that tone, Iago,' she said.

'Indeed not,' he said, mildly.

'My MOHmies are counting on me. They *know* I can solve it. Of course they love Eva, but I'm their *clever* daughter. I'm their *people-canny* daughter. They need me to be that. The future of the family depends upon me being that. This is my chance to prove it, really to prove it!'

'Proof,' said Iago, neutrally.

'So,' she said, sitting up straighter. Gravity was slightly less of an oppressive horror today. A few days more and she'd be gambolling about like a fawn. She hated to agree with her MOHmies, but they were right. A few daily hours in a centrifuge wasn't a patch on the total immersion of Earthly gravitational life. 'So – what *do* you think?'

'What do I *think*, Miss?'

'Go on – sit down. You're always standing about! It's a kind of showing-off you know. The rest of us have to sit down. You should too.'

'Should I be blamed for having unusually strong and healthy legs?' said Iago, with a twinkle in his eye. But he sat himself down nonetheless: cross-legged, on the sand. It brought him down to her level, which was better.

'The police believe the murderer to be one of the other servants,' Dia said. 'So do you.'

'I do?'

'Of course you do! It's the most obvious and plausible inference. But maybe *who* isn't so interesting as *why*. And there are various whys. For example: why should the murderer be the most obvious person? We might as well say the butler did it.'

'Indeed, Miss.'

'No – I *say*, no: it is something more unexpected than that. Believe me, I know how *these things* work. Who knows them better than I? And don't say Anna Tonks Yu, of the famous family Yu, who is my rival and my deadly and bitter enemy. Don't say her!'

'Her name shall never pass my lips, Miss. I only meant to point out that we're not in the Ideal Palace now.'

'You think the solution is banal and obvious, do you?' she asked.

'I only think that real life may not be as . . . *narratively satisfying* as a mystery written specifically for the IP. By a process of elimination, and since nobody else went into the house – discounting the theory that Jack Glass teleported magically into the storeroom – the murderer must have been somebody already inside. There were twenty servants in the house, and nobody else. Practically, it would have been an easy thing. One of them invites Leron into the storeroom at the back of the house. On some pretext – let's say, to fetch a piece of equipment.'

'Or offering him sexual *intercourse*,' said Diana. She loved being able to startle Iago with little improprieties like this. He was so stuffy and proper!

'Possibly that,' said Iago, with a frown. He cleared his throat. 'At any rate, we can imagine him going into the room, the murder scene. But straight away there are problems. The hammerblow that killed him was delivered from the front.' Iago touched a point on his own tall brow, near the hairline. 'The business-end of the hammerhead struck him right in the middle. As you'll know from the autopsy, on your bId, a splinter from the tree-wood handle was found in his nose.'

'Ow, ow, ow,' she drawled, in a bored voice.

'Of course splinters of tree wood in his nose,' said Iago, 'was the last thing on his mind. Indeed, by the time of the *follow-through* of the blow, which is what we're talking about here . . .

well, at that point he no longer had a mind to have a last thing on. If you see what I mean.'

'If you're trying to shock me with the grisly descriptions of vi-oh-*lence*,' Diana told him, 'then you'll have to 'try harder than that.'

'My point is this: the hammer is heavy. Leron was facing his murderer, looking straight *at* his killer. He did this, whilst they lifted a massy hammer *all the way up* and brought it crashing *down* into his face. Why? Why didn't he duck out of the way? Or try to wrestle his assailant? Or do anything except what he did do – just stand there, gawmping.'

'Is that even a word?' Diana said. 'Alright – that is a puzzle, I grant you. And there's another difficulty. Which again, clog-clever Iago, you raised before.'

'Miss?'

'All nineteen suspects came down at the same time as Eva and me. Before that, most of them had never set foot on Earth in their lives! You saw what they were like when they all came spilling out of the servant house – staggering and tumbling, barely able to walk. Not a one had even *begun* to acclimatize to a full g. How could any of them so much as *lift* that heavy hammer? Let alone bring it down with the force and precision to smash poor old Leroy's brains in.'

'Leron,' said Iago. 'You think this fact alone proves the inno-cence of all the servants?'

'L*eron*, that's right. Yes, I think that. It's their physical incapacity, *and* the fact that they were all vetted, for *crying* out as loud as you *like*! These were hand-picked handservants; they went through more layers of vetting and psychological profiling and checking than anyone else in the whole system. How could a *murderer* slip through that net? I mean it literally and actually and honestly: how could somebody with a history of violence, or with murder in their heart, end up as the personal handservant of Eva or myself?'

'Hard to see how,' Iago agreed.

'Never mind dosing our servants with high levels of loyalty drug. We check them rigorously physically and psychologically. You told me you were involved yourself. My MOHmies sign off on our handservants personally don't they? – I mean, the hand-servants assigned to Eva and myself?'

'Certainly they do,' said Iago. 'I personally liaised between the vetting teams and your parents, Miss.'

'You *personally* did – and yet you still think that one of them is a murderer!'

Iago looked at her, and then dropped his gaze.

Dia pressed on: 'None of those servants could lift that weight, Iago! And you saw for yourself, the gardening robot hadn't been activated in years. But an Earth native *could* lift the hammer. As for why L*eron* didn't fight him, or try a silly-old-runaway. Maybe *he* was too crushed and discombobulated and disoriented by the heavy gravity – eh? He'd never been downbelow before either, after all.'

'No native Earthling emerged from the house, Miss,' Iago pointed out. 'And the house was searched thoroughly after the murder happened: no native Earthling was found.'

'Doesn't that just suggest our murderer had a really good hiding place inside? Maybe he waited there all day – until the moment was auspicious for him to slip away?'

'How could he do so, without alerting the House AI?'

'I don't know.'

Iago pondered. 'And why would a native Earthling want to smash in the head of a servant who'd never even set foot here before?' he asked.

'Ah,' said Diana, knowingly. 'Motive! I'll come to that. But first, here's a thing: why choose a hammer? I mean: think of all the ways our murderer could have killed her-or-his victim. Why a hammer?'

'We can't argue with its effectiveness,' Iago noted. 'It proved more than capable of ending Leron.'

'You're not taking the force of my observation. Why choose

such a *big heavy* hammer – if not to give the impression that the murderer must be a big heavy person? A strong person, acclimatized to Earth gravity? You can't deny that's the impression it gives.'

Iago said nothing.

'I had a dream, the night after the murder,' Diana went on, meditatively. 'I dreamt I was a spaceship, about to fall *like a hammer* into the sun itself – and the sun was Leron's skull. I was the hammer.' She thought about this. 'The odd thing is, I was covered with fins. Wings in space. Vanes and fins and wings.'

'Curious,' said Iago, neutrally.

'Anyway, I was called FTL,' said Diana absently. 'Fins and vanes and wings,' she added, as if it were a charm. 'Fins. And Wings. I need to sleep, Iago.'

'Here, Miss?'

'No. Take me back to the house. This killing gravity. I can only get a proper dream-sleep in a gel-bed.'

'Very well, Miss.'

As Jong-il and Berthezene came down from the rocks, she said to Iago: 'could a servant hide murder in their hearts and pass unnoticed through our selection processes?'

'No, Miss,' said Iago. 'They couldn't.'

'You're sure? The human heart is a mysterious chamber, after all.'

'They couldn't do it. We have the most rigorous selection processes in the whole system. You really think your MOHmies could put you at any risk? Of course not. I personally assure you.'

'Well,' said Dia, sinking into the seat of the car. 'That rather suggests my theory is correct – don't you think?'

'You are the information problem solver, Miss,' said Iago, smoothly. 'Not I.'

She looked at the sky. Blue, and blue, and blue.

'I want to go home,' she said. She was feeling sleepy. Some dreaming would help her sort through her theories and come to some conclusion.

She couldn't be bothered to strap her crawlipers back to her legs, so made her way back to the car by leaning on Iago's shoulder. For an old man, the muscles of his arm and shoulders were certainly pretty toned.

When everybody was inside, the car climbed gingerly back up the rocky slope and settled itself back on the road. Acceleration tugged in her gravity-weary torso like a blanket settling over her. Her eyelids felt deliciously honeyed and heavy.

On the way home they drove past a procession: a dozen or more people, the woman at the front carrying an iCon of the Virgin – the local goddess. Hymns were being sung. Diana could hear nothing, of course, through the perfect seal of the car windows; but she could see their mouths working. And they walked with a slow, deliberate step, on their way to, or perhaps on their way from, a church, and a service, and prayers. The iCon of the Virgin was fashioned, of course, in the likeness of Dia's MOHmies. Which is to say, in the likeness of Diana herself. It was only moderately uncanny to see her image there. They weren't worshipping *her*, of course. They were worshipping the Platonic form of her, the embodied goddess. Still.

The car swept past, and away.

'I'm getting the impression,' Iago prompted, gently. 'That you have already solved this mystery.'

'You think you know me,' Diana replied, frowning. 'You don't really know me.' In her head, the mantra: fins and vanes and wings.

'Of course,' said Iago.

'It's a lot of contradictory data,' Diana replied, sulkily. 'And I *know* what you're going to say. You're going to say: it's what is supposed to make me special, my ability to see a straight path through the sorts of data self-contradiction and iChaos that baffle AIs. But AIs don't have to *sleep*.'

'The Model-F ones do,' put in Berthezene, irrelevantly.

'A man is murdered,' said Diana, her eyes closed, her head

jiggling gently from side to side in time to the motion of the car. 'The facts aren't the problem. The interlocking *contexts* are the problem.'

'Contexts?' prompted Iago.

She was on the event horizon of sleep; but held herself, just, on the waking side. 'Interlocking and incompatible contexts. Situating the murder in the context – let's say – of servant life; of the attitudes and mores of shanty globe existence; of larger Solar System politics up-to-and-including treachery against the Ulanovs themselves, and planning revolution and so on . . . and Ms Joad didn't come all the way down here for the hell of it, after all.' In her head the nursery-chant of it went round and round:

Fins and vanes and wings
Fins and vanes and wings
Fins and vanes and wings

She should see that Iago believed her to be asleep. So she spoke up again, just to surprise him. 'But there are the *other* contexts of Argent MOHfamily dynamics, and our relationship to the Ulanovs. But also the contexts of faster-than-light travel, of all the *random* things. And, for all I know, the context of Eva's *champagnely* exploding supernovae too – though it's hard to see how they have anything to *do* with it. Doodly-oh. But, I guess, the context of *physics*, yes. Not to mention Jack Glass. Not all of these contexts can be relevant to the solution of the mystery. Not *all* of them. The challenge is knowing which ones to discard.'

'So – you have an answer?' said Iago.

Diana opened one eye, and looked at him. 'Of course I do,' she said, sourly. 'How do you think I got my reputation as the Solar System's number one mystery and whodunit solver?'

Iago did his one-eyebrow-raising thing again. 'And?'

'My dear Iago, the information is all there, and you've seen all the clues I have. *You* ought to be able to solve this murder just as I have done.'

'My skills, Miss Diana,' said Iago, going all Jeeves-formal. 'Lie elsewhere.' His silly-old feelings were hurt, maybe, so Diana pulled herself more upright in the seat and said: 'don't be like that, ee-aa-oo, *please* don't! You are an *invaluable* member of the team, you really are. When I'm running the family I shall keep you on as a functionary or gardener or potboy or something. But *I* am the one bred by my MOHmies to solve mysteries. Aren't I?'

'You've solved the how *and* the why?'

'Why,' she replied, meditatively. 'Yes. Indeed, yes. Let us both bathe in the deep blue sea of *why.*'

'We're here,' said Jong-il. The car pulled up at the main compound, and Iago helped her inside.

She went through first; Berthezene and Jong-il followed behind, making the front door squeal with outrage at the metal guns they both carried. Jong-il stayed there, running their security clearance once again through the purview of the suspicious House AI, so as to permit them to carry their weapons indoors. Berthezene took up a post in the corridor outside Diana's room, and Iago helped her through and onto the gel-bed.

Klang, klang, klang. Noisy old door.

'An afternoon nap,' she murmured. 'Just a little sleep.'

She closed her eyes, and then she opened them again. 'When I wake up, I want to start planning my *party*,' she said. 'You understand? It will need a lot of planning.'

'Yes, Miss,' said Iago.

'And *what* do you mean by *that*?'

'Only what you know very well, that we cannot invite anybody, either in person or in virtual form, without compromising the secrecy of your being here.'

This annoyed Diana just enough to lift her up over the tug of sleep, if only for a moment. 'Nonsense,' she said. 'Not-sense, no-sense, un-sense. *Any* information agent could squirrel out the information.'

'I doubt that, Miss. We go to great lengths to keep you and your MOHsister safe.'

Diana wrinkled her nose. 'It ever occur to you I don't need your help? Did you ever think I'm the one keeping *you* safe?'

'In the sense that my safety depends upon the strength of the Argent family, and its proximity to the centres of power in the system – that is, of course, true. Nonetheless, we cannot compromise your safety. Nobody must know exactly where you are.'

'That foul Ms *Joad* knew where I was,' grumbled Dia, closing her eyes again.

'A personal agent of the Ulanovs is a different matter, of course.'

'I'm asleep,' said Diana.

'Very good, Miss.'

'I really am. Go away, you horrible, crack-skinned, ancient old relic.'

'Since you *are* asleep—' said Iago, moving towards the door.

'I am!'

'—then you won't hear me saying that we intercepted a message from Anna Tonks Yu.'

Diana opened one eye. 'That minx,' she said. 'What has she to say for herself?'

'We did not access the content of the message, naturally; in case it contained a seeker virus that would track back through the relays and reveal your location.'

Diana's heart was lolloping a little faster. 'You scanned it? *Is* there one?'

'That's not the point,' said Iago, gently, from his position by the door. 'And you know it. Miss Diana, you are clever – cleverer than anybody on this island with the possible exception of your sister. You don't need to *prove* that fact to anybody.'

Diana closed her eyes very tightly. 'Don't know what you mean.'

'Smuggling a message out to a member of a rival family – a *real* danger, potentially an immense danger. This is not Romeo and Juliet.'

'I'm asleep,' repeated Diana, with her eyes very tightly closed. 'I'm not even *going* to check the bId for the meaning of that reference.'

'You understand me very well, Miss. All I'm saying is – please, take this circumstance seriously. Danger surrounds us all the time. If any of the other MOHfamilies could *get to you* – or any organisation from a lower tier of power, any Gongsi or mafia or militia – it would be . . .'

'I'm asleep!' she snapped. 'Can't you see it? Don't you know what sleep looks like?'

'You're asleep,' said Iago. He left the room.

9

Eva Acts

Iago made his way – a little stiffly, for the gravity was oppressive – across to Eva's room. He lodged a request at the door of her IP, and, a little grumpily, she came out and into the real world. Iago went into her room. Sitting in her gel-couch, she opened her eyes, and wrath flashed in them.

'What is it?' she demanded. 'Shouldn't you be lurking about my sister?'

'I'm Tutor to the both of you,' he pointed out, mildly.

'Tutor,' Eva scoffed. 'What nonsense, Iago.'

At this Iago smiled. 'Would you prefer – flunkey?'

'Jeeves,' said Eva, scornfully. 'Of course I'm not privy to everything my MOHmies do. But neither am I a kid to be patronised, like . . .' She stopped, abruptly. 'What do you want, anyway? I'm in the middle of something. I have a PhD to finish.'

'Diana will be sixteen in a few weeks,' said Iago.

'She'll *still* be a kid. She'll be a kid at sixty-one. She has kid all the way through her, like a seam of silver running through an asteroid.'

'Let's hope,' said Iago, leaning himself back against the wall to take some of the crushing gravitational pressure off his legs, 'that we all survive long enough to enjoy her birthday party.'

'Sure we could all die at any time,' snapped Eva. 'Which only makes it more imperative that I get back to my research. I'd hate to leave it loose-endy.' But she stopped. 'You mean something more specific, don't you? You mean an actual threat?'

'Your MOHparents have good evidence to that effect.'

'Is it,' Eva said, trying for a flush of humour, 'what Joad said? Is the legendary Jack Glass coming down to kill us?'

'Personally I do not believe that the legendary Jack Glass is coming down to kill us,' said Iago in a level voice.

Eva sighed. 'Sit down, Iago,' she said. 'I suppose you'd better sit down. Is the attack imminent? Do we have to move again right now?'

Iago lowered himself, creakily, into a chair. 'Not right now. Probably next week; maybe in a fortnight. Certainly before your MOHsister's birthday. Both the Mrs Argents are agreed, though, that an attack is likely. They suspect the Clan Yu, but, speaking personally, I wonder if it will come from another direction.'

'Is that why Joad came down?'

Iago put his head a little to one side. As a general policy, he considered it was better not to answer questions the sisters put to him. Answering questions was *their* purpose in life after all. It was what they were made for.

'Politics,' said Eva, eventually. Then, surprisingly, she launched into an unexpected tangent: 'are my MOHmies *disappointed* in me, do you think?'

Iago considered. 'You could ask them.'

But Eva lifted her left arm, and let it fall under the influence of gravity. 'Even if they *were* disappointed, they wouldn't tell me. Not because they'd want to spare my feelings, of course; but because, like Dia, I am what they made me. To be disappointed in me would be for them to be disappointed in themselves. And though they *are* brilliant in many ways, my dear MOHmies are not good at honest self-criticism. The deep dark truthful mirror.'

For a moment they were both silent. Through the window, endless light fell upon the prone land; the ancient Earth yellow and brown and exhausted green beneath its holy blue sky. A figure went hurrying past in the middle distance, from left to right, plunging through the longer grass beneath the olive trees. Such strenuous exercise in the heat of the day! The motion of boots in the grass threw up a cloud of butterflies, winking taupe and brilliant green-blue in variegated motion as they scattered into the air between the trees.

Eventually Iago drew breath and spoke. 'Diana says she has solved the mystery of Leron's death.'

Eva's eyes flickered as her bId prompted her memory. 'The dead servant. I solved that yesterday, I believe. One of the *other* servants did it.'

Iago didn't reply, so Eva went on: 'has she? Solved it, I mean?'

'She hasn't told me the solution,' said Iago. 'And she claimed there were a few details she needed to slot into place, she said. But, I think – yes, she has.'

'One of the other handservants,' said Eva. 'Unless you believe Ms Joad, and it was the magically teleporting Jack Glass. One of the two.' She looked straight into Iago's eyes. 'Why did Joad tell us that Hen-and-Cow story?'

Iago waited.

Eva's eyelids sank a little. 'Why do I get the feeling this is a test? This whole thing? Choosing between one or other solution, it hardly matters. It's only one dead servant.'

'A fully grown human being,' said Iago, in a sad voice. 'With all the emotional and intellectual and practical capacity that entails.'

'There are trillions of human beings just like him in the Sump,' said Eva. 'But *that's* not it, is it? We both know that's not it. The test – is it her or me?'

'My understanding is that your parents earnestly desire the two of you to work *together*,' said Iago. 'That sounds like a platitude, I daresay. But they mean it. They really do.'

'That's just a long-winded way of saying that she passes the test and I don't,' said Eva, sulkily.

'You—' Iago began. But Eva cut across him. 'Don't condescend to me, Iago. I really won't bear that.'

He dipped his head.

Eva looked again through the viewing wall. The cypresses looked unnaturally upright and stiff against the sky, like dog's ears, perked and ready for bad news. But Eva knew the moment had already passed, the tide had rushed in between herself and Diana, and she had been stranded on the *wrong* side. The odd thing was that she experienced that realisation, in the moment, as a mode of relief. Presumably this was relief that the more acute pain associated with the moment of crisis was already behind her. But oceanic disappointment and gloom were poised, too, to wash over her. That, of course, would come.

'What was it?' she asked eventually. 'Was it the politics?'

'It's always politics,' said Iago. 'Politics is everything. The status of the Argent Clan depends upon riding the turbulence of politics, every hour of every day.'

'I *can* understand politics,' said Eva, unable to keep a tone of pleading from her voice. 'As a system I *do*. I don't meant to sound plaintive, but I *can* do it! Oh, maybe I don't have the empathetic instincts she does. I wasn't made that way. But my capacity for probabilistic solutioneering is . . .' She stopped. There was no point in berating Iago. He was only the messenger, after all. 'I'll finish this PhD,' she added, sulkily. 'I don't care what you say.'

'I know you will.'

'What is it with you and my MOHmies, anyway? You're old-school loyal to them, aren't you?'

'I owe them a great deal,' said Iago. 'They took me in. Plus, of course, we are working for the same thing. The stakes are enormously high.'

'Really? Isn't that just your usual political boilerplate claptrap?'

'No,' said Iago, looking very serious. 'It's the cold truth. It's the truth of the grave. The stakes are higher than they have ever been. The risk is greater than humanity has ever faced before.'

'I don't want to know,' said Eva. To her credit, she really didn't.

'You *feel* nothing for Leron, dead on the floor,' said Iago. 'And why should you? You never knew him. You see him as one atom in a quasi-gaseous accumulation of – as you say – trillions of human beings. And for Diana, the problem has precisely been coming round to your point of view. It's seeing those trillions as a resource, and not as a congregation of humanity.'

'You've delivered your message,' said Eva. 'I'd like you to leave me now, so I can get back to my research.'

Iago got awkwardly to his feet, his kneecaps popping. 'Diana will probably want to explain the solution to the mystery to you after she wakes up. She's proud of herself for figuring it out.'

'Yes, yes,' said Eva. 'We can all gather in the library and learn precisely *how* the butler did it – or the doctor. Was it the doctor? I seem to remember that it's always the *doctor* who is the murderer in these stories.'

He got to the door of her room before she called after him. 'Having failed the test,' she said. 'I suppose I'm entitled to know. Was the FTL thing a red herring?'

'It wasn't,' said Iago. 'I'm sorry to say.'

Eva sniffed, dismissively. 'The FTL murders!' she declared. 'And the murderer. *Was* it one of the handservants, like I said? Or was it Jack Glass, as Ms Joad insisted? I don't doubt that my little MOHsis picked the right one. But I can't shake the feeling that if I'd chosen *either* of them, I would have been wrong.'

Iago nodded.

'I knew it!' said Eva. 'It's *neither* of them!'

'Or both,' said Iago. 'Good afternoon, Miss.'

*

Eva retreated to her IP. She was disappointed; there was no point in pretending otherwise. It is always galling to fail a test, and it was made much *more* galling by realising only belatedly that it *had* been a test. Of course, she wouldn't be expelled from the inner sanctum of the Clan. Her wiser angel tried to suggest she see it as a blessing – for it would leave her more time to pursue her properly astroscientific research. And she could not begrudge her MOHsister her triumph (did Dia even realise that she *had* triumphed?). The disaffection she felt was, she decided, *something else*.

She tried to settle to her Champagne Supernova work, but the idiot word 'politics' kept yapping through her mind. 'Politics'! In the absolution of cold and distance politics meant nothing at all. The object of her study was further removed from politics than anything had ever been.

She went into her IP, and, steeling herself, went (as it were) through a door. It was no ordinary virtuality door; it was, on the contrary, a carefully *concealed* portal at the rear of the IP. A person couldn't wait, passively, forever. Sometimes action is required.

Eva acted.

The man running through the olive grove, a little while earlier, when the day was hottest and exercise hardest. Why was he in such a hurry?

Diana was in her room. She made a small window in her wall for a while; a porthole looking up at the plastic immensity of blue sky (blue! . . . such a *strange* colour for sky, when you came to think of it – such a weirdly thin dilution of the natural black). She widened the porthole, made it a wider picture window, and turned the sound up. It was late afternoon now. Korkura heat-haze and stillness possessed the scene. The only sounds were the distant breath-sounds of surf on an unseen beach, and the languid fizzle of cicadas hidden in the grass. Nothing moved. The sky looked like a screen. Two chopsticks of white were drawn upon it, converging towards the apex as two scramjets flew towards the same point, or at least appeared to do, from Dia's perspective. Even in the climate-balanced calm of her room she somehow *felt* the heat.

She deleted the window and settled into her gel-bed.

Sleep came straight away.

She dreamed of Iago. This was an odd thing: she rarely dreamt of any of the servants. She was standing on a small green hill: Earth, to judge by the gravity, but a colder and rainier latitude than Korkura's. The grass was trimmed neat, but the stalks had enough movement left in their abbreviated bodies to respond to the invisible pressure of the wind. All around were green fields, and to the left a wide expanse of blue-green woodland, like a cloud nestling flat against the ground. It was cold. The sky was white and grey, and the air in her nostrils smelt of rain. She knew, somehow, that this hill had once sported a tall tower, now ruinous. When she looked down Dia could see the stumps of granite brick only partly buried in the turf: the remnants of what had once been a mighty structure.

Iago was standing a few metres from her. 'Where am I?' she asked him; and then, without waiting for his reply she asked: 'what are you doing here? I *never* dream of you.'

'Asking the dream to interpret the dream is liable to lead to a short circuit,' he replied, in his croaky old voice.

Beside him was a RACdroid, its metal body gleaming dully in the winter light. 'Why have you brought a RACdroid? Are we going to witness a contract, you and I?'

'You passed the test. Your sister didn't. You are to be sworn in as the official heir of the Clan Argent.'

'You haven't even heard my solution!' she said. Then: 'it's a shame for my sister.'

'We must hope she accepts her shame,' Iago said, mysteriously.

'I didn't mean shame in that sense!' Then: 'ruins. Here – and you. Why am I dreaming about ruins?'

'It's all in the way a question is phrased, isn't it?'

She tried again. 'Alright. *What* is ruined, that I should dream about it?'

'That's better!' he said, and she experienced a mild shock of annoyance at his condescending manner.

She looked up. The sky was filling with storm clouds: imperial purple, darkest blue and black. They were great chunks of cloud, moving like solid objects, like portions of architectural masonry. They moved in with more-than-natural speed.

Then Iago said something unexpected. 'The stars are ruined. There is no warning, they are rent in pieces and hurtle out faster than the light they shed.' What a strange thing to say! The storm-clouds wholly filled the sky now. The quality of light changed.

'Their own light,' she said. Raindrops began to plummet, heavy as metal. The turf generated a surroundsound drumming noise. Dia had a flash of insight: the raindrops were, each of them, little hammerheads; and every strand of grass was a human being; and – ¡*flash*! – what was that? Lightning! So it came again – ¡*flash*! – and Diana looked across to Iago. Her face was wet and her flesh was shivering with cold. Soaked! She could hardly see him through the semiopacity of the rainfall. A lightning flash, its brillianting fishbone structure visible for a microsecond, but living on spectrally on the retinas. Each flash was the inexplicable death of a star.

'*What* is ruined?' Iago was saying, shaking his head as the rainfall bounced off his pate and droplets swarmed down about him like a mist. 'We are.'

You must understand: Dia was not used to having this kind of dream. Frankly it unnerved her. What made things worse is that she was *forcibly woken* in the middle of it by somebody else – and this was an *unprecedented* invasion of her privacy. She came out of sleep snarling, wheeling her arms in an attempt at fighting off this monster, this violator. But gravity was too debilitating, and her blows bounced feebly off the chest of whoever was rousing her.

'Miss! Miss Diana!'

'How dare you,' she gasped, her mouth dry. 'Interrupt my dreaming! I need my dreams to process my data—'

'Miss, we have to *go*.'

It was Jong-il. Even as her fury buzzed in her head she knew that something must be very wrong. 'Jong-il,' she croaked. 'What is it?'

'It's not safe for you here, Miss,' said the bodyguard, helping her out of the gel-bed. 'We have to leave now.'

Her rage drained away. 'Do I have time for a wash,' she snapped, '—or must I run away with specks of *gel* sticking to me?'

'Please, Miss, Miss, be quick,' Jong-il urged.

She was: the wash took only moments, and fitting the crawlipers moments more. 'Are we actually under attack?' she asked, as she followed Jong-il out of her bedroom. Iago was in the hall outside, looking (despite the absence of rain) distractingly like her dream version of him.

'I'm afraid so, Miss Diana,' he said. 'I apologise for waking you, but it is imperative we leave Korkura right away.'

'Who is it?'

'That's a little unclear: either Clan Aparaceido, or perhaps Clan Yu, using Aparaceido ordnance.'

'Is it war?'

Iago shook his head. 'I doubt that. It may be, of course; but I believe it's much more *likely* to be an opportunistic strike. They chanced upon information that identified you and your sister as being here, on this island. They're acting on it in the hope that they can take you both out. That would inconvenience your parents greatly.'

'It would inconvenience me more,' Diana retorted, drily. 'Is it certain? Is it happening now?'

'Not now. But our intelligence says it will happen within the next twelve hours.'

'Odds?'

'Our best intelligence is: point five seven.'

She nodded. It was certainly good enough reason to evacuate the island. 'Where's Eva?' she asked.

'You and she will leave separately,' said Iago. 'Your parents are adamant about that. They can't risk you both in one craft at the same time.'

It made sense. 'Then let me say goodbye to her, and let's get on with it,' she said.

The three of them went along to Eva's room, and the two sisters embraced. Both were wearing the same expression: sober, but focused. 'I'm sorry I couldn't be Hastings to your Holmes,' said Eva. 'It was petulant of me.'

'It hardly matters,' said Diana. 'And it's Mycroft. Hastings goes with Poirot.'

'So you worked out who actually killed the handservant?' Eva asked.

'You were right,' said Diana. 'It was another one of the handservants. Who else would it be?'

'Hah!' Eva laughed. 'So did I pass the test after all? A touch ironic, in the circumstances.'

'It's more complex than that,' said Diana. And then: 'what do you mean?'

'Nothing. Only, maybe I should do more of these murder mystery thingies? I could challenge you for your crown. You and that girl you have that crush on, the one you're so secretive about, who also plays them. What's her name?'

Diana winced, and looked away, and Eva suddenly understood. 'Never mind,' she said, wanting genuinely to console her MOH-sister. 'Danger is *good* for us. It's like gravity – if you live your life wholly without it, you grow feeble. We'll be alright.'

But Diana was blushing. 'Will you permit me to apologise to you?'

Eva considered this gravely for a while. 'Alright.'

They embraced again. 'Love makes you do reckless things,' said Dia. 'I know,' said Eva.

'We *must* leave, Miss,' said Jong-il, leaning in. 'I am miserably sorry, but it must be.'

'We have ballistic craft here on the island, of course,' murmured Iago. 'But a direct launch – given that the enemy probably knows where we are – would be too dangerous. We have half a dozen plasmaser installations on the Mediterranean coast, and it would be safer to go up in a car. Miss Eva and Jong-il will go down to Tobruk, and ride up from there. Miss Diana, Deño and I will ride up on an Italian plasmaser a little later.'

'I don't see that a plasmaser car is any harder to shoot down than a ballistic craft,' said Eva.

'It isn't.' Iago nodded once to acknowledge the correctness of Eva's observation. 'Indeed,' he added, 'it is larger, and travels more slowly, making it quite a lot easier to shoot, actually. But the car will be full of valuable cargo and also of many other people, so shooting it would be unambiguously an act of war. Shooting a private ballistic transport would be a different matter. More deniable; easier to explain away if need be. We do not believe the aggressors here – whichever Clan it is – wish actually to declare war.'

And Eva had no more questions. She left immediately with Jong-il.

10

Gravity or Guilt?

Diana was anxious to go; but she accepted that she had to wait until her sister was well away. So she went outside and sat in a recliner on the main lawn, whilst Berthezene took up a discrete position twenty metres away, with his gun out. She felt impatient, but she didn't feel afraid. Had being under constant guard blunted her capacity for feeling fear? She regarded the future blithely enough, certainly.

She saw Eva's plane zip away, skimming low over the tops of the olive trees with a muffled whiffling sound, leaving the orchard threshing behind it in its turbulence.

Gone.

It was late in the afternoon. Iago brought Diana a glass of iced water and a selection of fruit pieces. 'I saw Eva go.'

'Your parents do not want both of you in the air at the same time. It's only a precaution. When Miss Eva is on the ground at Tobruk and we have confirmation that the plasmaser car is ready, we will leave.'

'How long?' she asked.

'Not long,' he replied. 'Twenty minutes.'

'Can we be sure who has betrayed us?'

'We cannot be *sure*,' he said.

She sipped the water, and ate a piece of apple. Its texture was firmly spongy, wet, flavoursome. She had another piece. 'I know you think it was me,' she said, shortly, not looking him in the face. 'Contacting Anna, I mean. I know you think that's what has . . . brought this about. But you ought at least to entertain the *possibility* that somebody else is responsible. Quite apart from the servants we brought down here with us, there must be thirty people on this island who know we are here. Any of them could have betrayed us.'

'They are all dosed heavily with CRF. This makes them rather dopey, robs them of initiative, makes them rather emotional, all of which isn't ideal in terms of actually – you know: *running* the place. But it means they could never consciously *betray* you.'

'Unconsciously, perhaps? By accident?'

'We have the place locked down, as far as all forms of communication go. Nobody could accidentally betray the location. It would have had to be done deliberately.'

She thought about this for a while, and ate a particularly sweet piece of pear. How beautiful that taste! The piece was the colour, and shape and (for all she knew) the true flavour of the moon. She stared westward, over the sea. Clouds were starting to gather near the western horizon as the effortfully reddening sun bogged further and further down in the sky.

'What about those two policepersons? The ones who came in, after Leron was found murdered? Of course we had to follow the letter of the Ulanov law, and of course we could not deny access to properly constituted policeperson authority. But they weren't handservants, were they? They could easily have got a message to the others.'

Iago shook his head. 'They are also both dosed on CRF, perfectly loyal to the Clan.'

'Really?' Thinking back, they *had* seemed rather slow, initiativeless individuals. CRF would explain that. 'Doesn't it take a week or so to work on the brain,' she asked? 'Even at high dose?'

'Yes. But both the individuals in question were dosed in advance.'

'Goddess! Really? What – better safe than sorry, is it?'

He looked at her, seemed to be gauging her reaction, and then said. 'It hardly matters, now, Miss.' She knew he was referring to the message she had smuggled out. Once again she blushed. Then she tried to compose herself.

'I'm a fool,' she told him, feeling her own words stinging her – though they were the truth. 'Not yet sixteen – but that's no excuse. If I misjudged Anna . . . then, well—' She trailed off.

'You were in love,' said Iago, simply.

Diana's pressed her lips tight together, and clenched her hands, and stared back at him. But it was the truth. It was the idiotic and humiliating truth. It was the glorious, beautiful truth. She unclenched her hands and laid them on the table. Opened her mouth and sucked in a deep breath. 'Nice use of the past tense, there, Iago-go-go.'

'Love is a – complicating emotion.'

'Complicated, did you say? It is certainly that.'

'Complicating,' repeated Iago.

'We've a little time,' Diana said. 'Bring me up that hand-servant girl, Sapho.'

Iago looked sharply at her. 'Why?'

'I have some more questions for her.'

'I thought you said you had solved the mystery of the dead handservant?'

'So I have. But there are one or two little details that I haven't yet slotted into place in my mind. You know me, ear-gah. I like to tidy all the loose ends away. I like to cross the "t"s and dot the lower-case "j"s.'

Awkwardly, Iago bowed. 'I'll have her driven over here, Miss. Only—'

'Only what?'

'Only we can't take her *with* us, you know.'

'I don't intend to take her with us!' Diana retorted, genuinely startled at the suggestion.

Iago bowed again, and stepped away. Diana slumped deeper into her gel-chair and stared at the increasingly splendid western sky. Sunset opening the furnace door. All those gorgeous smelting colours of lava-red and flame-orange. The clouds crouched along the horizon, making their obeisance. She ate another piece of fruit.

Four minutes later a car appeared, buzzing along the coast road and dragging a dark comet-tail of dust behind it. Sunset light rubied off its windshield. It drove into the main compound and stopped two hundred metres away, and it discharged two people: a policeperson – zooming it with her bId Diana could see that it was Officer Avraam Kawa – and the handservant Sapho. He was supporting her upright by fitting his shoulder jigsaw-wise into her armpit. Together they made their way slowly across the lawn.

Iago had reappeared at her side: shimmered silently into place, like that Jeeves-butler chap in those funny stories. 'You understand, Miss,' he said, 'that we have a quarter-hour, no more.'

'It won't take long, Iago,' she replied.

Sapho, panting, was deposited in a chair opposite Diana.

Officer Kawa stood beside her, as if remaining upright in full g were the easiest thing in the world – which of course it was, to him. So Diana sent him back to the car and told him to drive off – 'we'll call you when we're ready'. And – after glancing at Iago – he went.

The buzz of the disappearing car mingled with the susurration of the surf.

'So, Sapho,' said Diana. 'Fruit?'

The servant looked at her, gap-eyed. 'Miss?'

'Try the pear. It's real pear, grown down here on Earth. Not like the stuff you get in a shanty globe, I'll wager.'

Cautiously Sapho reached out a trembling hand (was it trembling with gravity? Or guilt?), took a piece of pear, and manoeuvred it into her mouth.

'Nice?'

'Yes, Miss,' said the handservant. Then, looking unhappily up at Iago, and back at her mistress, she added: 'we have cats.'

'Cats?'

'In Smirr – my home globe, Miss. We have many mice, an infestation in fact. And so we have cats.'

Diana nodded. 'You think that's what I'm doing here? You think I'm a cat toying with a mouse? It's not that. Quite apart from anything we don't have time for that. I only have fifteen minutes—'

'Twelve minutes,' said Iago.

'Twelve minutes. I just wanted a quick chat, that's all.'

Away to the left, Berthezene moved from his position. She glanced over at him, wondering idly what had disturbed him. Following the direction of his gaze she saw Deño, standing on the coast road looking out to sea. They were getting ready to whisk her away, she supposed. Still, she had time.

'Here's something I found buried in the data,' she said. 'Your religious affiliation is Ra'allah.'

'Yes, Miss,' said Sapho.

'Tell me what that entails.'

She said: 'it's not a secret cult, Miss. It is not illegal. Information about our faith is freely available.'

'Tell me in your own words.'

Sapho looked to the setting sun. 'Ra is the sun, Miss,' she said. 'Allah is the God of the universe, the principle of law and compassion, of mercy of might. Mohammed was his prophet on Earth, but we do not live upon Earth. For us Ra is more than a prophet; more than an angel. Ra is the light of Allah, pouring into the cosmos.'

'Sun-worship?'

'We worship Ra'allah. We worship God, the only, and we recognise that the sun is the New Mecca, the New Metatron.'

'What of the Ulanovs?'

Sapho looked, sharply, at her. 'What of them, Miss? They are only human beings, like you and me, Miss. We do not worship them.'

'But isn't it the case,' she said, glancing at Iago, standing impassively beside her, 'that you consider the Ulanovs holy and blessed? Over and above obeying the Lex Ulanova and so on?'

'The Ulanovs,' said Sapho, slowly, 'have forbidden close approach to the Holy Face of the Sun.'

'They have made it illegal to fly inside the orbit of Venus, yes – but that's because they want to keep Mercury to themselves. For reasons of commercial exploitation, you know. It's pretty much solid iron, that world. A fantastically valuable resource.'

'We are not concerned with such things,' said Sapho.

'You know the Ulanovs have their own ships mining Mercury as we speak? Not to mention all the police cruisers and remotes necessary for maintaining the legal blockade. They fly within Venus's orbit. They don't bother you?'

'If some other power took over the Solar System,' said Sapho, 'and threw down the Ulanovs – do you think they would keep the space around the Holy face of the Sun so free of contamination? Relatively free, I mean, Miss, because you're right it is not a perfect emptiness. Only, I would say, things are better than they might be.'

Dia nodded slowly. 'I understand,' she said. 'But here's the thing: Leron wasn't a follower of Ra'allah, was he?'

Sapho immediately dropped her gaze. 'No, Miss.'

'What was he?'

'He worshipped Godravity. It is a terrible faith, the faith of bullies and pagans.'

Her bId fed her some details. 'Terrible because they deny your God?'

'They deny the *oneness* of God. They think of gravity as the divine principle in the universe: that only gravity gives shape and order to the cosmos. They think every particle of matter has the potential to be divine, but that when it accumulates beyond a certain point it acquires literal godhood. They worship black holes – the devourers – as the true gods, and this means that they worship *ten million* gods. They believe *all* these devil objects will form one giant God at the end of time, and He will be called Fenrir, and will swallow us all. It is a savage religion, Miss. Leron believed that only *force* gave shape, order and meaning to nature. He believed force to be beautiful.' All this came out in a long, rapidly-spoken monologue, and after she had finished speaking she looked flushed and unhappy.

'Did he force himself on *you*, Sapho?'

'Miss,' she assented. She closed her eyes, and opened her mouth. Her lower lip was shivering with grief, or perhaps just under the unforgiving tug of gravity.

'It seems a strange thing,' mused Diana, 'for two such antithetical religions to occupy the same shanty bubble. Usually – as I understand it – each bubble contains one community, and one faith. It's not as if there's a great deal of space for anything more.'

'Leron and his family came from another globe, Miss,' said Sapho, pulling herself a little straighter in her chair. 'It was destroyed by a police cruiser, and they took refuge with us.'

'Good of you to give them a home.'

'Ra'allah rewards compassion,' said Sapho. 'And besides: they paid.'

'Why did a police cruiser burst their home globe?'

'Because,' said Sapho, glancing up at Iago. 'Because they are rebels and vile people. They do not respect the authority of the Ulanovs, as we do. They plot revolution. They are friends of Jack Glass, they are followers of the principle of political *force majeure*.'

'What a curious thing!' said Diana, also looking up at the standing Iago. 'For a man who personally vetted these twenty handservants – to allow through an individual with such criminal and dangerous political views?'

'Two minutes, Miss,' said Iago, impassively.

'You were aware, Iago, that the deceased Leron was a followed of Godravity?'

'Of course I was, Miss Diana,' said Iago. 'Sapho, here, exaggerates the revolutionary leanings of that particular faith. Some followers of Godravity harbour terroristical views, I concede. But most don't.'

'Still – to recruit handservants from a shanty bubble containing two competing faiths, each at war with the other,' said Diana. She eyed him knowingly. 'Odd, no?'

Iago was looking over towards the sea, where Deño could be seen, still standing. '*Less* than two minutes, Miss,' he said.

'Sapho,' said Dia, turning her attention back to the handservant. 'I'm afraid in a moment I must leave. But I want you to understand something. I know that Leron sexually assaulted you.'

Sapho looked levelly back. 'Miss.'

'I believe it. I am going to do what I can to have your punishment kept to a minimum.'

'My – punishment, Miss?' Sapho faltered.

'Killing a human being is still killing a human being, even if the human being you killed was vile. And the Lex Ulanova cannot be circumvented, of course. But I think I *can* use my influence to have the sentence extenuated. It seems my influence is, um, um, on the *grow*.'

Sapho looked at her with her tired eyes. For a moment, perhaps, she hovered on the edge of denying everything. But the moment passed. She lowered her gaze again, and spoke in an exhausted voice. 'The punishment for murder is death,' she said. 'Death is beyond extenuation.'

'Not necessarily. With extenuation you will instead get imprisonment, I think,' said Diana. 'He had raped you before. I assume he was trying to rape you again when you killed him?'

The setting sun was shining across her face, smoothing out the irregularities of colour and giving the whole a wholesome ruddiness. Despite the grim shapes into which gravity was sagging her face, she looked almost beautiful. 'Yes,' she said.

Diana said: 'I looked around the store-room – where it happened – a couple of times.' She was speaking for Iago's benefit, although still looking at Sapho. 'At first I was distracted by a foolish theory that the murderer had activated a gardening robot to commit the crime; but of course that wasn't it. And although I ignored it at first, the crucial detail did stick in my head. I couldn't stop thinking about it. The way the walls were adorned with *fins* – vanes – stubby little wings. I couldn't immediately think why, and I didn't initially pay it much attention. Not being used to them, you see. Not needing them upland. But it came to me in the car yesterday. I knew what those fins, vanes, wings *were*. They are called *shelves*. People down here use them to store things on. You can put something on a shelf, you see, and gravity will keep it there. You can store light things upon them. Or heavy things.'

Iago was looking at her, but his eyes were unfocused. Checking something on his bId.

'Sapho,' said Diana. 'Leron chased you, didn't he?'

'He wished me to do certain things to him, sexual things, whilst he lay on his back,' said Sapho. 'I did not want to, and he grew angry. So he came after me and I ran away – though the running was hard, and we both moved stilted and slow, like through water, like in a nightmare, because of the gravity.'

'You ran into the storeroom.'

'Yes, Miss.'

'And he almost caught you – but you scrambled up the carapace of one of the robots stored there.'

'I wished to evade him, Miss.'

'It must have been hard, in the gravity! But somehow you managed it – a foot on the robot elbow, another on its shoulder, and then up onto the shelf fixed into the wall. Was he too worn out, gravity-tired, to climb up after you?'

'Yes, Miss.'

'So I suppose he stood there – taunted you. Told you to come down?'

'Yes, Miss.'

Diana smiled. 'Perhaps we should tell the authorities that what happened next was an accident. It could easily have *been* an accident, you know.'

'It was not an accident. I saw the hammer at the far end of the shelf, and so I scurried along – like a mouse. And below, Leron lolloped to follow me. He was very angry. He was calling up to me, and puffing, and wheezing with the effort of doing so. He told me: remember what Petero and I did to you in the dizzy dummies? Remember how that hurt, and made blood came out of you? I shall do *worse* to you now, he said.'

'So you killed him?'

'I got between the wall and where the hammer was, and pushed my arms out. I had to judge it just so, Miss. It was not easy. But Leron was standing below me, and I got the heavy chuck of the hammer to fall straight down – and it made a *thoc* sound, like a butcher's cleaver striking a rack of raw meat. The weight of it broke through his skull; for a life without gravity makes bones weaker. It felled him; his knees bent and his torso went straight down, and then keeled back and his legs kicked out. The hammer fell away and clanged on the floor. A great deal of blood came out of Leron's head – but it didn't turn to droplets as

212

it normally does. Instead it formed a flat plate of dark red, and swelled on the floor like a tumour.'

'Yes.'

'I climbed back the way I came,' said Sapho. 'I was crying and shaking, Miss, and in my heart I felt the mixture of glee and *fear*. I stumbled back through to my room, and fell on the bed. But it was not long before the other handservants went through. It was not the yelling that attracted their attention, you see. The yelling was just Leron enjoying himself, and the others thought it best to leave him alone. It was not the yelling that made them go through; it was the suddenness of the silence.'

'Iago,' said Diana. 'Surely my two minutes were up ages ago? Shouldn't we be on our way?'

Iago looked down at her. 'Things are considerably worse than we realised, Miss,' he said, gravely. 'I'm afraid we must change our plans.'

Diana read his expression, and her heart seized sharply in her chest. 'Eva?' she asked.

'Alive,' he replied, at once. 'Free and unhurt. But the Tobruk Plasmaser Elevator has been sabotaged.'

Diana went straight to her bId, and caught the data as Iago sent it to her. She saw the twin towers structure of the Tobruk Plasmaser housing; and the yellow desert, and the blue sky. The technology was simple enough: the descent of the down-car, buoyed on a semi-aligned column of plasma, forced the material down into one side of the large Ц-shaped structure of the main housing. The plasma was manipulated there via a fusion-level containment field, and fed out up through the other funnel to lift the up-car. As a fully laden car brought passengers or cargo down from orbit on one side, another car was pushed up by the counterforce on the other. It was so efficient a system that only a very little extra energy needed to be generated at ground level to boost the upward plasma column sufficiently to lift any Elevator car clean into orbit. But the pressure and heat inside the main housing was very high, which meant that the structures were particularly vulnerable to attack, and very difficult to repair once breached.

Diana's bId showed her the damage. There was an irregular oval hole in the flank of the main housing, with blackened flower-petal sections bent outward – a great poll of vitrified sand. Craft buzzed through the air. Figures were visible on the ground.

'Eva is still grounded?'

'Yes, Miss,' said Iago. He waved Berthezene over towards them. 'I'm afraid this may well be war, after all. It's a foolish play, by whichever Clan is responsible, and in the longer run I am confident it will work in our favour. But for now we must get you away from the island. The initial twelve-hour window was much too optimistic. They could strike here at any moment. If it *is* war, then all bets are off.'

Diana got to her feet, feeling a little dazed (although maybe that was because the blood fled from her head to her legs as she stood). The handservant, Sapho, was blinking and looking around her.

'I have notified a policeperson to reclaim Miss Sapho,' said Iago, as Berthezene arrived, breathing heavily.

'What's going to happen to me, Miss?' Sapho asked, in a strained voice.

'For now,' Iago answered her, 'nothing. Your confession here is a private matter. The police will return you to custody. At the moment larger matters are ongoing. When things have settled your fate will be decided.'

'Is there really going to be a war?' Diana asked.

'War will be brisk,' said Iago, confidently. 'Clan Yu have over-reached themselves badly here. I'm surprised, actually, at their strategy. If we can keep you two alive, I can't see any way for them to win. But we can worry about that later. The most important thing right now is to get you to safety.'

'We need to—' Berthezene began to say. But Iago stopped him, raising one hand. He pointed, and they all looked. Dominico Deño was coming towards them; and he was not alone.

'Things are either considerably better or much worse than I thought,' said Iago.

Walking across the grass, with a characteristically unfathomable expression on her face, was Ms Joad.

11

Ms Joad Again

'Good evening, my dear girl,' said Ms Joad. 'And look at us! All standing about on the ground in the open air, as if gravity were *nothing* to us! All except this scrap of a thing – who are you, dear?'

'This is one of my handservants,' said Dia, looking from Berthezene to Iago.

'Slouching in a chair?' tutted Ms Joad. 'You treat your servants with more latitude than I do mine. You stay here,' she told Sapho. 'Your mistress and I are going inside the house to have a chat.' She started off towards the main entrance.

Stalking after her on her crawlipers, Dia caught up with her. 'What are you doing here, Ms Joad? Not that it isn't lovely to see you, but your timing is unlucky. There are rumours of war – the plasmaser elevator at Tobruk has just been . . .'

'I know, my dear,' said Ms Joad, offhand. 'I know all about that. Come inside and we'll chat about it. I'm really most *excited* to hear your version of events.'

Dia glanced back. Berthezene, Deño and Iago were coming with her; and Sapho, still sitting in the chair by the table, a plate of fruit pieces beside her, sat. 'Should we just . . . leave her there?'

'A policeperson is on his way for her,' said Iago. 'She's not going anywhere. The appearance of Ms Joad is a much more important matter.' He looked worn.

'It *is*, isn't it, though?' said Ms Joad. 'Come inside – after you, my dear.'

Diana stepped through the main door. In her mind, she ran through the possible reasons the Ulanovs might have to send their sinister deputy down to Korkura not once, but *twice* in as many days. Would it benefit *them* to sabotage one of the Argent's plasmaser elevators? Surely not! Presumably that attack had nothing to do with the Ulanovs.

Iago followed. And behind him came Ms Joad. As had happened the last time she had visited, the main door squealed and shook as she stepped through it. Berthezene was right behind her – the alarm sounded at his weapon too, of course, but he had the gun out and began clearing it as an accredited weapon with the House AI. The alarm continued sounding.

'My weapon,' said Ms Joad, with exactly the same tone of fictional surprise she had used the last time.

Deño came through, and the door complained yet again. He brought out his own gun for the House AI to check. Berthezene had the smartcloth pouch in his hand. 'Your gun, Ms Joad?' he said.

'Must I?' she drawled, bringing the plasmetal pistol into view from beneath her shift.

'I'm afraid so, ma'am,' said Berthezene, holding the pouch towards her.

'*You* don't have to undergo this demeaning procedure, Mr Iago,' Joad observed. 'Because you are unarmed. Isn't it odd for a bodyguard to go about unarmed?'

'I'm no bodyguard, Ma'am' said Iago.

'No, that's right, isn't it. You're the *Tutor*. I might ask what you *tute*, as it were. But I'm not sure you even know yourself. No,' she said, regarding the proffered smartcloth bag. 'I don't think so.'

'It's mandatory, I'm afraid, Miss' said Berthezene.

'Really? Well if I must . . .' She held the gun out, and with a quick flick of her wrist discharged it. The report was no louder than a pair of hands clapping together, but the effect on Berthezene was dramatic.

The round went into his right cheek, *snik*, and it left a little black-red dent there. At the same time it came out of the back-left of his skull with a louder *thunk*, and the rainfall sound of many droplets spattering against the wall behind. A conic spray of red and grey sprouted from the back of his head, a brief ponytail of matter. He jumped backwards. His eyes were full of surprise. Conceivably they were full of pain, for pain *is* a surprising thing. But, really, he looked more astonished than anything else. His jaw swung open, but no sound emerged. A half-instant later he banged hard against the wall behind him, and the spectral red ponytail was gone, and his arms flew out, and he slid down to the ground.

Diana shrieked in astonishment and alarm.

Iago took one step forward and stopped. Deño's weapon was aimed directly at him. Aimed, Dia saw straight away, *at him* and not at Miss Joad at all. Deño! Her mind was skilled at putting pieces together, quickly and under pressure, but even an idiot could have seen *this* bigger picture. The attack was not coming from either the Clan Aparaceido or the Clan Yu. Diana's secret love-message to Anna had *not* betrayed their location (and even in the middle of these terrible new developments she felt a twinge of relief at this). Things were much worse. It was the Ulanovs themselves. The Ulanovs themselves were moving against Clan Argent. Diana thought, rapidly: were her MOHmies safe? Were they seizing Eva right now? Was it all over?

Her mind was doing that human-weakness thing: repeating *there must be some mistake* over and over.

Ms Joad peered at the corpse of Berthezene, propped slovenly in at the coign of floor and wall. Red was tracking down the wall in tendrils. Then she spoke: '*he's* unarmed.' She meant: Iago. Then she spoke again: 'take him down – don't kill him, though. I'll want to talk to him later.'

Iago, began to speak: 'Dominico, wait—'. But Deño fired,

shooting him in the right foot. He hit him square in the middle of the foot, the round blasting it to shreds. Iago danced cumbrously, rotated through a quarter-turn, and fell. He hit the floor with a louder clatter than Berthezene had done, clutching his wounded leg, his face white as ash. But he didn't cry out. His lips were tight. His breathing was suddenly loud as cicadas.

He was down.

And now Deño's gun was aimed at Diana's chest. She couldn't help herself; her heart started beating like a pulsar, hard and quick, and the adrenaline prickled through her skin and made her scalp fidget and buzz.

'You're not ours,' Dia said, to Deño. 'You belong to the Ulanovs.'

'My dear girl,' said Ms Joad, removing her gaze from Berthezene's body and stepping over to stand in front of her. 'Don't we all? And of course we *have* people everywhere. You'd expect nothing less.'

'Are you arresting me?' Diana asked.

'The *legal* route?' said Ms Joad, smiling broadly. 'Gracious.' She tucked her firearm away and folded her hands together in front of her. 'The stakes are *very* high, my dear; and sometimes events move too fast for all that . . . rigmarole. We had forces waiting for your sister at Tobruk, but your people blew the main building and so got away. But – really. Where are they going to go?' She shook her head. 'We will have her very soon. And although your parents have made you so as to be resistant to the various truth pharmakons and interrogations drugs, we can always fall back on older-fashioned modes of questioning. Can't we? I think that if I torture your MOHsister to death in front of you, you *will* tell me what I want to know.'

In Dia's head: *I can't believe this is happening! This can't be happening!*

Dia's heart thrummed faster still. She knew that Ms Joad was capable of this; and she knew she would not be able to bear it. 'There's no need for that,' she said, trying to keep her voice from burbling with fear. 'I'll answer any questions I can. I'll do it now if you like.'

'Excellent!' Ms Joad held up one finger. 'No jousting, though.'

'Jousting?'

'Game playing. None of that! Your brain is a thing of wonder, certainly, and *could* be very useful to us. But the rest of your body is nothing more than a machine for generating agony for you, and I am happy to activate *that* machine. Oh! Oh, if you try to play *games* with me, I'll demonstrate what I mean.'

Despite her fear, Diana's heart was returning to a normal rhythm as the initial flush of adrenaline diluted in her bloodstream. Her legs ached. 'I understand,' she said. 'May I sit down? This gravity is oppressive.'

'You may not,' said Ms Joad, with a wicked smile. 'Here's my first question: where is it?'

The blood in Diana's ears was thrumming. 'That is a rather general question,' she said.

'Deño, aim your weapon at Miss Diana's knee, if you will be so kind.' Deño obliged, swivelling his aim downward. 'I shall ask you again, my dear, and you will either answer me, or my-man Dominico will discharge a round into your knee. It will be extraordinarily painful I assure you! – ask your butler, there, Mr Iago, sprawled on the floor! And we only shot him in the *foot*! A knee is much worse. Still, you will need to be stronger than your pain, because I will ask one further time. And if you do not answer me, I shall have Deño turn you over to shoot you in the *back* of the knee. The first shot, entering the patella directly, will drill a hole in the bone and kick out some flesh behind. This is very painful, but the patella would be salvageable. The second, though, would blow your kneecap to shards and spit them bloody all across the floor. You'll lose the leg. Do you believe I would do this to you?'

'Absolutely I believe it,' said Diana.

'*Very* well. Where *is* it?'

The strange part of all this was that Diana was beginning to feel *sleepy*. It wasn't that she was fearless: on the contrary, the fear was an acute, throbbing pressure in her chest. She was breathing shallowly, her forehead tickling with sweat. But nonetheless, the urge simply to go to sleep possessed her. *Bad idea*, she told herself. Berthezene's body was right there, as if she needed further proof that Ms Joad was murderously genuine. Iago's body, wounded but still alive, was somewhere – she couldn't see him, he must be behind her. To fall asleep would only enrage Joad. The sleep would be short-lived. And yet the urge was *there*.

For Diana, of course, sleeping was something she associated particularly with problem solving. And perhaps there was nothing more to it than that: presented, as she was, with an acute problem – answer Joad's question or be mutilated and crippled! – her mind was trying to retreat into its habitual problem-solving mode. It would not do her any good, of course. She had no idea what the question was asking, let alone what the answer might be. Where is *what*? *Keep awake*, she told herself. To stave off the sleep she pictured to herself the projectile leaving the end of Deño's gun, and speeding rapidly as a photon to her leg. She saw, in her mind's eye, the circular sun-face of her knee cap shatter under the force of the blow. She visualised it exploding out in every direction in a blast of super-new light. She thought of the acronym.

'FTL,' she said, with a wobbly voice.

'Exactly,' said Ms Joad. 'But *where* is it?'

There were several things she could do; but none of them were going to be any use. Saying she didn't know – though it was the truth – would cost her a kneecap. Inventing an answer might spare her, at least temporarily, but then she would be required to name a plausible hiding place, and she had no idea what that might be. How could FTL be in any one place, anyway? Was Joad asking for a working interstellar spaceship, parked in the asteroid belt? Or a set of equations and technical specifications on a datachip? Would an answer of the 'inside the head of the such-and-such a person' type satisfy her? Diana couldn't think of any likely-sounding lie along those lines. So she opened her mouth to speak with her mind completely blank, and when the words came out they surprised her as much as anyone. In the corner of her eye she saw the upward motion of an object. But she wasn't looking there. She was staring right into Joad's eyes. And she said: 'I've come to the conclusion, Ms Joad, that I don't *like* you very much.'

She braced herself. Or tried to. How does one brace oneself, anyway?

Hell.

There was a slapping sound, and the gun discharged. Deño's aim delivered the round into the floor with a resonant *thud*. Diana realised, a beat later: somebody had slapped Deño's arm down, just before he fired.

Then everything happened very quickly, a staccato succession of actions. First Deño's head clicking back, his chin pointing at the ceiling, and a vivid splurt of red; then Deño's whole torso spinning on its right foot, rotating about and then backing towards Ms Joad. Ms Joad was expressionless; but she *was* reaching into her holster for her weapon. Deño's was glaring at the ceiling, red gushing down his front. His lurching body collided with Ms Joad. She staggered, went onto her back foot, and Iago was there – right in front of her. Diana couldn't see *how* he had got there. He seemed to appear from nowhere, standing upright. He punched forward, aiming his fist at Joad's sternum. His fist went in, and when it came back blood was gurgling from Ms Joad's chest.

For the first time, Ms Joad's expression betrayed something less than self-assurance. She looked incommoded and angry. Her eyes were on Diana's. 'I shall see you,' she said, '*again*.' But on 'again' blood bubbled from her mouth, and the word was half drowned, and she fell to the left and hit the floor with a crash.

Diana breathed in, and then out.

Her heart was galloping.

She breathed in again. Out again.

She looked down at the floor. Three human beings, sprawled over the white stone. A patch of oily-looking red liquid was expanding across the flags. The borderline of this growing area came close to her shoes, and she stepped backward to avoid getting them dirty.

Diana looked up. Iago was standing there. The lack of a right foot was a surreal sight: the leg ended in a flange just below the ankle. But there was no blood.

'Iago, you do not have a gun,' she said.

'Indeed not, Miss Diana,' he said, stepping over the legs of Deño's supine form and taking her hand. His stride was rendered uneven by the lack of the foot, but he seemed to be able to put his weight squarely on the bottom of the severed stump without discomfort.

'The door would have registered it if you had had a weapon,' Diana repeated, a little stupidly. Then she said: 'you are lucky the bullet missed *all* the blood vessels in your foot.' But as she said it, she realised it was a foolish thing to say – she saw that it did not in the least explain the state of affairs.

'We must leave at once,' Iago said, his voice perfectly level.

A fuller understanding of what had happened was just dawning upon Diana. 'What did you do?' she cried out. 'You killed Deño! My goddess, you actually *killed* him!'

'Would you rather him shoot you in the leg?'

'Leg,' she said, staring again, with a new kindling sense of horror, at the absence at the end of Iago's leg. 'Leg! Leg!'

'As you can see, my legs *are* artificial, Miss Diana,' Iago said. 'Both of them. Having a chunk knocked off the end of one is inconvenient, but the machinery still seems to work.' And Diana's problem-solving mind went: so *that* was how he was able to stand around so insouciantly in this crushing gravity.

It hardly mattered now.

She gulped, gulped again. 'Goddess. Oh, oh, Iago,' said Diana, taking another deep breath, and looking at the bodies. 'You struck them down. How did you strike them both down?'

But she could see the answer to this question. In his spare hand he was holding a knife.

'Why didn't the door register that as a weapon?' she said, pointing. 'Surely it would register a metal knife as easily as a metal gun.'

'A metal one, yes,' said Iago. 'But this knife is made from glass. Come along, Miss.'

12

Flight

They went back outside, into a fragrant Korkuran dusk. Sapho – the handservant – was still sitting in the chair. She looked up at them, startled, as they came out.

'Everything is different now,' said Iago, fitting his knife back into its sheath. 'This isn't inter-Clan rivalry. The *Ulanovs themselves* are coming after you. We need to get upland, and we can't trust *any* of the Argent facilities. And we certainly can't trust any of the other MOHclans; they'll be rubbing their hands with glee at the opportunities opening up for them. This is a very serious state of affairs, I'm afraid.'

'Are my MOHmies alright? Is Eva alright?'

'We must trust them to look after themselves. Right now we need to get away. We'll go to Al Anfal; I have friends there. Once we're there, we'll figure out a way to get back upstairs. Come along.'

'She comes with us,' said Diana.

Iago looked at the handservant, seated, staring up at them. 'No she doesn't.'

'Yes she does.'

'She will slow us down. She is safer here.'

'Clearly she's not!'

'Quite apart from anything else,' said Iago, grouchily, 'she *is* a murderer.'

'Oh, Iago,' she said. 'We both know that's not true.'

Iago was looking shrewdly at her. 'Yes you're good,' he conceded. 'Even though I'm guessing you don't know the whole story.'

'Indeed not,' she admitted. 'I couldn't, for instance, have answered Ms Joad's terrible question – back there. Could you?'

He shook his head.

'She comes with us,' Diana said again.

Iago gave up fighting it. 'Alright. Come along we *three*.' He helped the handservant out of her seat. The three of them made their way through the thickening darkness, halting and slow. By the time they cleared the lawn dusk had thickened into actual night. The house was black behind them. Away across the bay, prickles of illumination adorned the town. But the shadows swallowed everything up.

Stars were visible overhead.

They got in amongst the shadows of the olive grove, where they rested for a moment. But no sooner did they stop than, behind them, two cradles of light and noise were lowered through the evening sky down onto the lawn in front of the house.

Hiding behind a tree, Diana saw the two craft settle into the turf. Their doors opened, and a half-dozen strong-limbed agents, or soldiers, or policepersons (or *whatever* they were) dashed out and ran straight into the house.

'Quietly,' hissed Iago into her ear, putting a hand on her shoulder; 'but *quickly*.'

They all three slipped through the olive forest, and came out the other side behind a low wall of uncemented plates of slate-stone. Getting beyond this obstacle was not easy, despite its modest dimensions, but they managed it. Iago had to help Sapho up onto the top, and down on the far side. Puff, pant, puff. The black-purple sky. On the far side they crossed a road, the tarmac warm, still hoarding the day's heat. Dia's crawlipers clacked softly. Iago limped rapidly on, his right arm helping Sapho stay upright. Then they were across, and making their way over a wide downward-sloping field of lavender. The scent of the dark stalks was very strong, a clean, beautiful fragrance. Overhead the stars were distilling into full clarity. The spilled glitter of the milky way. The million cursor-points of bright stars. Somewhere in all that profusion was the single Champagne Supernova upon which Eva had been working. And this thought sent a small pang through Diana's breast. Would her MOHsister ever finish that work?

Behind them, something whooshed up into the air – one of the two craft that had landed outside the main house. They all turned; the machine, pricking with illumination and humming as it flew, was hovering above the house. A megaphone of light appeared at the underbelly, swivelling from left to right as the authorities swept the ground, looking for them. It rolled towards the coast, away from them.

'We need to get off this island,' panted Diana.

'Agreed,' said Iago.

On the far side of the lavender field was another road, and Iago led them a hundred metres or so along it before turning off into a much larger area of forest. These trees were much taller than olives; and the scent of pine, fierce in the nostrils though pleasant, was very strong. It was now so dark that they could see nothing, and moved with arms outstretched, passing themselves from tree trunk to tree trunk. The ground beneath their feet was spongy with pineneedles. For what seemed to Diana a very long time they passed, painstakingly, through this blind environment.

Finally they came into a clearing; stars visible again above them. Iago pulled a fabric web off a small flycar, and keyed the door open.

'I didn't know you'd hidden a flitter here,' said Diana.

They all clambered inside. The smell of plastic. Iago closed the door, and put the inside light on – eye-stinging yellow. It was a cupboard-sized space; there was barely room inside for all three of them. 'When we actually get going, I'll have to drive without lights,' Iago said; 'and low. It may be a little hair-raising, I warn you.'

'How far will this toy take us?' Diana asked as she fastened her clenchbelt. In the pale lemon-coloured light of the flycar's cabin, Sapho was sitting awkwardly, hugging herself and looking wide-eyed. 'You need to fix your belt – I'll show you,' said Diana.

'Thank you, Miss,' the handservant said, sitting passively as Dia fixed her clenchbelt for her. 'What you said – back at the house, Miss?'

'What did I say?'

'The gentleman said I was a murderer, and you said, no.' Sapho looked to Iago, who was booting up the interface from the driving seat. 'He was right, Miss. I am a murderer.'

'It's more complicated than that, Sapho,' Diana said. At that moment, Iago extinguished the interior lights, and Dia felt the unpleasant stretching sensation in her gut as the flycar rose into the night.

'Where did you say we're going, Iago?' she asked, into the dark.

Iago rendered all the walls transparent, like a tourist bark, the better to be able to navigate by the faint starlight. Diana saw, indistinctly, his silhouette, blacker against this dark ground.

'We're going,' he replied, 'to Al Anfal Li'llah. It's beyond Turque.'

'Will this car get us there?'

'No, it's too far. But it will get us off the island, which is the more pressing concern.'

They swished away through the air, flying so low that the tops of the pine trees spanked the bottom of the car with intermittent, shuddery, resonant slaps. Then they were clear of the forest, and passed down a long sloping trajectory that missed the lip of the coastline by a metre or less. The transparency of the flycar walls was a disconcerting thing, adding to Diana's sense of exposure and vulnerability; but at least it gave them a superb view of this portion of the island. Many lights were on at the main house now, and one of the Ulanovs' crafts still parked on the lawn. The other was visible in the sky, away to the east, moving meticulously forward, sweeping its searchlight back and forth like a pendulum.

In the bay west of the island a large ship was anchored, balanced on the gleaming constellation of its own lit reflection. The ship had not been there before. 'Is it Ulanov?' Diana said as they passed, low and quiet, half a thousand metres away from the ship.

'I presume so,' said Iago.

They left the ship behind them and Iago flew the car round the headland. Diana's bId buzzed with a call waiting, and before she thought what she was doing she answered it.

There, shining right in the middle of the car, was Ms Joad. 'My dear girl,' she said. 'What do you think you're *doing*?'

'Turn that off,' Iago instructed her.

'Don't trust *him*!' said Joad. 'Don't you know who he *is*?'

'I know!' retorted Diana.

'Well how can you know *who he is* and then still trust him? How can you do anything apart from run in terror?'

'I should trust *you*?' returned Diana, a flush of anger overriding her common sense. 'You were going to cripple me!'

'Nonsense. You're much too valuable intact – *that* was just playacting. And look at me now, poor lonely Ms Joad with one collapsed lung! But *you*, my dear, you are currently fleeing into the night with the single most dangerous man in the entire solar *system*! Come back, and here's the deal: Clan Argent to retain their position of eminence at the Ulanovs' right hand, yourself in the *as*-it-were throne, whatever your sister might expect – in return we take Mr Glass into custody. Simple as that.'

'Diana,' said Iago. 'Please turn that off.'

'You will regret—' Ms Joad began to say, in her pleasantly modulated voice, as Diana severed the connection.

'They'll know our heading now,' said Iago, as he rolled the car into a tight turn. Diana's stomach heaved and yawed. 'It makes getting away more of a gamble.'

'I'm sorry,' said Diana. 'I shouldn't have answered it.'

'No,' agreed Iago. 'You shouldn't.'

Diana felt the sting of this rebuke. 'It was an automatic reaction.'

'I'm afraid you'll have to close down your bId,' said Iago. 'It is compromised. If you use it at all, for even the most trivial reason, the Ulanovs will locate you. Can I ask you please to lock it down and erase access?'

Diana was going to object that this would leave her entirely and literally isolated – she hadn't done without bId since she was a toddler. But there were no grounds to argue. Iago was correct. So she closed it all down, and tickled the erase codes from their reluctant caches.

Being bIdless magnified her sense of vulnerability.

She asked Sapho if she were fitted with a bId, but of course she had nothing like that: she was only a servant, and a shanty bubble kid, after all.

They flew on, Iago keeping close to the coast and finally striking out towards open sea. After twenty minutes or so, Diana began to believe that they had indeed slipped away.

She slept fitfully, sitting up, her head at an awkward angle. When she woke her neck was sore, but the sky to the east was glorious with the colour of oranges. Sapho was snoring, her body in harness but her head lolling forward. Iago was still at the controls. 'Are you alright?' she asked.

'Yes,' he said. 'We will stop soon, and I'll find a craft suitable for the longer journey.'

'My mouth is dry,' she reported. 'And I need to relieve my bladder.'

'A contradictory state of affairs, it might be thought.'

'Does this car not have facilities?'

'It's too small for such luxuries, I'm afraid. A short-hop model only. Another ten minutes,' he added, 'and I'll come down.'

They passed over a dun-coloured landscape, sharp-edged

escarpments and inky hollows, as the eastern light slowly gathered itself ready for another dawn. It wasn't clear where Iago was going until the last minute, when they popped over a ridge and landed in the yard of a large farmhouse. This consisted of a lead-coloured, seven-storey barn, with a star-and-crescent logo painted upon it. Four agri-pros were parked outside – the place was very evidently fully automated. Nevertheless a human being was standing in the yard waiting for them. 'How did she know to be here?' Diana asked as they touched down.

'He. And he knew because I called ahead.'

'Why haven't you erased your bId? It will be just as compromised as mine.'

'The system I'm carrying,' he said, 'is not bId.'

Iago opened the door. They roused Sapho, and all three clambered stiffly from the car into the cool predawn. Iago went over and spoke to the stranger, as Diana and Sapho stretched their limbs. 'Where are we, Miss?' Sapho asked. 'I've no more idea than you, Sapho,' Dia replied.

Iago returned. 'My friend has brought a larger craft,' he said. 'But we've no time to hang about.'

The three of them went round the corner of the barn to find a proper-sized machine; stealth aerials all over it. Iago opened the side and all three climbed in. Diana made first use of the toilet cubicle, with Sapho going in after. Iago was priming and launching several dozen decoy drones in several directions. Diana explored the small kitchen and dug out some supplies. She drank some sugarjuice, and ate a strawberry muffin. It was a little stale but took the edge off her hunger. Iago came back, took a long draft of water, and went back up to the cabin. Diana had to chivvy Sapho into breaking her fast.

Dawn was heating the bar of the eastern horizon red hot by the time they were airborne. They flew straight east and the air clarified and brightened all around them.

*

Diana had never travelled in quite so primitive a craft before. The engine made a continuous sequence of crunching noises, as if its business was breaking its own innards. Small shard-puffs of smoke came out of its exhaust. Diana pondered what manner of engine it could possibly be. Something from the bronze age, maybe; something from the time of Homer. Something.

Sunlight the colour and thickness of honey.

From their elevated perspective the landscape approached cartographic simplification: interlocking shapes of light and dark. Innumerable hexagon-fields of wheat. A stumpy range of half-mountains passed below them, and on the far side of that a wide expanse of ash-coloured crops – edible cotton, she guessed.

They approached an eastern coastline. Northward and southward the sea bunched itself like blue cloth into a great many ruffles and pleats. They overflew the beach and left the land wholly behind. A great slab of sea lay immobile beneath them.

They flew for a long time over the sea.

The sun was high in the sky by the time the continental coastline appeared beneath them: Turque, and beyond that presumably the realm of Al Anfal Li'llah where they were going. The mountains came bulging up as they approached; flanks marbled with brown and black, and summits capped in great panes of ash-blonde snow. Diana thought to herself: the sun is always true north, irrespective of the vagaries of mundane electro-magnetic orientations. The sun is always at the bottom of the well. The sun is the one true point in all this uncertainty.

She spent some time gazing at the endlessly renewing sky; and then watching the pattern of shadows the sun inked upon the landscape. The mountains below them were a mode of monotony. Nothing could grow upon them. Most food came from the uplands, of course, from the innumerable Facs and globes. Some luxury products, and some subsistence crops, were grown below. But a large portion of the lowlands were lying fallow. Or were giving way to desertification.

She left the sun, white as paper, and the sky, blue as water, and closed her eyes. Sleep didn't come. Instead the ghostly shapes of her MOHmies loomed alarmingly, and she had to open her eyes. Here was the cabin. She put her hand on the wall beside her, and she could feel it shivering.

She was crying.

This would never do.

So she sat down and told herself: she had no reason to believe her MOHmies were dead. She had no evidence that Eva was dead, or even that she had been taken into Ulanov custody. She had to show herself as somebody possessing the character to endure adversity and triumph over it. Crying would not do.

So, to distract herself from her own self-pity, she went and sat next to Iago. The view from the cockpit was the same as the view from the cabin windows: parti-coloured mountains; valleys in which giant firs loomed minaret-like over the canopies of regular trees. The same sky, the inescapable sun. The sun was grief. Grief was as hot and as unavoidable as the sun. It is what we all rotate our lives about, whether we realise it or not.

'So,' she said. 'You are Jack Glass.'

He hummed for a while: a tune she did not recognise, four notes the same followed by a downward melody with a trill in the middle. Then he said: 'some people call me that.'

'Joad said it wasn't your real name.'

'The whole concept of real names,' Iago said, 'isn't a terribly coherent one, I think.'

'And you have killed people. Thousands of people!'

'Millions,' he said, glancing at her. 'If you believe some stories.'

She thought about this. 'You haven't killed millions of people.'

'No.'

'Or thousands?'

'No.'

'You have killed people, though?'

'You yourself just witnessed me putting an end to Dominico Deño's life. That was a shame. I liked him. He and I played Go together.'

'And I saw you stab Ms Joad. But you didn't kill her.'

'I could have done that better, I agree. But nobody's perfect.'

'Do my MOHmies know who you are?'

'They do.'

'They hired you anyway? You expect me to believe that they were happy to hire you to work in close proximity to their daughters?'

'They hired me not despite who I was, but because of it. They paid for these legs, and arranged for my face to be surgically reconfigured. They know what I've done and why I've done it. The plain fact is the Clan Argent and I share a similar goal; and that protecting you and Eva is part of achieving that goal.'

'The Ulanovs,' Diana said.

'Exactly. Their downfall. And, as for placing me near you and your MOHsister – well, I do have certain skills. As I've just demonstrated with Ms Joad and her agent. Though *skills* is a tendentious way of putting it, I suppose. I'd say a skill ought to be something constructive. What I've just done is hardly that.'

'My knees thank you,' she said. 'At any rate.'

And he smiled.

'I can't believe my MOHmies could have been planning something so – seismic.'

'You can't believe it? Or you can't believe you weren't in on it?'

Diana stared out of the window. 'I'm not even sixteen,' she said.

'Indeed. But you can see, given the stakes, why your MOHparents found it necessary to accelerate the whole question of settling on a successor. It wasn't their choice. Events have forced their hand.'

'But,' she said. 'You are a revolutionary! I can believe my MOHmies might want to topple the Ulanovs – but revolutionaries want to dismantle *all* the structures of power. Don't they? All the structures including the MOHfamilies! Why would my MOHmies ally themselves with somebody dedicated to their *own* overthrow?'

'There are as many different revolutionary creeds as there are religions,' Iago said. 'Some want to level the entire System, sure. Others are happy to work with the hierarchies that exist, to purge them of injustice and the Ulanovian tyranny, and to transition humanity towards stability and prosperity. For myself, I have – personal as well as ideological reasons to hate the Ulanovs. But it seems to me that any system, even a utopian one, will need efficient civil servants – and that's what the MOHfamilies are, really.' He coughed, or laughed, Diana couldn't tell which. Then he said: 'but, of course, there's a more pressing reason.'

'What do you mean? Reason for what?'

'Reason why your MOHparents would take somebody like me into their confidence, make an alliance with me and the forces I represent.'

She felt a tingle in her scalp, a yawing inside her stomach, as if she trembled on the brink of some great revelation. 'What reason?'

He looked at her. 'A new threat, large enough to overshadow any notion of political power-plays. Even for individuals such as your parents.'

'What threat?'

'The end of humanity.'

She had nothing to say to this. It seemed so improbably overstated, particularly for somebody like Iago, she wondered almost as if it were a joke.

'How long will we have to stay in this Al Anfal of yours?' she asked him, shortly.

He looked at her, a long, careful, appraising look. 'Not forever,' he said. And she saw that he meant: *a long time*. 'If the Ulanovs are truly moving against the Clan, then – well, things are clearly *volatile* at the moment. In the uplands, I mean. And throughout the System. And that means that things are volatile down here, since what is the Earth but a plughole down which all the shit of the System washes?'

The profanity startled her. 'Ee-*are*-gow!' she said. 'Such language!'

'I apologise, Diana,' he said, gravely, turning to look frontward. He didn't, she noticed, call her *Miss* any more.

It was midday before they came down, Iago guiding the craft into a narrow, precipitously-walled valley somewhere in the midst of Anatolia.

13

Of Multitudes

The house was primitive, but comfortable: two storeys, built close against the rocky west wall of the valley and hidden from all but the most specific searches from above. Diana had no idea where they were, and she didn't like the fact that (with no bId access) she couldn't find out. How close the nearest conurbation was, where their food would come from when the house supplies ran out – these were mysteries. Water came from a *well*, an actual well, just as in the days of Homer and *Homo erectus*: a shaft drilled through bronze-coloured rock, its contents pumped up into the house. 'How do you *know* it is clean?' she asked; but all Iago said was: 'it is clean alright.'

He fastened a hollow plastic globe to the bottom of his leg. It was cruder than a foot, but that fact seemed not to incommode him. He walked now with only the slightest of limps. 'Could you not,' Diana asked, still thinking with the assumptions of the very rich, 'get yourself a proper replacement foot?' 'These legs,' he replied, 'and indeed this face, this new face – they were very expensive, specialised pieces of work. I cannot simply replace them at any craft stall. Your MOHparents paid, not only to have the work done, but to keep it secret. The second element was by far the more expensive.'

Dia sniffed sulkily. 'I used to wonder,' she said, 'why you were so wrinkled. At your age, to be so wrinkled!'

'We are capable of many amazing things,' Iago agreed. 'But scar tissue is a stubborn fact of our corporality. We can fold it away in microwrinkles, but we cannot simply break and remake skin like putty.'

'That's revolting,' she told him.

Her life moved on into its next phase. She did not, at the beginning, feel the deprivation of her wealth too acutely; that felt like an adventure holiday than actual impoverishment. The lack of access to her bId was more of an irritation.

The air was thinner and colder here than it had been on the island; but she acclimatised quickly. Another function of a life lived upland.

Sapho cooked for them all, and cleaned up afterwards. She kept herself to herself; slept in the house's smallest room (although there were larger rooms available for her use) and said little. Some nights, if Diana put enough pressure on her, she would take her evening meal with them.

For the first full day there Diana did nothing but brood. It was actively dislocating not to have access to her bId. The fact that she was unable to check facts, to satisfy her various curiosities, was of course an inconvenience; but it dawned on her that in this house there were no other datasifts of *any* kind – not a slate, or a terminal, not so much as an antique library of bound codices. She was data-naked; an unprecedented and extremely uncomfortable situation. The lack of external access was less of a problem, for she was used to being insulated from the larger network of contacts and news for security reasons. But in one particular she felt the privation very sharply: she had no idea what was happening to her Clan. She did not know whether her MOHmies were alive and well, or in Ulanov custody (she wondered: on what charge?) or even dead. She did not know whether Eva was alright; or what was happening to the tens of thousands of Clan members and affiliates. Iago could tell her little, although he did seem to have some kind of non-bId access to information.

The first night she slept poorly: the house was not furnished with gel-beds and she had to lie on a mattress. More: the walls did not regulate the temperature automatically; so she was too cold until she got up and dialled more heat from a specific device in the corner of the room. That did make things hotter, and then made them too hot and she had to get up and dial it down. She finally fell asleep properly just before dawn and despite waking from time to time, she slept until midday.

And so it was a new day. I'm still alive, she told herself. That's something.

The daylight was white-grey; clouded over. She made herself some coffee and ate a little pasta. After that she wandered through the house absent-mindedly. She found Iago sitting in a chair in the back sitting room, staring through the antique window into nothing.

Rain fell, but without any force. The colour grey had been liquefied and was drifting down upon them in myriad drops.

Diana sat in the chair next to his. Eventually she spoke: 'you *were* behind it,' she said.

He looked at her. 'I'm glad you figured it out. Although of course I expected it of you.'

'What was it? A birthday present?'

'It was,' he said.

She looked at him.

'Your parents think it was their idea; but it wasn't,' he said, shortly. 'I am the one who planted that idea. I'm the one who knows how passionately you love murder-mysteries. Solving them is a five-finger exercise to you, but you love it nonetheless. So I thought I'd set one up; a real-life one. For your birthday.'

'I knew something was odd about the situation,' Diana said. 'A servant was brutally killed, only a few metres from where Eva and I slept! In any other circumstances our MOHmies would have pulled us straight *out* of there. They're not coy about their paranoia when it comes to keeping the two of us safe. But they seemed so *blithe* about it. Violent murder? You stay right there, my chickadees.' She shook her head. 'It was – uncharacteristic. All that chaff about how CRF in the servants' bloodstream would keep us safe?'

'That *was* one of the failsafes,' said Iago. 'And you *were* well guarded. Or at least—' He winced at the memory of Dominico Deño – 'so we thought. And the murderer had no grudge against *you*. She had a particular animus against somebody else.'

'How did you select her?'

'I went looking for a likely situation. It wasn't hard to find. Shanty bubbles are claustrophobic spaces. Tensions build up. I chose half a dozen possible groups of servants, from hundreds of initial possibles, and put them all into gravity training and preparation. When that Petero man – a horrible fellow, really – got killed, I looked into it. That was when I saw the potential in Sapho. That, really, made the decision for me.'

'You couldn't be *sure* she would kill Leron.'

'No,' he conceded. 'But it was very likely. I knew the dynamic in that group. And we had three weeks before your actual birth-day, after all. At some point he would press his attentions and she would not accept it. Or she would act pre-emptively. My main worry was that it would be too cut-and-dried a murder; too obvious for you. But even then, you would still have had to solve the larger mystery. I expected you to see early on that Sapho was the actual killer; but I wanted to see if you would be able to work out who was really behind it all. Me.'

'That wasn't hard,' she said, sulkily. Then in an outburst of tired wrath: 'A birthday present? That's a pretty sick sort of birthday present – don't you think? Give a girl, for her sixteenth birthday – a *corpse*.'

'This,' he said, turning his hands so that both palms faced her. 'This is the point of it.'

'*This* is? My anger?'

'Yes.'

Her rage flared up inside her, like a flame. 'You evil man,' she said. 'This is the *point* of it? A human being is dead! He wasn't a saint, maybe – but then, who is? You're certainly not! Goddess, are *any* of us? And he is *dead*.' The more she spoke, the more her rhetoric fed back into her anger. 'It's not a *game*. I nearly died!'

Iago shook his head. 'Joad would never have killed you. You're too valuable to the Ulanovs alive. Your sister likewise.'

'Shut up! A killer pointed a *gun* at me and smiled! I'm not even sixteen yet, but I felt death as a proximate thing. That's not a game. How dare you—' she was speaking loudly now, though croakily; a great reservoir of fury and resentment and bitterness inside her was flowing out of her. And she hadn't even known it was there! 'How dare you – play with life and death as a *game*? As a *birthday present*?'

His impassive face. She couldn't stand it any longer. Getting to her feet in this ridiculous gravity was a struggle, as ever, but she managed it, and she stormed out. Sapho was at the door, looking through, drawn by the sound of raised voices. But Dia didn't want to speak to her either (although it was hardly *her* fault) and instead she went through to her room and wrapped herself in a blanket. It was cold. It was late summer, and yet it was cold. Everything about this place was wrong. Everything in her life had gone wrong.

They were high up. This was the weather of tall mountains.

Look *down* from high places. Her anger flew like an eagle. How *dare* he? Toying with her, using living human beings as chesspieces. Did he really think she would be pleased that her sixteenth-birthday present was *a corpse*?

One of the curiosities of anger, of course, is that the more you focus it outward, firing it at the injustices of the world, the more it actually parses your own self-pity and resentment. Was she angry that Iago had treated Leron's life and death with such existential disrespect? Of course not. A moment's thought told her that. How could she be moved by a man whom she had never known, except in the abstract? Anger, after all, is not kindled by abstracts. So: what was so enraging? Her own life. The prison of her existence, guarded by gaolers who called themselves body-guards. The lack of anything that might be considered *a free choice*. Perhaps this wasn't Iago's fault, except insofar as he was part of the larger structure of control. Except that it was his fault. And he was the one with whom she was furious.

She thought of the multitude.

Trillions of human beings, wrapped like a fog about their home star. The mind collapsed at the scale and the numbers. But if ethics meant anything at all, it meant not letting the largeness of the human population overwhelm our moral knowledge that life is lived individually, and that even when agglomerated into billions and trillions individual human beings deserve better than being used as tools. That the overwhelming majority of this vast mass of humanity was poor, living precarious and subsistence lives in leaky shanty bubbles, eating ghunk and drinking recycled water – this made this more, not less, true. These were the people least able to help themselves. They should be helped, not exploited.

Now, the patterning genius for which she had been bred and in which she had been trained, her ability to see problems three-dimensionally and by superposing all possibilities into the same conceptual grid – this same ability immediately challenged her own outrage. It said: what have you done to help the trillions out of their absolute poverty? It said: what *could ever* be done? Nothing, nothing, nothing. Have you ever, before this moment, spared these trillions even a passing thought? You have not. You have never. Is your outrage here really an ethical reflex, or is it something simpler and baser and more human – your individual feeling of having been slighted? A wound upon the skin of your pride?

Furious, foetally positioned on the bed, wrapped in her blanket, she fell asleep. Of course she did.

As she had done a thousand times before, she dreamed. She dreamed of: interiors.

Her MOHmies were standing in a large Louis Vingt-Deux

hallway, all light brown wood, and chrome curlicues and floor-to-ceiling mirrors on every wall. Large windows let in light as white as a fresh snowfall, so bright that it hurt the eyes. The light moved with weird, sticky slowness; what Diana first took to be dust motes in the air were actually photons: swollen by some mysterious physical process and drifting with leisurely insolence. Because light was flowing so slowly, time was all wrong: somehow simultaneously zipping by too quickly *and* passing much too slowly. It felt nightmarishly carceral. It was disturbing. But her MOHmies were smiling. 'What is going on?' she asked.

They answered in so perfect a unison that there was no double-tracking of their respective voices. 'Your rage has slowed time,' they said.

'And is my anger not justified? He had no right to treat me like that!'

'*You?*'

She felt this as rebuke. 'No. Not me. The dead man – Leron. How could he treat a person like that? Even a man from the Sump. Even,' she went on, although her anger was shrinking inside her, 'a bad man, like him. It's not right. A human being is a human being. A human being is not a toy.'

'We cannot *help* but use the people below us as a resource, my love,' said her two MOHmies, as one. 'That is what it means to be in power. Your choice is to relinquish power forever, or to accept that and use people for good.'

She looked from wall to wall, from mirror to mirror. Mirrors. Her MOHmies were (of course) reflected in them; but Diana did not seem to be. She peered, trying to check whether this was just a feature of her point of view, or whether, in this dream, she was actually invisible.

'If we are powerful,' sang her MOHmies, 'we can make things better, but we are made unclean by the fact that we have power. If we are powerless we remain clean, but we cannot make things better.' Their voices, together, had a weird depth and resonance to them.

'It's a false dilemma,' she said.

'Precisely! *That* is what he is trying to teach you. That was your birthday present.'

Diana took a step forward. With a sensation of slippage inside her, she realised, belatedly, that there *were* no mirrors in this bright-lit hall. Every mirror was actually a broad doorway, and what she had assumed were reflections were actually other figures – her MOHmies, replicated into dozens of versions of themselves. Through every door a new room, and her MOHmies in every room, and behind them another door and another perspective on her MOHmies. She had the insight that she was seeing an infinite regression of rooms. There were trillions of human beings in the Sump, but there were an infinite number of her own parents.

And with that insight, she woke up.

She sat up in bed, pulling the blanket more tightly around her shoulders. Is there a more primitive form of technology than a blanket? Something queer about the light: a more metallic whiteness to it. It took her a moment to realise that it was snowing.

Snow.

She went back through to the sitting room. Iago was still there, and sitting across from him was Sapho. She looked up guiltily as Diana entered, got awkwardly to her feet, nodded and hurried away. Diana came over and sat in the seat she had recently occupied. It was still warm. 'Why did she start like a guilty thing?'

'She overheard what we were saying,' said Iago, in a level voice. 'She wanted to know what was going on, and I suppose she's entitled to know – her, above all. I was telling her that she was not responsible for killing Leron. Though she struck the blow, I was the one who set it up. I told her that I knew he had been abusing her, and that I used her as the means by which justice could be done.'

Diana thought about this. 'She believed you?'

'Why wouldn't she? She wept, actually. I think it relieved, to some extent, her feelings of guilt.'

'Iago,' said Diana. 'I'm sorry. I shouldn't have lost my temper with you.'

He opened his eyes fractionally wider. Then he said. 'Thank you.'

'You're surprised?'

'Let's say,' he replied, 'that you have reached this place quicker than I anticipated.'

She ignored this. 'The point was not just a birthday present, was it?' she said. 'Which is to say: it was. But it was very specifically a *sixteenth* birthday. It was about adulthood. Yes?'

Iago replied with characteristic obliqueness. 'Of course it is not comfortable to think that human beings, who breathe and feel and hope as we do, are a resource we exploit. It is a very terrible thing. But the alternative is: to live a hermit life. And the stakes are too high for that.' She took this for: *yes*.

'So,' she said. 'This is what I deduce. Your birthday gift to me was a real-life murder mystery. You expected me to solve this mystery.'

'Of course.'

'But that wasn't the real present, was it? You expected me to solve the mystery, and then you expected me to uncover what was behind it – you expected me to work out your involvement.'

He was looking at her. Slowly he nodded.

'You *wanted* me,' she said, 'to be angry. You wanted me to feel used, to be outraged at the disposal of a live human being into such a game. You wanted me to feel *that*, so I would confront this fact of power. That to rule means to treat people in that way.'

'The thing is,' Iago repeated. 'The stakes are very high.'

'Overthrowing the Ulanovs?'

'Ha!' His laugh took her by surprise. 'No, no. That would be power politics – a very desirable outcome I think, overthrowing tyranny; and I genuinely hope we can bring it about. And what your MOHparents hope, too. But that is the oldest currency in human affairs. Power politics, I mean. It happens, or it doesn't happen, and *Homo sapiens* carries on. No, I mean something much more important than that.'

'What?' Diana asked. Iago was looking through the window: snowflakes descending. Each was smaller than a fingernail, and thinner, and less durable. But they were coming in greater and greater numbers. The world outside was turning white. In summer, too!

'Let's talk about that,' he said.

14
The Third Letter of the Alphabet

'Joad wanted to know where *it* is,' Iago said. '*It* is something unimaginably dangerous, something worth unimaginable sums of money. It being—'

'FTL,' she said.

He hummed assent. 'More to the point, *it* is a particular thing, hidden in plain view. It's floating in space. Joad is searching for a single fish in that immeasurable ocean.' He looked at his finger-nails, compared the row of left to right. Then he said: 'no – it's more difficult to find than that. Space is inconceivably bigger than any ocean.'

'Space is big. How big is this object, thing – whatever it is we're looking for?'

'The size of a human being. Exactly that size. Do you know what? – this interests me, actually. Do you know that the median point between the mass of a proton and the mass of the entire universe is the mass of an average human female? Had you heard that fact? That factoid?'

'*Is* it a human female?' Diana asked him. There was a strange kerfuffle in her chest, her heart scurrying. And there was something else. Her head felt as if it were simultaneously swelling and shrinking, an odd hallucinatory effect. The smell of baked bread was somewhere about. She wondered what all this sudden excitement in her body was about, but at the same time she didn't need to wonder because she knew – she knew what the secret voice was uttering in the gravity well hidden in the centre of her weightless mind. It was saying: *you, you, it's you.* It was saying: *this thing they have been looking for, this artefact that is worth killing so many people for, this unimaginable precious thing, this unimaginably dangerous thing – it's you.* 'A human female,' she said again, with a shimmer in her voice.

'What?' Iago said, looking at her.

'I know I'm not an ordinary human female,' she said, in a rapid voice. 'Of course I've read up about the possibilities enabled by MOH-conception. And, I'll tell you – and I've always had the sense of . . . don't laugh, but I've always had the sense of a *special destiny* associated with my life—'

'A man,' said Iago.

'No, not that . Oh, I don't mean to choose celibacy, and I've no objection to dialling my sexuality that way. But men are nothing, less than nothing really.' She pulled herself up short, for it occurred suddenly to her that this might be an insensitive thing to say to Iago. 'All I mean to say,' she added, by way of qualification, 'is that the old Romantic Love dream is – well, that's a *man's* dream. It's a way of locking the female principle into limits that—'

He interrupted her then, but gently. 'I'm not being clear,' he said. 'A dead man.'

'A dead man,' she repeated. Then, in the tone of belated comprehension. 'A dead human male? That's what Joad is looking for?'

'That's what we're all looking for. His corpse, floating somewhere in all this immensity of space.'

'Oh,' she said. 'Oh I feel foolish!'

'There's no need to,' said Iago with a wry smile.

'I jumped to conclusions.'

She looked through the window to the barren ground outside. Breathing, in and out, the hiss of silk-on-silk. No matter how long you stayed downbelow, no matter how acclimatised you thought you had become, the truth was that drawing breath was a blur of effort and residual pain. She wanted to go home. She wanted very much to go back up. Human beings really did not belong in this laborious place. Snow. This is frozen water fluffed into popcorn-sized white cinders by the meteorological processes of the Earthen atmosphere. A sparse down-procession of flakes drifting mazily down on the far side of the glass, and then suddenly there was a great swarm of them. They moved in an insulting half-hearted imitation of weightlessness, sometimes buoying up only to fall slowly again.

The quality of light in the room had changed from yellow-white to a silver oxide, to an argent vividness and chill. Iago spoke to bring up the interior lighting, but Diana spoke it back off again. She liked the quality of cold dusk at midday. She liked it.

'I'm sorry,' he said. 'I said human female only because that's the way the maths comes out – slightly smaller than the average human male.'

'Average is a nonsense. How do we even *know* the average when the population is counted in trillions, and the majority are scattered through billions of reclusive bubbles?' But that sounded rather more hostile than she felt, so she said: 'I'm a bit of an egotist, I'm afraid. It's foolish of me to react like this. Foolish to be disappointed to hear that I'm – not – after all – the messiah.' She chuckled at the vainglory of the thought, now that she had actually uttered it

Iago smiled. Then he said. 'I would say that you're remarkably *un*-egotistical.' But, then, the barb: 'for one of the rich, I mean.'

Suddenly the grey light all around her seemed monstrous, as if the whole room had been plunged below the surface of an Earthen ocean. That's what it was. She was sick of being *low*, of being cast into the profound depths of the shaft of the planet's gravity – and the last thing she wanted was to sink further still.

She spoke the lights in the room up, bright and on they came, tart as fresh lemon juice. And then she sat herself up straighter, and drew a long, breath.

'Tell me about this deceased male human,' she said. 'The stakes are so very high, you say? How can one person's corpse mean so much?'

'He is called Mkoko,' said Iago. '*Was* called that, I mean, when alive.'

'And who was he?'

'He was a crewperson on a sloop called *Hesperus*. Strictly it was called *Hesperus 33a10*, there being a large number of spaceships with that name. Engineers are not a very imaginative bunch when it comes to names.'

'And how came he to be floating dead in space?'

'There was a shipboard fire and he was killed. Burnt to death, unfortunately for him. The surviving crew buried him at space.'

'Buried him at space,' Diana repeated. 'Sounds like a waste of good carbon.'

'Well, yes. But I'll tell you something else about engineers. They're almost all religious. Often religious in old-school ways, such that – an outsider might think – their religious beliefs *must* bring them into conflict with their own scientific and technical knowledge-bases. But there's something *in* the sort of god-obsessed imagination that excels at engineering. I don't know what it is. And the various fleets wouldn't run without them, of course; so they have latitude when it comes to religious freedoms and practices.' He cleared his throat. Diana looked at him. With his face lit brightly from above she saw again how *old* he was. Lines on his white face like the cracks on Callisto's round white surface.

'So this Mkoko got killed on some sloop and his body was chucked into vacuum,' said Diana. 'Alright: now tell me why he is so important.'

Iago said: 'he's *not* important.'

'Eye-ah-*go*,' she rebuked him. 'You're being evasive, and it's tiresome.'

'I don't know very much about Mkoko, actually,' Iago said. 'It's not him. It's something he has about his person. His corpse. You see, also serving on the ship was another engineer, called McAuley. Now *he* – well, he was something else.'

'Who? Wait.' She tried to remember. 'The name rings a bell. If I still had access to my bId I could check. *Do* I know him? Have I ever heard of him?'

'Perhaps not. It doesn't matter. He invented something, that's all. And then he thought better of it.'

'He invented something, and then changed his mind?'

'Exactly.'

'What did he invent?'

'He wouldn't say.'

'People asked him?'

At this Iago suddenly laughed. It was such a strange, uncharacteristic noise to come out of his mouth that Dia flinched. 'I'm sorry,' he said, controlling himself. 'I'm sorry. But yes – people asked him. People asked him over and over again. They kept asking him. They pressed him hard on the matter. So hard that he died.'

'Oh,' said Diana, understanding.

'It was . . . clumsy and stupid of them, quite apart from being,' and he looked into the corner of the ceiling and spoke the word as if trying it out: 'immoral. But now McAuley is dead, and he can tell us nothing more about his invention.'

'He revealed nothing at all about it under . . . interrogation?'

'He was much more stubborn than his interrogators realised. Religious faith, you see. Old school. They weren't ready for it. He decided that he truly would rather die than say. Do you know what vacuumboarding is?'

'No,' she said.

'You expose a person's face to the vacuum of space – the whole face. You have a special little porthole in your – interrogation cabin. It's very unpleasant. Obviously, you can't breathe, and that is scary; and it's cold in ways you cannot easily imagine. And very painful, as blood vessels burst and your eyes bulge and your lips freeze solid. The – subject – usually struggles, clenches her eyes shut, holds her breath. Then after a while you pull them back in. They'll often tell you what you want to know then, especially if they've been prepped with the right Oxys first. Your trick is to get the information out of them quickly, because soon after that their bruises will start to swell their face and they quickly become incoherent. Often, depending on how long you vacuumboard them for, the flesh of their lips dies, necroses, blackens with frostbite and comes away. They tend to lose the sight in one or both eyes.'

'I am not going to ask,' she said, 'how you know all this.'

'Oh I've never been an interrogator,' he said. 'I've never had the stomach for *that*.'

'You!' she said, with a brief laugh, although saying that one syllable, *you*, made her scalp shiver and the hairs thrill on the back of her neck.

He smiled. 'Iago Glass,' he said. 'Iago, Jago, Jac – I know. I *have* killed, yes.' As he spoke, she listened carefully, but his voice sounded no more hollow than it usually did. 'It is one of the lamentable truths of my nature that I am good at killing people. But I take no pleasure in *hurting* people. Killing is clean, but torture is messy, and I deplore mess. Killing is enclosure, a shutting down. But hurting people is a ghastly form of disclosure, an opening up – often in a literal sense. That is . . . anathema to me.' He looked at her. 'I don't say this to try and endear myself to you. I am what I am.'

'A equals A,' she said. 'I assume you don't care what I think, anyway.'

'Oh I do!' he said, earnestly. 'Truly I do. I don't want *you* to shun me.'

'Of course you don't,' she said. 'You're dosed with the finest CRFs my MOHmies could afford.'

'I've never taken CRFs,' he said. 'Your parents trust me absolutely; and with good cause. All the other servants are, of course, dosed up; but giving me those drugs would be a mistake. You need my initiative and, ah, distinctiveness.'

'Oh,' she said.

'A equals A. Quite right,' he said. 'Yes, I have killed people, but I have tried to do it as cleanly as possible. I take no pride in what I do, because pride is the flipside of guilt, and that particular emotional matrix is alien to my nature.' He put his hands together, palm to palm, a Namaste. 'Nobody – by which I mean, nobody who knew who I really was – would employ *me* as a torturer. Regular interrogators were hired to question McAuley. And they didn't understand him. He was – a remarkable man. So they dosed him with exactly the Oxys you would expect, being predictable sorts; it did them no good. So they thought: pain, and the terror of death, will get him to speak – there's no way to prepare a conscious human body with countermeasures to those quantities, after all. They tortured him, and he held out. They vacuumboarded him, and instead of struggling he expelled all the air in his lungs. He was singing, I think.'

'Singing?'

'Singing a hymn to the glory of God, at the top of his voice, into the perfectly muffling medium of outer space. A silent hymn sung with all the volume he could muster. They didn't realise. Subjects don't usually react that way. And it must have hurt like – hell. It must have felt as if the devil's own frozen hand were reaching down his windpipe into his lungs and ripping the flesh free.' Iago shook his head, and folded his arms. 'But he had – willpower. By the time they realised what he was doing and drew him back in, he was two-thirds brain dead.'

'And his secret died with him?'

'Ah. That brings us back to Mkoko. You see, it seems that

McAuley loaded the details of his invention onto a datachip, and hid it about the body of Mkoko before ditching him overboard.'

'Why?'

Iago made a little o with his lips and shook his head. 'He had his reasons, I suppose.'

'So the secret is out there – if we can only find the corpse?'

'Exactly.'

'And the secret is FTL?'

'I said we don't know the details, the ins-and-outs, the specifics. We don't know how McAuley solved the problems that stood in his way. But, yes. His invention was a blueprint for a new kind of spaceship drive. Faster-than-light travel.'

'So it's true,' said Dia, the hairs tingling on the back of her neck. 'That's amazing. I mean *if* it's really true. But it can't be true, can it?'

'Why not?'

'What I mean is: *is* there a way to travel faster than light?'

'McAuley found a way.'

'But that's wonderful news!' said Diana, in a loud voice. Her heart was quickening within her. Quickening means *coming alive*. 'That's – incredible news!'

'Wonderful,' said Iago, in a neutral voice. 'No, no, I don't think so.'

'You wouldn't call it wonderful?'

'I would call it terrifying.'

'But this is the ticket to the rest of the universe! This takes the lid off the solar system! The teeming trillions can spread to every star! They can escape the rule of the Ulanovs, they can slip the leash. Terrifying? On the contrary, this is the start of a new golden age!'

Iago was looking closely at her. 'You are excited,' he observed.

'Of course I am! To discover that it's possible after all? It's freedom! It's the ultimate freedom!'

'Death,' said Iago. The snow outside had stopped falling. A

250

snake of white slept on the outside windowsill, and the bare yard beyond had been softened and blanched.

'Oh don't be absurd!' she cried. 'It would be death to *stay*. In the long run – it will be stagnation and death to stay here!' She paused. 'McAuley must have shared his invention with somebody. He refused to tell his interrogators, alright. But friends? Colleagues?'

'No,' said Iago. 'The thing you need to understand about McAuley is that he was a genius. He had his madness, his religious mania. But that enabled rather than interfered with his capacity for invention. A friend of mine once said: McAuley had the finest mind since Newton. That's right, I think.'

'So he makes this extraordinary thing. He invents the key that will unlock mankind's prison cell. And then he prefers to *die* rather than tell people about it?'

'I suppose,' said Iago, 'that when the idea occurred to him, perhaps he felt a wave of euphoria. Maybe he did dream a brilliant future for humanity, spread throughout every star in the cosmos – all the things you have just said. The lid off, and so on. Maybe that lifted him up, spiritually, as he worked out the details. But then very soon he changed his mind. He decided that, were his work to become known, it would be a disaster. So he destroyed the data.'

'But,' said Diana. 'Why?'

'Well, actually he didn't destroy all copies. And, really, that's a better question. Why *didn't* he? He eradicated all traces except one: the datachip, which he fixed to the body of his friend Mkoko and kicked out into space. I suppose,' Iago went on, 'that he was making an offering to chance. The God he believed in would be the final arbiter as to whether the corpse is ever discovered. Maybe he couldn't bring himself to completely destroy what was – obviously – his greatest achievement. Something humanity has dreamt about for hundreds of years. He had enough pride left to want to leave one copy surviving.'

'No,' said Diana. 'I'd still say my question is the right one.

Why did he want to deprive humanity of this gift? Was it money? – because surely he could have sold the technology for any price he cared to set!'

'It wasn't money. He came from a wealthy family. He walked away from his inheritance – he was working as second engineer on a clapped-out sloop, after all. He disdained money. That was another part of the logic of his religion.'

'Then why?' Diana said. She slumped back in her chair. 'This is insane. A moment ago I had no idea that such a thing was even possible! FTL! Good grief.'

'You're not thinking it through,' said Iago, mildly.

This stung. 'Alright, I'll think it through – professor. I'll run through the possible negatives. But do you know what? I *know*, I know *in advance* that they are all massively outweighed by the advantages of opening up the whole universe to human settle-ment. So.' She laid a thumb in at the cleft of her chin. 'I suppose, a technology like this would be fought over. There might be struggles. Wars, even. The Lex Ulanova has preserved order in the system for so long we've forgotten what full-scale war is like, I don't doubt. Is it that?' But before Iago could reply, she answered herself. 'But, no, that's crazy. Who's going to fight over it? Disseminate the data everywhere, place copies all over the IP, copy it a trillion times. Set it free and there's nothing to fight over. So what else? Is it – is it that the drive is very polluting?'

'Not so far as I know,' replied Iago.

'Then *what*? What is the downside of letting humanity spread through the stars? Are you worried about alien encounter?'

'Not at all.'

'Then I *don't* understand. There! I said it.'

Iago was looking through the window. 'It's snowing again,' he said. And so it was: thinner flakes this time, and fewer. A few knocked themselves like cold moths against the window. Iago and Dia watched for a while. Then Iago said: 'that last act of McAuley, his hymn, has become something of a myth. A story.

Amongst those that know, I mean. Which is a select group. What precisely *was* he singing, with his terminal breath?'

'How can we know?'

'Exactly,' said Iago. 'Exactly. But people speculate, nonetheless. One person I know has a whole elaborate theory – wrote it as a story. He thinks that McAuley was racked by the belief that his pride was sinful; that God had set the speed of light as a constant and that to exceed it was blasphemous.'

'Really?' said Dia. 'That doesn't sound very plausible.'

'You say so because you don't share the particular religious beliefs McAuley did. But, actually, yes, I agree with you. Perhaps it played a part. But it's speculation. And we don't need speculation. We don't need to attribute his reluctance to disseminate his FTL technology to his religion. Because I don't share his religious belief; but I *do* share his reluctance.'

'*You* do?' Dia was flabbergasted. 'Why?'

'You're not thinking it through,' he said again, gravely.

'I don't see it,' she agreed. 'I don't see the downside.'

'We're going to have to leave soon,' said Iago. Then he said: 'you learned about Einstein at kindergarten, of course. But as with lots of kindergarten stuff, we tend to forget what it means, in the fullest sense. We take it for granted.'

'Forget what *what* means?'

'Forget what it means to say "the speed of light is the fastest we can travel". It's not an arbitrary limit, like a speed limit on a road. Rather it's an expression of the fundamental geometry of the universe.'

'You sound like Eva,' said Diana. 'She always insisted vehemently on the impossibility of FTL.'

'And why was that?'

'If I had my bId, I'd recite all the relevant . . .' Diana started to say. Then she said. 'Not that I need it! OK, I'll play along. All the vectors in spacetime are aspects of *the same* vector: an arrow that sums the total of your motion through the eight aspects – west/east, north/south, up/down, forward-in-time/backwards-in-time

253

– those eight coordinates that altogether constitute spacetime. If you were completely motionless in space, the arrow would point directly along the axis forward-in-time, because you are travelling, one hour per hour, as "fast" forward in time as it is possible to go. If you start to move eastward, accelerating faster and faster towards the east, then the arrow swings a little towards the east axis, and the vector of your forward-in-timeness reduces a little. This is the time-dilation effect Einstein discovered. Move faster in an eastward direction and the arrow swings further that way, and accordingly you move less precipitously forward in the direction of forward-in-time. Eventually the arrow will be pointing directly 'east', and you will be travelling at c in that direction, and not moving forward in time at all. In order to travel "faster than light" you would somehow have to rotate the arrow *more horizontally than horizontal*. It's easy to see how stupid *that* is. Saying "faster than light" is like saying "more straight than perfectly straight". Looking for it is like looking for the fourth side of a triangle. Looking for it means that *you haven't understood what a triangle is*. This is, as you said, kindergarten stuff.'

'What follows?'

'How do you mean?'

'I'm asking you to think through the implications.'

'Of FTL? You mean – hypothetically? I suppose that to travel faster than light would mean generating a new, localised spacetime geometry.'

Iago waved that aside with a condescending gesture. 'Obviously that. I don't mean that.'

'Alright,' said Dia, crossly. 'What *do* you mean?'

'You can't exceed c, any more than you can rotate through more than three-sixty-degrees. So the only alternative is: to change c. And that means . . .' She was about to say 'freedom' when the truth of it clattered, shockingly, into her mind. 'Oh,' she said, her face falling. 'Oh!'

He nodded. 'You make your McAuley machine. OK. Then

what? You might make it into a spaceship and travel to Orion. Or you might make it into—'

'A bomb,' she breathed.

She understood, finally, the stakes for which they had been playing.

'Drop it in the sun,' he agreed. 'Think about $E=mc^2$. Say your McAuley machine resets c a million times higher – the sort of ratio you'd need to cover interstellar space in a reasonable time: 120 light years is a million light-hours, after all. So you reset c a million times higher. Feed that into Einstein's equation. Think what it would do to the energy output of our star.'

'A bomb,' she said again.

'The biggest bomb there's ever been. Such ordnance is the *necessary* correlative of FTL. It's an inevitable feature of the technology.'

'Good goddess,' said Diana, in a low voice.

'You can see what I mean when I say that the stakes are high. You can see why the loss of one life, or even dozens of individual lives, might be a price worth paying – to save trillions.'

Diana shivered.

'I believe that when McAuley developed his technology he was thinking in terms of unlocking the prison door, and letting humanity out into the cosmos. Like you said. Maybe that thought blinded him. But he was no fool. I'll tell you what he actually invented. He had invented a way of increasing c. Of course that meant he had invented a way of turning $E=mc^2$ into a *species-killing* weapon.'

'Nobody would use it,' said Diana. 'You would have to be insane! Nobody would *be* so mad.'

'Is it a chance we can take?' said Iago. 'You think it would be a good idea for this technology to fall into Ulanov hands? Or – anybody else's?'

'Oh Lady of the Cosmos.'

The question dominated the afternoon, hanging in the air,

buzzing at Dia's mind even though, or perhaps because, its answer was so obviously *no*.

She located a cache of woollen and plasfabric sweaters, coats, hats and scarves under the stairs, dressed herself in them (though they were rather too short for her upland-lengthened limbs) and went outside for a walk. Sharply cold. Hers was a slow, cumbrous procession; the ground uneven beneath her feet. When the path went up it was enormously strenuous work ascending it, and left her gasping in pseudo-asthmatic panic. And when the path went down it was perhaps even harder, although in a different way: her passage always on the alarming edge of tripping and tumbling towards a painful fall and probably a broken bone. The air seemed something the opposite of a clean and penetrable medium: cold to an almost gelid degree, spotted with drifting ice-flakes falling languidly towards the beige ground. On the other hand, being *in amongst* the mountains, rather than seeing them from her usual perspective of high above, gave her some insight into why mountains had, historically speaking, so obsessed humanity. Their prodigious size and mass had a sort of divine *indifference* about it. They had the appearance of a kind of *absolute* solidity. Impossible to imagine them ever passing away. And yet − she reminded herself, not only the mountains but the entirety of the Earth, and its moon, and Mars, and the trillions upon trillions of people living in their various mansions and houses and shanty bubbles orbiting the sun − all of it could be wiped out in moments, if what Iago said was true.

Frost on a boulder looked like scales. On she went, struggling against her own limitations. It didn't bear thinking about, but she couldn't stop thinking, and that meant she couldn't stop thinking about it.

Eventually, panting like a dog, she reached the edge of the estate: a brick wall twice her height, and an old iron gate − brown metal speckled all over with tomato-coloured rust. She sat on an old stone stump and got her breath back, wondering if it was a portion of some ancient Greek temple column, or a piece of modern masonry, or perhaps just a chunk of rock shaped by random action into a cylinder. No way to tell. Through the bars of the gate she saw the road going down into a shallow valley of cold, dry stones.

She got back to the house in time for supper. 'Good,' she said in a hearty voice, as Sapho put bowls on the table. 'I *have* worked up an appetite.'

But all three were in a sombre mood that evening. In the darkness of its mountainous location, the interior of the house illuminated only by a couple of light poles, it felt terribly remote.

'I realised something,' said Diana. 'When I was out walking.' Iago and Sapho looked at her, patiently, expectantly, and she thought: this is what I do. This is what they expect of me. Seeing through the tangle to the heart of the mystery. Her whole torso tingled. 'I realised that Eva was *right*.'

'Right?' repeated Iago.

'She had a dream in which she learned that the solution to the murder mystery was directly connected to her own research. Her latest PhD on those "Champagne Supernovae", those instances of stars that explode with supernova brightness even though they lack the necessary mass?'

'Yes,' said Iago, nodding his head very slowly. An ocean tide was turning about in his gaze. 'Yes,' he said again, putting a hand to the side of his face. 'Of course.'

He looked, in the polelight, very old.

Diana said: 'She refused to believe it herself, but she was right! Every Champagne Supernova, every single one – is the funeral pyre of an alien civilisation. Each one marks a life-form that advanced to the point where they discovered whatever it was that McAuley discovered. And then, and *then*, by accident or by deliberate act of war, by malice or through misguided religious beliefs, the technology was turned on the life-form's own home star. Its energy output increased instantly by a million times: just as you said! Goddess have mercy.'

For a long time they were silent. Then Iago said, with a wry smile: 'I have to say, *that* had not occurred to me.'

'You don't think it is right?'

'I'm sure it is. It explains the otherwise inexplicable supernovae that Miss Eva was studying. I'm sure it explains some more conventional supernovae as well. Only, think of it! Whole civilisations burnt up in an instant. On old Earth they used to worry that simple atomics would destroy humanity. But atomic weapons are firecrackers compared to *this*.'

'It is a monstrous thing,' said Sapho. Diana looked from her to Iago, and back again. Here she was, with two actual murderers; yet both were touched in their tender consciences by the possibilities of human death. And she, who had never murdered anybody in her life, felt a blankness in her heart when she contemplated it.

'It makes me feel,' she said, groping for the right word. 'Old.'

Iago nodded sombrely.

'Maybe it *is* inevitable,' Diana said, carefully. 'This McAuley fellow – *he* discovered the technology. And those, those, who-ever-they-were, those *unknown* alien scientists too. Even if we don't locate the revenant of McAuley's research, the datachip, the thing everyone is looking for – well, even then, eventually some-body amongst our trillionfold population of ingenious monkeys will replicate McAuley's research. Maybe we are simply . . . doomed.'

'The Fermi paradox,' said Iago.

'The what?' asked Sapho.

'Imagine,' Diana agreed, 'that life *is* common in the universe, and that when it reaches a certain level of technological advance it inevitably develops FTL capacity. But that in doing so it inevitably destroys itself. That would be why we have never encountered the aliens.'

Sapho shook her head, slowly. 'Goddess preserve us,' she said again.

'It's not a consoling thought,' Iago agreed. 'But it doesn't mean we should just give up. On the contrary, I tend to feel that any effort, any cost, is worth it – if it preserves mankind from this threat.'

'Even the cost of people all across the system thinking you are a monster?' Diana asked him.

'A small price to pay,' he said. 'Considering the stakes. Besides – there are people who know the real me.'

After Sapho had cleared the bowls, and was washing them in the kitchen, Iago said: 'we can't stay here much longer. We need to go upland.'

'Are they coming?'

'It's awkward keeping tabs on what's going on in the wider world without letting the Ulanov forces know that I'm doing so. But I have the sense they're narrowing in. They're devoting enormous resources to finding us, after all. Because they believe we have the blueprint. They believe you know it, or you know where I am – Jack Glass, that is to say – and that *I* know it.'

'And do you?'

'Of course not. But that doesn't matter; the important thing is that the Ulanovs *believe* it to be the case. They'll do anything – absolutely anything – to get hold of us.'

'They want it in the first instance to stop anybody else getting it,' Diana said, automatically. 'And in the second instance because they think faster-than-light travel will unlock prodigious new opportunities for wealth and power. Do you think they realise the destructive potential, though?'

'You realised it, a very short time after being told about the technology,' said Iago. 'You think they won't make the same deduction? We are talking about massively increasing c; and $E=mc^2$ is hardly an obscure or little-known equation, after all. I realised it as soon as I became aware of the possibility. I didn't make the connection with your sister's research, although now that you point it out, it acts as a terrible confirmation.'

'I shouldn't be naive,' Diana said. 'Of course, realising its destructive power only makes them want it more. Of course. Even more than great wealth, power craves technologies of destruction. Good to be wealthy, but better to remain in power – and the more awe-inspiring the weaponry at your disposal, the better able you are to do that.'

Iago nodded. 'The surface of the Earth is extensive,' he said, 'and I have many friends here. But a better hiding place is in amongst the greenbelt.'

'You mean, the Sump?'

'In amongst the trillions, yes. Tomorrow.'

'Sapho too?'

'She can come with us, or we can leave her to make her own way across the uplands. But the important thing is – to get away.'

'Tomorrow,' said Diana, thinking of Eva's Champagne Supernova stars: each one the candle lit upon the mass grave of an entire civilisation – maybe several civilisations, on several planets, but all eliminated together, at a stroke. Her breath caught in her throat. 'Tomorrow,' she said again.

part III

•

THE IMPOSSIBLE GUN

So it ends
As it begins
Off we climb
And no one wins.

Thom Gunn, 'Seesaw'

1

The Mystery of the Rogue RACdroid

'It is about going *back* in time to an age when *democracy* was the way humanity governed itself! It is about going *back to that Eden*, one human one vote!' Those physically gathered about the speaker began chanting, a low murmur, more like a religious ritual than a political rally, 'OHOV, OHOV'. The speaker wasn't really addressing them, of course; he was speaking through technology to the thousands in every suburb of the large sphere – and also to the seven bubbles linked by scramble tunnels, and to any other habitations or communications in the local area.

It was happening in real-time, in the open air. There were of course many more efficient ways of addressing a large audience, in a variety of secure worldtuals. But the imitation of an old-style Earth democratic hustings was an integral part of the performance.

'Democracy is our birthright as human beings!' the speaker cried, raising her voice to be heard clearly over the murmurous chant of the crowd. 'It has been *stolen* from us, by the Gongsi, by the MOHfamilies, but above all – by the Ulanovs!' At this, the chanting was replaced by a great cheer. Badmouthing the MOH-families might not be politic, but it wasn't illegal: but bad-mouthing the Ulanovs was, legally, treason. That was what the crowd wanted to hear. Here in the depths of the Sump, they felt safe enough openly to flout the Lex Ulanova.

'They call it revolution!' cried the speaker, over the hoots and chants, through which the chants of OHOV could still be heard. 'They call it revolution and say it is against the law! I say it *is* the law – the true law of humanity. I say it *is* revolution – as planets and worlds revolve about the sun and return to the original point on their circle, so humanity shall return to its true inheritance! Ancient Greece! The Roman Senate! The British Parliament! The American Revolution! The Velvet and Jasmine Revolutions! A return to our birthright!'

A large crowd surrendering to its own ecstasy in zero-g is a striking sight. People had originally gathered in a loose pattern determined by guy-ropes and wall-fixtures, so as to permit the greatest visibility to the greatest number. But as levels of right-eous frenzy increased, people loosed their hold, and floated or swam in a fishlike swarm. The view of the speaker was obscured. The chanting rose in volume, others began shouting 'Mithras! Mithras!' with an inspired vehemence. Cameras were knocked – advertently or otherwise – from position, and the whole meeting disintegrated into chaos. Or, if you prefer, integrated from rigidity into true human, democratic fluidity.

From the other side of the space, not more than two hundred metres away, many people watched, with approval, or interest, or disgust. And amongst those many were three of particular con-cern to us: two young women, both with dark hair, and an older man with a face you might call careworn. Were you to look closely at him, you might notice grains of rust in at the roots of his hair – as if he had been dirtied with something, and had not had time properly to wash it all out again. As it happened, the thing with which he had been dirtied was not rust, but blood.

This was not his own blood.

Behind them was a RACdroid – one of those devices for witnessing and affirming contracts. Why they should bring such a piece of machinery to such a place was not immediately clear. One glance made it obvious that the entire place had been given over to a carnivalesque celebration of democratic revolution.

One of the women said to the man: 'this place is pretty frenzied.'

And he to her: 'they are true believers.'

'So are you, Jack,' she said. And then: 'should I call you Jack? It doesn't chime right.'

'Stick with what you know,' he advised.

'They did find your house, after all,' said the other. 'Do you think they'll trace us here?'

'We can't stay here long, certainly. But we need fuel. We need to find Aishwarya as quickly as possible, and have this RACdroid looked at. And then we need to move on.'

'And find out who killed Bar-le-duc,' said Diana.

'Bar-le-duc,' said the other woman. 'The most famous policeman in the System, and it falls to us to investigate his death.' She tutted.

'I'm less worried about his death, Sapho,' said Iago. 'I care more for the authenticity of this RACdroid.'

'The droid carries the answer to Bar-le-duc's death,' Sapho replied.

'If it's kosher. *If.* Come on.'

They had flown in piloting a small sloop, a private craft: blocky, about the size of a freight container and not much more elegantly styled. Its name was *Red Rum 2020*. The docking area was cluttered with nearly a hundred craft, disposed higgledy-piggledy: they nudged in as close as they could to the nest of globes, but still had to unroll their own crawl-tube more than twenty metres before they could find an access point. This was one of those aspects of her new life to which Diana found it very hard to become accustomed. As the privileged daughter of a great and powerful house she had always been used to privileged docking – passing from ship to house or back again had only ever been simply a question of stepping across a threshold. Out in the Sump, however, she always seemed to find herself pulling through the interior of some scanty umbilicus or other; and every time she did so the thought went through her mind: only a few millimetres of eminently penetrable material separates me from the death of vacuum. Her experiences in Dunronin – only days before – had made this fear more acute.

This particular cluster of shanty bubbles was called Garland 400. It was deep inside the Sump, a longtime home to anti-Ulanov sentiment and illegal democratic agitation; only its remoteness had protected it from the attention of the police. That and the relatively low-key nature of the revolutionary scheming. The police burst thousands of globes every year, exemplary punishments for breaches in the Lex Ulanova. But Garland 400 had been one of the millions of delinquent communities that had not drawn attention to itself.

It was hard to see how they had evaded notice. As Iago, Diana, Sapho and their RACdroid pulled their way along the guy-ropes of the main bubble, they were surrounded on all sides by ecstatic revolutionaries: drunk on alcohol or cannaboids, blissed out with corticotopian connections, zapped on diamondanes. There were people to the left and right, before and behind them, above and below, chanting 'OHOV! OHOV! OHOV!' or singing hymns to Mithras, or bellowing the Marseillaise (or versions thereof). Many were naked, and some were copulating, in writhing clusters. It was a cacophonous obstacle course. Perhaps the speaker was still speaking: if so, it was no longer possible to hear her. A superbly wrinkled old woman, naked from the waist up, floated towards them repeatedly offering to buy their droid. Several people tried to tag them.

They made it through in the end, through the crawl tube into the second globe – smaller, and much quieter. It was clear the party was going on in the main space. There was some merry-making above them: a long bar, linking curving wall to curving wall, was serving alcohol; several score people had their arms hooked about the metal, drinking and watching the goings-on next door on screens or via IP access, discussing it animatedly with their friends, and singing.

'This one?' Diana asked, glad to be out of the riotous space.

'Next one along.'

266

'It's amazing the police don't close this down,' she cried. She had to raise her voice to be heard over the din.

'If they knew about it,' said Iago, 'they would.'

'It makes me shudder with horrible recognition,' said Sapho. 'I grew up in places like this – riotous, ungodly places. Ra'allah does not smile on drunkenness. He kindles sugar in the grape, but the grape can only make alcohol if it be hidden from his light.'

They pushed off and flew straight to one of a number of exits, Iago guided by memory, or perhaps by access to his mysterious bId-that-wasn't-bId. They passed through a short tunnel and found themselves in a green space: vegetation all around them, feeding directly off sunlight or clustering around light tubes. It took Diana's eyes a moment to adjust to the marine quality of the light. She began to pick out various huts in amongst the foliage.

'Aishwarya,' said Iago, gesturing with his hand. Or, waving to her as the individual so named floated over towards them. The sounds of revelry from the first, biggest sphere were still clearly audible; but somehow they didn't disturb the peace of this place. Faces appeared in the doorways to huts, and then disappeared back inside again. The guy-ropes stretched from wall to wall were garnished with vines. Tomatoes grew upon long pendant strips, like giant red flies snagged on huge stretches of flypapers.

'Jack Glass,' said Aishwarya, coming close. She did not sound pleased to see him. 'You look different.'

'Trivial adjustments to the face,' he said. 'Not the eyes, though.'

'No,' she agreed, looking at him. 'The eyes are the same.'

She was a very elderly individual; her close-trimmed hair was a pattern of white dots over dark brown scalp, her limbs long and spindle thin, her skin marked with interconnected patterns of lines, swirls and grooves like a magnified image of a fingerprint. It had evidently been a very long time, if ever, since she had spent time at the bottom of any gravity well. Her nose was a rather magnificent horn-shaped appendage, downward curving, and marred only by an oval area of pinkness where (a common sight in the uplands) a tumour had at some point in the past been cut away. But it was her eyes that held your attention. Though countersunk into the head, and surrounded by dark, puckered skin, they possessed a fierce, almost immortal brightness – proper ancient mariner eyes.

'Aishwarya,' said Iago. 'I wanted to introduce you to Diana, here. She is the first person I have met in many decades who may be cleverer than you.'

Aishwarya pulled a sour face. 'Her? She's a mayfly. How old are you, sweetpea?'

'Sixteen,' said Diana.

'True wisdom comes with age, my darling, and – oh! oho! Wait. You are Diana *Argent?*'

Dia looked to Iago first, but answered: 'I am.'

'Good gracious! I forgive you, Jack Glass, for bothering me, since you have introduced me to such a human being! And you? Her servant?'

'My name is Sapho,' said Sapho, a little fiercely.

'I see. *Not* a servant?'

'Sapho hasn't been taking her CRFs for some months now,' said Iago. 'Not since we all had to leave Earth in, uh, a hurry. But she's still loyal to the Argent Clan. Aren't you?'

'Of course,' Sapho said, grumpily.

'CRF withdrawal has a *complex* of emotional effects,' said the old woman knowingly. 'Still, you're better off without those pharmakons in your system, my dear. They blunt your initiative. And we all need our initiative, don't we? We're all living through interesting times, after all.'

'They certainly seem to think so,' said Iago, gesturing with his thumb behind him.

This appeared only to annoy Aishwarya. '*Such* idiots. I don't mind idiots, generally; but they have to be so extreme about it! They will bring destruction down upon us all. I have a sloop ready to run at the first sniff of a police craft.'

'You think it will come to that?'

The old woman sniffed. 'Maybe not. But they are *such* idiots!

Now that they're drunk, they think the time for revolution has arrived. When they sober up tomorrow they'll go back to whining and stealing from their neighbours – not that there's anything worth stealing. A life of pointless gang squabbles and living like beasts. I spent a week growing some special tomatoes, last month, and a group of teenagers smashed them! They didn't even steal them and eat them! Or steal them and sell them back to me, like smart little gangsters! They just smashed them up for the hell of it.'

'Poverty degrades people, that's true,' said Iago. 'But perhaps we should at least *consider* that they may be right about one thing.'

'What one thing?'

'Timing. Maybe it *is* time for revolution.'

She snorted. 'Of course it isn't! What, you think the present political *instabilities* could help germinate actual System-wide revolt? No, no. What we are witnessing is – saving your presence, my dear – one of the occasional pecking-order struggles that *defines* the hierarchy. The twin heads of the Argent Clan have gone into hiding; one of the heirs is who-knows-where, the other is . . . here, directly in front of my own eyes, bless me! Of course the other MOHhouses are – what's the phrase? Jockeying for position. Of *course* the Ulanovs are throwing their weight around. It's not *revolution*. It's business as usual. But those idiots – they think Mithras is about to manifest himself and lead a wildfire revolt across the whole System!'

A flock of duck chose that moment to dash away, squealing and parping and flurrying as they wagged their wings in a curious series of motions to move through the weightless air. They leapt from the walls of the world near where Aishwarya was standing, flew cumbrously through the middle of the globe and landed on the far side.

The bubble's scrubbers were designed to resemble little model trees and bushes. Sections of the globe were planted with toy forests. Broccoli clumps of green and yellow. Ash, oak, simultree, tree ferns of an unnatural, bright, plastic green.

'And there was me thinking you were a devotee,' said Iago. 'I'm sure you *used* to be.'

'Of *Mithras*?' she shrieked, slapping at Iago's chest with her hands and lurching half-a-metre backwards herself in equal-and-opposite motion. Without looking round, she found a foothold on a guy-wire, and pushed herself back. 'Don't insult me, Jack Glass. You know I follow Christ the Hindu.'

'Isn't that the same fellow?' It was only at this point that Diana realised Iago was deliberately teasing the old woman.

'That's tantamount to blas*phemious* blasphemy,' cackled Aishwarya. 'Those Mithras fools don't even *know* their history! They think the Romans were democrats! They cite the Roman senate as one of their models . . . as if anybody *voted* for Roman senators! But they have to do the doublethink they do, because Mithras was originally a Roman god, you know. Christ knew otherwise: he fought the Romans, because they were the Ulanovs of their day. Christ knew that true democracy begins with the democracy of the spirit, and spreads outward in communist apostledom. Christ organises a properly democratic congress of all three hundred and thirty million gods!'

'Very good,' said Iago. 'Though *they're* the ones having the party.'

'They ought to be more careful,' was Sapho's opinion. 'Worship of Mithras is proscribed.'

'Oh they know it, I know it' said Aishwarya. 'Everybody knows it. They think they don't have to keep it hidden any longer. OHOV is not an illegal chant – only because the Ulanovs don't know what it means – but the ones shouting "Mithras, Mithras, Mithras" are just getting carried away. Well, we shall have to hope the police are too busy with other things to come and break up this riotous assembly. You expect me to invite you both into my hut?'

'Yes,' said Iago.

'Well I won't. I didn't ask you to come here. You just turned up. What do you want?'

Diana looked to Iago again, but he was smiling. 'This is a RACdroid,' he said.

'I can see it's a RACdroid,' barked Aishwarya, slapping him again on his shoulder so hard she knocked him through a quarter turn and he had to reorient himself. 'You ride on a pale horse, Jack Glass, and death comes with you. Why are you bringing a RACdroid to me? You don't wish to affirm a contract, I suppose.'

'It may be a rogue,' said Diana. 'Its seals *seem* to be in order – though I'm no expert. But its data is all jumbled.'

'I need to know if its seals are indeed in order,' said Iago.

'Oho!' said Aishwarya, who found this last statement oddly hilarious. 'And you can't simply take it to the authorities! Oh! Oho!' She laughed to herself for a while. 'Well, well, I can have a look. What will you pay?'

'What will you charge?'

'Hundred credits.'

'Eighty.'

'Ninety,' said the old woman. 'Tampering with a RACdroid's a serious offence under the Lex.'

'We're not asking you to tamper with it – just check its seals.'

'Quibbles! I'm not an authorised RACdroid agent under the law, and you're asking me to do something illegal.'

'Listen to that chanting,' Iago observed. 'They are literally fomenting revolution next door. And you're worried about performing an illegal RACdroid examination? Eighty credits.'

'Eighty five.'

'Eighty,' repeated Iago.

For a brief moment, a demon of fury passed visible across the old woman's face. 'May the Mahadeva Jesus Christ rain *destruction* upon your wicked head, Jack Glass, for cheating an old woman of five credits!' But an instant later the rage had passed entirely away, and she was smiling again. 'Eighty it is,' she said, blithely. 'Come along then.'

Aishwarya led them, and the RACdroid, over towards a hut. She disappeared inside, reappearing a moment later with a glove on her right hand. With this she began fondling the device. It observed her with its impassive exhaustless machine patience. 'Seals seem alright,' she said. 'Kosher machine. The real thing. Oh! I see that *this* RACdroid belongs to the celebrated Bar-le-duc.'

'You know him?' Diana asked.

'Of course I do! He's the most famous of the Ulanovs' senior policemen! Ah but you mean, do I know him *personally*? And actually, and oddly enough, he was here a few days ago. Nevertheless you should ask your companion. Bar-le-duc is an old friend of yours, isn't he, Jack Glass? So you have his RACdroid. How is Bar?'

'Dead,' said Iago.

The smile went from Aishwarya's face. 'Really?'

'Yes.'

'When?'

'Two days ago. And since you want to know how, I shall tell you. He was cut in half.'

'He was *cut in half*?' repeated Aishwarya. When she frowned, as she was now doing, adding wrinkles to wrinkles, her eyes almost entirely disappeared into her head.

'Vaporised. Smashed to atoms. He was shot with an impossible gun.'

The old woman thought about this. 'What do you mean, Jack Glass, when you say an impossible gun?'

'A projectile weapon of some kind,' said Diana. 'Except that the projectile vanished. Impossibly.'

'Or else the *shooter* did,' said Iago. 'It is fair to say that the circumstances of his death are – mysterious. This is one reason why we need to access the data contained inside this RACdroid. It was there. It was a witness.'

'But – *murder*?' breathed Aishwarya.

'Yes, the murder. But something else,' said Iago. 'Before Bar-le-duc was killed, he and I agreed a contract. A legally binding contract. That was why he brought the RACdroid along – to affirm it. The contract guaranteed the immunity from prosecution of my companion, Diana here. I'd like to make sure that that contract still holds.'

'Did he have the authority to make such a deal?' Aishwarya asked, in an amazed voice.

'He had the Ulanovs' direct authority.'

'Gracious me. Saraswati protect me. And he came here! A week ago! He was floating right where you are! It's a good job those fools weren't chanting "Mithras-Mithras" *then*, since I now see he must have been on the Ulanovs' official business!'

'Why did he come here?' Iago asked.

'He was looking for you, Jack Glass.'

'Did you tell him where to find me?'

'I did not! The idea! How would I *know*? But he found you anyway, I guess.'

'Of all the places in the System to visit,' said Iago, wrinkle-browed. 'Of all the gin joints. *This* one? And then – straight to my house? It's fishy, you must agree.'

'I must nothing. I suppose he was following the trail. I guess he was visiting your old friends,' said Aishwarya with a shrug.

'I have lots of old friends,' said Iago; 'and they're well scattered.'

'And now he's dead,' said Aishwarya. 'Truly, death follows where you travel, Jack Glass.'

'Oh, but *Jack* didn't kill him,' said Diana. 'He was standing right next to me when it happened. The RACdroid was there too: you can see, in the datapool, the three of us standing together. We were both sprayed with his blood. Whoever fired the fatal shot must have had *all* of us in her sights. But she chose to kill only Bar-le-duc.'

'She?'

'Or he, of course.'

'Why?'

'I don't know,' said Diana. 'And we don't know who she or he was – or for whom they were working. Naturally, we analysed the open RACdroid's datapool, hoping it would provide us with clues. But it only made things more confusing. Specifically, its data seems to be corrupted. But how can its data be corrupted if its seals are kosher? Could it be a production flaw?'

'If its seals *are* kosher,' said Iago, 'then at least its testimony will stand up in court. At least the contract will still hold. Although I suppose the court may be confused by what it says.'

'After what fashion is its data corrupt?' asked Aishwarya.

'It gets the order of things . . . wrong,' said Iago.

'You mean its records disagree with what you recall?' said Aishwarya. 'In that case, I'd respectfully suggest it is your memory that is at fault.'

'Its records disagree with the laws of physics and causality,' said Iago. 'But that's the least of it, really. The whole thing is an imposs-i-*bility*. Bar-le-duc died inside a sealed bubble, a small home-sphere – in fact, my own house. Whoever killed him must have been inside that sphere when they committed the crime. There was no way they could have got out of the sphere after the crime. It's a small bubble, with only one airlock. The RACdroid had it in view the whole time, and nobody left through it. There are no other exits from the house, and the skin of the bubble remains intact. Accordingly, whoever killed Bar-le-duc must still have been there *after* the crime. But we searched that bubble very thoroughly, and there was nobody there. It's like the murderer vanished into thin air.'

'A locked-room mystery,' said Aishwarya, nodding. She frowned deeply, and then smiled brightly. 'Oh I'm *sorry* for old Bar-le-duc! Though I remind myself that he devoted his life to working for the Ulanovs! And that fact makes me a little bit less sorry, and a little bit more glad. Still, it would be good to know who killed him.'

'Of course,' agreed Iago. 'It is a particularly puzzling mystery. More puzzling still if the data of this RACdroid is to be believed.'

'This RACdroid is no rogue,' said Aishwarya. 'I'll double-check the seals, of course, but I'm telling you now, it's a kosher machine. We can review the data together, if you like. Diana Argent, upon my soul! Here in my very own front yard. So sweet-pea: Jack Glass once called me the cleverest woman in the System, and now he says that *you're* cleverer. Well: don't you think between us we can get to the bottom of this?'

2

The Nightmare at Gideon

We have to go backwards in order to understand how we got here. To trace the line from the death to death: from Leron, Berthezene and Deño ending their days down at the bottom of Earth's gravity-hole, to the explosive death of Bar-le-duc, out in freefall space. We can join the dots.

This is what happened. Pay attention. Diana and Iago had passed through a hundred islands, from grand asteroid-carved mansions to strings of shanty bubbles and even to solitary globes thousands of kilometres from anywhere else. Sapho went with them; praying to her God, Ra'allah, to preserve them all. For the time being, at least, those prayers seemed to be working.

In most of these places Iago had at least one friend. The longer Diana spent in his company, the more she was struck by how little she really knew him. He was a different man in each environment, and none of these personas had anything in common with the deferential servant who had been so constant a presence in Dia's former life.

Her former life. She thought about it, often, of course. Six months had passed since everything she knew had been turned upside down, but already that former life had acquired a distant, almost an historical patina. Had she really lived so sheltered an existence? The least glance in the mirror naturally reminded her of her sister – or, adding a few imaginary lines, her parents. Yet she was conscious in herself only of a kind of hermetic detachment. 'Should I not miss them more?' she asked Iago, one day, as they waited out another two-day flight from bubble to bubble. 'You'll see them again,' he had replied. Only later, as she wrapped herself in a blanket and tied herself by a belt to the wall, readying herself for sleep, did it occur to her that his answer had not addressed her question at all.

She thought, too, of the sudden explosion of violence that had happened on Korkura. It also seemed unreal, in her memory; virtual rather than actual.

Then she had her first nightmare.

The first of them happened in a cluster of bubbles called Gideon. This was a mixed community of several thousand, the majority of whom worshipped a deity they called The Temporal Christ. Iago docked to buy supplies, and Diana and Sapho were both of them glad to escape the confinement of *Red Rum 2020*.

The bubbles' theology was explicated at length by a very elderly woman, dressed modestly in a blue scarf and long-sleeved top from the waist up, but with nothing but skimpy hot-pants below. The oval and circular marks of removed tumours were visible at several places on her legs. Her name, improbably enough, was Delphinium Junceum; and she had evidently known Iago a long time. Certainly she chatted happily with them as they shared a meal of treated ghunk and bubble-grown fruit. 'Our belief,' she said, 'is *not* that time is an illusion – whatever our enemies say!' 'I certainly never thought so,' Diana assured her, gravely; although she had heard of this sect for the first time only half an hour before. 'No!' Delphinium, insisted. 'We do not believe that time is an illusion! Rather, we believe that time *only existed* for thirty-three years, when God himself fell into the temporal element. Time ended when he ascended to heaven.'

'It didn't exist before?'

'No – when Christ was born in Bethlehem, so too was the whole world. His birth was the creation. Of course, the cosmos was created with the traces of its imagined past: fossils were created inside the rocks at that moment; the memories of past time, archaeological records and books – like the Talmud. But none of this actually happened. It was all just an imaginary backstory, embedded within the world when it was created.'

Delphinium explained the iconography of her brooch: a cross contained within a circle. 'The circle is the female physical aperture through which Christ came into the cosmos, the cross the instrument upon which he was crucified and so departed from the cosmos. Together they are the clock face. In Christ it is always noon and three and six and nine o'clock, just as it is always quarter past these hours, and half past, and quarter to. It is all time, all the time, in Christ.'

'I see,' said Diana. Without her bId, she was compelled to dredge her memory for such knowledge as she possessed about antique clock face arrangements.

They drank soursweet local wine together, and Diana became a little tipsy. Other inhabitants of Gideon floated over and joined the discussion. It appeared there was doctrinal dissension on the topic of what had happened to time *after* Christ's crucifixion and resurrection. Some claimed that time had indeed stopped, but that it had recently started again – once more, with the illusory backstory of the preceding two and a half millennia embedded in it – which they took to be evidence that the second coming of Christ was underway. Others insisted that time had not started again, that we were indeed living in a timeless cosmos, and that the appearance of the passage of time was merely an illusion, a sort of distant echo of the rich plenitude of actual Christ-time, which had set up some kind of standing wave in the medium of existence. Diana discovered that she enjoyed teasing out the arcane implications of these conflicting theologies, exploring the limits of a self-supporting, unfalsifiable but of course illusory conceptual structure. It was a kind of problem-solving. Afterwards they sang songs, and played human pinball amongst the branching baobab branches. When she finally tied herself to a branch and settled to sleep, Diana was smiling.

Having a nightmare was, accordingly, unexpected. She was standing back in the oppressive gravity of Earth, upon the marble floor of the Korkura house. Ms Joad was there, and beside her an indistinct entity who was – somehow Diana knew – *also* Ms Joad, although she appeared to share none of her physical particularities. Iago was dead on the floor, his own blood crawling across the floor in a hideous, monstrous, simulacrum of life. It was like a giant flatworm, glistening and red-black. Then, horribly, it turned back and crawled over Iago's corpse. It seemed to be devouring him. It was inexpressibly repulsive to watch. Diana looked about her, and saw that she was not after all in the Korkura house. It scared her to think that she didn't know where she was. Ms Joad spoke, and as she did so little sparks and licks of flame played about the corners of her mouth. 'Feathers or lead?' she asked. 'You *must* choose my dear. Feathers or lead?' Diana knew that either answer would bring a terrible consequence upon her. 'Oh, please,' she cried, in a terror of anticipation, tears bubbling from her eyes, '*please* may I avoid the question altogether?' But Joad only repeated: 'feathers or lead?' And she had in her hand a knife, fashioned of rough unpolished glass, which she held close to Diana's face. Somewhere, behind her, a great roar was building, like the sound of a descending elevator air-braking, the noise growing louder and louder and more and more terrible, and Diana thought: I cannot avoid answering this question, and either answer is as likely to be wrong as right. So, although it is alien to everything I *am* and everything I can *do*, I must guess. I must simply guess. She opened her mouth to answer the impossible question, and at precisely that moment she understood what the roaring was. It was the sound of her own death, which she was somehow hearing out of time, perceiving the afterwards of the event before the event. And the blood slug leapt with a whipcrack sound from Iago's corpse and sealed over her face and crammed into her mouth.

She woke coughing, and screaming hoarsely in broken breaths between coughs. Her lungs were on *fire*. Sapho was beside her. 'What wrong, Miss? What is it?'

But the terror had pierced Diana's soul, and she was not in charge of herself. For a long time all she could say was: 'blood! Blood! Blood!' – punctuating the raspy utterance with coughs. The repetition alarmed Sapho enough to make her wake Iago up. He brought her a globe of coke-water, which helped her calm her coughing. 'What was it?' he asked. 'A nightmare?'

She nodded.

'Only a nightmare,' he said, in what perhaps was intended as a soothing voice. 'Not real!'

'You don't understand,' she gasped. 'Dreams are a crucial part of how I . . . how I do what I do. A dream like this . . . it is death! It is *death*, it is destruction coming.' She was crying a little as she said this, but putting it into words helped clarify her thoughts. The memory of Joad's cruel face; of the strange inchoate creature of black blood, of the feeling of suffocation, was very vivid in her mind. 'I never have nightmares,' she said. 'I *never* have them! Dreams are my workspace.'

The interior of the globe was as bright as day; though almost all the population were asleep.

'Too much soursweet wine,' was Iago's opinion.

Sapho tied herself to Diana's branch and the two embraced, which did manage to calm Dia a little. Soon enough Sapho went back to sleep, and Diana did not. Presently she began to find the other girl's presence constricting. She disentangled herself from Sapho's limbs, and moved herself along the branch. Eventually, after a long, fretful interlude, she went back to sleep.

In the morning Iago spent an hour in close conference with a dozen Gideonites. Diana and Sapho explored the walls of the world in Delphinium's company. Dia was unhappy at the previous night's dream, still jangled and unnerved. 'It means death,' she said to Sapho. 'It means death is coming.'

'Death is always coming, Miss' said Sapho. 'Ra'allah permits us to know as much. All he withholds is the when.'

'The when,' said Diana, in a small voice, 'is: soon.'

When Iago emerged from the sphere's main yurt he looked vaguely troubled. 'What was that about?' Diana asked. 'Revolution,' he replied. 'They want it to happen now. They don't want to hear the time's not right.'

'They're looking to *you* to initiate it?' Sapho asked, disbelievingly.

They left Gideon that afternoon, after haggling over the price of a block of fuel. The haggling was, of course, a constant of life in the Sump. It was usually undertaken vocally, with great vehemence and passion. In Gideon, though, Iago's offers were met with choral chanting of the bubble's counter-offers. It was rather charming; although the negotiation was no less forceful for its musical delivery.

Time to go. They all strapped into to their g-couches, and hauled away again on a snail-shell-shape spiral. After the initial burn, Diana made her way to the porthole and stared at the vacancy outside. It ought to be possible to see the burn-signatures of ships, freighters and sloops. To see the scattered glory of billions of bubbles. But all she saw was a blackness insufficiently alleviated with stars.

'Where are we going?' she asked Iago.

'To visit some *good* friends of mine,' Iago said. But after a day and a half's travel they arrived to find their destination deserted, and no hint as to where the occupants had gone. It was a string of four bubbles, of which three were breached and empty. Light strips still beamed in the innards, but vegetation was freeze-dried and detritus swirled very slowly in the vacuum. 'What happened here?' Dia asked, as the *Red Rum* drifted past this wreckage.

'Police,' Iago replied. 'I suppose.' The fourth bubble was still intact, and lit within; but when they docked and opened the door they found a space choked with unmannerly vegetation, and without human habitation. The air was heady, over-oxygenated. 'I suppose the police breached the other three globes to herd the population into this one,' said Iago. 'When your globe bursts, as they sometimes do, you scurry like rats through the escape schutes, and into the next one. The police just need to pop them in sequence to corral all the population in one place. Then they could arrest them, ship them off.' 'Why?' asked Diana, putting her palm over her nose. The stink of the plants was surprisingly intense, and, oddly, more animal than vegetable. Some genetically modified bulb or fruit, she supposed, designed to supplement the dreary diet of ghunk. 'I mean – what for?'

'Who knows? The legal rubric was probably political dissent. Although maybe it was trade fraud. There's a huge amount of barter in the Sump, and since barter is, strictly speaking, illegal, it gives the police a pretext at any time they need one.'

'But why *bother*?'

'They may have had a specific reason. Or they may just have needed to hit targets, for prison labour, or indenture service. Speak to regular policepeople, and they'll complain about how their lives are ridden by quotas. Plus, confiscating stuff from houses is sometimes lucrative. Though it's usually not. People out here are too poor to own anything particularly valuable.'

Iago put a slow quarter-burn on to move them into open space. For a while they all just lay, enduring the drag of acceleration. Eventually the burn ended, and they were able to dismount their g-couches. 'I've picked up some news,' Iago announced. 'Well, gossip. Or perhaps it's the same thing?'

'What news?' asked Diana.

'First, your parents are well. I deduce this from the fact that they are still undetected by the authorities, despite some furious activity. Secondly, Miss Joad – you recall her?'

Diana smiled mirthlessly

'Well,' said Iago. 'She has been punished for her failure to apprehend us. The Ulanovs were not happy with her.'

Diana felt joy flush through her chest at this news. 'Really? Did they execute her?'

'Not that. But she has been demoted a long way down the hierarchy.'

The nightmares still came, though. That very night Diana woke from dreams of blood and death, orchestrated by her sub-consciousness's eidolon of Miss Joad. She was less debilitated by this one than her first, but it was still intensely unpleasant.

It was two days' flight to their next destination: a Fac. Not, Iago assured them, an illegal operation, though it was remote enough from the usual trajectories of police sloops to be, he said, one shade of grey. But in fact the crew largely maintained a *legal* operation.

The Fac was a linked series of pressurised ovals, inside of which meat was being grown in semisentient slabs. Iago greeted the human crew – a dozen men, no women, all with the sunblast sigil of Ra'allah tattooed onto their foreheads. Sapho greeted them with smiles, and they sang a solar chant together. Then they all drank bovrilcohol, played mahjong together, and there was a great deal of laughter and singing.

'The seventy-percent rule has hurt us badly,' said Samm, one of the more animated of the farmers.

'The seventy-percent rule?'

'The Lex Ulanova assumes that thirty percent of all trans-actions in the Sump are fraudulent,' explained a man called Chilli, whose paper-white skin was marked with multiple circles and ovals of pale pink scarflesh where tumours had been removed. 'It's a concession of reality, I suppose, but also it's an arbitrary figure – deeper in the Sump and pretty much *all* the trade is fraudulent: if you can call growing figs and tomatoes and swap-ping them with neighbours for roasted beetle or powdered urea *illegal*. But for most of the Sump life is subsistence; ghunk, sunlight, there's no surplus there *for* trade. On the other hand, out here, nearer Earth-moon – well, if we could get away with thirty percent black trade, we'd be happy. We can't, though. Pretty much all the meat we grow is sold in bulk contracts, and the money passes through kosher accounts, and all tariffs and duties are deducted automatically by AI. We're almost entirely legal, I'm sorry to say.'

'That's good, though, isn't it?' asked Diana. 'I mean, at least you're clear of the attentions of the police?'

Samm scowled. 'The seventy percent rule is enshrinéd in law,' he said, with a trisyllabic flourish on *enshrined*. 'That's the thing about the Lex – it even regulates the bounds of illegality. So: we are taxed not from 100% of our gross, but from 143%. To take into account our supposed involvement in the black market. It means our tax burden is much higher than it would otherwise be.'

'You still clear a profit, though?'

'Barely,' said Chilli. 'I'm part-owner here; I ought to be swanning about in a luxury O with other captains of industry, drinking and taking soma. Instead I live over the shop, and eat ghunk, and send all my surplus to my wife and daughter on Mars. She's in the Arean Academy, you know. The fees are – but, look, enough of my troubles.'

'The truth is,' said Samm, 'if the police wanted to roll us over, they could. It's just that they've no *reason* to, we're too small for them to bother about. We just need to hang on.'

'Until?'

'Until I have enough for my own house,' said Samm.

'When I hit my target, I'll sell, and move to a more respectable orbit,' agreed Chilli. 'But that's years away.'

Eventually the crew of the Fac gave Iago three bales of preserved meat and other foodstuffs, and in return he gave them a metre-square tablet of mysterious provenance and functionality. Barter, the oldest mode of human trade; now – since all *actual* money was tagged so it could be taxed as it passed through bank accounts, or suchlike databases – more common than ever before. Back aboard *Red Rum 2010* Diana discovered that Iago had also traded, or begged, or otherwise obtained a hefty chunk of ice, cabled to the exterior of the boat. 'We're going somewhere for a long while,' Diana deduced. 'I say so because – well, that's a lot of ice.'

'The genius of deduction,' beamed Iago.

'Where *are* we going?' Sapho asked. 'Are we just going to drift from bubble to bubble?'

'I'm taking you to *my* house,' said Iago. 'Nobody has ever been there before. Except me, I mean. It's the most private place I know. But first – I want to use this Fac's datasift to piggyback a message.'

'A message?' asked Diana.

'I've located your sister.'

Diana's heart leapt up. 'Is she safe? Where is she?'

'She's on Mars – or at least, she's on her *way* there. It's been months since she set off; she'll nearly be there now. And yes, she's safe. She's taking care to stay *on the move*, and so must we. It'll be a while before I can reunite you two physically, I'm afraid. Your parents prepared the way pretty carefully, and a good proportion of the strength of your Clan managed to slip through the Ulanov net. But things are very uncomfortable right now: the other Clans jockeying for position, the Ulanovs putting enormous resources into suppressing Clan Argent – really, quite staggering amounts of money.'

'Can I speak with her?'

Iago scratched his head. 'There is a risk,' he said, cautiously, 'when it comes to setting up a line of communication, of course. If we tip off the authorities, they will bend space itself to get to us. If they could seize your sister they would have an advantage; but if they could seize both of you the game would be over.'

'Is that yes? Or no?'

'It is yes. Your bId was contaminated, and I assume hers is too; but we can use my network – it's nonstandard, unique to me, and I'm scrupulous about keeping it clean. Plus we'll piggyback upon the system here, aboard this Fac. And we're well-enough placed to sever the connection and nip away if there's any sign that things have been compromised.'

Diana spent an hour online, from which she obtained a few minutes of old-style face-to-face talk. The communication lag was fifteen minutes there-and-back, which was frustrating because time was so short. It was not a properly worldtual encounter, either, so she couldn't even hug her MOHsister. But she *could* see her, and speak to her, and that was enough to get both of them weeping and grinning. Eva filled her in on her adventures: arriving at the Tobruk Plasmaser, and almost immediately finding herself in the middle of a firefight. 'Luckily we were able to get away, south. I eventually rode an old ballistic vessel into orbit from Ivoire.' 'It's precarious, isn't it?' said Diana, smiling through her tears. 'Iago and I were shot from a g-cannon on Mount Abora! When the engines on the boat kicked in I thought we were literally going to shake to pieces!' 'I'm so relieved you're alright, my love!' Eva said. 'We both need to hide until things have blown over a little. MOHmies are both fine – I've seen them, in the flesh, and they're fine. But they're hiding, and so will I and so must you. I won't ask where you will hide, because it's better you don't tell anybody, not even me – though I love you more than I can say.' Diana wiped her eyes with a fold of her tunic. 'I will. I'll be safe until—'

A sandstorm of interference froze the image of Eva's face, and scratched hundreds of straggly neon lines across it. 'That's it,' said Iago. 'The connection is broken.'

3

Dunronin

So they climbed into the narrow g-couches of the *Red Rum* cabin
(there was room for four, although even with only three the space
felt crowded) and shot away. Diana, grimacing under acceleration's squeeze and squash, wept again with happiness to think
that her sister was safe. Presently, she dozed – too flattened by the
forces to sleep properly. She was in the hinterland of sleep, a dusk
of the mind, and a flash of light gleamed suddenly. She thought:
perhaps it is a Champagne Supernova a thousand light years
distant, or perhaps it is a tiny will-wisp flicker a metre away, and I
could reach out my hand and touch it. But how can I know? The
muscles in her arm flexed and bulged, but it was impossible to
raise the limb against the haul of the g-force. Then she heard the
grumbling noise she heard in her nightmares, and its slow
accumulation of volume made her very afraid. It was the sound
of a massive explosion, but played backwards, so that it grew and
gathered towards a climactic cacophony rather than falling away
from it. There were things in the darkness that wished her ill.
The flash might have been light glinting on the cutting edge of a
blade, aimed at her eyes. Abruptly the noise was very loud, and
tremors were shaking her, and she was straining every sinew to
scream, but no sound emerged from her mouth. She woke, still
squashed and squeezed by acceleration. Or else she was still
asleep, and this was part of her nightmare.

But then the g-force went soggy, and then dissipated altogether. She opened her eyes and discovered that she was gasping
the word 'hurt' over and over.

Sapho helped her out of the couch. The *Red Rum* was coasting
now, gravity-free and quiet. 'Three days until we get to where

286

we're going,' Iago said, hanging upside down from the ceiling like a bat. 'Did you have another nightmare?'

'I wasn't properly asleep,' gasped Diana. But she was sweaty all over her skin; and since sweat dissipates poorly in zero-g she felt uncomfortably hot. Her face was red. 'I don't understand it. I've never had nightmares before, in all my life.'

'All your long life,' said Iago, smiling.

'But I saw – I don't know.'

'What?'

'Death. Doubles. Pain.'

'Perhaps,' suggested Sapho, 'a sedative? To help you sleep?'

'I can't take any sedative,' said Diana, reflexly. 'Dreams are one of the key ways I process and problem-solve. I can't tinker with my sleep. I can't smother my dreams in opiates.'

'There are no problems to be solved over the next three days,' said Iago. 'We're just biding time until we arrive at my house.'

'Oh Iago,' she said, with the patronising tone unique to teenagers rebuking their elders. 'There are always problems to solve!'

The nightmares did not recur during the flight, provided they were travelling in zero-g. As they coasted, she slept very peacefully. But on the occasions when they had to get into the g-couches in order to put a prudent zig or a zag into their trajectory the sensation of weight in her bones and on her chest made her aware again of her fear. And the final deceleration was a nerve-jangling half-hour; claustrophobic (she had *never* experienced claustrophobia before!), panicky, horrible. It had, in other words, something to do with gravity. Or perhaps it was merely a question of bad associations between Earth's ground-level pull and sudden, alarming violence.

Otherwise the voyage was as uneventful as the dozen that preceded it. At one point Iago thought they were being followed, but after poring over the input data he decided it was simply a sensor-echo. 'It can't be a police ship,' he said. 'Not just because they can't know where we are; but because the reading suggests the trailing ship is exactly like us. I mean – exactly. Like a doppelganger. It's a blip.'

After six hours the blip vanished from the sensors, which tended to confirm Iago's theory.

Finally they arrived. They docked at the single doorway to a small bubble, glinting green in the black sky.

'Diana, Sapho,' Iago announced. 'This is my house. This, in point of fact, is my *retreat*. You are the first human beings, apart from myself, to come here. It is, I hope, a safe place to stay, at least for the time being. The Ulanovs have some high-powered AIs monitoring all the billions of objects in solar orbit, of course; but I have worked hard and spent a lot of money to ensure that Dunronin looks just like any of a billion Sump smallholdings. As far as the authorities are concerned, this place is home to perfectly unexceptional folk, just like a trillion other ordinary people, living on ghunk and sunlight, growing what vegetables they can to supplement their diet, worshipping whatever strange gods they worship. We shall hide in the crowd.'

' "Dunronin"?' asked Diana.

'That's what I call it. A kind of joke. I suppose it is. Anyway; the house isn't large – but it's a damn sight bigger than the cabin of the *Red Rum 2020*, so let's get *out* of this racehorse belly and stretch our legs.'

It *was* small, inside: a one-hundred-metre diameter, the walls given over either to low-maintenance scrub or transparent panels. They were close enough to the orbit of Venus for the sun to be markedly larger and brighter, and shadows moved with ink-block distinctness over the interior as the globe went through its slow rotation. There were vegetable beds, but these were home to nothing but weeds. 'I haven't been here in many years,' Iago noted. 'But we can get trays cleaned out and growing pretty quickly, I think. We'll bring some of the ice in here. And look at the fruit tree! I bought it in part because of its slow-grow gene tweak, since I'm not often here to prune it. But even with the tweak, it must have *quadrupled* its size since I last saw it!'

288

Diana would not have recognised the briar-patch tangle of black branches ending in tongue-sized, rubbery white blossom petals *as* a fruit tree. 'There's no fruit on it,' she complained, 'for one thing.'

'I can turn the fruiting gene on, now that we're here,' said Iago. 'There's a phial of the needful in one of the storage cases by the door. Sprinkle it in at the roots. We'll have fresh fruit in a matter of weeks.'

They unloaded the *Red Rum*, which didn't take long. After that Diana explored the new space. For structure and ease of locomotion there were eight guy-ropes, none of which passed through the central space of the sphere. A hundred-metre diameter gave the house a surface area – the inside of its curving walls – of over 30,000 m². Some people might consider that big enough; and it took her a while to check out all the different features, patches of vegetation, and shelters: the bedrooms, the toilet closets, the various stores, the exercise grids.

'I know you're used to larger mansions,' Iago said, floating over towards her.

'This is plenty large enough,' she said. 'By which I mean – I'll get used to it. To be honest, Iago, I'm more worried about getting bored bored *bored*.'

'Without your bId, bId, *bId*,' Iago replied. 'I understand. There are books in storage; and some old-fashioned sealed-world IP environments. But I'm afraid we are going to be doing a fair amount of simply hanging about. I find the best thing is to spend time cultivating the garden. There's no need to hurry it; and three hectares of ground can absorb a lot of work, even when the plants are designed to be low-maintenance. It'll take us a week to tidy up, for instance; before we even think about reseeding, or turfing, or new crops or anything like that.'

'I don't mean to sound ungrateful,' she said, wriggling herself through the air to give him a hug. 'I'm still getting used to being, you know. Off the grid. I'll adjust.'

'There's plenty of time,' said Iago.

He was wrong, though. In the event, there was very little time. They had a day and a night, both equally bright, and that was all. They spent the time tidying, eating stores and chatting, playing games. But it was early on the second day when the authorities caught up with them.

You spend six months fleeing, keeping out of the way of the Law. Finally you arrive at a safe place, and that is when the Law catches you.

It is frustrating.

The first Diana, Sapho and Iago knew was a flash, visible very clearly through the house walls. They were weeding, and all three stopped what they were doing and looked. 'What was that?' Diana asked. She had that sudden tingling intimation that things were about to change.

Iago checked the House AI. 'Very close. Between twenty and thirty thousand kilometres away – no more,' he said. 'That's not good news.'

'What is it?'

'I don't know.'

'Something's not right,' said Diana.

'Could it be the exhaust of a ship accelerating?' asked Sapho.

'Rather bright for that,' said Iago, looking troubled. He peered into the palms of his hands, as if the answer were written there. 'Also much too close – too close for comfort.'

'Was it something blowing up?' Diana suggested.

Iago ran a more detailed check on space in that direction. The AI was slow, relatively, but it turned up the ship quickly enough.

'A sloop,' said Iago. He sighed. 'A police sloop, and coming towards us. It's pretty well chameleonised; but when you look straight at it you can make it out. And it's *definitely* coming this way.'

'How?' Diana squealed. 'You said this place was—'

'It is!' Pride gave his voice sudden ferocity.

'Then how have they found us?'

'I don't *know* how. But they're definitely coming. If it weren't for the flash, I wouldn't have noticed the approach.'

'Why would they give themselves away like that?'

'I *don't* know.'

'Thirty thousand kilometres, you said,' Diana pressed. 'Does that give us time to evacuate? Into the *Red Rum* – can they outrun us, if we make a sprint for it?'

'They'd catch us easily,' said Iago. 'And anyway, they're almost here! This ship isn't connected with the flash. At least I don't think so – a different direction.' He cursed. 'We don't have time even to *try* and get away.'

'But then what *is* the flash? The two things must be connected.'

'It would be an improbable coincidence otherwise,' said Iago. 'Although it's hard to see what could connect them.'

'Was it a . . . flare, perhaps?'

'Police sloops are not in the habit of alerting their prey by firing flares,' said Iago.

'Well then – some other ship, some friendly individual is trying to warn us – to help us. Is there *another* ship out there?'

'No,' said Iago, checking the House AI again. 'Nothing else out there. Just the police sloop.' He closed his eyes. 'I feel very old,' he said. 'This is terrible news. We *cannot* fall into the hands of the Ulanovs. It would be a disaster for your family if *you* do, Diana. And if *I* do – well, it would be a disaster for all humanity.'

'Not,' said Diana, drily, 'to overstate it.'

'No!' said Iago, with sudden vehemence. 'For years I have gone to extreme lengths to avoid falling into the hands of the Ulanovs. I have done some genuinely terrible things. And I have done so not to save my own skin – what does my own skin, matter, after all? I have *done* so because the entire future of the human race is at stake! It has not been a personal matter. It has been a species imperative. I have never found anything I could, in conscience, put before that imperative. Not,' he added, looking around at his own bubble, 'not until now.'

'What can we do?'

'Our options,' Iago said, in a low voice, '*are* limited. We can't fight them. We can't run away.'

'We're caught!' cried Sapho.

Iago stretched himself in mid-air. 'We need,' he said. 'We need more information.'

But he did nothing more active than floating to a spigot, washing his hands, rubbing them in a cluster of pearl-bright beads of water and drying them. Dia and Sapho followed suit. Then Iago kicked off from the guy-rope and flew to the door to set up such defences as the house possessed. 'It's not much,' he said. 'I have two rail-guns, but they aren't going to trouble something as large as a police sloop.'

Then, as Sapho and Diana floated beside him, he dialled a line through to the ship.

A face appeared: long-featured and lugubrious-looking. 'Jack Glass as I live and breathe,' said the face, in an unsurprised voice.

'Bar-le-duc,' replied Iago. 'It *is* you!' He sounded so energised by the sight of him that Diana, momentarily, thought this new-comer might not be a threat after all. This impression did not last long, however.

'I was going to say *it's been a long time, Jack*,' Bar-le-duc replied, slowly. 'But time is a slippery concept, where you're concerned – isn't it?'

'You have come to arrest me,' said Iago.

'I have. The authorities *have* you now, my friend. They'll torture you, and probably kill you, and that will be your end. But you've known for a long while that that's where you're heading. No need for me to Tiresias excessively on *that* score.'

'You haven't taken me yet, Bar,' said Iago. But he spoke without defiance. He sounded, on the contrary, rather worn down and weary.

'True! Somehow, despite our stealth approach, you spotted us a little *ahead* of time. My plan was to board you, utilising the element of surprise – burn through some emergency entrance holes and rush you. But you spotted us! Well done.'

'If you didn't want to be spotted, why let off that flare?'

'Flare?' said Bar-le-duc. 'We let off no flare! Do you think we're idiots? I assumed *you* let off that flare, to inform us that you had *seen* us. I'm more interested in – what gave us away? I was coming in, silent running, very cautious. Another few minutes and we would have *had* you.'

'Serendipity favours the angels,' said Iago.

'I congratulate you, anyway,' said Bar-le-duc. 'I can afford to be magnanimous, now! Now that I have finally caught you!'

'Your career hasn't suffered, Bar, since the last time we met?' Iago asked, with mock solicitude.

'What?'

'I was anxious that our previous encounter might have harmed your prospects. Perhaps you have heard about Ms Joad? She used to be one of the Ulanovs' favoured agents. Then she failed to arrest me, and now she's been banished to the outer darkness.'

'I heard about her, yes,' replied Bar-le-duc, with respectful gloom in his voice. 'A shame. To go from being a somebody to being a nobody would be hard for anyone; it is doubly so for her. Well, thank you for your concern, my friend! Having you slip through my fingers certainly didn't *help* my promotion possibilities.' He spoke with a slow, deliberate, rather depressive intonation, as if any kind of communication with other people was a mournful duty. 'Still,' he added, smiling thinly, 'I have you now.'

'Who *is* this man?' Diana asked.

'You haven't heard of the celebrated Bar-le-duc?' said the hologrammatic representation of the celebrated Bar-le-duc, mournfully.

'He's *police*, is who he is,' said Iago.

'Really!' objected the head. 'Much *more* than police.'

'He works for the Ulanovs. He specialises in arrests. Search

293

and capture. He tried to arrest me once before. He failed, though.'

'I've tried more than *once*, dear man,' said Bar-le-duc.

'And you failed more than once, too. Maybe you'll fail again.'

'I don't think *so*,' Bar-le-duc murmured. 'Not this time. You can't run. You can't fight. There's nothing you *can* do.'

'I could match your bounty, and pay you more,' suggested Iago. 'Pay you – shall we say, three times?'

'No,' said Bar-le-duc, simply.

Something structural in Iago's spirit sagged, visibly; you could see it in his face. 'Well, here's another option. I simply shan't let you into my house. Huff and puff all you like.'

'I think you *will* let us in,' said Bar-le-duc, sadly. 'From where I'm sitting your bubble looks eminently poppable.'

'Pop the bubble?' Iago said, peering through the window to get a glimpse of the sloop. 'Do that and we'll die, and if we die you get nothing.'

'I'm confident we could fish you out of the vacuum. Though I couldn't say the same for your friend. Or we could harpoon you. This sloop has Tachyon Thrust you know – plenty powerful enough to tow you all the way back Lagrangeward.'

'You try that, and I'll burst the bubble *myself*,' Iago warned.

'I believe you would, too,' said Bar-le-duc, in his slow, mournful voice. 'You're very blinkered when it comes to the possibilities of life, Jack. In that respect you're almost a *child*. One thing at a time in your mind, eh? Oh so ignorant about life; although of course there's nothing about death you *don't* know. Of course you'd kill yourself. But – her?'

Iago glanced over at the *her*, and Diana felt a ghastly tightening in her stomach. It occurred to her suddenly: *this is really happening*. It had crept up so unexpectedly; and her life lately had been such a succession of weird meetings and unexpected developments that it took an effort to persuade herself this was different. But, suddenly, Diana was aware of the possibility that *she could die*. They could all die, here and right now. This could be where it ends. She tried to think through the options – that being her speciality, of course – but she couldn't see past it. There are only two ways this plays out, she thought: either the police arrest us, and turn us over to who-knows-what horrors; or we all die, right here and now.

Neither alternative was good.

'How do you know about her, anyway?' Iago snapped. 'How did you find out where I live? How have you *done* this, Bar?'

'I have my sources,' said Bar-le-duc. 'You don't need to worry about them. But you *do* have to come along with me, my little thomas-rhymer. You *have* to harp-and-carp. Options exhausted, I'm sorry to say.' He did sound sorry, too.

Iago looked about himself, turned himself entirely about in mid-air. He appeared to be surveying his domain. But there was nothing in here that could help him. 'It was foolish of me to come here,' he said, perhaps to himself. 'We should simply have gone on from bubble to bubble – we should have kept moving. If I could turn back time I'd do it differently.'

'Not even you can turn back time,' said Bar-le-duc.

Iago faced the hologram again. 'I want this absolutely clear,' he said, decisively. 'I will go with you so long as you guarantee that *she* be untouched – left alive, and free.'

'Iago!' said Diana.

'*If,*' Iago said again, not looking at her. 'She can go free.'

'Free,' said Bar-le-duc, as if the word were literally incomprehensible to him.

'You know what I mean. Able to go where she chooses, at liberty.'

'Why should I?'

'Because otherwise I'll kill us all.'

'But if I agree to let her go?'

'Then,' said Iago, 'I'll come willingly with you.'

The projection was of a head weighing up his options. Then, Bar-le-duc smiled his thin smile. 'By all means,' he said. 'If that concept means anything to you – or to her – then fair enough.

But after all, we're *all* in prison. What is it the old poet said, about the solar system being a prison, with many cells in it, existentially equivalent to living inside a walnut shell? Who was that – Shakespeare? It's usually Shakespeare.'

'No equivocation,' said Iago. 'I'm happy to agree the Solar System is, in the largest sense, a prison. But you must agree that you will permit Diana to go into whichever portion of it she chooses, unmolested.'

'Very well. But do you know what, my friend?'

'What?'

'If what they say about you is true – why, then the System will no longer *be* a prison! You can open the door, and humanity can flood out into the cosmos as a whole!'

'I wouldn't believe everything they say about me,' Iago muttered. Then, speaking directly: 'how shall I trust you? Do you have a RACdroid aboard that sloop?'

'Of course I do. I am an accredited senior officer of the Lex Ulanova. It can witness our contract. Still: a contract to let a wanted criminal go free? I'm not sure that's wholly legal.'

'It's not the legality I'm worried about,' said Iago. 'It's having it *recorded*. So that, at a later date, it is not simply your word against mine.'

Even Bar-le-duc's laugh sounded sad; a slow series of clucking noises. 'And you think there will *be* any later date, for you! My poor friend.'

'Just bring the RACdroid with you.'

'So then we are clear,' said Bar-le-duc. 'I shall leave your Clan Argent friend to her own destiny, and in return I shall take *you* off to the authorities, and *they* will dismantle you organ by organ, in a welter of blood, to get at what is in your head. You're quite sure you want to go ahead with this? I ask, for old time's sake.'

Iago took a deep breath. 'Just bring the RACdroid. I'll deal with, with the *rest* of it if-and-when.'

'Deal with it!' repeated Bar-le-duc, chuckling sorrowfully. 'My dear friend. I've spent such a portion of my life hunting you! I'm almost sorry it comes to this.'

'*You* can come through, Bar. Bring the droid. There's only one entrance to this globe, and my sloop is already docked there; so you'll have to dock with the rear hatch of my ship and come through that to get inside. I'll instruct the AI to unlock it.'

'Very well.'

'Come alone, Bar. Just you and the RACdroid.'

'No, my dear man, no! Come alone into your lion's den? You think I don't know how *many* people you have killed? No. I shall bring four people with me, to protect my tender flesh against your glass knifeblade.'

'You can bring two,' said Iago.

'Four.'

The hologram vanished. The conversation was at an end.

'Iago,' Diana said. 'Jack, I mean – you're not really thinking of giving yourself up to him? You heard what he said!'

'Right now,' he said, glancing over at Sapho, 'the choices are: either I go with them or everybody inside this bubble dies.'

'Only Ra'allah can help us now,' said Sapho.

'I need to know how they found us!' Iago said. 'I make it my business not to be found, and yet – here they are.' He looked at his two companions. 'Don't worry about me; I've escaped from prison before. I can do it again.'

4

The End of Bar-le-duc

Bar-le-duc's sloop was much larger than the *Red Rum*. Diana, Iago and Sapho watched it manoeuvre cumbrously to present one of its doors to the little craft's rear lock. It was not well done. At one point the flank of the sloop banged against the walls of the house, causing the whole structure to deform and bulge, ringing with a resonant, deep *boing* sound and shaking leaves and debris into the central space to float and swirl.

'Steady!' muttered Iago.

But eventually it was done. The great sword-shaped length of the police sloop dominated the view from the house windows; a fat tangent line drawn off the curve of the sphere. The sound of *Red Rum*'s back door being opened echoed around the space.

'Here they come,' muttered Iago.

The first thing to emerge from the airlock was the RACdroid itself; a circular silverblue face, blankly inexpressive, above an ovoid torso and four flexible gel limbs; it clambered into the sphere and made its way along one of the guy-cables, stopping halfway along. Bar-le-duc came next. In person he was a tall, distinguished-looking man. His long hair floated distractingly bouffant in zero-gravity and perhaps his features were slightly too large for his pale brown face. But his triangular wedge of a nose was certainly impressively aristocratic-looking, and his eyes had an eagle's directness. He was carrying a gun which he kept unerringly directed at Iago as he negotiated the airlock and came into the larger space. 'Jack!' he said, smiling. But then his face grew stern. 'Three of you? I thought it was just you and Ms Argent?'

'Your sources are not infallible, then,' said Iago. 'I'm pleased to hear that. This is Sapho. She's no threat to you.'

'Ra'allah protect us,' muttered Sapho.

'No *threat*?' repeated Bar-le-duc. 'Well, well, perhaps so. Nonetheless, I must ask you, Ms Sapho, to *go away* – go over there, to where those purple-leaved bushes are. Stay visible, if you please, but do remove yourself from my immediate vicinity. I will shoot you if you make any sudden moves – believe me.'

'I believe you,' said Sapho, and pulled herself along a guy-rope until she reached the wall over by Bar-le-duc's left. When he was happy she was far enough away, he called to her to stop.

Meanwhile, Bar-le-duc's four figures (all men) were coming through one after the other. Diana's heart was beating more rapidly. It was actually happening. It was *really* happening. She had no weapon; and she could not see how Iago could take on *five* armed and trained commandos. It was starting to look as though he was actually going to be taken into custody. And then, what followed? Hadn't Bar-le-duc said it himself? The authorities would dismantle him organ by organ, in a waterfall of blood, to get at what was in his head. 'Iago,' she said, urgently. 'What shall we do?'

'We shall stay calm,' said Iago, levelly.

'Good advice, Ms Argent,' said Bar-le-duc. He kicked off gently from a guy-cable, and floated through plain air towards them. Ten metres away to the left, a little below them, the RACdroid perched, recording everything.

'I brought the droid, as you can see,' said Bar-le-duc. 'Though now that we're *here*, I'm not sure we really need it.'

'This is the deal,' said Iago, in a clear, loud voice, for the benefit of the Droid. 'It takes the form of a contract. You, Bar-le-duc, agree, by the legal powers invested in you, to let Ms Diana Argent go free. You will leave her in this place with her companion, Sapho, and the functioning space sloop currently docked – the ship is called the *Red Rum 2020*. Both the two of them, and the ship, are specifically identified in this contract. You agree to leave this sphere and this ship in good order, *and* you agree to leave both Ms Argent and her friend unmolested, cleared of legal taint. In return, I agree to go with you without violence.'

'*No* violence,' repeated Bar-le-duc, forcefully.

'None. I contract to make no assault upon you, your men or your equipment, and to accompany you to whichever destination you choose.'

'I could simply take you, Jack,' said Bar-le-duc, wagging a finger.

'You could try,' said Iago. 'But you cannot afford to kill me, since you need what is in my head. And I am very skilled at

299

causing death and damage to other human beings. This means I could make the passage very . . . troublesome for you.'

Bar-le-duc looked at him. His eyes, a striking violet-blue, neither blinked nor wavered. 'And if I agree to your contract?'

'Then I shall come with you, as I have specified, and do you no harm. The details are in the RACdroid now.'

'RACdroids can be destroyed,' Bar-le-duc said.

'If that happens then Ms Argent's legal immunity is destroyed too. Believe me, that's the last thing I want to happen. So I have no incentive to do you any harm, or to damage the droid. I'm proposing to legally link *my* good behaviour to *her* immunity. That is the contract. Do you agree to it?'

After a pause, Bar-le-duc said: 'yes.' Then speaking more loudly, for the benefit of the droid, he said: 'I, André Bar-le-duc, contract as Jack Glass has specified.'

'Iago,' said Diana. 'You can't go with him. You're going to your own death!'

'It looks like a heroic gesture, doesn't it?' said Bar-le-duc, speaking not with sarcastic mockery, but rather with a dignified and mournful precision. 'Self-sacrifice. But I have known Jack for longer than you. He is planning something – he has something up his sleeve. Isn't that so Jack?'

'All I care about,' said Iago, 'is that Diana's legal immunity is assured.' He was looking at each of the men Bar-le-duc had brought in, one after the other, as if sizing them up. But what could he possibly do? All were armed, trained, and loyal to their master – their loyalty reinforced with CRFs.

'It is done,' said Bar-le-duc. 'The RACdroid has the contract. I must say, Jack, this has gone smoother than I thought it might.'

Diana felt panic rising inside her. 'Don't leave me,' she said.

'You are free, Diana,' Iago said. But he didn't look at her.

Bar-le-duc shook his head. 'It's poor form of you, Jack – toying with this girl's heart!'

'Oh, *what* do you mean?' Iago snapped at him. 'Don't talk nonsense.' He sounded genuinely annoyed.

Bar-le-duc, addressed Diana. 'Ms Argent, my dear,' he said. 'Believe me when I tell you: Jack Glass looks at people in the way an artist or an architect looks at his raw materials. He is not interested in them – in you – he is only interested in what he can *do* with them, with you. Now, perhaps he feels that what he is going to do with these people, these trillions of human beings, *is* worthwhile, or virtuous, or in the service of the greater good. Maybe he genuinely thinks so! But it seems to me that this does not excuse his behaviour. Means do not justify the end. People must not be used as tools. They must, rather, be treated as people.'

'You intend to treat *me* as a person, do you?' said Iago, evidently annoyed by this lecture.

'That *is* different. You know it, just as I do. I serve justice, and the law – order. If we did not have strict and just punishment for transgression, then what would we . . .'

That was the precise moment Bar-le-duc was cut in two – slain, killed, destroyed.

Everything inside the bubble went crazy. Explosive decompression. All the air inside the globe convulsed with a great recursive lurch.

Diana was wrenched and dragged sideways. She wheeled dizzyingly full circle and kept on spinning. The abrupt rapidity of the motion threw her arms and legs out, starfishwise.

Chaos.

It was chaos, and old night.

Despite the unexpected suddenness Diana instantly understood what was going on. As she shot through the air and bounced hard against the fabric of the bubble, knocking the breath from her, she realised that the side of the bubble had split open. She realised that Bar-le-duc's torso had been turned into an expanding cloud of red droplets.

Uh!

There was something more, immediately before the explosion, something else. Who was it said it originally? – Shakespeare was it? Searching her bId-less memory for the source of the quotation, she alighted on Shakespeare: *the code got all weird*. That was the best way she could think of describing it. She felt some strangeness, some occlusion in her ability not just to process but even to *parse* reality. For a moment, reality had acquired the unmistakeable flavour of a Worldtuality; before snapping (almost *tangibly* snapping) back to actual reality. A bulge, or shrinkage; fear clutching the brain. Perhaps, she thought, it was her own senses, so finely tuned, so thoroughly bred into her. They gave her an intimation that this thing was about to happen. And it did.

Somebody had shot Bar-le-duc with a piece of heavy ordnance. This had literally, and horribly, chopped his body in two. The shot had broken in through the wall of the bubble – and smashed the docked sloop in half too. Using goddess-alone-knew-what advanced targeting technology, somebody *outside* the bubble had locked onto Bar-le-duc, and fired a superfast projectile through the wall of the globe *right through him*.

Almost as pressing a question as *who?* was – *how?* But more pressing than either was: what shall we do to stop this haemorrhage of air?

Diana saw that she was being sucked towards the breach in the wall of the globe. She saw three of Bar-le-duc's men wriggling in flight, all pulled along the same trajectory. The fourth man was nowhere to be seen. He had been standing, she recalled, near where the gash in the side of the wall now was, so presumably he had been obliterated.

Whirlwind.

The RACdroid was leaning in their direction, although it had anchored itself automatically to the guy-cable.

Sapho, weirdly parti-coloured – sprayed red down one side only – was flying at a tangent to Diana. Dia saw her land in amongst the threshing bushes, waving her arms to absorb the impact, and struggling to hold on.

The vagaries of the impact had thrown Iago in the *opposite* direction to the breach – Diana saw him disappear into the miniature forest. Like Sapho, he looked as though a spray gun had coated him with a fine mist of red paint.

That red had been Bar-le-duc, moments before.

It occurred to Diana that Iago must be being sucked out of the *second* hole. Because there must be an exit breach to correspond to the entry point. The projectile having entered and bisected the globe must have punched through on the far side – that was why Iago was sucked away in that direction. That meant his death. He had vanished; he must be floating airless and blasted in empty vacuum. But it meant *their* deaths too – no globe this size could survive two major breaches. The air would drain like water through a sieve. They had moments, only, left.

They were all going to die. The thought crystallised briefly in Diana's mind: Iago said *this* was the choice! To go with Bar-le-duc, or for everybody to die.

She collided against the side of the sphere with enough force to punch the air out of her lungs. Rebound-bounced. Span three sixty. She caught sight of one of Bar-le-duc's men vanishing into the projectile's entry-hole. The fellow threw his arms wide, his face a rictus of panic, and clawed at the lip of the hole, trying to hold on. But the sides were slippery, the curved edge of the gash worked against him, and the force of air too strong. He scrabbled for a moment, and then he was gone. As she hurtled diagonally across the mouth of the hole Diana saw, briefly, right down it – into a chaos of swirling spaceship metal fragments and rubbish, and beyond that into blackness.

A hole in the fabric of the world and all air and heat and life swooshing through it.

All around her people were yelling; their mouths working and flexing. She could even, just about, hear the wah-wah-wah of their words, though smothered and distorted beyond com-prehension by the huge noise of gushing air.

A second impact, cushioned by the foliage. Diana clung to the springy branches, and felt the whole stretch of bush heave as if about to come away from the wall. But it stayed where it was, and she clung for her life. The two remaining Bar-le-duc men had found similar gripping points.

As she turned her head to scan the chaos inside the dome, she saw something massy and angular fly through the air. This object, whatever it was, struck one of the two men on the head. The collision deflected it only marginally – it was clearly very massy – and it zoomed towards the breach.

Had it reached the gap face on, it would have slipped straight through. But Providence, or the goddess, determined that it reached the gap in such an orientation that its angular corners jammed in the aperture. The ambient roar of air changed timbre, rose a little. The wall bulged; but the obstacle stayed put.

There was still a great wind, tugging at Diana and trying to suck her into space, and death; but now that the hole was partially blocked, its force was diminished somewhat.

And, unexpectedly (wait a minute! Shouldn't he be *dead*?) – here was Iago himself. Alive! *Not* sucked into space through the exit breach after all, but flying from the far side of the bubble and holding in his arms a gelsheet.

He reached the breach, and covered the whole area with the sheet, in one smooth motion. The sheet spread itself, its edges searching for the circumference of the gap, not in the least incommoded by the heavy object rammed in there.

In a moment the breach was sealed.

Silence rang like a bell in Diana's ears.

She was gasping hard, pulling at the air with lungs that didn't seem to be working.

Iago kicked off again, and passed in straight-line flight to a storage chest set in amongst a patch of heather against the wall. It took him only a moment to dial up the reservoir-air, and with a gorgeous gushing sound the pressure inside the bubble began to rise.

White noise. Breathing slowly became easier.

*

Breathe.

Breathe.

Diana gulped. Her inner ear snapped right, left, and the quality of sound shifted downward. Her heart was wiggling frantically in her breast.

She gathered enough of her wits to take stock. The space inside Iago's 'Dunronin' looked like a shaken snowglobe: all manner of floating detritus and leaves and (ugh!) globules of blood circling slowly through sluggish air.

Sapho was clinging to a bush on the far side of the bubble. At least *she* was safe! Two of Bar-le-duc's original four men had vanished into space, but that still left two inside the house with them. One was hanging on a branch not far from Diana; the other was in motion, scrambling away to the far side of the world, with his weapon in his hand.

They were armed, of course. Her heart gulped and hurried.

And there was Iago: his face a mask of intense fury. She had never seen him look so *fierce* before. He kicked off against the storage trunk, and flew straight towards her. Grabbed her shoulders. 'Are you alright?' he demanded. 'Are you hurt?'

'I'm fine,' she said, breathlessly. 'How did you seal the second hole?'

'Second hole?'

'The exit hole – oh, *yargo*, I thought you'd been sucked out! I thought you'd been sucked out of the far side and were dead!'

'There's no exit hole,' he said, looking briefly puzzled. And then, kicking off against the side, he leapt to the man hanging nearby. He grabbed him not by the shoulders but the neck.

'How?' he yelled. Diana had never seem him lose his temper before – she had lived with him, effectively, for *years* – close-quarters – and she had never seen him lose his temper before. The effect was made more appalling by the fact that he was painted all over with a glistening, scarlet, sticky coating. '*How*? How did he know where I was?'

'He knows you have the FTL,' the man gasped.

Iago's eyes widened momentarily. Then he said: 'What?'

'He *said* so. He said it! The Ulanovs don't know, or they'd have sent an army to take this place. Monsieur wanted to seize you by himself, and take you as a prize to his masters.'

This was the man who had been thumped by the chunk of flying debris – whatever that had been. The gash was deep in his forehead, and prongs and dabs of blood oozed from it. Globs broke from the end of this liquid extrusion to join the general aerial throng of scarlet droplets. Indeed, the blow seemed to have stunned him. He glanced across at his colleague. He had one arm hooked around a bush, and in his other hand he held his weapon. But he looked unsure what to do with it.

Iago didn't let go of the man's neck. 'What's your name?'

'My name?' he repeated, stupidly.

'*Yes* your name!' yelled Iago.

'Mahyadi Panggabean,' said the man.

'Indonesian?'

'I come,' Mahyadi Panggabean said, slurring the words a little, 'from a settlement called Access 17, which orbits . . .'

'Don't be an *idiot*,' snarled Iago. 'You know what I *mean*. Your line traces back to Indonesia?'

The man tried to wipe blood from his eyes, and in doing so only spread it more completely about his face. Blinking and wrinkling up his brow into ridges and valleys. He made a series of whimpering sounds. 'I know what you're really asking,' he said. 'I know. There *are* lots of Indonesians working for Clan Yu, it's true. But there are Indonesians working for *all* the Clans – Gongsi, too.'

There was a really *bestial* ferocity in Iago's manner. Diana actually flinched a little, just watching it. He took hold of Mahyadi Panggabean's head and shook the fellow's whole body, like a doll, in mid-air. The fellow moaned, and blood began coming more fluently from his head wound. 'Is this a *Transport* move?' Iago shouted. '*Is* this the Clan Yu trying to grab the FTL for themselves? *Is that why you came?*'

'Sukarno!' Mahyadi Panggabean wailed, evidently calling to his colleague. But although the other man had a weapon in his hand, he did nothing but cower deeper into the foliage growing against the wall.

'He won't shoot,' Iago snarled. 'He won't shoot me, because he's been told either I'm taken alive or he'll be killed himself. Am I right, Sukarno?' he called across. 'They want me alive or they will be wroth. They want me alive for what they *think* is in my head. And he Sukarno won't shoot anybody *else* here, because he knows,' Iago was yelling. 'He knows that if he does I – will – literally – *cut the flesh from his bones*. I will flay him alive with my sharp-edged glass knife.' Sukarno shrank deeper into the greenery. 'Tell me who *sponsored* this raid?'

'Don't—' cried the man.

'Was it Clan Yu? Tell me.'

'Clan Argent!' Mahyadi Panggabean screamed, as if the words were being wrenched from him. 'They will *execute* me for telling you! It was them!'

Iago released the man. The fellow started rotating slowly in space, his hands to his face, making no effort to reach out and correct his orientation.

'Clan Argent,' Iago said, in a steady voice. All the rage had instantly vanished from his manner.

'Everything is in turmoil. The Ulanovs have recognised a new head of the Clan – the two old leaders have vanished, the rumours say dead,' gabbled the rotating man. 'Something so dangerous, this new weapon – the survival of *humanity*. That's what Monsieur said! It cannot be uninvented, sir. So which is a better environment in which to contain so terrible a thing? The new leader of the Clan will support the Ulanovs, repressive though they be. Better *that* than the chaos of civil war, or revolution – and such a weapon in general circulation? If the Ulanovs are deposed, it will be war System-wide. In such a maelstrom, what if one faction or another chances upon . . . this *thing*?'

'This thing,' repeated Iago.

'This FTL,' gasped the fellow.

With a series of deliberate gestures, Iago wiped the smeary blood from his face and hands. He looked up and down the interior of his ruined house.

'Mr Sukarno,' Iago shouted, without turning his head to look at the bushes where the man was hiding. 'You can come out, now. I'm not going to harm you.'

'I *have* a gun, Mr Glass!' came Sukarno's quavery voice from out of the vegetation.

'I know you do. That doesn't make any difference now.'

'I *have* killed men, Mr Glass!'

'But you're not going to kill anybody here today,' Iago replied. 'Come out of the bushes. I shall not kill you. It is true that I will have to leave you here. In my house I mean, for a few weeks at least. But there's plenty of ghunk, and it's a pleasant environment, and fruit will start growing in a week or so. I promise you I will alert the authorities and they will rescue you. Although presumably they know you are here.'

'I don't believe they do,' said Sukarno. 'Mr Bar-le-duc wanted to capture you himself, and receive all the bounty. I don't believe he informed the authorities where he was going.'

'It that case I shall notify them that you are here.'

There was a pause. 'They will not be pleased to discover that Mr Bar-le-duc is dead!'

'No,' said Iago. 'No they will not.'

Sukarno came out of the bushes, and gave himself a gentle foot-push to fly over to where the others were. There was so much red in the air that he could not avoid becoming coated in it as he passed.

'I apologise for the damage to your house, sir. Only Mr Bar-le-duc said he was *certain* that you did possess the FTL,' said

Mahyadi Panggabean. His injured head wobbled awkwardly on its neck. 'He was *quite* certain of that.'

Did he tell you the nature of our relationship?' Iago asked.

'He did – sir.' It was remarkable, to Diana, how easily these two men had fallen into roles subordinate to her Iago. That she still tended to think of him as a servant made this odder. But she knew what was happening, of course. Bar-le-duc had dosed his men with CRFs. This made them loyal, and eroded their capacity for initiative and independent action. Now that their master was dead they were at a loss. By acting decisively, Iago tapped into their raw certainty-seeking brain chemistry.

'Mr Glass,' said Sukarno, taking hold of his colleague, to stop his slow drift and spin. 'Permit me to ask. *Do* you have the FTL?'

A flicker of Iago's former fury sparked again. 'Do you *honestly* think I'd be sitting around here if I had a functioning faster-than-light drive? You think I'd be risking torture and death at the hands of the Ulanovs? If I did possess FTL, I'd have a ship that could outrun any Tachyon Thrust, wouldn't I? No police sloop could ever catch me. I could leave altogether. I could shake the dust of the Solar System from my boots and explore the whole galaxy. Couldn't I? Wouldn't *you*?'

The men looked at their own boots.

'Is that *really* what you would do?' Diana asked.

'Wouldn't it solve two problems in one go?' he replied. 'Assume I possess a working FTL, and the knowledge how to make it. By flying to a distant star I would remove the danger of both from humanity; and keep myself safe, at the same time.'

'You don't have the FTL,' said Diana. 'So why did this Bar-le-duc think you did?'

'Another question,' Iago returned. 'An even more pressing one.'

'What?'

'Who killed him?'

The first thing was to check the damage. Iago unpacked a giant filter fan, and began drawing the air inside the bubble through its meshes. Slowly at first, but then with greater rapidity, the rubbish and blood droplets in the air were cleaned away. Breathing no longer involved coughing on fragments of leaves, or choking (horribly) on iron-tasting gobs of red. In fact, the device's filter clogged up not once but three times as it strained to clean the whole, so cluttered was the space inside that sphere. Each time it jammed Iago slid the filter free and scraped a goo of lumpy black into a plastic sack. Meanwhile, Sapho wrapped a bandage around Mahyadi Panggabean's injured head, folding it and arranging it to leave his eyes clear, like a white balaclava.

The seal around the breach was sound. There was a small panic when the airlock door – ten metres or so from the breach – refused to open. It took a good deal of wrenching to get it to swing free. 'The metal of the joint and the hinges has been deformed,' Iago said, holding his crowbar like a sword. 'Unsurprising considering the violent forces that have acted upon this sphere.'

But they got it open in the end. That meant they could see that the *Red Rum*, on the far side, was undamaged. Its air pressure was still good, and all its electrics were working. But the ship on which Bar-le-duc had arrived was completely shattered. The path of the fatal projectile – whatever it was – had intersected Bar-le-Duc's ship as well as his body, spilling its contents in a glittery cloud and rending the remaining spaceship metal in great petal-edged gapes. The decompression over there had been complete; the structural failure instantaneous and catastrophic. Nobody could have survived.

All five of them crowded inside the *Rum*'s hold and gawped at the damage. Iago asked the House AI to check for activity outside, but it reported nothing. 'That only means,' said Diana, 'that the sloop that shot at us is well camouflaged. That's all that *that* means.'

'Bar-le-duc's ship was connected to ours,' Diana said, gazing in horror. 'It's lucky it didn't simply rip *Red Rum* off the airlock, or we would have been stranded here.'

'It *will* have applied unusual structural stresses to the *Rum*,' said Iago. 'We'll have to check it carefully before we think of flying away. But that's not my main worry.'

'What is your main worry?'

'Look at the damage,' was Iago's instruction. 'Do you see?'

Diana didn't see at first, and looked again. Then she saw. 'Oh goddess,' she muttered, turning to look back through the airlock into the bubble.

Sukarno was also there, as were Mahyadi Panggabean and Sapho. 'We should leave now,' said Sukarno. 'Whoever is out there might shoot again at any moment.'

'Fool,' said Sapho. 'They can shoot a space ship, as it runs, as easily as they can shoot a shanty bubble.'

Mahyadi Panggabean spoke slowly. 'Perhaps the ship that launched this attack upon your bubble has flown away? For indeed, if it is still out there in space, we might wonder why it has not fired again.'

'Think,' said Iago. 'Look at the evidence. The beam of this weapon, or the path of this projectile, was powerful enough completely to *smash* your sloop, to punch through the wall of my home bubble, and to turn your late employer into red steam. Such a blast would *easily* be powerful enough to smash through the antipode point on my sphere. It would, in point of fact, necessarily have drilled right through.'

'But it didn't,' said Sapho, in tones of dawning realisation.

'Perhaps it just so happened to run out of momentum,' said Mahyadi Panggabean. 'As it struck . . . or . . . I feel . . . unwell. I can see two of everything.'

'Come come! *Look* at what it did to Bar-le-duc,' said Diana. 'It didn't just shoot him, it vaporised him. It was hardly running out of momentum when it hit. And look at the damage to this side of the bubble – and to your ship. See how the fabric is bent outward? These are exit wounds.' She stopped. 'Do I mean wounds? I suppose the word is *wounds*.'

'The conclusion,' said Iago, is clear enough. 'This was *not* a shot fired from outside the sphere to its inside. On the contrary, it was fired from the *inside* of the sphere to the outside. Which means—'

'Which means whoever fired it is still inside the house. They cannot have got away, and so they are still inside.'

The presence of five human beings made the main cabin of the *Red Rum* feel very cramped; but all five looked back through the hatchway with trepidation.

5

The Search

'Respectfully, sir, I may say,' said Sukarno, 'that we must leave now. We should leave without delay. Close the hatch and cast off this craft, before whosoever *is* inside your house shoots his weapon again,' said Sukarno. He had his gun out again, and was pointing it towards the open airlock.

'Out of the question,' said Iago.

'Please, sir, with respect once again – why not?'

'For one thing, I'm not leaving without that RACdroid. For another, the ship isn't provisioned. It's three days at full accel to the nearest friendly house; a week to a proper cluster large enough to resupply us. Look around you, Sukarno. Five of us, four g-couches. If I took your suggestion seriously, I'd have to limit myself to acceleration of little more than a couple of g – it would be weeks before we got *anywhere*. No.'

But Sukarno did not give up. 'There might be discomfort,' he said. 'But the individual who killed our master is still inside your house. If we leave now, we trap him, or her, inside. We can notify the authorities to return and arrest the malefactor.'

'There was no ship docked at the door when we arrived, yet the malefactor – as you put it – was already inside. How do you think she managed that?'

'Somebody must have delivered her,' said Sapho.

'It's the only logical explanation,' agreed Diana. 'Assuming they didn't just *teleport* inside. But if somebody dropped them off, then that same somebody could come collect her again. So your idea of trapping them inside doesn't work.'

The speech made Diana cough. The odour of blood and sweat and something else, something scorched and foul, was strong in her nostrils.

'*How* did they drop this individual off?' said Iago, pulling himself over to the hatch and putting his head through. 'The locks on my door are manifold, carefully encrypted and they were all unbroken. If somebody dropped off a murderer, they did so without triggering any of my security measures.'

'Somebody clever enough to fool your locks?' said Diana.

'The locks respond only to me,' insisted Iago. 'And I haven't been here in years.'

'Perhaps they didn't come through the door?' Sukarno suggested.

'Then how? Perhaps: when we find this person, whoever she is – well, then we can ask them.'

'You mean search the house?' said a fearful-sounding Mahyadi Panggabean. His words were slurred.

'Sir,' said Sukarno. 'Respectfully, it would be a risk that amounted almost to suicide for us to go back into that enclosed space! To chase a murderous individual armed with what is, evidently, a very powerful gun? You cannot expect it of us!'

'This individual, whoever she is, could easily have killed us already,' Iago said, peering through the hatch into the interior of his own house. 'She, or he, did not. Why would she kill us now, if she didn't before?'

'Again, with respect – sir,' said Sukarta. 'We weren't *hunting* them before. A person hunted reacts differently.'

'Irregardless,' said Iago.

'You're right,' said Diana, pulling herself across the cabin to float beside Iago. 'Whoever they are, they could have killed all of us. They didn't. I don't believe she acted randomly. I believe she waited until you were about to be taken into custody, Iago. I believe she shot your jailer. I think she has your best interests at heart.'

'Or the best interests of humanity,' Iago said.

'It's a bad habit you've gotten into,' said Diana. 'Assuming that your personal safety and the fate of the whole Solar System are one and the same.'

'I shall meditate upon the difference,' said Iago. 'When I've a moment.' Diana looked at him. He looked grim – the blood and dirt wiped smearily away from his face, but still horribly present on the rest of his clothing. And then he smiled. 'You're the intuitive problem solver. Who do you think is out there?'

Diana wasn't sure where the words came from; but with a sudden tingle of insight she said: 'Ms Joad. She didn't want Bar-le-duc taking you – because she wants to arrest you herself. To redeem herself in the eyes of her former masters.'

'How could it possibly be her?' he asked, absently, peering through the hatch.

'I don't know.'

'Then that's just groundless speculation. You can do better than that. Let's *find* the malefactor, and then we can get some answers. Come on.' He put his foot against the lip of the hatch and kicked off, sailing in a straight line right through the centre of his house. The others hurried to the doorway and looked through. Iago had grabbed onto a guy-rope, and was now hanging, surveying the low scrub directly across from the doorway.

'Well,' said Diana. 'Come along, everybody.'

Mahyadi Panggabean, all agreed, was too poorly to take part. He was positioned near the door and told to keep his eyes open. The RACdroid was moved over there too: quietly and efficiently recording everything; keeping visual lock on the four of them.

314

Iago set it to sound the alarm if a sixth figure moved anywhere inside the house.

'Let's go,' said Iago.

It is a feature of a sphere that any place on the interior wall is as good as any other for obtaining a panoptic view of every other point on the wall. The four searchers started from the door and moved methodically at four ninety-degree orthogonal paths. 'Shouldn't we be armed?' Sapho asked, rather nervously, looking across at Sukarno. 'No,' Iago replied, in a loud voice, making sure he was audible through the entire sphere. 'We're not looking to hurt anybody. We only want to know with whom we are sharing our space – and maybe to talk.'

There was no reply.

In fact, it was obvious from the start that the only place the shooter could have been situated – when she fired her shot, that is to say – was a patch of two-metre-high bushy scrub, a couple of hundred square metres in extent, more or less diametrically opposite the doorway. She could have moved since then, of course; and the four of them made their way, hand over hand, along their different trajectories carefully examining all possible hiding places. The fruit tree offered the best cover: Diana climbed into its thickest portion and through every angle and curl of branches. Nobody there. By the time she came out the other side, the others were on the edge of the scrub. She made her way across the backs of the empty vegetable trays until she had joined them.

'She must be in there,' said Iago, gesturing towards the scrub. 'If she's anywhere.'

'Unless she has magically teleported out of this space,' said Diana. Sapho looked at her. 'There's no such thing as tele-portation,' she added, feeling foolish for having spoken.

'Come out,' Sukarno cried into the vegetation. 'I have a gun!'

'Mr Sukarno,' said Iago, without looking at him. 'You are, if you don't mind me saying, too fond of shouting "*I have a gun.*"'

'If they are in there,' said Sapho. 'This person, this killer, and we encounter them – what should we do?'

Nobody said anything to this. Then Diana called: 'whoever you are – we don't want to hurt you. You've done us a favour, saved Iago here from being arrested. We just want to talk!'

Still no reply. Gobs of blood and debris and loose foliage still swirled lazily through the air.

Everybody looked at the thicket. 'I can see some of the way in,' noted Diana. 'But not all the way through.'

'We need to go inside to be sure,' said Iago. 'Please put your weapon away, Mr Sukarno. You're likely to shoot one of us with it.'

Sukarno, fumbling, fitted his gun away into his holster.

'Well,' said Iago, taking a breath. 'Let's look.' They all moved into the thicket.

Given how limited it appeared in extent from the outside it surprised Diana how capacious the thicket's interior was. She scrambled into a maze-like network of holey spaces. The branches and strands of the vegetation were smooth, though stiff; covered with a waxy layer to preserve moisture. The leaves were mostly stiff nubbins, and there were many areas too dense to move through. But nevertheless there were numerous cavities and ways of passage. Dia pulled herself easily through. The vibration of the others' movements communicated itself to her through the stems as she grasped them. The space was dark and green.

Movement: a leg, thrusting through and towards her. She lashed out, a clean punch that connected with a solid thwack, pushing her, action-reaction, back against the wall of vegetation. 'Hey! It's me,' Iago called. 'It's me – what's the matter.'

Diana was breathing hard. 'I knew it was you,' she gasped. 'Your damn tin *leg*.'

'A bit more expensive than tin,' he said, pulling himself through the L-shaped cavity.

Sapho put her head, upside down from Diana's perspective, into the space. 'Miss?'

'I'm sorry,' Diana said. 'Iago startled me.'

They were silent. Then Iago said: 'there's nobody here. This thicket is empty.'

'I found a – tube,' said Sapho, uncertainly. 'I don't mean an actual tube. Not a thing. A *lack* of things.'

'You're not making sense!' snapped Iago. 'What?'

'I mean a *pathway*,' said Sapho. 'Cut through the mass of vegetation. But if you look, you can see. Look through it and it is angled towards the door.'

'Show me,' said Iago. He wriggled after her. Forcing her breathing into a slower rhythm, Diana came too. She passed about a kind of U-bend and put her head into a bulk-shaped space, large enough to contain both Sapho and Iago. A moment later, Sukarno popped up.

As Sapho had said, there was a sort of chimney out through the dense vegetation. 'It could be the trajectory of a projectile,' Iago was saying, his face to the wall of green. 'Or it could just be a natural pathway.'

'Its edges seemed – scorched? No?'

'Hard to tell,' said Iago, laying his fingers along the edges of the hollowed-out space. 'It's not hot. Rather the reverse.'

'If this is where the killer sat,' said Sukarno, 'then the killer is here no longer.'

'In which case Mahyadi Panggabean would have seen them,' noted Iago. 'I can see *him*, actually, through this tube: by the door. Mahyadi Panggabean!' he called. 'Have you seen anybody coming out of the thicket?'

There was no reply. Wrigglingly extricating themselves from the thicket, and kicking themselves across to him they found that he had fallen asleep. 'His wound,' Sukarno said, apologetically. 'It has made him weary.'

'*Is* he asleep? Is he unconscious?' Iago asked. By dint of shaking and slapping they roused him, and he glowered at them. 'I am tired,' he said.

They let him go back to sleep.

'The RACdroid,' said Sapho. 'It does not sleep.'

'Let's have a look at what it saw,' agreed Iago.

Getting the machine to replay its visual data was a simple matter. Accessing functionality in anything but view-only format would have been much trickier, of course. And any infraction of the device's complex nesting of seals would have marked all its data as corrupt. But as it was, they didn't need to do anything more difficult than press play. The device recognised Sukarno's DNA as an authorised user, and complied.

The image that resulted was high-quality, both in terms of its resolution and its temporal slicing. A top-range Droid, evidently; expensive. Sukarno played back the recent files. The bright-printed pattern of light and shade moved with smooth rapidity over the scene, in the wrong direction. They saw themselves disappear backwards into the thicket; and after a period of weird jerky rustling, saw themselves appearing again.

'We didn't flush anybody out,' Diana observed. 'There was nobody in there *to* flush out.' Then, with a dawning realisation: 'there was never anybody in there.'

'Then – who fired the shot?' asked Sapho. 'The invisible woman?'

'Whoever did fire the shot has *somehow* escaped from this house,' was Sukarno's opinion. 'Though I don't know *how*. There are no other ships nearby – and we would have seen them.'

'Are the walls intact?' Diana asked, thinking through the possibilities.

'According to the House AI,' said Iago, 'with the exception of the breach by the airlock, the entire house skin is sound and unbreached.'

'This, it seems, is a locked-room mystery and a *half*,' Diana said, looking at Iago with a wry expression. 'Somebody got into the bubble *without* coming through the only door but also without breaking the walls and without being seen. They hid in the bushes over there, shot Mr Bar-le-duc, and then departed the bubble: again without using the door or breaching the walls. And, once again, without being seen.'

'It is impossible,' said Sapho.

'The logical inference is that they have *not* departed,' was Iago's opinion.

'Then – where are they?'

'Where didn't we look?' Iago asked.

They went round the house again, opening every container no matter how small or impossible it was in terms of fitting a human being inside. It occurred to Dia that they had not looked inside the still-empty vegetable trays. It was just-about conceivable a person – a very thin person – might have squeezed themselves into one of these narrow pallets; but Sukarno, Iago and she opened every one, and the only thing inside was blackponic pseudosoil.

Two hours later it was clear that the only people inside the bubble were the five of them.

'Run the RACdroid back further,' Diana said. 'It must have recorded the murder itself. It may well have recorded an image of the murderer.'

Sukarno did so. Images zipped rapidly backwards through a strange scene: human beings – they themselves – disappearing through the front door. The house empty and quiet in their absence. Then they all re-emerged, backwards, and began nipping up-down, back-forth, left-right, apparently taking nets and sponges of bloody rubbish and scattering it at every coordinate in the globe. Then they came together, and separated, floating randomly about the place. Iago leapt away from Mahyadi Panggabean and grasped Diana. Then he leapt to the door, and abruptly the whole scene was furious Brownian-motion and chaos. 'Slow it down,' suggested Iago. '*That's* the blow-out – right there.'

'Sir?' said Sukarno.

'Run it back to just before the murder, and then play it forward?'

The image spooled back, and froze. There they all were, motionless: Bar-le-duc in the middle, looking lugubrious and complacent. There was the hint of a smile at the two edges of his long mouth; like serif on a font. His right hand was a little forward, his left hung by his side. He was looking directly at Iago. Behind him, over by the wall, Sapho was clearly visible: arms folded, floating. Diana was close beside Iago. And Iago had his head slightly to one side, a sceptical expression on his face – listening to Bar-le-duc. He had his arms loosely by his side, fingers unclenched, ten centimetres at least away from his body. And, finally, Bar-le-duc's four minders were visible, at various places around the sphere. Mahyadi Panggabean was on the side of Sapho; Sukarno on the other side of the globe. And the two other men, whose name Dia had never known, and who she would now never meet, stood nearer the door.

Sukarno played the scene on. This was the moment of death. Bar-le-duc vanished in a spreading cloud of dark red. It happened instantaneously – no breaking apart, an immediate transition from a solid to a gaseous state. It was bewildering. And everything inside the house was chaos; bodies thrashing and hurtling, leaves and droplets of blood swooshing in every direction.

'Stop,' said Iago. 'Run it back. Go through it more slowly.'

Sukarno did so. He took the image back to the initial conditions; and then ran it forward. Again, Bar-le-duc vanished without intermediary condition into a blast of red mist. 'He was hit,' Iago said, 'with a great *deal* of force. Or perhaps with a very focused beam of heat. Can we make it slower yet?'

'I'll slow it as much as the device allows,' said Sukarno.

There was something hypnotic in watching events over and over again. The transition from a living, coherent organic being to a disorganised mess. Mortality focused into an interstitial blip.

The third time through, events took so long to unfold that Diana began to grow bored. Certain things were evident, however. Somebody had fired the shot that caused Bar-le-duc's violent death, it was none of the seven other people who were clearly visible on the recording – Bar's four bodyguards, Iago, Diana and Sapho were all in plain view, and doing nothing, as the thing happened. One of the bodyguards did have his weapon out, but it was angled away from Bar-le-duc, and it was clear to see that it had not been discharged.

They watched, and it happened again. The wall cracked open and simultaneously Bar-le-duc's torso began to dissolve into red. The image froze.

'High-velocity projectile', noted Iago. The Iago in the recording was still looking sardonically at the face of Bar-le-duc, entirely unaware that anything was amiss. That is how instantaneously it had happened. Even Bar-le-duc himself – weirdly, horribly – seemed blithely unaware of what was happening to his own midriff. His face was calm, even as his belly was mashed and evaporated, as if his end had overtaken him more quickly than his nerve impulses.

The recording moved on, and the red cloud ate up the whole of Bar-le-duc. A moment later and the facial expressions of Iago and Diana changed, both together, to startled disgust. Diana watched Iago's: there was no faking that flinch; he was as surprised by this horrible event as she had been herself.

'Check the thicket,' Iago suggested. 'We ought at least to be able to see a muzzleflash.'

'I can't see anything in the bushes,' said Sapho. 'Movement, or muzzleflash, or anything like that.'

'Me neither,' confirmed Sukarno.

Diana's scalp was tingling. Something was amiss. 'Go back,' she told Sukarno.

He pulled the image back in time, slowly, slowly; and the cloud of red shrank down to reveal Bar-le-duc's head and feet; and then his arms and hips. 'Try to stop it at the exact moment the projectile hits him,' she said.

Moving the image a little further back, the cloud of red shrank further, tightening, and focusing on one point just below his diaphragm. This red shrank away, and at the very moment Sukarno halted the image.

'There,' said Diana.

'But,' said Sukarno, looking. 'How can that *be?*'

They were looking at a recorded image of Bar-le-duc the tiniest possible fraction of a second *before* he had been shot. Nobody was visible in the bushes on the far side of the globe. The other seven human beings present were all hanging in space, doing nothing. Bar-le-duc had not yet been shot. He was on the very verge of being shot, like Zeno's hare at the limit point of overtaking the tortoise. Yet, clearly visible – a faint red line linking his solar plexus to the wall beside the door. And that wall already breached.

'That's why we found nobody in the thicket,' said Diana. 'Bar-le-duc was shot from outside after all. There's the trajectory of the projectile.'

'It looks like a focused energy beam,' said Sukarno.

Iago looked at the image. 'But *how?*' he asked.

'Somebody followed you – a ship. Who knows the location of this house?' Dia asked.

'I do,' Iago insisted. 'I'm the only one.'

'Then you followed yourself,' said Sapho.

Diana shook her head. 'Bar-le-duc found you. If he did, somebody else *could*. A ship, standing sentinel, outside. It saw you were in danger, and acted to remove that threat – by killing Bar-le-duc.'

But Iago was shaking his head. 'But that doesn't explain how did the damage outside end up bent the wrong way? The rips in the plasmetal of that spaceship bend *out*, not in. And – why didn't the bullet punch straight through the far side of my house? What happened to it?'

'How to explain the disappearing bullet,' said Diana. 'That *is* a challenge, yes.'

6

The Disappearing Bullet

Iago had decided they all should eat. 'A problem is rarely solved on an empty stomach,' he announced, opening a storebox and heating some vegetables. 'There's some wine somewhere,' he said, to Sapho. 'And you can use the showerbag fully clothed or naked – if the former, it will clean your clothes too, although it won't get you *quite* so clean. There's only one bag, though, and using it on all of us will overload it, I suppose. This is supposed to be a one-person house.'

'So none of us gets perfectly clean,' said Sapho. 'So what?'

Sapho folded the bag around Mahyadi Panggabean up to his neck. This left the bandages undisturbed whilst it cleaned his body. Then the four others took turns in the bag. Iago went last, when the device was dirtiest and partially clogged, so he wasn't washed very efficiently. But everybody looked better afterwards than they had done before.

Mahyadi Panggabean drank an entire globe of juice. Everybody else sipped wine and ate packets of heated noodles.

It was Sapho who broke the silence: 'What does it *mean*?'

'It means our searching through the shrubbery was a wild comet chase,' said Diana. She sighed. 'The shooter was never inside this house to begin with. The image shows the trajectory of the bullet between the wall and Bar-le-duc's body *before* it hits him – that blurred dark-orange line. The shot came from outside.'

'To repeat myself: *if* that's true,' noted Iago, 'then how are the ripped edges of the wall bent outwards? Why was Bar-le-duc's ship forced *away* from the house by the projectile that destroyed it? And most of all – *what happened to the bullet?* You saw the force with which it vaporised poor old Bar.'

'Maybe it was a miracle,' said Sapho, in a small voice. 'Ra'allah sometimes intervenes to punish the wicked.'

'Let us put miracles to one side,' suggested Iago. 'By way of explanation. A projectile capable of ripping an entire sloop into rags of spaceship metal; and turning a human body into red steam – such a projectile fired from outside the bubble into its interior *could not* vanish into thin air. It must have continued through, punched a second hole in the opposite side of the globe and gone on its way. This did not happen.'

'I can't explain it,' conceded Diana, looking unhappy. 'But look at it this way: we have to choose between a disappearing bullet – or an entire disappearing human being.'

'Entire human being?'

'The person we were searching the thicket for!' said Diana. 'Theory A is a disappearing bullet. Theory B is Person Unknown killed Bar and then themself vanished into thin air. Ockham's razor suggests the former is less of an affront to logic than the latter.'

'Ockham's razor,' scoffed Iago. 'The most ridiculous use of metaphorical steel in the history of thought.'

Diana shook her head. 'Oh we mustn't let go of logic. Logic is all we have. The RACdroid shows that none of *us* killed Bar-le-duc. We're all hanging right there, doing nothing, as he gets blown apart before our eyes. There *is* nobody else inside the sphere. We've searched it thoroughly. The only *logical* conclusion is that the murderer was never inside this globe.'

Iago looked steadily at her. 'There's another possible explanation you're not considering,' he said.

'What?'

'What if the recording is in error?' he said. 'I believed Bar-le-duc when he said this RACdroid was kosher. What if it isn't? What if it is some kind of rogue? Perhaps its data has been falsified entirely, or more likely some algorithm inside the droid has distorted its data somehow. In that case . . . well, in that case, the contract I agreed with Bar-le-duc, just before his death, would have no legal force.'

Diana sniffed dismissively. 'I'd forgotten about the silly contract,' she said.

'You should not forget about it, Miss Diana,' said Iago, sternly. 'It is the legal guarantee of your continuing freedom. You should not be so quick to rubbish it.'

There was a silence.

'Surely it should be easy to tell,' Sapho put it, wiping her mouth on a rectangle of smartcloth, 'whether the RACdroid is a rogue or not?'

'It *looks* kosher,' said Iago. 'But I'm no expert. On the other hand, I know somebody who is.' He stretched his spine, lengthening his legs and arms. Then he rubbed his face. 'We have to leave this place anyway,' he went on. 'It is no longer secure. We have to go – Diana, and Sapho.'

'I won't be sorry to leave this place,' said Diana. 'I would sleep easier without the reek of blood in my nostrils.'

Iago grunted agreement.

'Sir?' said Sukarno, looking mournful. 'I concede that it is the large amount of CRF in my system that prompts me to this – but I beg of you to consider taking Mahyadi Panggabean and myself with you as well.'

'No,' said Iago. 'We cannot. You must stay here, until you are retrieved. I will inform the authorities of your location. But if things are they way I suspect them to be – well, the authorities will soon be here anyway.'

'I understand sir,' said Sukarno, his eyes shiny. Away to the left, Mahyadi Panggabean began to sob quietly.

Sapho and Iago loaded the *Rum* with various supplies. Diana did not help. She parted some of the vegetation and looked out through the transparency. All that black; the luxurious mess of stars. Then the bubble turned and the sun appeared and the stars withdrew their horns into their black shells.

Watching the sun move sideways across the sky, she tried to let her mind tune in to the hidden rhythms of the problem. The sunlight was bright yellow-white, except for the central belt where there was the vague hint of a very pale green. The blackness all about. The nourishing void, the devouring void.

Concentrate, she told herself. But the problem seemed trapped between two impossibilities – the disappearing murderer on the one hand, the disappearing bullet on the other. A true solution would have to dissolve one or other impossibility, but it wasn't obvious which was the more tractable. She let her mind drift. The *suddenness* of Bar-le-duc's demise. The misty, fine red line. How might one make something disappear?

Explode it. Atomise it.

They hadn't searched for Bar because they'd been convinced he'd been turned into droplets.

She felt the tingle in her gut. This was – something. The little hairs on the back of her neck shivered.

What if the two problems – the disappearing person, the disappearing weapon – *cancelled one another out?* It was not clear to her how this might be; but she had that sense that the solution to the mystery lay along this line . . . somehow.

Then she thought: two things exploded: Bar-le-duc and the skin of the globe. What if the latter were not a side effect of the man's death – but *its cause?* She tried to imagine a weapon embedded in the fabric of the house; firing with asymmetric force, just enough inward trajectory to blow Bar-le-duc to pieces; and with much greater outward force, enough to tear his ship in half. Was that possible?

Was it plausible?

It felt wrong, somehow, as a solution; incomplete, or orthogonal to a more elegant answer. But not *wholly* wrong, she thought. Something about it was right. One thing Diana had always been good at was intuiting the general rightness or otherwise of a solution, even before she had the supporting details in place.

This line of thought carried one rather significant correlative, of course. Who would have placed such a weapon in the wall of the house?

Who else but its owner?

Iago floated over to hang beside her. 'I'll be sorry to lose this house,' he said. 'Since I suppose I can never return here.

'That's a pity,' she said, tight-lipped.

'We shall have to,' he said, an uncharacteristic note of hesitation in his voice, 'travel from place to place for a while. Diana, I apologise if that makes you angry with me.'

She glanced at him, and then looked outside again. 'Don't be absurd,' she said, angrily. 'Why should that make me angry? *I'm* not angry.'

'You heard what Mahyadi Panggabean said earlier?'

At this she felt only tiredness and boredom, and turned her face away. 'Bar-le-duc was being authorised by my own Clan. Yes I heard. It's not that surprising, though, is it? Power abhors the vacuum. The Ulanovs would hardly dismantle the entire structure of the Clan. They've put some puppet in the pilot's seat – or else, some enterprising Clan member has seized power, and made a deal with the Ulanovs. As long as my parents are OK, and my sister, I can't care too much.'

'Diana,' he started to say.

'I'd prefer to be alone now, Iago,' she snapped.

He didn't force the issue: let her be, and went back to packing the *Rum*.

The last thing to be loaded was the RACdroid, and then – with a brisk farewell to the Mahyadi Panggabean and Sukarno, he, Sapho and a sulky Diana went on board and shut the main door behind them.

Departure was delayed, however, by the difficulty they had in jettisoning Bar-le-duc's ruined craft. This had docked straight-forwardly at the *Rum*'s rear hatch, but whatever had wrecked the craft had deformed the link, bent the whole assemblage of door and door five degrees or so away from true. It took a half-hour, and a power wrench, to force the resilient spaceship metal back towards its original configuration. It proved impossible to line it up as it had been before, but at least they got it back to an arrangement in which the mechanism could at least be disengaged. Iago layered sheets of sealant over the whole portal, and finally they pulled away from Dunronin and accelerated at one third g into blankness.

7

To Garland 400

It was a three-day journey straight to Garland 400, the cluster of Antinomian bubbles in which lived (Iago promised) a RACdroid expert who could determine, once and for all, whether their machine was rogue or not. Iago decided to start the voyage by flying a decoy trajectory for six hours, at full burn; so the early stage of the flight was a very uncomfortable period inside the g-couches. Then there was an hour of weightless flight, which gave them time for a little food. And then, to make up the time, another four-hour full-burn stint in the g-couches. Diana was miserable, halfway between awake and asleep, in unyielding discomfort. Her thoughts were trapped in a loop: Bar-le-duc was dead, Bar-le-duc wasn't dead, Bar-le-duc was dead, Bar-le-duc couldn't be dead. *Feathers or lead?* she thought. *Feathers or lead? Feathers or lead?* Had Bar been exploded by the weapon, or had he exploded the weapon? It had to be one or the other. Did it have to be one or the other? Even the question as to whether it had to be one or the other *had to be one or the other*! Feathers or lead? Feathers or lead?

By the time they were set in their actual trajectory, and the g-force melted away, Diana was cranky and exhausted. She took a light supper; watched a book by herself, trying to ignore Iago and Sapho's conversation. Sapho wanted to learn how to fly a ship of this type; Iago was talking her through the interface, discussing its cranks and hiccoughs, discussing the fuel-to-ice ratio and so on.

Finally Diana hooked herself to the side and went to sleep. Iago dimmed the interior lights, and went to sleep himself. Sapho too.

But Diana slept only fitfully, waking at odd moments, hanging there doing nothing more than watching the motionless cabin: the bone-pale dashboard glow; hearing the hum. She slept again, woke uneasily, and slept again.

Now she dreamt. It was a complicated series of interlocking set-piece dream-stories, gothically ornate and grisly – but she remembered almost none of the details, only that it was so complicated. This in itself was a disturbing thing. She *always* remembered her dreams. Remembering her dreams was a necessary part of her problem-solving. But on this occasion the only bit of the dream she could recall afterwards was the very last portion. There were three of them: Diana and Ms Joad and a third person, behind her, whom she could not see or name. They were all standing on the shore of a red sea, bright red, tomato red, artificially red. It was blood, this sea, a great pool of blood under the influence of gravity. Little waves broke on the shore at her feet, with horrid, slurpy, chuckling sounds. The sand was hard and compacted. 'With a little heat,' Ms Joad was saying, 'you know what this sand will turn into? With a little atomic blast? We'll detonate, we'll detonate.' 'But first we must have time to get away,' said Diana, feeling anxious, worried that if they were being reckless, then disaster must follow. '*Under* the waves, my dear,' said Ms Joad. 'That's where we'll go! You must learn to breathe it. It was what you did in your maternal womb, wasn't it? You breathed the life-fluid of your mother then – it is simply a question of *going back to that time*. You. Will. Remember.' 'No,' Diana cried; but the red fluid rose up in front of her in a red wave, and then it was all about her; she was kicking her limbs in an epilepsy of panic, and the stuff went in at her mouth.

She woke sweating, gasping. Her heart was hammering. Sleep was out of the question; so she unfastened herself and floated through the cabin. She drank a little water; and then – because she thought it might help her skittering thoughts and fearful heart – she drank a little rice vodka. But that only made her feel sick. The view through the main windows had that eerie motionless quality spacetravel almost always presents to its travellers. However many thousand kilometres a second you are actually travelling, it always looks as if you are perfectly motionless. Diana thought to herself: I breathed vaporised Bar-le-duc into my lungs. We all did. I absorbed him. Unconscious cannibalism. That's what I was dreaming about.

She began to cry.

It felt as if she would never control her sobs; but eventually she stopped crying. Of course she did. She floated back over to her perch, hooked herself on again and lay still. The hours moved in their mysterious, unmeasurable way.

The next day passed in a daze. The next night she was so exhausted she slept eleven hours, and upon waking was conscious of no dreams at all.

8

The Wrath of Diana

To go from the enforced stillness and low-key daily interactions of the *Rum*'s cabin into the crazy, drunken revels of the first of Garland 400's bubbles was something of a shock. They left Sapho on the ship, and made their way past the chanting, boozing, copulating crowds; through into the adjacent bubble and then again into the one after that. Here Iago introduced her to Aishwarya; and the old lady checked the RACdroid's seals carefully and pronounced it whole and kosher, and not a rogue at all.

Which meant that its data was to be trusted.

The four of them each drank a globe of cold, dark coca; and Diana felt the stimulant buzzing inside her veins. 'So the shot that killed Bar-le-duc must have come from outside the bubble after all,' said Iago.

'That flash,' Sapho reminded him. 'We saw the flash. That must have been part of it.'

'Maybe,' said Iago. 'Although the flash happened a good while before the impact.'

'Perhaps,' said Aishwarya, 'the flash was wholly unconnected with Monsieur Bar-le-duc's death. A quantum fluctuation. A piece of ice hit by a micrometeorite. It could be any one of a dozen things. Experience has taught me that we much more often see connection where there is only random copresence. Pattern-seeking consciousness, you know. Great plains ape, you know.'

'But this, this, this – I mean, the RACdroid's recording – is *data*. Inarguable,' said Iago. 'We can't argue with it. The shot was fired from outside.'

'Indeed,' agreed Aishwarya.

'So what happened to the bullet?' Iago pressed. 'It was forceful enough to tear an entire police sloop into shreds of spaceship metal, to punch through half a metre of house plastic, and to atomise Bar-le-duc. But then, instead of snapping through the other side of the bubble it . . . vanishes? How do you explain that?'

They sipped, and chewed, and were silent for a while.

'Shall I tell you what I think is interesting?' said Diana. 'The *timing* of it. Bar-le-duc's sloop has managed to evade your early warning systems, and is about to land, burn through your walls and take us all by surprise. Then a mysterious flash – quantum foam, sure; a random asteroid burn, whatever it was – but it *just happens* to burst like the Star of Bethlehem, to warn us.'

'Happenstance,' suggested Iago. 'As my good friend, here . . .'

Dia ignored him. 'And *then* Bar-le-duc boards us, with his thugs, and the best you can do by way of bargaining leverage is to negotiate a legal amnesty for me.'

'Nothing I could have said would have induced Bar to give *me* up,' said Iago. 'He'd been chasing me for many years. I was the great prize of his career.'

'Could you not have fought him?' Aishwarya asked. 'You surely haven't forgotten *how* to fight?'

'If I had fought him, we would all have died,' Iago said. 'That is certainly what would have happened. When he came aboard he was accompanied by four of his hired guns. And besides: the deal I struck with him – immunity from prosecution for Ms Argent, here – was dependent upon my not resisting arrest. The deal was important. Accordingly, I didn't resist arrest.'

'Exactly my point,' said Diana. 'The timing of it *must* be significant! You were just about to go off with him – and at *precisely that moment* an unknown individual flies past the house and blows him into a mist of blood and matter. Ms Aishwarya here believes in coincidence, and I am content to respect her superior experience of life. But it looks to me *too well timed* to be chance.'

'Chance,' said Iago, in a blank voice.

'You're holding something back, Jack,' Diana said.

'Am I?' he said. 'I usually find that a good strategy.'

'Oh I know *you* didn't kill him,' she said. 'I was hanging right beside you – the RACdroid confirms it. But if you didn't actually shoot him, I still wonder if you're not behind it somehow.'

'Miss Diana!' objected Sapho, surprisingly. 'How can you say such a thing?'

But Iago only laughed, once again. 'You were there, Diana. You're my alibi! If even my *alibi* thinks I'm guilty, then what chance—'

'The RACdroid too,' put in Aishwarya.

'What?'

'It is also your alibi.'

'That too. An infallible alibi, too. Ah, but this is an *immensely* valuable machine,' Iago said, reaching across and patting its metallic surface. 'You see: quite apart from anything – *if* I killed Bar it would constitute resisting arrest, and as such would invalidate the contract. Your immunity would no longer be valid.'

'My immunity!' repeated Diana, scornfully.

'Believe me,' he said, earnestly. 'I would do anything to avoid invalidating your legal immunity.'

She had been able to contain her annoyance up to this point, but this was too much. This was the final straw. Diana had had enough of this chaff, pushed off hard with both legs and floated away, without saying goodbye. It was rude, of course. But she no longer cared.

Iago had the sense to leave Diana to herself for a while. She explored all across the curving walls of that greenspace. Then she spent half an hour staring out into space. Natives stared at her, from their branches, or on the variously angled porches and windows, and this spooked her. Nobody approached her, much less offered her any violence, but their mute surveillance struck Diana as oppressive. 'Miss Diana?' It was Sapho.

'He infuriates me,' she said. 'He just *infuriates* me.'

'Jack? Surely he wants the best for you.'

'How can you defend him?' she snapped at the other girl. 'He set up that situation, on Korkura. He put you in the closed room with the man who raped you. It was a *game* to him!'

'It was justice,' Sapho retorted, with dignity.

At another time these words, and the way Sapho delivered them, might have brought Diana up short. But she was being carried along on the juggernaut of her own anger. 'Justice? It was horrible – it has given me nightmares! Blood, death and mutilation. Horrible.'

'You think it wasn't horrible for me?' said Sapho, flushing. 'I was the one who pushed the hammer onto his skull. It was horrible for me too. But I come from a world where people are not insulated from horrors the way the rich are.'

'Sapho!' cried Diana, shocked. 'You're rude.'

Sapho's dark face darkened further, and her hands trembled. 'He understands justice,' she said. 'You do not. You don't understand him at all.'

'Good goddess, Sapho – is this some reaction to going cold-turkey on your CRFs?'

'Your goddess is a sham,' Sapho retorted. 'Ra'allah will burn her to ashes with the light of His majesty.' And then, because the pharmakon was not entirely metabolised out of her system, and because acting in so insubordinate a way to a member of the Clan Argent went against all her training, Sapho burst into tears. 'Miss! I'm sorry – I'm sorry. I'm sorry!'

'Really, Sapho!' said Diana, her eyes wide. 'You're not yourself!'

'It's true. It's the truth. I'm sorry Miss – I'm sorry. I'm going back to the *Rum*. I'm going back to the *Rum* until I have taken a hold of myself. Until I have recovered my courtesy, Miss.' And with a strong kick-out of her legs Sapho shot through the doorway out of the bubble.

Diana was left jangled by this encounter – servants did not speak in such a way to their mistresses. Everybody dosed their staff with CRFs, of course; but nobody liked to think that the pharmakon was the only reason for loyalty.

Iago floated across. 'Was that Sapho, I saw, leaving the bubble?' he asked. 'Where's she going?'

Diana snapped. 'You want to know why I am angry with you?' she said.

He looked rather surprised at this, but nodded.

'It's not that you have a guardian angel,' she said. 'Having a guardian angel, keeping you out of prison, disposing of your enemies – that's obviously a *terribly* useful thing to have. It's not that.'

'Dia – what's the matter?'

'It's the way you insist on seeing things from a perspective of angelic *elevation*. It's inhuman.'

'You are going to have to, uh, unpack that for me a little,' Iago said, cautiously.

'Am I? Listen: on Korkura, you gave me the birthday present of a real-life murder mystery. You knew I liked whodunits. More than that. You knew I had a *passion* for murder mysteries. So you gave me the death of a human being.'

Her brusqueness began to apply heat to Iago's own temper. 'What did I do? I arranged for a rapist to be put in the way of one of his victims. I set things up so that the victim was able to pay him back. You're telling me that was wrong.'

'I'm not pretending that he—' She reached, an automatic mental gesture, into her bId to supply the missing name, but of course she was unplugged from all that. So instead she stalled, losing the momentum of her fury as she rifled her memory for . . . 'Leron. Leron, him, I'm not pretending that *he* was some kind of innocent martyr. But *you* didn't have to arrange for his death! What made it *your* business? There *is* such a thing as the Lex Ulanova, and rape is one of the crimes it covers. You could have alerted the proper authorities.'

'Really, Diana?' he replied. 'You think the Ulanov law is interested in petty infractions in the depths of the Sump?'

'Rape is hardly a petty infraction!'

'Be realistic, Diana! You know what the bulk of prosecutions under the Lex are for? Commercial fraud. Lesser corporations and gangs and occasionally lone traders evading trading duties and sales taxes. In the Sump, where barter is common and policing stretched thin, they concern themselves with the more egregious infractions of the 70% rule. Every now and again they mount big raids and arrest people who show any disparity between material wealth and monies declared and passed through legitimate accounts. Other crimes only tend to get punished if they are committed in respectable locations. You *really* think the police would be interested in the distress of an individual like Sapho?'

'You gave that man's death to me *as a gift*! A sixteen-year-old girl! You thought that was *appropriate*?'

Iago was losing his composure. 'Don't pretend you don't *love* murder mysteries? You've immersed yourself in thousands. Murder is your *passion*.'

'For the puzzle of it,' she said, in a too-loud voice. 'Not for the *death*. I'm not morbid, Iago. I like to solve the puzzle! Solving puzzles is how I'm made.'

'If that were true,' he growled, 'you'd spend your time solving the mystery of the stolen Imperial Diamond, or the mystery of the kidnapped heiress. You'd be like Eva, and try to solve purely intellectual mysteries, like the Champagne Supernovae. But you don't. You come back, again and again, to this one particular kind of mystery. Sure, you like the puzzle element – but you know it's more than that. It's death that fascinates you. By puzzling out individual deaths you come closer to trying to plumb the biggest puzzle of all – mortality itself.'

She looked at him, her anger deflated, and said, in a slow, unconvinced voice: 'No.'

'Come along, Diana! Can you *honestly* say to me that you would find the same *satisfaction* in solving the crime story to do with theft or embezzlement? When you heard that Leron had been killed, what did you think? Did you grieve, for no woman is an island and every human death diminishes you? Or were you *excited*?'

'No wavy *way*. You gave me a *death* for my sixteenth birthday,' Diana said again. 'Can't you see how grotesque that is?'

'Your outrage is a purely intellectual response,' Iago said. 'You feel no in-the-gut revulsion. Bar-le-duc said that death is my medium. It's never been my choice, but maybe he was right. Well I shall tell you something: it's yours, too.'

'No,' she replied. 'No. Wavy. *Way*.'

'We're the same. It doesn't make you a psychopath. You don't *seek out* the death of others. But you are the heir to a wealthy and powerful Clan, and death is the currency of power. If you were too squeamish to deal with that, on an emotional level, then . . .'

'Then what? I shouldn't take charge of the MOHclan?' Diana shook her head. 'When has that ever been a choice, for me?'

Iago's own fury had drained away too. He put his left hand on the top of his head; and with his right he took hold of his chin. It was an odd gesture, contemplative in an ape-like kind of way. 'There are lots of hiding holes in the System, I suppose,' he said. 'But it would be exile. An evasion. Individually speaking, death is always a rupture, a violence. But taking a total view, death is the bell curve upon which the cosmos is balanced. Without it, nothing would work, everything would collapse, clogged and stagnant. Death is *flow*. It is the necessary lubrication of universal motion. It is, in itself, neither praiseworthy nor blameworthy.'

'Death is always individual, though,' she objected, in a low voice. 'To the person dying.'

'You're right,' he agreed. Now he clasped his hands before him, zipping all his fingers into one another. 'We do need to be able to see it on both scales, you're right. If you could only see the large-scale aspect of death you'd be some kind of monster. But by the same token: if all you can see is the *personal*, then politics, on the scale of the human trillions that inhabit this system, will be opacity to you.'

'Ruthless,' Diana said.

'Nobody can overthrow the fascist dictator by being nicer than him. The reason for this is: by definition everybody is always already nicer than the fascist dictator.'

'I'm too young to lead a revolution,' said Diana.

'Hah!' said Iago, smiling. 'Your *age* isn't the issue. Your state of *mind* is the issue. It's a matter of . . . toughness, of course. So, I have some news for you, and I think you will take it well. But I cannot be sure.'

'What news?'

Iago didn't reply at first. He looked around the bubble.

Aishwarya, or perhaps the other inhabitants, had arranged a great many prisms and transparent balls around the walls in strings and constellations. As the whole structure turned, and the sunlight came through the windows these crystals squeezed out a succession of rainbow strips and patches of brightness, blood-red through to yellow and green up to the indigo of which the vacuum of space was but a more intense distillation. These splotches and grills of colour played unpredictably upon the various greens of the inner foliage.

'Bar-le-duc came straight to my house,' Iago said. 'He arrived pretty much as soon as we docked and unloaded. He *knew* we were there. How could he know? I didn't tell him, and Sapho *couldn't* have told him. She didn't have access to the means to communicate with him even if she had wanted to.'

'Well *I* didn't tell him!' Diana objected.

'Yes you did, though,' said Iago. 'You didn't *mean* to. But you spoke to Eva. She used that conversation to plant a tracker in the ship AI. A ferociously clever piece of kit, actually. Which is to say: I was expecting her to do it, and I put in play a code-chaser, one of the best there is. The virus shrapnelled into something like eight million separate prions, and it ran *everywhere*. An amazingly difficult code to cleanse. I thought I'd got it all out, but in the event – obviously – I did not. '

Diana was staring intently at him. 'This is a counterfactual, or joke, or some other kind of – is it?'

'It's as real as it gets.'

'We're talking about my sister.'

'I'm—' Iago looked about him, at the various buildings and struts and ropes, at the hundred shades of green, and the bright, arc-edged trapezoid of illumination coming through the main window as the structure turned slowly. 'I am sorry,' he finished, eventually.

'Is the trace still active?'

'No. I mean, I hope not. I mean, I sincerely don't think so. It was piggybacking on *Red Rum*'s standard datasift peg. I usually keep that running because – well, because it looks more suspicious for a ship to be *un*plugged than connected to the general datasift like the majority. But I rooted out the trace, and I've unplugged the *Rum*, so I don't think we can be traced now.'

'Eva,' said Diana, speaking slowly and distinctly, as if there were some danger that Iago might not follow, 'is my sister, and more than my sister. Why would she do this? *If* she did this?'

'The conditional tense,' noted Iago. 'And, you see, *that's* what I'm talking about. The System is brutal and unforgiving. If you refuse to accept it on its own terms it will destroy you. So the question is: how quickly can your mind adapt to the brutality? That was the real nature of my gift to you, for your last birthday. To see what happened to your data-assimilation and problem-solving abilities when the *if* turned to *is*. When the fiction of one possible murder-mystery in one-of-a-trillion possible worlds turned into an actual corpse, on your doorstep.'

'Why would Eva do this?' Diana repeated, in a level voice. 'My *sister*. *My* sister.'

'Why? Power, I suppose. After all. The idea that the Ulanovs would blow up the Tobruk Plasmaser station just to stop Eva getting into space – that never *fitted*. Why not just arrest her? It was a smokescreen. Screens make me suspicious.'

'You've suspected her all this time?'

He nodded. 'I think you have too, although you may not have permitted yourself to realise it, consciously.'

Diana said: 'but she's my sister.'

'And you were hers. And *she* was facing the prospect of being your number two when your parents stepped down.'

'Eva is perfectly content with her academic research,' said Diana. 'She just isn't interested in power. As I say those sentences,' she added, clasping her knees to her chest, 'I can tell they're both wrong. Aren't they? Of course she's interested in power.'

'She's a human being,' agreed Iago.

'Of course she is not content to be nothing more than her research,' Diana said. 'So. What did she do?'

'I assume she made a deal with the Ulanovs. It would suit them rather better, I think, if they could keep the Clan Argent in place in its subordinate tier. But they no longer trust your parents, and they don't trust you either. Eva, of course, would be a better bet than an outsider, or quisling. I suppose the Ulanovs think she is more straightforward, easier to parse, politically than her parents, or you. She must have agreed to give them you, and your parents – I can't believe the Ulanovs would have agreed otherwise. She probably contracted to more stringent tithes, increased access to Argent data stores. In return they have told her she can lead the Clan.'

Diana was feeling a vague swirling sensation, somewhere in her solar plexus. It was not pleasant, though neither was it especially debilitating.

'I don't believe it,' she said. But of course she did. She grokked its rightness right away. So, always punctilious in such matters, she amended: 'or perhaps, I suppose I *do* believe it. But I don't see that . . .' She couldn't go on. The truth of it was that she did see. She saw the game laid out, entire.

Iago finished her sentence: 'you don't see that she would do you any harm? I'm sure she'd *prefer* not to, if circumstance permits it. But I don't see how she can leave you at liberty.'

Diana's anger had sublimed, now, into a solid pressure of tears inside her chest. With an action of will she elected not to cry. Instead she opened her mouth, and said: 'my whole life has been upended and eviscerated.' She was on the edge of crying, but fought it down. 'And for what? Tectonic realignment of the blocs of power? Clan Onbekend are on the rise, Clan Argent on the decline? The *randomness* of it is the most infuriating part.'

'FTL was the catalyst – or, the rumour of FTL,' said Iago. 'The prospect of a weapon that could destroy the sun. The thought of being able to flee to the stars. How could it not shake up the status quo?'

'But it's not *real!*' said Diana, her anger flaring back up and replacing the desire to cry with the urge to punch somebody. 'It is not theoretically possible, and it's certainly not *actual*! They're chasing you because they think you have McAuley's blueprints inside your mind . . . And you don't! Do you?'

'No,' he said. 'I don't.'

'The Ulanovs have grown so used to policing the Lex Ulanova in terms of its infractions, that they think the laws of physics are similarly friable. It's so – provoking!'

She caught sight of the way he was looking at her, and, from nowhere, she began to laugh. 'I know!' she said, putting a hand in front of her mouth. 'That they believe it – that's what matters. Not the truth of it. But to be chased and ruined and threatened over a *rumour*. It's so absurd.'

She laughed, and he smiled; and in that moment she felt no anger at all. She and Iago hugged.

'Of course, it's a question of the stakes involved,' said Iago. 'Not *that* it is practicable; but *if* it is. *If* is a potent realpolitik pivot.' He stretched his legs in mid-air, and yawned. 'I'm going to go back to the *Rum* for a bit. I'm going to check up on Sapho, see if her prayers to Ra'allah are over. Make sure the revellers in that bubble aren't causing her any annoyance. Will you come?'

Diana took stock. She did feel a little lighter inside, though she couldn't exactly fathom why. But at least the anger and the weepiness had withdrawn inside her, as a snail's horns are retracted. 'I'll come later,' she said. 'I'm going to stay here for a while.'

'Very good, Miss,' said Iago, in imitation of his old manner.

'After all,' she said. 'Somebody killed Bar-le-duc. I can't see how it was done, let along who did it. And that irks me.'

'Ah, Miss Diana of the Clan Argent, bred to solve problems – if *you* can't solve it, nobody can. Shall I leave the RACdroid with you?'

'Yes. I want to look again at the recording.'

'Bring it back to the *Rum* when you have finished, will you? I'd rather keep it locked away and secure. According to Aishwarya there's every chance the revellers next door will try and steal it as soon as they get sober enough to think it might be valuable.'

He left her alone.

9

Solving the Mystery

A sharp-edged block of sunlight slid very slowly over the leaves and the mossy turf. Ducks, invisible in the foliage, played their kazoos. She breathed in the oxygen. Things might look bleak, but as long as she could still *solve problems* she would be alright. What else was the future, but a series of as yet unsolved problems?

On the other hand, not every mystery has a solution.

The pattern refused to coalesce in her mind. Something was getting in the way. Her recovered good mood started to sag again.

She went over the data in the RACdroid one more time. Insofar as she could tell there *was* nobody in the undergrowth. The shot that killed Bar-le-duc couldn't have come from there. None of Bar's henchmen fired it, any more than did Iago, Sapho or Diana herself. So much was clear. But no matter how she manipulated the data she could not tell whether the fatal shot had come from outside the bubble, or from the wall itself.

Aishwarya floated over to see what she was doing. 'Going over the last moments of the life of Bar-le-duc, I see.'

'I'm trying to work out what happened,' Diana said. 'Whoever killed him can't have been inside the house. It must have been a shot from outside. It was a blow powerful enough to break apart an entire spaceship, to rip through the side of the side of the house and turn Bar-le-duc into red mist. So why didn't it just shoot straight through the opposite wall?'

Aishwarya shrugged. 'You think *that's* the interesting question?'

'It's,' Diana replied, cautiously, '*a* question, certainly. Where did the projectile go?'

'Maybe it caught a lucky rebound and shot back out the way it came,' said Aishwarya. 'Maybe it was some special kind of bolt keyed to dissolve when it struck flesh.'

'*Are* there such bullets?' Diana asked, wide-eyed.

'Well *I* don't know!' said Aishwarya. 'I'm no armourer! That kind of tech-chatter bores me to *ice*. Things aren't as compelling as people.'

'Alright,' said Diana. 'I'll go along with you. The timing of the killing *is* interesting. Bar-le-duc was just about to take Iago – Jack, I mean – away. Now, either the timing of this killing is perfectly coincidental; or else the killer chose her moment precisely to *stop* that eventuality coming to pass.'

'But who would want to keep Jack Glass out of prison?' asked Aishwarya. 'Prison is where he belongs.'

'Who indeed?' asked Diana. She felt that tingling in her scalp, and down the back of her neck, that suggested she was close to something important. 'His friends? Fellow revolutionaries?'

'Why keep it secret, though, if it's them? Assume an antinomian sloop just happened to be passing, saw – Christ-the-Hindu knows how, but let's assume it – saw that Jack was about to be apprehended by the Ulanovs' most famous policeman. So they fired their magic bullet from their impossible gun, and killed the arresting officer. Wouldn't they make themselves known, afterwards? "Hey, Jack, we saved your life . . ."?'

'That scenario,' said Diana, feeling the tingling sensation recede, 'doesn't *feel* right. Doesn't feel plausible.'

Aishwarya shrugged again. 'Doubtless not. It's a hypothetical, though. Yes? Bar-le-duc and Jack were friends, you know. A long, long time ago. But Bar had been working for the Ulanovs a long time.'

Something lay, just out of reach of her conscious mind, on the fringes of her thought. She had almost had it. Almost! But it was gone, now. The impossible gun, she thought. The impossible bullet. She was missing *something*. Bar-le-duc was dead. She knew that because – because what?

How did she know that?

'There is still some of his blood in Iago's hair,' she said aloud.

'What's that?' asked Aishwarya.

'I've been assuming that Bar-le-duc is dead. It certainly *looks* as though he is. But only a fool trusts assumptions. Tell me, Miss Aishwarya: could you analyse DNA from dried blood?'

'I could, if I had the equipment,' Aishwarya replied. 'But the hooligans in these damn shanty-bubbles stole all my valuable kit a long time ago. You know who you should go visit? Northface. She's a friend of mine. You go speak to her – two days' flight at 1g, not far. Her bubble is called "Penny Lane". Approach her carefully, though; she's not fond of Jack. But she'll run your DNA. Very reasonable rates.'

'Thank you,' said Diana.

Diana took hold of the RACdroid and manoeuvred it through the gate into the adjacent bubble, and from there into the main sphere, where the party was still ongoing. The revellers had got past the stage of speechifying by now. Many were floating blind-drunk, their arms and legs spread, their faces stupid in unconsciousness. A few other couples were having sex, though not so many as before. There were fewer clusters of people grasping one another like frogs in spawn. Diana navigated past all this with the droid, and into the docking hallway.

The hatch to the *Rum* was shut, which was presumably Sapho being understandably cautious. She smacked her palm on the curve of spaceship metal, and heard her knock echoing inside.

The mechanism snapped free. The door opened.

Sapho was there. She was crying: her face crumpled and red. That should have alerted Diana straight away, of course; but emotions had been running so high that day it didn't really seem that out of place. 'Sapho,' she said. 'Could you put this RAC-droid in storage please?'

Diana pushed the droid through, and followed after. Inside the *Rum*, Iago was reaching for something. Or else some oddity in the angle of her perception made his body look longer than it was. But this impression lasted barely a second, and she saw that it wasn't Iago at all, as Sapho shut the hatch and bundled herself against her. 'Oh mistress,' the girl cried, clasping her.

The figure in the cabin was Ms Joad. 'Hello, my dear,' she said.

'How are *you* here?' asked Diana.

'Naturally it counts as *loyalty*,' said Ms Joad. 'After all, I am now working for your sister. And Sapho, here, would sooner die than betray the Clan! But your Jack Glass is not a member of *that* family – is he?'

'You're working for Eva,' said Diana, processing the new information. 'What have you done with Iago?'

'Jack? Anxious about him, are you? Well I haven't killed him, at any rate. Not *yet*. No. I stung him with a little jabber I carry about me; muscular paralysis. It's selective; I forget the specific vertebrae it targets, but he can still breathe – and talk. I've stowed him in one of the g-couches. For *safe* keeping.'

Diana turned, pulling herself round on a wall handle: and there indeed was Iago, laid out in the g-couch for all the world like a corpse in a coffin.

'I shall tell you straight here and now that I *don't* believe in wasting time,' said Ms Joad. 'It was a near-thing – young Sapho here, bless her loyalty, explained how close that horrible Bar-le-duc came to snatching Jack. He was working for Eva, you know. Your own MOHsister! Of course, I am too. I'm just retracing his steps. Making assurance doubly sure.'

'I can't believe Eva has employed *you*!'

'You hurt my feelings, dear girl! True, after my performance on Korkura I was demoted. The truth of it is: I was going to be sent to the belt, some low-grade diplomatic work. No thank you! But I had been highly enough placed to see what was going on. I took the opportunity to leap before I was pushed. I approached your sister, and was taken into her employ. She's a canny woman, Eva Argent. She knows, for instance, how *precarious* her position is at present. But – ah, if she can lay her hands on the recipe for FTL . . . that would strengthen her hand *immeasurably*.'

'Iago doesn't have the secret to FTL.'

'Of course he does! He knew McAuley personally, after all. He must have told you so? No? Perhaps he didn't trust you. People who are themselves untrustworthy often find it hard to trust others.'

Diana felt the tumbling, various data falling through her. 'It would not have served your purposes for Bar-le-duc to capture Jack,' she said, to Ms Joad. 'Would it? *You* wanted to be the one to bring Iago back to my sister. To consolidate your position.'

'You should thank me, my dear,' said Ms Joad, favouring Diana with her superbly chilly smile. 'Better *your* family gets the FTL than the Ulanovs, surely? Even if *you* won't be running the Clan, after all. Still, I'm sure exile won't be too incommoding for you. Some prisons are *quite* comfortable.'

Diana said: '*you* killed Bar-le-duc. Bar-le-duc was coming for us, and you were following him. That flash, outside the house: that was you! You had some . . . what? Targeted projectile, and blew him to pieces. And then you followed our sloop here. But you took a risk, didn't you? What if your weapon had split the whole house? What if we hadn't been able to control the decompression? We could all have died – and you wouldn't have had Iago as a bargaining chip. But perhaps that was a risk worth taking?'

'My dear,' said Ms Joad, looking bored. 'I honestly have no idea what you're chattering about. Now, will you come freely? Or must I jab you too? Either way, you're going *into* a g-couch, and we're going to fly *as fast as we can*. I shall piggyback my ship on Jack's one, until we use up all of his fuel. We have a long way to go – all the way to Mars! – and we need to move quickly. You look dismayed, my dear! But perhaps your sister will show you

346

mercy. True, she'll lock you up. At least for a few years, until her grip on power has been more firmly established. But it is *probably* in her interest not simply to kill you.'

'Never underestimate the bond between MOHsisters,' said Iago, in a creaky voice, behind her.

Diana was at the side of the g-couch in moments. Inside, with straps across his chest, and an ill-looking, bluish sheen to his skin, was Jack Glass. She could see that he was paralysed, trapped, caught like a bug in a spider's web, cocooned and restrained past all hope of escape. Even if she got the straps off him, his muscles were clenched and nerveless, unmoveable. 'I'm still alive,' said Iago, moving his mouth with difficulty. There were straps across his neck and forehead too.

'I can't believe it ends like this,' Diana cried.

Ms Joad chuckled, coldly. 'Get in the g-couch, my dear,' she said. 'You too, Miss Sapho.'

'Do as she says,' rasped Iago.

'Yes. Take his advice, my dear, and *do as I say.*'

'She'll jab you if you don't,' breathed Iago. 'Believe me: it's not pleasant. It . . . *burns* as well as paralyses. I need *you* in a g-couch. I need *her* to move the ship.'

'*You* need?' repeated Ms Joad, who had floated over to the g-couch, and was holding a pen-shaped object in her right hand. 'By all means let us consult *your* needs! So long as they overlap precisely with my needs, I'm sure we can accommodate them.'

There was no helping it. Diana pulled herself over to a free couch. As she manoeuvred herself inside, her mind moved everything about, and tried to connect every datum with every other one. But it was impossible. It was *impossible* that Iago could escape from this situation. Paralysed with a neurotoxin that would keep his muscles frozen for days. Strapped in a g-couch. Flown to an unknown destination, where agents of her own family waited.

She laid herself flat in the couch. Ms Joad loomed over her at the lid. With a few swift, precise gestures she fixed the straps about Diana's torso and tied her arms down. She tied her left leg, and then her right. She looped a strap about Diana's neck, and another over her forehead.

'Hush now,' said Ms Joad. For an instant their eyes locked, and Diana experienced a weird fluxion in her own thought patterns. How old was this woman? How long had she been alive?

Diana was gifted a vertiginous sense of future retrospect. She saw a future Joad, gloating: *he led us a merry dance, from world to world, through myriad bubbles – but we caught him. I caught him. I jabbed him and sealed him away and brought him back; and we were able to extract the formula for FTL from him, before he died. And now the Clan has a bomb with which to blackmail Ulanovs, and the whole of humanity!* It could lead only to disaster.

'There's no glory in this, Ms Joad,' she said.

'Glory is a combustion,' the older woman replied. 'The rapid interaction of like and unlike, cancelling one another out in fire.' She smiled a deathly smile, and then she disappeared from Diana's constrained point of view. Presumably she went to strap Sapho into her couch. From where she lay, Diana could see only one window, which gave out a view of the green curve of the main Garland 400 bubble. Bright sunlight fell upon it.

There was nothing to do.

Soon, Diana felt the jar and the pull as the ship disengaged. The green arc slid out of the frame of the window. With a distant sense of motion in her ears and stomach, she watched as a portion of another ship filled the frame, and then passed out of view again. That was Ms Joad's own craft, presumably. The hissing of attitudinal jets. The clunk, resonantly audible, as the nose of the *Rum* connected with the nose of Ms Joad's one-person sloop.

'Ms Joad?' wheezed Iago, from his couch.

'You *will* try my patience,' came her voice, from outside Diana's field of view, 'if you insist on interrupting me.' The grumble of the main thrust firing up; the orientation of the shadows on that portion of the cabin wall that Diana could see.

The *nowness* of now. The vivid intensity of being alive. 'You'd better have something important to say to me, young man.'

'I do,' Iago rasped.

'What?'

'I wanted to say,' said Iago. He sighed, and went on: 'that I'm ready for you now.'

The next part was a jumble. The lids of the g-couch slammed instantly shut, with a jarring clunk. Diana was aware of being shaken *very* violently – and this despite the fact that she was cocooned inside a g-couch, strapped down and restrained. Yet she felt as if her limbs were going to be shaken apart from her torso, and as if her eyeballs were being scrambled inside her head, the shaking was so intense. It lasted for a long time. Eventually the shaking died down, and finally it stopped. All she could do was lie there. The lights inside the couch had gone out, and her own breathing sounded loud in her ears, and every now and again some piece of debris banged hard against the side of her couch, sending a cacophonous noise through the little space. Otherwise there was nothing.

It was perfectly dark and very quiet for a long time. The sound of her own breathing, and (as she strained her ears) of her own heartbeat. These two slowly settled into a calmer rhythm. It did occur to her, although without any particular sensation of alarm, that she might be dead. Possibly her body had died and her consciousness was continuing inside this box because – the notion was fanciful, but somehow it appealed to her – her soul couldn't get out. Eventually the box would be opened, she thought, and then maybe that would be an end to it. Her spirit would fly off to some other realm. Eva had conspired against her, and against their parents. The world had been turned upside down. But it was foolish to say so, because there was no up and down in space.

In that space her mind kept working. She was bred to solve problems, after all.

The awkward thing was the way the problems kept resolving

themselves into opposite pairs of impossibility. The death of Bar-le-duc had been caused by an impossible assailant, or else by an impossible gun. FTL was an impossibility by the laws of physics; yet the Champagne Supernovae that Eva herself had been studying were candles lit in the impossible distance to the fact that this technology was not only possibly, but had been – madly, dangerously – invented by a dozen separate alien civilisations.

She was supposed to be good at solving problems. And now, here she was.

The whole cosmos had shrunk down to her, in the dark. To her thoughts.

The dark calmed her. She slept. She dreamt that she was not in a g-couch at all, but the barrel of a gigantic pistol. Iago was there with her. 'This is the biggest gun,' she said. 'Bigger than any other gun.' 'Size is a relative concept,' he replied. 'We must always ask: big in relation to what?'

The barrel's diameter was even bigger than she first thought: a hundred metres across. She stood up, and Iago stood beside her. Bright light was coming in from the mouth of the pistol. Their shadows were as long as totem poles before them, and Diana turned to watch the sun through the perfect circle of the barrel's mouth. 'Is it a good idea,' she asked. 'To aim this gun at *that* target?' 'How strange it is,' said Iago, in reply, 'that the moon has phases and the sun has not!' His voice was not his own. He was speaking with the voice of Ms Joad. Diana thought to herself: he is doing a surprisingly good vocal impression of Ms Joad! And then, she thought: but how can I know if it is Iago doing an impression of Ms Joad, or Miss Joad doing an impression of Iago? 'Quite right,' came a voice in the darkness. The light had gone. Everything was dark. She was waking up. But she heard the voice, nonetheless. 'A person impersonating another person is exactly halfway between two people. An impossible asymptote!'

She was awake again. 'Hello?' she cried, and was startled by the nearness and loudness of her own voice in that enclosed space.

There was no way out.

It was, to put it simply, difficult to tell when she was awake, and when asleep. She thought she heard Sapho saying: 'you have all the information you need to solve this mystery.' But that didn't sound like the sort of thing Sapho would say.

She must have been asleep, because it looked as if the darkness around her was dissolving into an eye-stinging spread of bright dots: green and cyan, white and yellow, a huge sediment of particles, each one of which was a human life – each of which was *many* human lives, all clustered together.

But then she heard Aishwarya's voice saying: 'did you make the mistake of underestimating my Jack Glass?' 'No,' she said. 'No, I didn't.' But the voice went on: 'the people here believe in ghosts, or at least in ghost-like spirits they call *bhuts*. You are not supposed to add to their population without consulting them first!' 'I added nothing,' replied Diana, a little panicky. 'No,' said the voice. '*You're* not the murderer, are you – '

'Are you?'

'Are you?'

'Are?'

'Ah.'

'Ah.'

And the lights coalesced into a swordblade of brilliance, and then Diana was blinking and wincing in *actual* light. The g-couch lid had been opened. Somebody was loosening the bonds that held her, and it was Aishwarya herself, large as life and twice as natural. 'What's at *stake* here?' Diana was saying, or trying to say, but her throat was sore, and the words didn't come out properly. 'What's at stake here?' 'There you go, my lovely,' said Aishwarya, roughly but not unkindly. 'Come out of there. You're one lucky rich person, and no mistake.'

10

Aboard the *Библиотека 4*

People in Garland 400, recovering from their exertions of the day before, asked fewer questions than Diana thought they might. Several had watched with their own eyes as the *Rum*'s snout exploded, turning several of the smaller craft also docked there into a swirling confetti of spaceship metal. But the explosion had been in keeping with the general debauch, or at least had not impinged on drugged and drunken consciousnesses as anything *too* unusual. To those who asked, Aishwarya and Diana said it had been a faulty docking connection, and a catastrophic decompression – not much of an explanation, of course, but enough to keep people from pestering them. Naturally, nobody in Garland 400 wanted to get the police involved. Luckily the *Rum*'s nose had been pointing away from the place when it blew, so no harm had been done.

'Luck having,' said Iago, 'nothing to do *with* it.'

Sapho was unharmed, although she was very jumpy and prone to tears. Iago, though – the famous Jack Glass himself – was *not* in a good way. His artificial legs had been annihilated from the knee down and wrecked from the knee up. The sensible thing would have been simply to remove them, but they were plumbed into his nervous system in complicated ways, and Aishwarya did not possess the expertise, even if she had possessed the machinery, to unpick them. Not that he needed legs, of course, in zero g; but it was messy-looking.

More worryingly, he had suffered some freeze-burns and vacuum exposure around his lower torso, and Aishwarya expressed worry that his kidneys might be damaged. It was hard to know, because the effects of Ms Joad's neurotoxin still held his muscles motionless.

Aishwarya kept him in her house – a bare, but comfortable space – and personally put pieces of fruit into his mouth to feed him. It took almost two complete days for the paralysis to recede, and only by the end of the third was he moving around with something of the agility he had once known.

The RACdroid was undamaged. Iago was pleased about that.

With the *Rum* permanently out of commission, they had no way of leaving Garland 400. Aishwarya's own craft – the one she had used to come out to them and bring them back to Garland – was (she told them, fiercely) *not* at their disposal. It didn't matter, Iago said.

In the end they hitched a ride with an itinerant doctor; a woman called Lydia Zinovieff. Her business was in travelling from house to house, from bubble-cluster to cluster, offering her services. 'It's mostly tumours,' she said. 'The wealthier can afford the implants, and ward off the worst of it. But in the Sump it's a different matter. People get all sorts of skin and other cancers in the high radiation, and often the most they can afford is excision. You see all manner of human beings with those egg-shaped or circular patches on their skin – and those are the easy ones! It's the inner tumours that are the trickiest. They want the best medical treatment of course, but can't pay for it.'

Her vessel was called the *Библиотека 4*. There were no g-couches, because Dr Zinovieff claimed never to travel at more than 'a g or two'. And indeed, the journey from Garland 400, via two large single bubble houses, and on to a cluster of twelve called The Sun Pole took nearly two weeks. But the sloop was more spacious inside than the *Rum* had been, and since the good doctor liked to spend most of her time inside a nesting IP, linked to the Corticotopia, Sapho, Diana and Iago had plenty of privacy.

They took the RACdroid with them.

Whilst they flew, Iago borrowed some tools and pared down or cut away the more ragged undersides of his severed stump-legs; just (he said) for neatness sake. 'So, you kept the gun inside there?' Diana asked him.

'Not that it *was* a gun, exactly,' he replied. 'Which is to say: it *was* a gun, though it didn't in the least look like one. A small sphere, conker-sized. And the bullet it fired was very small indeed: no more than a clump of atoms. It wasn't the bullet itself that caused so much damage. It was the *speed* at which the bullet travelled.'

'The impossible gun,' said Diana. 'Hah! Do my parents know you have it?'

'I *don't* have it any more, in point of fact,' he corrected. 'It's smithereens now. But the answer to your question is: no. They knew that I had been friends with McAuley, and they believed that he had confided his secret to me. Which, in a manner of speaking, he did. But they did not know that I possessed an actual functioning machine.'

'You were just carrying it around with you!' said Diana, admiringly. 'All this time, I thought the Ulanovs were chasing a spectre, a nonsense. The chimera of FTL. But you had an actual, functioning FTL pistol about your person.'

'Once you go beyond c,' said Iago, applying a finger-sized auto-file to his right stump and sending a sprig of white-fiery sparks from it away into the cabin, 'well, physics gets weird. As an object moves more and more rapidly, time appears – from its point of view, relative to an external observer – to pass more slowly. The closer you approach to the asymptote of absolute speed, the more slowly time passes. For a photon, travelling at the speed of light, time doesn't pass at all – it seems to us that the light from the Andromeda galaxy takes millions of years to reach us, but to the light itself it is there and it is here with no time passing. So what happens when you go *faster* than light? Time reverses, of course. At 2c, time travels one second per second *backwards*, if you see what I mean. It must be this way, in part to preserve general causality. But that has some – odd effects.'

'A bullet shot faster than light moves backwards in time,' said Diana. 'It's kindergarten physics, of course.'

'As to whether *human beings* could ever travel so fast . . .

frankly, I don't know. McAuley thought they could. But I wonder if forcing a human being backwards in time wouldn't scramble her consciousness. After all, our minds have evolved with extraordinary finesse to inhabit the medium of *forward-moving* time.'

'We couldn't use it to escape the solar system,' said Diana. 'But we could still use it to turn our sun into a Champagne Supernova.'

'It is desperately dangerous, yes,' agreed Iago, bending a protruding strut and tucking it away. 'It works, as it were, by altering c. It could provoke a catastrophic chain-reaction if it were dropped into the sun. As to whether it could ever transport humanity – maybe it could. I don't know.'

'Where did you get your impossible gun from?'

'McAuley. Where else?'

'He built it?'

'It's beyond my skill,' said Iago. He floated over to a storage drawer put the tools away. 'Do you know the funny thing? I did not *choose* to shoot Bar-le-duc. Which is to say, I don't *think* I did. Which is to say, I don't know, I suppose I must have done.' He scratched his head. 'I was as surprised as you when he exploded into a cloud of red right beside me. The bubble was breached, and I was knocked back into the foliage on the far side. And then the gun was in my hand. It was in my hand before I knew it. At that point, did it seem I had a choice? I don't know. The impossible bullet had already been fired. I pulled the trigger, then, but it had already happened.'

'It meant that you evaded capture,' Diana pointed out. 'It was in your interest to do it; and you did it. Doesn't that amount to choice?'

He frowned, briefly. 'I suppose it doesn't matter so much as the act itself. Bar *is* dead, after all.'

'And Ms Joad, too.'

'Hmm.' He looked blankly at her. 'That was more – premeditated. I couldn't be sure what would happen in that situation, actually. That was a wilder chance I took. She paralysed me pretty thoroughly. I suppose she assumed the nerve controls for my legs were plugged into the base of my spine, instead of more directly into my brain. She doesn't understand modern prosthetics, I suppose. Still, it was tricky, using one foot to press into the cavity in my other leg. The irony is that it was Joad's fault that my right foot had been knocked off in the first place – without that, I wouldn't have been able to get to the weapon at all.'

'It could have been that firing the gun inside your leg would have blown you and us and the whole shop to fragments,' she said.

'It could have been. But I was alive as I squeezed the device with my left toe. Things were lively – we were bouncing around a great deal. But I was still alive. So, you see, I knew we would survive. Because pulling the trigger is the end of the process of firing an FTL pistol, not the beginning.'

'Odd,' she said.

'Exactly. When I killed Bar-le-duc: the first thing we saw – long minutes before Bar even arrived – was the flash.'

'That's right!' said Diana. 'The *flash*.'

'That was the impossible bullet falling *back* into sub-light travel. A sort of photonic boom. By then it was safe: just a very small projectile travelling very fast. If we reconstruct the sequence of events, it runs, from our perspective, backwards. First we saw the flash. Then in very quick succession, the shattering of Bar's ship, the breach in the side of my house, Bar himself being atomised, and finally – me, in the bushes, pulling the trigger.'

They stopped talking then, because Dr Zinovieff emerged from her worldtual to fetch herself some tea. She made some for her passengers, and chatted with them. She complimented Iago on the neat job he had done with his stumps. 'They're fancy prostheses,' she observed. 'Must have cost you a lot.' 'A goodly sum,' Iago agreed.

Shortly, the good doctor went back to her virtual world.

'Jack – I don't want this to sound petulant,' said Diana shortly. 'Or little-girl-ish. But why didn't you *tell* me?'

He took a deep breath. 'You need to understand, Diana,' he said. 'The RACdroid we are carrying with us is *immensely valuable*. It is a powerful bargaining tool for guaranteeing your safety. But it only works if the contract it carries is *inviolate*. If I breach the terms of the agreement, the contract becomes null – useless.'

'And,' said Diana, nodding, 'of course you *did* breach those terms. You resisted arrest.'

'But only you and I know that,' said Iago, in a low voice. 'I can't stress how important it is nobody *else* learns the truth. As long as nobody knows I killed Bar – well, then the contact is still viable.'

Diana felt a hundred years old. 'Iago. Or Jack. Jack, I don't think I understand you at *all*,' she said.

'I'm not so hard to understand,' he said.

'Really?'

He was quiet for a long time. When he started speaking again, it was in a low tone, monotonous, but quietly urgent. 'I have placed my life in the service of one thing. Revolution. Only when the myriad peoples of the Sump have some *collective* say in their own future will they be lifted out of misery. Only when the prison guards of Ulanov tyranny have been eliminated, and the prison of poverty itself dismantled, can humanity achieve its potential. *Then* we'll be ready for the stars – not before! If McAuley's technology is disseminated now, one faction or other of the endless warring tribes of humanity will use it to destroy us all. But once we are free . . . once we have evolved beyond the old medieval power structures and the medieval internecine violence they create, *then* we'll be able to use the technology responsibly. Everything depends on that. Have I killed people? – I have. But only in the service of that higher cause.'

'I still find it hard to believe my MOHmies employed you, knowing you were a revolutionary.'

'Your parents are more flexible than you give them credit,' said

Iago. 'They know that the Clan Argent couldn't hold absolute power under the current system; not alone – and they don't trust any of the other MOHfamilies to go into alliance with them. No, once the Ulanovs go everything changes. Your parents see advantage in that as well as danger. And they see – or more accurately, they foresaw – that the Ulanovs would eventually move against them.'

He was silent for a while. Then he spoke: 'years ago, before your MOHparents gave me employment, and a new identity, long before that, I was in the Sump.'

'As Jack Glass?'

'Oh, a completely different pseudonym. Of course. Anyway, I was working on my networks, moving from bubble-cluster to bubble-cluster, laying long-term plans for revolution, planning sedition in a dozen forms. I worked hard to protect my anonymity. But nonetheless I was betrayed, somehow . . . I've never worked out how. The police arrived in seven cruisers. I was in a place called "God's Prepuce", a single bubble of antinomians, a religious community, devotees of Shiva Christ the Terror. Dedicated anti-Ulanovians, of course; but not so deep in the Sump that they could afford to be blatant about it. Nonetheless, the police came and arrested the entire population of the place: eight hundred and ninety people. They came because somebody had tipped them off that Jack Glass was one of that eight hundred and ninety. And I was. You know who commanded that force?'

'Bar-le-duc?'

'The very same. They came in large numbers: pierced the bubble with lances and pumped stultant gas into the space. They surprised us. We couldn't fight them. They melted boarding-doors through the walls and swarmed in, wearing masks. Everyone was arrested and threatened with summary execution – unless the celebrated Jack Glass identified himself and allowed himself to be taken into custody. A man called Chag Sameach put his hand up. I hadn't discussed this with him, or with anybody there. But they all knew I could not afford to be taken into custody, knowing what I know. So I let him do it, his I-am-Spartacus performance, and Bar-le-duc took him away in his personal sloop.'

'Didn't they DNA him?'

'They DNAd all of us, of course, but no database had Jack Glass's code. Not back then, at any rate. And Chag had no legs – that's not uncommon in the uplands, of course. So they were persuaded. As for the rest of us: well, we were all sentenced, on the spot, to eleven years each, for political agitation and sedition. Every single one of us. We were loaded into carriers. A Gongsi called 344 Diyīrén bought our prisoner rights, and shipped us uphill to carve lucrative des-reses out of orbiting rocks. Three hard months in an acceleration couch, hauling out to the asteroid field; holding at a facility called 8Flora. The prisoners were all randomly mixed, of course, to minimise the dangers of association. And finally I was dumped with six other men, in a cavity in the side of a tiny asteroid called Lamy306 – a couple-hundred metres across, and me in there with six violent men.'

'But surely they realised they didn't have Jack Glass pretty quickly?' Diana asked. 'Wouldn't they realise as soon as it was clear this Chag Sameach couldn't tell them anything?'

'Of course. By then I was in prison, burrowing rooms out of the rock of Lamy306. And all the time I was thinking precisely that: they would soon discover that Chag was an imposter. Then their *next* move would be to go through the other 889 prisoners they had seized in God's P. They wouldn't need to hurry it – for after all, we weren't going anywhere. But neither would they stint. The Gongsi has records of every rock to which that batch of prisoners had been distributed; and eventually they would get round to my one. Once they took me it was all over. They would have me, and then they would have applied irresistible pressures to my mind, and the story of humanity would enter its closing straight. I had to get out.'

'Joad mentioned it, that time on Korkura,' said Diana, in a low voice. 'The breakout that so baffled the authorities.'

'That's what she was talking about. I worked as quickly as I could, but it took time. And eventually I had to kill my fellow prisoners, in order to be able to make good my escape. I wasn't happy about it.'

'Six men. You killed them all?'

'No,' he said, a little too quickly. Then: 'Some of them were already dead. There was . . . fighting within the little group. Some of them killed some others of them. But afterwards I killed the remainder. I took no pleasure in it. I did it only because it was perfectly unavoidable. If I had stayed, if I had decided just to serve out my sentence, then the Ulanovs would have got hold of me. And then things would have gone very badly for the whole human species.'

'Because you had the gun?'

'I didn't have it about my person, not then. But I knew where it was cached. And they would have got that information out of me.'

'But, wait a minute,' she said. Her brain was lining up all the elements in the story, and snagging on those that didn't fit. 'When Bar-le-duc caught up with you again, in your own dome, you were willing to go along with him. The danger was the same: it was worse, because you had the actual gun about your person. The danger for the entire species. Wouldn't you destroy yourself rather than fall into his hands?'

In all the years Diana had known Iago she had never seen him do what he did next. He blushed. His cheeks darkened, red, and his eyeline moved away from her. 'That was different,' he said.

'Different.'

'As I told Aishwarya, fighting him would have meant not only killing me; but killing you too.'

'So? What do you mean, different? *How* was it different? You killed those other men in prison quick enough. The future of the whole species was at stake, you say! So, how was it any less at stake when Bar-le-duc pitched up at your house? How could your individual life, or mine, or Sapho's possibly weigh in the balance against *that* outcome?'

'The agreement I made with Bar-le-duc was *the contract recorded in that RACdroid*. That guarantees your safety. That was paramount.'

'Goddess, why? Why was *that* worth giving yourself up for?' she pressed. 'Are you saying that stupid contract was worth putting the entire System at risk? The lives of *trillions*?'

He made as if to speak, but swallowed the words. Then he ran the palm of his hand over his bristly hair, and closed his eyes. Finally he said: 'yes.'

'Have you lost your mind? The entire population of humanity – the whole *System*? Trillions of lives, in exchange for my safety?'

Iago said: 'because I love you.'

It made her feel angry to hear him say this. She wanted to counter immediately with 'don't be absurd' or 'idiot!' or something of that nature. But looking at him she found she couldn't simply rebuke him. A sword was sheathed, suddenly, in her heart; but it was pity, not love. Oh, it was uncomfortable, and acute, and worst of all *unfitting*. She thought to herself: I'm only sixteen! He's a *generation* older than me. He's the one who ought to know better, not me. And in an attempt to move the exchange into less emotionally dangerous territory, but knowing as she did so that it would make no difference, she said: 'your loyalty to my family is a commendable thing, Iago. But nonetheless—'

'It has nothing to do with loyalty.'

'Don't be foolish,' she chided, vaguely.

'It's you,' he said. 'I love you.'

'You told me you don't even *have* any CRFs in your system. You told me my MOHmies didn't dose you with them, because they needed your initiative and trusted your loyalty without them and all that.'

'All that is true. When I say I love you, it's – you know. My self speaking.'

She looked at him. Politeness doubtless called for a neutral expression, but the horrible thrill of revulsion went through her, and her features creased. She composed herself, with some difficulty. 'Well,' she said, shortly. 'Don't.'

A sad kind of smile broke across his face. 'It's not a matter of my *volition* I'm afraid.'

'Now,' she scolded him, 'you know that I can't feel that way about you – don't you? I never could. It's not just the fact that you're male. It's not just the age difference – if I'm honest, both those things play a part. But I don't want you to think the impediments to, uh, us are, uh, *details* like that. Fond of you though I am, there is no marriage of true minds between you and I.'

'I know,' he said, simply. 'It's a love without hope. But love is not a fire that needs the oxygen of hope to burn. It is a different sort of combustion altogether. I can't extinguish the way I feel about you.'

Diana opened her mouth and closed it again. This was a problem of a different kind altogether. She tried to consult her feelings on the matter, but discovered she didn't know what she felt. Something occurred to her: 'Is it a sexual thing?'

'No,' he said. 'Oh, it is not.'

'You're bound to say that,' she said. But looking at him, she saw he was genuine. And since sex played, as yet, so minimal a part in her life, she was quite prepared to believe that it wasn't quite the big human deal a person might think, from observing art and accessing gossip. But 'sex' at least would enable her to categorise the nature of Iago's feelings for her. Without that, perhaps counter-intuitively, his feelings for her became more unsettling, not less. So she said again; 'you're bound to say that, aren't you?'

He wasn't looking at her. He was blushing. She had seen him blush before.

'Why? Is it because of my position?'

'You are you,' he said. 'That's why. Not that you're clever, and beautiful, though you are: because lots of people are that. But only you are you.'

'I think perhaps you need to read up on Modulated Ova Haptide technology,' she said. But she knew, herself, that this was no answer. 'Jack,' she said, because using his real name struck her as the right thing to do at a moment like this (although as she did so she found herself thinking: how do I know whether even that is his real name?). 'You've explained yourself concisely, and I think I understand. So you'll let me reply concisely too, won't you?'

'Your concision is, no, I think,' he said.

'Yes,' she agreed. 'I mean no.' His blush deepened, and after a moment, it faded a little. 'Goddess, I don't know what I mean.'

'I understand,' he said.

After that Jack Glass slept. He was still recuperating: his wounds were not trivial, and the residue of the nerve toxin made him continually tired.

Diana thought about what he said. Of course she did. She left him, and went off to play Go with the ship AI. Four matches told her that with an eight-stone advantage she could always beat the machine, but with seven or fewer the machine won.

Eventually the *Библиотека 4* arrived at a long string of bubbles called Judasalem, where Iago claimed to have reliable friends. They finally took their leave from the good doctor herself. Sapho made enquiries, and rented a house for the three of them – a simple limpet property, against the wall of the third bubble. Iago, who had paid the doctor her fee, also put up the money for this rental.

That evening, they ate at a restaurant: fish, grown, the owner boasted, in Judasalem's own aquarium. Sapho did not stay long; she was still feeling the coldturkey effects of the removal of her dosage, and went back to the house to sleep. But Diana felt her whole mood lifting. It had been so long since she had encountered anything so evidently civilised, so dependent upon at least a modicum of law and order, that Diana felt a wash of painful nostalgia for the way her life had been before.

Iago looked sad, though. She knew that things between them had changed in an irrevocable way.

They ate with their knees tucked under a bar. The fish was served wrapped in leaves, and accompanied by globes of hash-wine. Their view was of the wide inward curving wall of the bubble, patched over variously with green vegetation and blue habitations.

She asked him: 'What is it like?' she asked. 'Killing people?'

'What a question!' he replied, obviously startled.

'I mean it genuinely. I feel like the outsider here. Sapho killed someone, and you have killed someone. Or many someones.'

Iago thought for a while before answering. 'It is not pleasurable,' he said. 'There is a part of me, as there is of many people, capable of doing it. But I keep that part locked away inside me. It feels like there's a – box. A box, inside me.'

'And inside the box?'

He looked at her. 'Combustion,' he said. 'You're going to tell me we must separate, aren't you.'

The directness of this startled her; but she maintained her composure. Her question to him had been an attempt to startle *him*, after all. 'Why?' she stuttered. 'Why do you say that?' But immediately she decided there was no point in fencing with him. 'No, you're right. I have been thinking. I have been thinking that.'

'Because?'

'Oh, Iago,' she said, feeling tears somewhere inside her, ready-to-hand, prepared to emerge. But she held them back. 'After what you told me, on Doctor Zinovieff's ship? I'm *very* fond of you.'

'That's a degree towards love,' he pointed out.

'Perhaps it is! I suppose it is. We do have a . . . bond, I suppose, you could say. I *owe* you a great deal. But you and I could never – just, never – oh, dear Iago! Even if we were young, how could we?'

'Even if we were young, how could we,' he repeated, in a neutral voice. 'The conditional again. You're fond of the conditional tense.' He sighed. 'Ah well, my darling,' he said, lifting the globe of hashwine. 'I will do as you think best.' To hear herself called darling was like a mild electrical shock. It was impossible to say whether it was a pleasant or an unpleasant experience. 'Where will you go, though?' he asked.

'I don't know. Sapho will come with me, of course. I suppose,' she said, the thought just occurring to her, 'that I will need money.'

'I can help you with that,' said Iago.

'I will go find my parents, I think,' said Diana, staring past Iago to the green motley of the sphere's far wall. 'They have hidden themselves away, true, and it won't be easy to find them. But what is that, except a problem to be solved? And what am I, if not good at solving problems? I may also go visit Anna Tonks Yu, in the flesh. Why not?'

Iago looked away. It was not possible to see, from where Diana was sitting, whether his eyes were brimming, or not. 'All this would break my heart,' he said, in a level voice. 'If I had a heart.'

'Don't be like that, Iago. The mouth can say never, and the rational mind can predict it. But never isn't part of the heart's vocabulary.'

He brightened at this, a little: nodded, and even smiled. But he didn't meet her gaze. 'There's a bigger problem to solve than the location of your parents, I think,' he said, shortly. 'That's the problem of the system as a whole. Revolution. Historically, I suppose revolution has been driven by despair, when a people have nowhere lower to sink and nothing to lose. But ghunk, and living space have made it harder to fall so low. The problem is: how can we make people make things better for themselves?'

'Hope,' she said.

'Exactly,' said Iago. 'Of course I am aware of the dangers. It is an understatement to say: *the stakes are high*. If the FTL pistol had fallen into Ulanov hands – or into the hands of your MOHsister – or any other faction, it could easily have been a disaster, and on the largest scale. Maybe it would have been more politic simply to destroy the device. But I didn't do that. I didn't, because it represents the seed of hope – that people might be able to leave this System altogether, and go whither they choose.'

'Freedom,' said Diana. They sipped their globes for a while, and Diana felt simultaneously excited and mournful, a kind of painful thrill at the open-ended nature of her future. Very grown up. Very much so. 'And if we're to spread hope around the entire solar system,' she added. 'Then we can certainly spare a little hope for you. Don't you think?'

He smiled again, but again didn't meet her eyes. 'That would be nice.'

'You say you have no heart,' she added, feeling her way with her words. 'But I don't believe you. You have a great heart. You're resourceful, and clever, and you have brought me life. That's probably a cause of hope. Wouldn't you say?'

'Wouldn't I say?' Jack repeated. 'It's one of the better conditionals, that wouldn't.'

They sat in silence for a while.

'You understand,' she asked, shortly, 'why I have to go off?'

'I accept it,' replied Iago, still not looking at her. 'Which is better.'

Coda

Sapho, however, refused to go with Diana Argent. Diana was surprised at this, but she ought not to have been. Sapho – or I should say, *I* (for I have been the doctorwatson here, as perhaps you have already guessed) – preferred to stay with Jack Glass, as his companion and amanuensis. He and I have things in common; and the more the CRF diminishes, unreplenished, in my bloodstream the less I experience that debilitating intensity of doggish loyalty to her and her family. This is not to say that I wished her ill. On the contrary. I helped Jack do what he could to prepare her for her journeys: we hired a bodyguard – an essential thing, of course – and rented space in a trading sloop. She went, finally, taking the RACdroid with her (for surety, Jack said); and I wept a little at her departure, and so did she, and only Jack did not, though I think he wished he could. But I have made my choice, now, which is to stay by *his* side. To listen to his account of his time, and his varied experiences. To tell his story.

To tell his story to you.

Jack Glass Glossary

Antinomians Umbrella term for the various groups opposed to the Lex Ulanova, or Ulanov law.

bId The Biolink iData point of connection with larger reservoirs of AI datapools.

Bovrilcohol Delicious meat-based alcoholic beverage.

Bubbles Orbital habitats, of varying size and degrees of luxury. Fashioned from a silicate-carbonchain weave (raw materials mined from asteroids or moons, augmented with long-string molecules derived from gen-engineered algae grown by many orbital Facs) in very large numbers, there are hundreds of millions of these simple transparent or semi-transparent globes orbiting the sun.

Corticotopia A widespread affiliation of drug-adapted 'mind citizens'. Members of this idealistic community put little store by their physical location, believing instead that true human social harmony can only be achieved by a particular regimen of brain alteration. The specific nature of this regimen is disputed amongst different Corticotopian sects.

CRF Corticotropin Releasing Factor. A modified pharmakon dispensed by some organisations to their staff to guarantee loyalty. It is most effective in cases where loyalty is particularised on a single family or (best of all) individual; although even in small doses the drug reduces initiative and independent motivation.

Gongsi Any commercial organisation, corporation or company of sufficient size and wealth, often monopolistic in nature. Any trading or manufacturing company might be called a 'Gongsi' depending on the scale of its operations. See also: **Merchant Houses**.

IP 'Ideal Palace'; a data-generated simulacrum or worldtual, inside which a user may model equations, experiments, discourses, games or anything else that takes her fancy. What distinguishes an IP from other worldtuals is that it is a sealed-away and secure environment, accessibly only to the one user.

Lex Ulanova After the Three Wars, the Ulanovs established their dominance over the entire System, reinforced by the establishment of a new overarching legal code, the Ulanov Law or Lex Ulanova. This superseded the hundred or so local codes, and was markedly stricter than most of them: enforcing the Lex, and punishing delinquents, became a major industry, and many of the third-tier organisations owe their prominence to its existence.

Merchant Houses. A strategic alliance of managerial MOH-individuals and Gongsi trading corporations. Originally the Ulanovs were themselves a Merchant House; but after the Merchant Wars, and their seizure of control, they broke up the old structures into constituent parts.

MOH The technology of Modulated Ova Haptide genetic manipulation.

Plasmaser Elevators A system of ground-to-space (or space-to-ground) mass transport. Elevator cars descend, buoyed on a semi-coherent column of laser-focused plasma; the downward force of this pools the material in the system's groundstation, and in turn is used to push *up* a counterweight car to orbit. More efficient and much cheaper to set-up than conventional space elevators, and much more so than ballistic orbital or re-entry systems.

369

Police The structures of System policing are complicated: police functions overlap largely with military and contract enforcement; and several largely independent forces – all notionally enforcing the Lex Ulanova – in practice compete with one another. Broadly, 'police' describes forces operating in space generally; 'policiers' (originally a belittling diminutive) operate on planets, 'militia', as a term, covers a wide range of armed officers.

Polloi The people.

RACdroid A 'Record & Contract' robotic device. Designed to both record as binding and store knowledge of any legal, personal or mercantile contract. RACdroids are connected to encrypted data reservoirs. Their integrity is crucial to their operation; if anyone so much as suspected a RACdroid of having been compromised, it would destroy their purpose.

The Sump The 'Sumpolloi' (what used to be called the *lumpenproletariat*); a contraction from 'sub-polloi'. By far the most populous element in the solar system population; most of the Sump live in cheap and precarious 'shanty bubbles'.

Tiers The unofficial hierarchy of power in the System. The Ulanovs occupy the top position as 'secretaries' of the System. Below them are the five MOH-families, sometimes called 'Clans' (Clan Argent, Clan Yu, Clan Kwong, Clan Aparaceido and Clan Onbekend). Each of these is a large, functioning organisation, with a variety of interests, although by convention each is also conceded particular expertise in one area (respectively: information, transportation, taxation, the military and the police) specific to upholding the Lex Ulanova and maintaining the status quo. Below this second tier is a third, occupied by the various large-scale commercial organisations and trading companies known as 'Gongsi'. Below this third is a fourth, occupied by various other cults, clans and groups, most of whom are concerned with law enforcement: police groups, mafias, cults, militia groups, bands, fame-ilies and so on. Below them are the Polloi, a large

assemblage of population of varying degrees of wealth and inde-
pendence, almost all committed and often legally indentured to
fourth- or third-tier organisations. Finally, not strictly part of the
tiers at all, is the Sump.

Worldtual Or 'worldtual reality'; a data-only environment, a
whole-world simulacrum generated by computing or other data
processing technologies. Worldtuals either take the form of a
Consense (a multiply linked cloudwork environment, in which
many different users interact) or else as a standalone, hermetic
'Ideal Palace' (see IP).

Acknowledgments

'Champagne Supernovae' are a real phenomenon, one that puzzles real astrophysicists, and which are, I'm sorry to say, really named after the Oasis song. Interested parties may read the relevant Wikipedia entry. Faster-than-light travel is, as this novel says plainly on several occasions, a physical impossibility; the same is true of teleportation.

I should like to thank Stephen Baxter for his practical advice with respect to the first portion of this narrative; and also Paul McAuley for letting me apply his surname to the Solar System's most brilliant scientist (the name 'McAndrew', the Kipling-esque original – from which, as it happens, the character was originally sketched – didn't have quite enough vowels to satisfy my rather exacting sense of euphony). The e-text of this novel includes two works, 'The Mary Anna' and 'McAuley's Hymn', originally published elsewhere; I would like to thank the editors of these prior appearances, and Ian Whates in particular. My wife Rachel is a pearl of great price and I'd like to thank her. I would also like to thank my genius editor Simon Spanton, and of course the Tron-like electronic editor Darren Nash, both at Gollancz.

The impulse for this novel was a desire to collide together some of the conventions of 'Golden Age' science fiction and 'Golden Age' detective fiction, with the emphasis more on the latter than the former. My introduction to this latter body of discourse, and especially to those authors whose influence is most obvious here

(Margery Allingham, Ngaio Marsh, Dorothy L. Sayers, Michael Innes), is something I owe to my mother, Merryl Wynne Roberts, who has read more such novels than I have had hot dinners. This novel is dedicated to her, with my love.